DARKNESS ON HIS BONES

A James Asher vampire novel

Barbara Hambly

This first world edition published 2015
in Great Britain and the USA by
SEVERN HOUSE PUBLISHERS LTD of
19 Cedar Road, Sutton, Surrey, England, SM2 5DA.
Trade paperback edition first published
in Great Britain and the USA 2015 by
SEVERN HOUSE PUBLISHERS LTD.

Hambly, Barbara author.
  Darkness on His Bones. – (The James Asher vampire novels)
  1. Asher, James (Fictitious character)–Fiction.
  2. Vampires–Fiction. 3. Horror tales.
  I. Title II. Series
  813.6-dc23

ISBN-13: 978-0-7278-8523-4 (cased)
ISBN-13: 978-1-84751-623-7 (trade paper)
ISBN-13: 978-1-78010-676-2 (e-book)

All Severn House titles are printed on acid-free paper.

Severn House Publishers support the Forest Stewardship Council™ [FSC™],
the leading international forest certification organisation. All our titles that
are printed on FSC certified paper carry the FSC logo.

Typeset by Palimpsest Book Production Ltd.,
Falkirk, Stirlingshire, Scotland.
Printed and bound in Great Britain by
TJ International, Padstow, Cornwall.

To Ravenna and Jaden

ONE

From: W.W. Streatham, Secretary for Information, British Embassy, 39 Rue du Faubourg Saint-Honoré, Paris

To: Mrs James Asher, 16 Holywell Street, Oxford, England

28 July, 1914

James Asher met with accident last night critical condition Hôpital Saint-Antoine stop come immediately stop contact me on arrival stop yours etc

*

Mrs James Asher
c/o Lady Louise Mountjoy
48c Avenue Kléber
16ème Arrondissement
Paris

Don Simon Ysidro
c/o Barclay and Company
Rome Central Office
Rome

30 July, 1914

Simon,

Something frightful has happened to Jamie. In the middle of last month he crossed to Paris, ostensibly to attend a conference on Magyar verb forms, but in truth, I think, at the behest of some of his former colleagues in the Department. He arrived there (here?) on the 23rd. On the 28th of July I received a cable from someone in the Paris embassy. James had been found unconscious

in the cemetery of the church of Sainte-Clare-Pieds-Nus, with a
fractured skull, multiple puncture wounds in his throat and arms,
and severe loss of blood, though no blood was found at the scene.

He has not yet recovered consciousness.

I have no idea where you are ~~living~~ to be found these days,
but I beg of you, if you are in Europe and able to come to me,
I am in desperate need of counsel and help.

I am staying with my Aunt Louise in the Avenue Kléber,
but mostly I can be found at the Hôpital Saint-Antoine. Please
come.

Ever,
L. Asher

TWO

'**D**on Simon said you were a man of courage.' The glow
of the candles James Asher had lit all around the small
salon – for the old *hôtel particulier* on the Rue des
Trois Anges had never even been equipped for gas, let alone
electricity – seemed to outline in gold the woman in the doorway,
and caught twin mirrors in her eyes, like a cat's, when she moved
her head.

If he concentrated he could see her fangs.

But he had to concentrate. There was a sort of dreamy inat-
tention that stole over one's thoughts when one dealt with
vampires, the forgetfulness that usually comes with being over-
tired or preoccupied with other matters . . . Asher had encountered
it before. He guessed there were others somewhere beyond the
dark doorways that led into the rest of the building and he'd
placed his chair with some care, his back to a corner and the
long windows that opened to the courtyard barely a yard from
his left hand.

It was a drop of about fifteen feet but that risk was nothing
compared to the danger he was in at the moment. He also knew
that there was no other way to do this.

'Lady Montadour.' He rose and bowed deeply to her without

stepping out of the circle of candelabra that ringed his chair. 'I hope you'll forgive my rudeness. I had no idea what your arrangements here were, and I feared that a note requesting an interview would result in either your retreat or my entrapment before I have a chance to explain to you the danger you're in.'

(Sunk deep in darkness his dreaming self shouted to him, *Run, you idiot! They're behind you, around you* . . . His mind groped for the recollection, like trying to piece together a jigsaw puzzle blindfolded. Cold hands gripping his arms, the razor pain of claws tearing open his throat. Colder lips against his skin as the blood welled forth. It slipped away.)

'*I?*' Elysée de Montadour crossed the salon and, dreaming, he both saw her and couldn't see her: the languourous glide of a ghost and then suddenly, unexpectedly, she was beside him in the circle of light. One hand in his and the other holding his arm, the fingers cold as marble (*she hasn't fed* . . .). The mingled scents of blood and Houbigant's Quelques Fleurs.

She's changed her dress, his dreaming self observed.

Or was it on some previous occasion that he'd seen her lying in a coffin, dark curls spread around her delicate triangular face, beautiful beyond words in the light of his lantern? He couldn't remember. *But if I saw her asleep in her crypt, why didn't I kill her?*

A murderess who deserves death a thousand times? Why warn her of danger?

The answer was important but he couldn't recall it.

Did I see her in her coffin before speaking with her, or after? He couldn't recall that, either.

In the coffin she'd worn something white and gauzy that had clung to her rich breasts and tiny waist. Now she was dressed in a tobacco-colored Patou walking suit; its green silk trim brightened the emerald of her eyes. Lydia had one very like it. She hadn't donned gloves yet and her inch-long claws were sharp as a cougar's against his skin.

'I hope you haven't forgotten what happened to the vampires of Paris, the last time German armies marched into the city.'

'The Boche?' Her silvery laugh was forced, like the theatrical toss of her head. 'Those stupid cabbage-eaters aren't going to get within a hundred miles of Paris. The armies of France will take Lorraine before they've advanced two miles. They'll be cut off, left lying in their blood—'

'The armies of France are going to miss them entirely,' replied Asher. 'They'll be racing east to reconquer Alsace and Lorraine while the Germans are rolling down to Paris from the north, through Belgium. They know you're here, madame. They want you working for them.'

Memory drowned the dream again. Memory of trying to flee in darkness, and knowing it would do him no good. *I was wearing silver in Elysée's salon . . .* But in his dream he felt the razor gash of teeth in his throat.

It was important to remember what had happened to the silver chains he'd worn.

Where was that?

Why did he remember walking down a turret stair with Elysée de Montadour carrying a branch of candles upraised behind him? Or was that part of another series of events altogether? One that might never have taken place?

There was a chapel . . . A bone chapel, such as he'd visited in Spain and in Rome. The light of his lantern played across skulls, vertebrae, pelvises, radii. A man stood beside the altar and held out his hand to him, clawed fingers stained with ink. In the chalk-white face the dark eyes were filled with grief, and reflected the lantern-glow like a hunting cat's.

He's here . . .

'Jamie?'

A voice – a woman's. *I know whose voice that is.* It came from far off.

From the land of the living.

He understood that the chapel was the realm of the dead.

'Jamie?'

Lydia Asher touched her husband's hand. The strong fingers were bruised and scratched, and claw gashes showed on either side of the bandages on his wrists. The windows of the ward stood open, the muggy August night suffocating. Even at this hour – and it was just after four in the morning – faint shouting drifted from the Rue Saint-Antoine, mingled with strains of 'La Marseillaise'. Tiny as seashells clacked on a nursery table-top she heard the hooves of a milk-cart's team; a distant taxicab hooted its horn. *Vive l'Alsace!* a drunken woman yelled, almost beneath the window. *À bas le Boche!*

The French army was readying for war.

And, Aunt Louise had remarked drily yesterday afternoon, it was preparing to leap eastward, to occupy the territory stolen from France in the previous war, at the first crack of a German shot which would exonerate them from the accusation that they were the ones who'd broken the peace. Leap eastward and leave Paris defended by only a handful.

Lydia had thought her husband had stirred, unshaven lips moving in his sleep. But he lay still as death, as he had last night and, the doctors told her, the night before, when they'd brought him in. His mustache and eyebrows, threaded with gray, looked nearly black in the glare of the ward's electric lighting. He'd had transfusions of blood but his face was still nearly as white as the bandages around his head, the dressings on his throat and arms that covered the slashes and punctures that she recognized as the marks of a vampire attack.

Jamie, no . . .

A year ago he had sworn to destroy them. Was that why he'd come to Paris? To seek them out, like a madman? Or had there been some other cause?

On the small stand between his bed and the next, in a hospital dish, gleamed two short silver chains, which the doctors had told her had been wrapped around his hands when he was found.

He usually wore them on his wrists. Lydia guessed they'd saved his life. The one that he habitually had around his throat was gone.

They have to know he isn't dead.

She settled herself in the stiff wooden chair beside his bed.

That means they'll be back.

By four thirty it was growing light. Lydia paced from her chair to the window and back, restless from the herbs she'd taken; on a journey to China two years ago, she'd had ample opportunity to investigate the curious medicines relied upon by the Chinese doctors. The physicians here – and at home in England as well – scoffed at Lydia's observations and experiments, but she'd found, at least, several powders and tisanes that stimulated the mind and held off sleep far more effectively than any amount of *café noir*. Sleep was the one thing she couldn't afford just now. Not if Jamie had been so mad as to enter into open war with those who hunted the night.

Young Dr Moflet, the night surgeon, had smiled condescendingly when Lydia informed him that she had a degree in medicine from Oxford. 'Indeed, I suppose the English do give out such degrees to young ladies . . .' But Dr Théodule, though he'd been practicing since the Franco-Prussian War, spoke as if he expected her to understand the effects and implications of head trauma and blood loss.

Neither man understood Lydia's insistence upon being at her husband's side from sundown till dawn.

Her desperation not to sleep.

Old M'sieu Potric in the bed across the aisle snuffled in his sleep. A few beds away, a working-man named Lecoq coughed, the gluey hack of pneumonia. Somewhere a band was still playing.

The door at the end of the long ward opened: Dr Moflet, trim and stylish with his close-clipped fair mustache and pomaded hair; Dr Théodule, stooped, white-haired, and resembling nothing so much as a wizard who has attempted to transform himself into a goat and had the spell fail halfway. The nurse Thérèse Sabatier followed them, grizzled and disapproving in her uniform of gray and white.

'Should Germany invade Belgium, I would consider it my duty to go.' Dr Moflet's voice was grave, and Dr Théodule sniffed.

'*Should*, he says. Of course they're going to invade, and be damned to their promises to respect Belgium's neutrality. It's the fastest route to Paris—'

Both men bowed at the sight of Lydia, who had whipped her spectacles off at the first echo of their voices in the hall. Bad enough, she reflected, that she'd been up all night and wasn't even wearing powder, much less the rouge and mascaro which usually mitigated her thin cheeks and unfashionable nose. There were only two people in the world she didn't mind seeing her with her glasses – *gig-lamps*, the other girls at Madame Chappedelaine's exclusive school for girls in Switzerland had called them – hanging on her face.

One of them lay unconscious at her side.

The other . . .

The other, reflected Lydia, with a feeling of strangeness at the thought, had been dead for many years.

'He has rested well, your husband?'

Dr Moflet answered Dr Théodule's question before Lydia could open her mouth. 'I'm quite certain he has.'

To Lydia, in what he clearly considered a kindly tone, he went on, 'There is no reason for you to remain, madame. Given the extent of Professor Asher's injury, it's unreasonable to expect him to recover consciousness for at least another few days.'

The man means well, Lydia told herself. She had to bite her lower lip in the effort not to retort, *Well, I'm only here because with war coming I thought the department stores would be too noisy to go shopping.* She took a deep breath and answered the older man. 'Sometimes he's seemed to be dreaming. To be trying to speak.'

'That's good.' Dr Théodule nodded encouragingly. 'Did you take his pulse at such times?'

'Sixty beats at just after eleven; at two, sixty-two.'

Dr Moflet's chiseled mouth tightened, as if he considered a patient's pulse the affair of the ward nurse, certainly not that of the patient's wife.

'And no other change?' The old doctor felt Asher's wrist as he spoke, turned back his eyelid, withdrew his stethoscope from his frock-coat pocket to listen to his chest.

Lydia shook her head.

'It's early days, as Dr Moflet has pointed out.' Dr Théodule straightened up. 'If – for whatever reason – your husband fell from the tower of St Clare's church, as I suspect he might have, it is only to be expected. I have seen many men make a full recovery from worse. Shall I have one of the orderlies fetch a cab for you, madame? You can be sure that if there is any change you will be summoned immediately.'

'I still don't understand why—' Moflet began, and Théodule lifted one knotted old hand.

'She troubles no one, Moflet. If madame will come with me . . .?'

After the stink of carbolic soap, iodine, and the sickly horror

of gangrene, even the smoke outside and the nearby river smelled
sweet. Though her degree was in medicine, Lydia was a researcher
to the marrow of her bones. She hated hospitals. Hated the sense
of helplessness, the grieving desperation of the bereft.

Pigeons circled in the gray sky, and from all directions bells
chimed for early Mass. It would probably be the best attended
morning service of the twentieth century, Lydia reflected. Wives,
mothers, sweethearts, flocking to pray for the men who were even
now packing their clothes, reporting to their areas of deployment,
receiving from quartermasters and clerks rifles, ammunition,
sturdy boots, and the bright blue-and-scarlet uniforms of which
the French were so proud. ('Idiots!' Aunt Louise had harrumphed.
'They'll stand out a mile! As well stick a dartboard on their
bottoms!')

The Métro still seemed to be open, though last night one of
the visitors to the ward had spoken of a rumor that it would be
shut down. In any case Lydia had no desire to descend to the
darkness underground, even at the threshold of dawn. Vampires,
she knew, had ways of remaining awake into the hours of daylight,
as long as they were protected from the sun's killing rays. And
she had learned also how common it was for vampires to have
human servants.

As Jamie was their servant, she thought, *back in London*.

In view of the patriotic hysteria that seemed to have electrified
the brain of every waiter, bus conductor, hospital orderly, and
newsboy Lydia had talked to for the past three days, it was
unlikely that anyone would even inquire were she to be 'acci-
dentally' run down in the street or pushed off a church tower.

So she climbed into the red-and-yellow taxicab that pulled up
before the hospital's steps, gave Aunt Louise's address, and
apologized to the dark-browed Neanderthal at the wheel for the
inconvenience of a journey across the center of Paris. '*Ce n'est
rien, madame*,' he returned in a voice like a friendly gravel-bucket.
'They've started requisitioning vehicles – trucks, automobiles,
they even tried to get the horse from my cousin's coal-cart – so
at least the journey will be swift. And just as well,' he added
grimly. 'The men in this city all started drinking last night, poor
saps, as soon as they heard the news. *Celebrating*! Damned fools.
Every café has been open all night, and stands open still. Me at

least no man will find pounding the door of their damn recruiting office.' He flipped a card from his pocket. 'The telephone number there is the café opposite the cab-stand, the Ax and Bow on the Avenue du Maine in Montparnasse. Ask for Stanislas Greuze.'

He walked her to the wide bronze doors of number forty-eight – possibly his willingness to be of service was related to the address on that most fashionable of streets, or to the exquisite quality of Lydia's jade-and-violet silk walking suit. Aunt Louise's companion, Mrs Flasket, was already awake and taking a cup of tea in the shadowy cavern of the apartment's salon when Lydia unlocked the door. 'How is he?' She set aside her newspapers and poured another cup of tea for Lydia. Mrs Flasket habitually read the *Times*, *Le Figaro*, and the *Berliner Tageblatt* before breakfast. Aunt Louise seldom gave her the time to do anything once she herself wakened at six with querulous demands for tea, toast, and company.

'Still unconscious.' They both spoke almost in whispers. Even asleep, Aunt Louise had sharp ears.

'Did you manage to speak to this Mr Streatham at the embassy yesterday, dear? I didn't think so – heaven knows who'd have time for a mere civilian attempt at murder. Did you hear that Germany's now declared war on Russia? The Germans are evidently claiming that French dirigibles bombed Nürnberg last night, so using German logic they're going to invade Belgium in order to defend themselves. I had no opportunity to say so yesterday—' she offered Lydia a small plate of toast, at which Lydia shook her head – 'but I am extremely sorry to hear of Professor Asher's injury.' Aunt Louise's harangue on the subject of Lydia's rashness had, on the previous morning, prevented any other discourse. 'Have they any idea yet what happened? The fourth arrondissement can be a dicey neighborhood.'

'Only that he was found in the old churchyard of St Clare's.' Lydia wondered if she could wake sufficiently early this afternoon to have a look at the place by daylight, before returning to the hospital. It might be safer to telephone the cab-driver Stanislas Greuze as a paid escort, rather than risk taking Aunt Louise's chauffeur Malraux, always supposing that Malraux hadn't volunteered for the army by teatime. 'Aunt Louise mentioned yesterday that Professor Asher called here when he arrived in town.'

Or was it the day before? The exhaustion of travel, the long night sitting at Jamie's side before she even came to her aunt's apartment, blurred events and times . . . and Aunt Louise regarded a mere lecturer at New College (and one who'd had the temerity to wed into the family of Lord Halfdene without Aunt Louise's permission, at that) as so far beneath her notice that she might well have neglected to mention Jamie's visit for forty-eight hours after the arrival of Jamie's terrified wife.

'To borrow your aunt's architecture guidebooks.'

Lydia's brows shot up, and she regarded the pleasant conglomeration of blurred pinks and blacks – all that she could readily distinguish of Mrs Flasket – with surprise.

'Architecture guidebooks?'

'She wouldn't lend them.' Mrs Flasket's soft contralto flexed with an unspoken comment on her employer. 'Fortunately, I had my own copies of several . . . I dare say they'll be in his rooms. You haven't yet found where he was staying?' Her breath blew out in a tiny, resigned sigh. 'I expect that's what he was doing at St Clare's. It was part of an old convent, you know, and quite the oldest church in the arrondissement. He asked me about the old *hôtels particuliers* in that district as well – it was the most fashionable part of town in the seventeenth century – and was I believe making inquiries about those who owned them these days.'

Lydia guessed what Jamie had been looking for, and her heart lurched in her chest. How he'd traced the Paris vampires to the fourth arrondissement she wasn't sure, but coming and going from the hospital she had seen any number of extremely old-looking buildings on the side-streets, baroque town palaces now surrounded by the cruder brick shops and houses of a working-men's suburb.

He has to have been looking for a vampire nest.

Oh, Jamie, no . . .!

Beyond the long windows, open already to the receding cool of the sticky morning, a boy's voice shouted the news against the church bells: 'France mobilizes! French armies to report to their staging points . . .'

From the bedroom came the silvery complaint of Aunt Louise's bell, followed by the old woman's harsh voice: 'Honoria!'

Mrs Flasket rose. 'Tell her I've gone to bed already,' said Lydia quickly.

'Of course, madam. I expect she'll want to go to the bank,' she added thoughtfully. 'You probably should, too. The government will almost certainly close them, to prevent a run . . .'

'Honoria!'

The door of the kitchen quarters opened and Aunt Louise's maid Marie hurried through. The young woman – whose name was actually Imèlde; Aunt Louise called all her maids Marie – carried the mahogany tray of breakfast: cocoa, crumpets, a few spoonfuls of clotted cream in one crystal dish and of marmalade in another. Aunt Louise considered silver inappropriate for early mornings.

'This came for you, Madame Asher.' Imèlde took an envelope from a corner of the tray. 'Have you heard? Germany invaded Luxembourg this morning.'

'Well,' Mrs Flasket said. 'That tears it.'

The handwriting on the envelope was the same as the one that had come for Lydia yesterday – she had to hold it almost to the end of her nose to read it.

The message inside was almost the same.

My dear Mrs Asher,

Might I beg the favor of a meeting with you? Information regarding your husband I have, which may mean the difference between life and death for him. At the base of the July Column, opposite the Rue de Lyon, at six this evening, in a cab I will be waiting. Forgive me these precautions: they are necessary. Please come alone, and tell no one of our rendezvous. Upon our meeting tonight all depends.

Sincerely,

William Johnson

Lydia's hand shook, and she turned away lest the maid see the tears that filled her eyes.

Information regarding your husband . . . the difference between life and death . . .

A lie? The truth? An unexpected ally or a trap? The sun would still be in the sky at six but even as there were vampires who could remain wakeful into the mornings – and longer, with the use of drugs – there were those who wakened a little before sunset from their impenetrable sleep.

And a living man in their pay would of course suffer no such peril.

This was the precise reason that the vampires of London had forced Jamie to work for them, seven years before.

Precautions . . . are necessary. Upon our meeting tonight all depends.

If it's a trap, Jamie will die. We'll both die.

If it's the truth, and I tear this up as I did yesterday's . . .

'Madam?'

She turned sharply, to see – albeit rather blurred, between myopia and tears – Mrs Flasket's worried face.

'May I be of help?'

She shook her head. 'I just don't know what to do. Whoever attacked him . . .'

She held out the note, and the widow re-donned her reading-glasses to scan it. 'I expect precautions *are* necessary,' Mrs Flasket remarked, 'given the mood of the people. Whatever this Mr "Johnson" says his name is, his handwriting is German. Look at the way he makes the capital "J" on "July Column"; only a German puts that slash to the side of it. And those "h"s in "husband" and "have" are characteristic, completely aside from that business of *Information . . . I have*, and *Upon our meeting . . . all depends*. I wasn't a governess in Potsdam for eighteen months for nothing.'

She frowned as she handed the letter back. 'This is not to say,' she went on carefully, 'that a German gentleman would not mean Professor Asher well as much as a Frenchman or Englishman might . . .'

The bell tinged even more insistently.

'You'd best go to her.' For a moment Lydia thought Mrs Flasket would linger for an answer, but after a troubled nod the older woman smoothed her dark-gray skirt and retreated in the direction of the bedroom.

Putting Aunt Louise in one of her passions wouldn't help Jamie – or anyone.

For a long time Lydia stood in the light of the wide windows, listening to the bells and the shouts of the paperboys below, staring sightlessly at the note in her hand. The German armies were on the march. They'd be attacking through Belgium . . . even as the French armies would be haring madly away to the Rhine, a hundred miles or more to the south.

They'll be in Paris inside a week, Jamie had often said.

And there would be men with the German army who would recognize James Asher, even unconscious and unshaven in a hospital bed.

Recognize him as a man who'd asked a lot of questions around Berlin in the past, though he hadn't been calling himself Asher then.

And the worst of it was, she suspected, those Germans wouldn't be the greatest danger.

She crumpled the paper in her hand and poked it into the heart of the cold hearth.

THREE

D reaming, he remembered the taste of tea.

Old Mama Karlebach, in that tall narrow house near the Spanish synagogue in Prague – a formidable scholar in her own right – made the most extraordinary tea for her husband's students, smoke-flavored and steeped with herbs and drunk, in the local fashion, from small engraved glasses held in cup-shaped silver holders, after one had tucked a cube of sugar in one's cheek.

Asher's fellow student Jürgen Schaumm wanted to know why one couldn't simply dissolve the sugar in the hot tea and sip it that way, as the English did. But Asher – always curious about different customs and moreover wanting to keep in Mama Karlebach's good graces – obediently popped the sugar-cube in and slurped through it. 'You're doing it wrong,' old Rebbe Karlebach had grumbled through the wilderness of his beard.

Drifting in darkness – knowing he lay on the wave-shore of death, waiting for the tide to rise and cover him – Asher found himself again in that musty parlor, crowded with books and curiosities and bunches of drying herbs. Looking back, he realized that old Solomon Karlebach – old already in 1884 when Asher had first come to him during the summer vacs from Oxford – knew perfectly well that the vampires that he spoke of to his students were real. That they watched the old house on Bilkova Ulice, and knew that some at least of its inhabitants were aware of their existence. Yet neither the old man nor his wife ever showed the least concern about walking abroad at night. Karlebach's sons and grandchildren lived in the house with them, noisy and lively and unaware that those who hunted the nights were any more genuine than the rusalkas in the rivers or Baba Yaga in the woods with her house that ran about on chicken legs, fables Mama Karlebach would tell them at bedtime.

Nor was I any more aware than they.

Asher saw himself in those days, tall and solemn with his thick brown hair falling into one eye and the long side-whiskers fashionable just then, sipping his tea in the parlor. Jürgen Schaumm, like a plump little gnome from some Black Forest tale, studiously jotted in his little green notebook every verb form usage that fell from the old woman's lips in Czech or Yiddish. Asher knew he should be making such notes as well – Czech and Central European Yiddish were what he'd come to Prague to study – but he was much too interested in whether Prince Vassili would succeed in answering the riddles of the old man by the stream . . .

And in his dream there was a sound at the window, the faint tapping of long claws on the distorted old glass. Rebbe Karlebach's dark gaze lifted for a moment from his book, as if to pierce the darkness outside. But when Asher looked, there was nothing.

Only the momentary gleam of eyes.

'Mistress?'

The word was barely the scratch of a dead leaf on pavement. Lydia jerked around with a gasp. The young man beside her was bleached as a ghost in the glare of the ward's electric lamps, skin tailored like white silk over aquiline bones, long hair wispy and colorless as spider-web around a thin face horribly scarred, as if razors had slashed open cheek and throat and the cuts had never healed properly. His eyes had a crystalline quality, sulfur and champagne.

The hands he held out to her were armed with inch-long claws, and when he said, 'Hush—' as she threw herself into his arms, she could see his fangs.

'Mistress, hush.'

Her arms locked around his waist and she pressed her cheek to his; they were of a height, five feet seven. His flesh, though without the limpness of the dead, was cold as that of a corpse, which was exactly what he was.

A corpse whose life had been extinguished in 1555.

A man who had become vampire. A vampire whom Jamie had vowed he would kill.

'Thank you!' she whispered. 'Oh, Simon, thank you, thank you—'

'Art well?' Don Simon Ysidro put his palm to the side of her face, drew back to regard her. 'Have they tried to come for you?'

She shook her head. 'But they must know I'm here. And I've had two notes, trying to get me alone—'

'Did you keep them? Silly girl,' he added when she shook her head again. He sat on the edge of Asher's bed, felt his hands and forehead, economical of movement as a dancer and with no more expression than an ivory image. Above a Jermyn Street suit of ash-gray wool and a silk tie precisely two shades lighter, his features were indefinably not of the newborn twentieth century nor yet of the one that had preceded it. Rather, they always reminded Lydia of old portraits, close-lipped and withdrawn, as befitted those who had grown up in the shadow of the Inquisition.

'Will he be all right?' Everything she had learned about head trauma in four years at the Radcliffe Infirmary, and in nine years of study thereafter, flooded to mind. 'Is he . . . is he *himself*, in there?'

The yellow gaze touched her like a measuring rod, then turned aside. She thought for an instant that some expression passed across his face. Resignation? Grief? Understanding? Then Ysidro placed both hands on Asher's face, shut his eyes, cocked his head as if deeply listening. Seeing into his dreams, as vampires could. Probing his thoughts in unguarded sleep.

When his eyes returned to hers she saw in them what she had

never seen before, and it shocked her to her soul that he would feel pity, and terrified her too.

'That I do not know, Mistress. Time only will tell.' She didn't see him do it – it was extremely difficult to see a vampire move any distance – but he was suddenly standing at her side (*when did he get up?*) holding another chair; he must have taken it from beside a bed further down the ward. He set it next to hers, sat in it, and took her hands.

'Tell me what befell him. I sought you in dreams the night I had your letter, yet you were waking till it grew light.'

'I didn't dare sleep.' She clenched her hands, aware that they were trembling and angered by this. The herbs had that effect sometimes, like cold and heat at once. 'Not at night. They have to know he isn't dead. Are they out there?'

'One only.' And he moved a finger slightly as she slewed around to glance at the long curtainless windows. 'Vampires are ever to be found near hospitals, Mistress. It may have naught to do with James. Tell me now . . .' Moth-light fingertips brushed eyelids and lips, and a line appeared between the vampire's pale brows. 'He cannot have run so mad as to hunt them? Surely he would not cross the Channel at such a time to do so?'

'I don't . . . I don't *think* so. I know what he said a year ago . . .' She shook her head. 'He had a letter – he'd received an invitation to a linguistics conference. I'm sure it was a put-up job by the Foreign Office, because the invitation came the day after the Germans started poking their fingers into that whole uproar about whoever it was who got himself shot in the Balkans . . . the Prince of Serbia?'

'The Archduke of the Austrian Empire.'

'He did tell me.' Lydia passed a tired hand over her forehead. 'It seems years ago, now . . . In any case, he tucked the invitation away and didn't even answer it. If it had been genuine – from a genuine linguistic society, I mean – he'd have written a refusal. Then about two weeks after that he got a letter from Rebbe Karlebach.'

A derisive pin-scratch appeared at the corner of Ysidro's mouth at the mention of the old vampire-hunter. If he had not long ago lost the capacity to breathe, he would have sniffed.

'He suddenly decided he'd go to the conference after all.'

'Ah.'

When Ysidro had been some minutes silent, thought running behind his eyes like the movement of water under ice, Lydia went on, 'The doctors say he can't be moved. I think they're right, but every hour we stay here . . .' She shivered. 'The doctors keep saying that if the Germans *do* declare war, they'll never get anywhere near Paris. But Jamie's always told me the Germans and the French are going to attack each other simultaneously, hundreds of miles apart. I don't know anything about war or international relations and my friend Josetta is always telling me what an idiot I am about politics, but that sounds completely daft even to me. Are the Germans going to invade?'

'Beyond doubt, lady.'

'Will you help me get him out?'

'When it becomes possible, of course.'

She took a shallow breath, let it out, feeling infinitely better. She had known what he was from the moment they'd met, seven years ago; knew, too, that because he had helped her – saved both her life and Jamie's – it did not alter what he was. Because he was what he was, she knew she shouldn't trust him, let alone like him, let alone . . .

She shook the thought away.

He's here. He'll help me. He came . . .

As she had known he would come.

She turned from him, her thoughts going back to Jamie, the man whose love and strength had been the sheet anchor of her life since the age of fifteen, and again for a moment had the sense that Ysidro was going to speak; but he didn't. 'I think Rebbe Karlebach must have heard something that concerned an offer by the Germans to the vampires of Paris,' she said at last. 'It's the only thing that would have brought Jamie to Paris now. But in another way it makes no sense. Why would the Paris vampires work for Germany? Why would vampires *care* who wins the war?

'My Aunt Louise's companion, Mrs Flasket, tells me Jamie was going about Paris looking at *hôtels particuliers*. When they found him he had these—' she produced from her handbag the silver wrist-chains – 'wrapped around his hands.'

The vampire considered them for a moment, not touching the

silver, then mimed the path of a strike, with a hand so wrapped, at the face of an assailant. Silver would burn vampire flesh like red-hot iron.

'He had this in his pocket.' From her handbag Lydia produced a card, one of her husband's – or at least one printed with one of the names her husband went by when he was, as they'd said when he'd worked for the Department, *abroad*. It said 'Sergius Donner', with addresses in Southampton and Prague.

On the back, in an unknown hand, was an address in the Rue Lagrange.

'I went there this afternoon. It's an antiquarian bookshop. The old man there said yes, Jamie had come in, asking about sixteenth-century religious tracts by someone named Constantine Angelus.'

Don Simon Ysidro said nothing – was silent for so long that Lydia wondered if he had heard some sound outside, some intimation of danger far off. He seemed to be listening, his cold yellow eyes unfocused and filled, she thought, with the echo of agonizing pain.

'Is Constantine Angelus one of the Paris vampires?'

'He was,' he replied at long last – at very long last.

And fell silent again, as if hearing the echo of distant voices.

Then his brows drew together with a puzzlement that pushed aside whatever it was he heard in his heart. 'The Paris vampires may care very much if German troops enter Paris, as they did in 1871. On that occasion, most of the Paris nest were so ill-advised as to remain in the city during the siege – I'm told the hunting was spectacularly good. With so many dying of cold and malnutrition, and such authorities as there were having other matters to think upon, there were none to inquire about the dead. But the citizens of Paris were sufficiently alert to the possibility of German spies that one morning all of the Paris nest was trapped and wiped out, with the exception of Elysée de Montadour, wife of the Master of Paris.'

'You think that's why the Paris vampires might seek the protection of the Germans?'

He took the card and ran a corner of it very gently along his lower lip, as if seeking some elusive scent or vibration in the pasteboard. 'Mayhap.'

'Can't they just leave?'

'They can,' he agreed. 'I would, in their place. Elysée now being Master of Paris in her husband's stead . . .'

His frown deepened.

'It may be that this letter James received from Karlebach concerned some plan by the Germans to back one of Elysée's fledglings, the moment Elysée does flee. The Masters of cities grow deeply protective of their home soil, and the Paris nest has always been an unruly one, rebellious and resentful. Elysée may fear that in departing she would surrender her territory, and have to fight to get it back. She has never impressed me as a particularly strong vampire.'

He sat for a time, head bowed, Jamie's faked calling card held between two fingers. In the opposite bed, old M'sieu Potric muttered in his sleep.

'I shall speak to whoever it is out there,' he promised at last. 'They may merely be hunting, of course, and know nothing of these matters. Elysée is ever careful to tell her fledglings as little as she can. Immortality has never conferred intelligence upon those who seize it. And I shall seek Elysée – I assume she still has that shocking bourgeois *hôtel* out in Passy. I trust you've searched James's lodgings?'

'I'm trying to find out where they were. He had a key in his pocket, which means a rented room rather than a hotel – but he never writes things down. I mean, only things like slang words in foreign languages, or superstitions, like seeing two people in a café and one of them won't hand the other a knife to butter the bread but sets it down for the other to pick up, that sort of thing. I suppose that comes of being a spy. Might that be the sort of thing he was looking for in these religious tracts by Constantine Angelus?'

Ysidro made the small movement which was for him a head shake, barely the flicker of his eyes. 'When Constantine wrote of superstitions he was more likely to be referring to the veneration of the saints.' Something – the reminiscence of a smile – for a moment touched the corner of his mouth.

'That's an odd thing for a vampire to write about . . . isn't it? Did you know him?'

'He was Master of Paris,' said Ysidro, 'when first I returned to this city as a vampire, in 1602. He was – dear to me.'

'Is that usual?' she asked, after considering these words. 'At least, you just said the master vampires are very . . . very territorial. What were you doing in Paris?'

'Trying to save my soul from Hell,' said the vampire at length, his eyes suddenly inhuman, and very old. 'Constantine Angelus was the only one among the vampires genuinely willing to help me do it.'

FOUR

'I've never been inside it, you understand.' La Belle Nicolette (as she was called in the *Guide Rose*) laid a lace-gloved hand on Asher's arm, and with him considered the soot-black facade of the old *hôtel particulier* across the cobbled street. 'You can't see it from here, but according to my Tante Camille, who grew up there, it takes up most of the block behind the other houses. My cousins – on the respectable side of the family – are forever petitioning Uncle Evrard to sell the place, because you could probably get three blocks of flats on the land and they could all have a *fortune*.'

'Is Uncle Evrard so sentimentally attached to the place?' Asher covered the little hand with his own and gave her a humorous twinkle. The beautifully matched horses attached to her open carriage would cost, he guessed, in the neighborhood of fifteen thousand francs, not even taking into account the salary of the liveried coachman on his high box, seemingly deaf to the conversation behind him. The gossip columns of *Le Figaro* speculated that La Belle Nicolette had so many lovers among the bankers and stockbrokers at the Bourse because no one man by himself could pay for her dresses, but Asher guessed that at the moment most of those wealthy gentlemen had other matters on their minds. And indeed, La Belle had been perfectly willing to be taken to an exclusive little café off the Jardin des Plantes in exchange for an hour's conversation about whatever her escort wished to discuss.

She made a gesture of throwing up her hands, rolled her eyes theatrically, and smiled back. Asher guessed her age at nineteen.

'Uncle Evrard! Nobody on my side of the family has seen Uncle Evrard for *decades*. He lives in Perpignan – heaven only knows where he gets his money from! – and does good deeds for the Church. He writes Mama and Tante Camille *endless* letters about their way of life, as if Mama hasn't been settled down with her M'sieu Hofstein for fifteen years and Tante Camille were walking the streets instead of living respectably on the dividends of American railway stock. Are you truly writing a book about old houses and old families of Paris?'

'I am, *ma belle*.' Asher kissed the girl's hand. A dozen feet up the narrow street the iron-backed carriage gate blocked the view of anything but a steep Renaissance roofline and the conical cap of what looked like a round tower, perhaps fifty feet back from the gate itself. So large a forecourt would be mirrored in a sizeable stable block. *No wonder the respectable cousins want Uncle Evrard to sell the place.* The Rue des Trois Anges was barely wider than an alley and the *hôtel* itself wasn't mentioned in any of the guidebooks to this once-fashionable quarter. Neither was the street.

This was one of the things that had drawn his attention to it.

'Does no one live there now? A caretaker . . .?'

'*Guards.*' She rolled the word on her tongue like an expensive *marchand de vin*.

'*Guards*?' Asher rewarded the melodramatic revelation with an expression of astonishment.

'Truly! The family all fled to Limoges when the Germans took Paris in seventy-one, and when they returned they found a letter from a solicitor, telling them they were to find somewhere else to live. Tante Camille tells me that money has continued to appear in Uncle Evrard's bank account ever since, though of course by that time Tante Camille had her own flat near the Bois . . .'

Paid for, Asher guessed, by a gentleman friend.

'The family weren't even permitted to get their clothing and dishes – and I must say it served them right! That was all shipped to them later. Uncle never would explain whose solicitor it was and why he let himself be turned out of his own house, and of course both sides of the family were *agog* with guesses.'

She nodded toward the lodge beside the porte-cochère, even its little window shut tight.

'Some of my friends – boys I wasn't even supposed to speak to! – used to walk past the place, and they said they'd seen guards in uniform come in and out; commissionaire's uniforms, you understand, not military. But big men, they said, and not from this neighborhood. They buy their cigarettes at the *tabac*.'

Her graceful gesture indicated something in the direction of the Rue Vieille du Temple. 'And sometimes they have a beer at the café. But you understand, I do not come to this district often. It is not what it was.' She wrinkled her nose in comic distaste. 'I'm sure they would be amenable—' her wink was a discreet reminder of the little token of esteem that he'd purchased for her at Tiffany's on the Rue de Rivoli after coffee – 'perhaps to an interview?'

'At some future date.' Asher had stuck his head into enough vampire nests to know that, even in daytime, even in sleep, the Undead did not really sleep. And even through the thickness of earth they could distinguish differences in the footsteps of passers-by, enough to recognize a stranger's.

Particularly if a paid guard later commented, *Someone was here asking questions . . .*

'You wouldn't know who pays these guards, would you? Not the same solicitor, surely, after all this time?'

She shook her head. Framed in a chignon of coffee-black curls – and shaded by a particularly hideous fringed hat reminiscent of a lampshade, which Asher recognized as being the *dernier cri* of fashion – her face was a symphony of ovals, the earrings he'd bought her at Tiffany's twinkling like the ocean. 'Well, not Uncle Evrard, at any rate. But every family has its oddities, has it not?'

Recalling the audience he'd had two days previously with Lydia's Aunt Louise in that great Versailles of a flat on the Avenue Kléber, Asher grinned. 'I understand that you must have other engagements this afternoon—' by the line of roof-shadow on the old walls around them he guessed it must be after four – 'but may I beg of you the final indulgence of an introduction to your Tante Camille? This is the most impressive example of Renaissance domestic architecture I have yet seen in Paris, and the most untouched. If I cannot see its interior for myself, I must and will have a description of it! May I count on your mercy for this plea?'

'But of course, m'sieu! It will be my pleasure. Jacques,' she called out to the driver. 'Tante Camille's . . .'

As the matched pair of chestnut geldings drew away from that locked carriage gate Asher glanced back at it, noting the ship under full sail carved on the keystone of the opening. For a moment – he frowned, troubled, knowing that his dream was starting to drift from the actual events of that July afternoon and back into the realm of what could have been fantasy – he thought that the gates stood open. Thought that a dark-haired man stood within them, watching him drive away. A man he had seen before, but could not remember where.

Is this only a fantasy, or were they following me, even then?

It was nearly midnight before Dr Théodule came into the ward. He looked exhausted; Lydia snatched off her glasses, sprang to her feet, and hurried the length of the room to meet him. 'Don't tell me you're still on duty, doctor!'

'I'm the only one still on duty.' Bitterness edged the old man's voice. 'Moflet's volunteered. The orderlies are all on their way to Lille with the army—'

'As they should be, doctor.' The nurse Thérèse Sabatier came into the ward behind him. 'It is the duty of a man, and a Frenchman, to spring into action when the trumpet sounds. You,' she added brusquely to the cleaning-woman who had followed her in, 'start changing these sheets as soon as you've mopped. It will be up to all of us to work harder, in honor of the heroes who've gone.' Her cold eyes scanned the sleeping men in the beds along the walls, as if suspecting each of malingering in the hour of La Belle France's need. 'And don't take all night about it.'

'No, madame,' murmured the woman meekly.

'And these men can simply take care of themselves?' Dr Théodule leaned over the first of the beds, listened to the patient's heart, checked the notes written on the chart at the bed's foot, and clicked his tongue. Glancing back Lydia saw that Ysidro was gone.

'A true man,' returned the nurse, 'will think his life well ended if the physician who could not be in two places at once chose the defense of his country over the care of men who may already be dying.'

'Did you write these notes, Dr Asher?' The old man gestured a little with the stiff paper. Lydia nodded. The evening, before Ysidro's appearance, had been long.

'When the orderlies didn't come in I thought the least I might do was check their heart rates and blood pressure.' She followed the doctor to the next bed, with Sister Sabatier glaring at her behind the physician's back. 'I can administer saline injections, if—'

'The saline will be needed for the men at the battle-front.'

'We are not at war yet, Sister,' retorted Théodule. 'Pray God they'll avert it, even now . . .'

'Fools.' The nurse sniffed. 'To hamper us in our best chance of victory by waiting for our enemies to choose the time and place of battle.'

Dr Théodule looked at Asher's notes, moved aside his pyjama-coat to listen to his heart, pushed up its sleeve to administer the saline injection that for five days now, Lydia knew, was the only thing that had been keeping him alive.

Her knees still ached from an hour of standing in the angry, anxious crowd at the bank that morning. She was grateful she'd done it for, as Mrs Flasket had predicted, that afternoon the government had closed the banks to keep gold from being sapped from the country in the time of emergency. *If fighting starts it won't be possible to purchase sodium, chloride, potassium.* The thought of combing Paris pharmacies for supplies of such things – *if I can find a pharmacy open tomorrow!* – made her heartsick, but she knew it would need to be done. *If the army doesn't commandeer those things I wouldn't put it past Sister Sabatier to steal them from the hospital stores and hand them over . . .*

'No change?'

Lydia shook her head. A few beds over M'sieu Lecoq began coughing again, and in the murky heat the ward was filled with the acrid smell of urine from sheets too long unchanged. At the far end of the room a man groaned as the cleaning-woman rolled him aside to pull the soiled linen free.

'Sometimes I think he's coming out of it,' she said. 'He'll move a little and whisper, as if he's dreaming. And then – nothing.'

Movement caught her attention, close by: a reflection on the black glass of one of the open windows. But she saw nothing in the ward itself that could have cast it. *If it wasn't my imagination . . .*

'Stay by him.' Already on his way to M'sieu Arnoux in the next bed, Théodule paused and took Lydia's hand between his own. 'You are a brave and faithful wife, madame.'

'They're not . . . You don't think the Germans are going to shell Paris or anything, do you?'

'Shell it from where?' Sister Sabatier, already three-quarters of the way down the ward, turned back to speak to them, heedless of the men asleep in between. 'What sort of guns do you think the Germans have, that can bombard a city more than a hundred miles away? This one's dead,' she added, and yanked the sheet over old M'sieu Potric.

Lydia felt a chill, for M'sieu Potric had spoken to her when she'd come in that evening, and she'd thought he was getting better. Théodule went to confirm the death. The cleaning-lady went on stoically gathering soiled sheets.

Lydia stood where she was, beside her husband's bed. M'sieu Potric had lain opposite the window where for a moment she had thought she'd seen something reflected in the inky glass.

She didn't see Ysidro for the remainder of the night. When she emerged from the hospital gates in the morning, exhausted and dreading the hunt for a pharmacy that would, she knew, occupy most of the day, the first person she encountered was a newsboy in the street, shouting that Germany had declared war on France.

FIVE

There were Albanian mercenaries – bashi-bazouks, Muslims – all over Bosnia in 1885 in spite of the fact that Austria had taken the area from the Sultan several years previously. Asher's Modern Languages tutor had shown up rather unexpectedly on Rebbe Karlebach's doorstep in Prague and

suggested that Asher come 'walking' with him in the area, to
learn the ways of the countryside. 'Invaluable if you're going
to be studying there,' Belleytre had added, with that glinting
twinkle in his gray eyes that Asher later came to know well.
Asher had done rough hiking in the Carpathians and the prospect
of physical exertion didn't trouble him. Belleytre taught him how
to blend in – not just in his speech but in his mannerisms and
hygiene – with the local polyglot population of Bosnian Muslims,
bearded Greek monks, swarthy gypsies, and staunchly Catholic
Croats, and had introduced him to bandit chiefs, arms smugglers,
the leaders of informal nationalist armies, and similar colorful
types. The following year Belleytre had suggested that he go
back – 'just to have a look about' – with Edward Brannert, one
of the senior men on Asher's stairway at Balliol. Up until that
time Asher had never dreamed that Brannert was connected with
what he suspected Belleytre was involved in.

'You're only there to get to know everyone,' Belleytre had
said when the two young men had come to tea in his chambers:
evasive as always, just as if they were going to enter the disputed
provinces legally and make Sunday calls on other well-bred
academics. 'Study the lie of the land, maybe keep your ear to
the ground a bit in the public houses, pick up some nibbles of
gossip. Maybe draw the odd map or two.' It went without saying
that these maps of the tangle of heavily forested gullies, gorges,
and valleys between Sarajevo and the Montenegro border had
better not be discovered in either of the travelers' pockets, should
they happen to encounter officials of the Austro-Hungarian or
Turkish empires – both of whom were claiming the territory.

Or if they should encounter the bashi-bazouks.

When Asher first began to suspect that there were mercenaries
in the neighborhood of the deserted hunting-camp where he and
Brannert had planned to rendezvous that evening, the first thing he
did was destroy his maps – four weeks' worth of painstaking work
– and abandon the camp. Thus, when he was caught by the mercenaries in the woods, he could convincingly protest that he was just
a Czech student from Prague (*thank you, Mama Karlebach!*) on
the tramp to Sarajevo where his cousin had offered him a chance
of work. Brannert, who'd walked into the hunting-camp shortly
after Asher had fled it, had still had his maps on him.

It was the first time Asher had seen a man tortured.

He'd gotten thoroughly sick but it never occurred to the mercenaries that he might be acquainted with this 'English spy'. He doubted that even Brannert had recognized him. The bashi-bazouks had teased him unmercifully about his weak stomach for the remainder of the night, and let him go in the morning. Looking back, he didn't know why he didn't tell Belleytre and his mysterious 'friends' in the Department to go to hell as soon as he returned to Oxford, but the thought never crossed his mind. Later he wrote to Brannert's family telling them their son had fallen down a gorge while hiking, and had been killed instantly.

Why do I remember this? he wondered, walking over the Charles Bridge into Prague, dirty and exhausted and still sick – nearly a week later – from the *rakia* the mercenaries had made him drink with them. The dark waters of the Vltava slid by under the arches like an oiled black sword blade; he knew he needed to turn right on to Bilkova Ulice to reach Rebbe Karlebach's house. To shelter under the old man's steep-slanted roof for a night or two before getting on the train for Calais, and so on to Oxford to report to Belleytre, which was what he knew he'd actually done . . .

Only the street wasn't as he remembered it. Instead of the graceful frontages of eighteenth-century stone he saw around him tall, slightly crooked shapes, a weird lacework of dark timbers and pale plaster glimmering through the mist. He knew he should be on the Parizska but there was a four-storied gable black against the sky where he knew the Spanish synagogue should be, the narrow throat of a court where, in his waking recollection, the glatt kosher shop of Mama Karlebach's nephews stood.

A young man walked ahead of him, long pale hair hanging on to slender shoulders of black velvet, and his face was familiar . . .

Where do I know him from?

Why am I dreaming of him?

Asher quickened his step to catch him up, trying to recall his name.

Stephen? Sylvester? Simon . . .

Simon . . .

The young man wore the archaic black robe of a scholar,

billowing loose around a close-fitting doublet and paned breeches. Embroidered gloves covered his hands. He turned down a narrow passageway to a court, and Asher followed. *This isn't Prague . . .*

Water glistened in the center of the dirt street, blobbed with excrement, animal and human; its stink overrode even the bitter chill of the night. Candle flame dimly illumined the windows of the upper floors, but the lower were all shuttered fast. *Where AM I?* It smelled like Constantinople at its most revolting, or the canals of Venice on a hot day, but the houses were all wrong. When the young man knocked at a door in the court beyond the passageway a servant opened it, and didn't seem to see Asher when Asher stepped quickly through almost upon the young man's heels.

The downstairs room was an abyss of shadow, sparse furnishings half-glimpsed in the serving-man's candle flame. Judging by the servant's clothing, and the young man's, Asher put the date at late in the sixteenth century or within the first decade of the seventeenth. *Why am I dreaming about the reign of Queen Elizabeth? Something to do with Shakespeare?* The stair was narrow as a coffin and turned twice around itself as it ascended.

In an upper room an old man sat at a desk writing, his dark soutane buttoned close, with a shawl worn on top for additional warmth. Asher half expected one of them to greet the other with familiar opening words: 'I know not why I am so sad' or 'Now is the winter of our discontent Made glorious summer by this sun of York'.

The candles showed the mist of the old man's breath as he turned his head and the younger crossed to him, holding out his hand.

The old man's quill dropped from fingers gone nerveless with shock. He'd been handsome as a young man, and had kept most of his teeth. His bones were beautiful still. His lips formed the word 'Simon?', soundless with incredulity.

The young man – Simon – fell to his knees, caught the old man's soft, wrinkled hands and pressed them to his cheek for a moment, then kissed them desperately, like a man begging for his life.

'Simon?' the old man whispered again, and put his palm to his visitor's cheek. 'Dear God, you—' He broke off, staring and staring. 'Fifty years,' he said at last, hoarse with disbelief. 'You died in—'

'Help me.' The young man's voice was barely a breath of sound. 'Jeffrey, help me. I beg you.'

'How is this possible? Is it really you, and not a – a spirit, a phantom . . .'

For answer Simon pulled off his gloves and held up his hands. His long, slim fingers were almost skeletal, but instead of nails they were tipped with claws. Tilting back his head he drew up his lips to show the gleam of fangs. He caught the man Jeffrey's hands when the old man would have pulled away from him in horror, and the candles on the desk reflected in his eyes as in a cat's.

'It is truly me,' he said. 'For almost fifty years I have been as you see me, dear friend. I have been the thing that you tell yourself cannot really exist. They say that God forgives, Jeffrey. Forgives anything, if it is asked with a contrite and willing heart. What must I do, to be forgiven?'

The man Jeffrey only touched Simon's cheek, like white silk colored gold by the firelight, a young man's cheek. 'It is true, then? There are such things as the vampire?'

'There are. I am.' He bowed his head again, pressed his face to his old friend's hands. 'Tell me what I must do, to ransom my soul back from Hell.'

'This isn't right.'

Like the scratch of a razor in bleached wax, a frown marked Ysidro's brow.

Lydia leaned forward, her heart in her throat. 'Is he . . .' The words dried in her mouth. 'He isn't . . .'

The yellow eyes met hers, momentarily impatient. 'He is as he was last night,' he said, as if Asher's future ability to think and reason, his intelligence, and the thousand things that made up the man Lydia loved were of only secondary importance, and she wanted to slap him, for all the good that was likely to do. ''Tis not his mind that I touch, but his dreams. His memories. The images of where he has been, and what he has seen. Yet he dreams of matters which are impossible for him to know. Recalls events at which he was not and could not have been present.'

'Are you sure of that?' She realized how foolish the words sounded even as they emerged from her mouth.

'To the best of my knowledge,' returned the vampire astringently, 'your husband was not in Paris in 1602, so yes, I am fairly certain of my ground here.' He considered the wasted face on the pillow, and for the first time Lydia saw not only puzzlement but also disconcerted alarm in his eyes. 'To the best of my knowledge,' he added, 'those are *my* memories in which he treads, in his dreams.'

Lydia only stared at him, as if he had spoken some foreign language. For a moment she wondered if she were dreaming herself. She was so exhausted, she was aware, that the shadowy hospital ward had a slightly phantasmical cast to it. She'd spent the afternoon being driven by Stanislas Greuze to every pharmacy in Paris, and in those which were not closed she had met – and argued with – elderly men, or the wives of the younger pharmacists, who had only spread their hands in resignation. 'It is of no use, madame. The army has sent for all supplies of drugs. If it should happen that a compromise is reached, perhaps next week . . .'

She'd returned to the Avenue Kléber and found her aunt's salon hip-deep in steamer trunks. In her own room, Imèlde was packing the small case that Lydia had brought from Oxford the previous week. 'I told 'em you were staying, miss,' her own maid Ellen had protested. 'But they wouldn't listen . . .'

'Nonsense, of course you're returning to England,' Aunt Louise had informed her – granite and steel swathed in patchouli and lace – and had slapped boat-train tickets into Lydia's hand. 'We need to be at the Gare du Nord at ten. It's the last train – *what* I went through, to get these!' Meaning, Lydia was well aware, what Honoria Flasket had gone through.

'Heaven only knows what the Gare will be like. *Military personnel only*, they're saying now. I guarantee you, Dieppe will be a madhouse.'

The ensuing argument had cost Lydia most of the sleep she'd been desperately looking forward to through the whole of the aching day, and she'd fled the apartment the moment her aunt went to her room to dress for dinner.

After examining seven or eight possible responses to the

vampire's words – picking each sentence up and mentally turning it over, like her Uncle Ambrose when he'd had too much cognac and was trying to select a music-box cylinder – she finally settled on, 'How is that possible?'

'It isn't.' Ysidro touched Asher's temple with the backs of his knuckles, the small straight line still etched between his brows. 'The only way he could have these things in his mind – in his dreams – is if he were in contact with Constantine Angelus.'

'The Master of Paris? The one who wrote religious tracts?'

'Even he.'

He was dear to me, Ysidro had said. Lydia was aware of how few – human or vampire – this man would speak of in those terms, in the three-plus centuries of his shadowy existence.

'He is the only one whose mind I would permit to enter into mine, in dreaming, as if he were my master who made me vampire . . .'

'Is it possible,' she asked, 'that he wasn't killed after all when the others were . . . in 1871, did you say?'

'No.' The sharpness of his voice was like the shutting of a gate. 'And he perished long ere that.'

In the silence that followed the grumble of truck engines rose from the Rue Saint-Antoine, the squeak of wagon-wheels, the *tock* of hooves. Reservists' voices, coming into town with their satchels of food and clean socks, at the deployment centers and train stations.

Two beds over, M'sieu Lecoq coughed, wet and labored. The only person Lydia had seen so far tonight had been Fantine, stoically mopping the corridor. Judging by the stale smells of soiled linen and vomit she hadn't made it to this ward yet tonight, and it was nearly midnight.

At length Ysidro set his thoughts, whatever they were, aside. 'But as Constantine could enter into my thoughts,' he said, 'I am well able to walk into James's dreams, as I can walk into the dreams of any one of the living into whose eyes I have looked. Last night James dreamed of a woman who from her manner and the over-emphatic style of her attire I assume to be one of the demi-monde – "eight-spring luxury model", as the fashionable say. Thus when I departed last night I repaired to such haunts of fashion as are still in operation in this city;

contrary to the assertions of Sister Sabatier, many in Paris still think more of seeing and being seen than of aiding La Patrie, and most of them were at Maxim's until a surprisingly advanced hour of the morning. By the time I located the woman with whom James had gone riding in a carriage through the old Marais district, 'twas near daylight and I was forced to return to my own lodgings by way of the sewers. But ere I left the restaurant I managed to send the woman a note by way of one of the waiters – a note containing five hundred francs – and she will be expecting you to call in the afternoon. Is this agreeable to you, Mistress?'

'It is.'

He drew from his pocket a visiting card, elaborate with copperplate lettering and embossed flowers, which bore the name 'La Belle Nicolette'.

An address on the Boulevard Haussmann had been penciled on the back. Lydia could only offer up a silent prayer of thanks that at this moment Aunt Louise was on her way to England, home, and glory.

'I would have called on her myself, tomorrow night,' the vampire went on, as Lydia took the card, 'rather than suggest that you go near such a woman. Yet my heart misgives me. I think we need to learn what this woman may know as soon as may be. Despite assurances from the government that France's armies will cut those of Germany to pieces, I suspect a great many people will be leaving Paris ere this morning's sun goes down. 'Twere better not to delay.'

'I agree.' Lydia slipped the card into her reticule and propped her spectacles more firmly on to her nose. Eight-spring luxury model or not, it never crossed her mind that Asher would have sought out or dreamed about a woman who wasn't somehow involved in the puzzle he had come to Paris to solve, whatever it was. 'Last night, did you – were there . . .' She regarded her friend hesitantly. It might have been he who killed poor M'sieu Potric, she reminded herself, whose empty bed stood like an accusation opposite the open window . . . Yet he had saved her life, and that of her daughter. And beyond that debt, she recalled all the nights she'd walked with him in the spring mists along the Embankment, or played cards with him on the train to

Constantinople. Remembered moments when he'd smile the smile of the man he'd once been.

And she hated herself for feeling what she felt.

For knowing herself a traitor to Jamie in her heart.

'Am I safe here, do you think? Is Jamie safe?'

'While the sun is down? No.' Lydia had not seen him move, but he stood now beside the window, looking down into the street. The chilly glare of the street lights outlined the aquiline nose, touched with frost his thin white eyelashes, his spider-web hair. 'Though I sensed their presence near the hospital last night I encountered none of the Paris nest. It may be that Elysée de Montadour is waiting to get at James again to finish what she began – if 'twas she. Or it could be one of her fledglings. As I said, Paris has long been a rebellious and troublesome nest. I would not leave either of you here alone.'

Fantine came in then with her bucket and mop, thin and stooped, though Lydia guessed she and this woman were nearly of an age. She left a great bundle of stinking linen outside the door and carried, awkwardly, another clean bundle jammed beneath her arm; not nearly enough, Lydia judged, to change all the sheets in the ward. Still, she went to her, helped her set the linen down and gave her a friendly 'Bonsoir, madame', and listened to her complaint of the army's depredations on the hospital stores.

'My brother's joined up,' the cleaning-woman said. 'I tried to tell him not to, for it won't be good for him. He's not so smart, my brother.' She frowned worriedly, and tapped her temple. 'He'll get hurt. And now they've took away most of the clean sheets as well.'

When Fantine moved off to the far end of the ward Ysidro seemed to re-materialize from the embrasure of the window; the hand he laid on Lydia's shoulder when she sat down was cold as death.

He hasn't fed.

Yet.

'Did you get money ere the banks closed?' he asked.

'Two thousand francs. That's all they'd give me.'

'A one-eyed man is king in the country of the blind. If you remain long in Paris you'll find many who are delighted to sell their services for whatever coin you choose to pay. Where do you stay? At your aunt's, still? Very good. In the hours of darkness I shall remain here with you insofar as is possible. In the earlier hours of evening I shall commence arrangements to flee the city as soon as James is well enough to be moved. Discover if you can what took James to where he was found in the fourth arrondissement. To the best of my knowledge, Elysée de Montadour dwells still in the nest her husband had, out on the Rue de Passy, but she may well have another in the older part of the city. If any more of these communications reach you from this "Mr Johnson", bring them to me.'

'I doubt any will, now that Aunt Louise has gone. They'll assume I left with her, which I suppose is what any sensible person would have done. You're not turning German spy-hunter, are you?' It was the last thing she'd have expected of the vampire.

'What I hunt,' Ysidro corrected gently, 'is word of why James was seeking the writings of Constantine Angelus. And how it is that he comes to dream of matters that only Constantine would have known of me.'

SIX

'I came to Paris in the winter of 1602,' said Ysidro, 'seeking the man who had been my confessor when first I arrived in England. His name was Jeffrey Sampson, a Jesuit and dear to me. A man of great intellectual attainment, yet of a kind and cheerful heart. Like many of the True Faith he was obliged to flee the country after the Pope issued a bull that called upon them to deprive the heretic usurper Elizabeth of her throne.'

'One can scarcely blame her for being irked,' pointed out Lydia.

A corner of the vampire's lips flexed for a moment. Without admitting the justice of this position he went on, 'When I came to Paris I had been vampire for nearly fifty years. I had done my best to take only the lives of those already damned – London crawled with heretics – yet my heart feared that this was not enough. I had heard all my life that 'twas Satan who created such creatures as myself, who walked the night and would be destroyed by God's daylight. As I grew to know those others of the London nest – and those who haunted the countryside like wolves in the hours of darkness – I could not shake from my soul the terror of damnation, and the fear that I would in time grow like them. Then, too' – he turned one hand over, where it lay on his knee, as if considering the length and sharpness of his claw-like nails and the worn gold of his signet-ring that gleamed in the dim light coming into the dark ward from the hall – 'I had by then seen many of the living I knew in London age and die. Long already had I ceased to frequent old haunts, for fear that Moll Butcher at the Left Leg in Shoreditch, or Mistress Quimmer at the Black Dog, would see my face a boy's face still and cry out that I had sold myself to the Devil for eternal youth.

'A fit jest,' he added, and looked down again at Asher's face. 'We who hunt the night are Dead Sea fruit. Colored dust. That those who behold us would call what they see "youth" is to me irrefutable proof that God exists and has a sense of humor.'

'Were there that many heretics in London?' Lydia had a momentary vision of acres of stakes, holocausts of flame.

''Twas illegal then in England to be anything else.'

By 'heretics', she realized, he meant Protestants. Church of England, like herself.

'In France the Catholic League had striven and failed to keep the leader of the French Protestants from taking the throne. I doubt a single soul believed King Henri's conversion to the True Faith was anything but a blasphemous ruse to silence opposition to his accession, and, I came to learn on my first night in Paris, even the Undead of Paris were divided between the faithful and the followers of Calvin and Luther. Thus I returned to the question that I asked Jeffrey, when at last I found him at his lodgings south of the river: can one be faithful, and yet damned?'

After a long silence Lydia asked, 'What did he say?'

Lydia returned to the Avenue Kléber at eight the next morning, with the thin mists just burning off the river. In the cab she asked Stanislas Greuze the question – wondering what a good socialist would reply – and, rather to her surprise, he told her the tale of

Tannehauser, the knight who sought out the goddess Venus in her secret realms below the earth. After three years of worshipping her there the knight was filled with remorse and left her, traveling to Rome to beg the Pope's forgiveness of his sins. 'With such sins as yours,' the Pope cried, 'it is far more likely that my walking stick will put forth flowers, than that you will ever be forgiven.' So Tannehauser knew he was damned, and left.

The cab-driver spun the wheel deftly, dodged between two trucks of a convoy in the Place du Théâtre Français, and fleeted up the half-deserted Avenue de l'Opéra. 'Three days later the Pope found his walking stick covered with spring flowers. He sent out men to fetch Tannehauser, to tell him that God's mercy was indeed infinite, but Tannehauser was never seen again. My granny used to tell me,' the driver went on, 'that it just goes to show you not to judge. Myself, I think it just means, "Never trust the Pope."'

Ellen let Lydia in with the information that after Lydia's departure the previous afternoon Aunt Louise had had the locks changed '"in case that foolish girl is so careless as to leave her key lying about," she said, the old witch!' fumed the maid, handing her a new key. 'The trouble I had getting these cut from the one Mrs Flasket slipped me at the train station! And what a horror that was, with soldiers all milling about and women crying and American tourists all fighting each other for a place standing up in the mail car. I'm to post it back to her,' Ellen added, 'at Halfdene, which is where she's going, and God help your poor uncle! How is Professor Asher, ma'am?'

'The same,' Lydia whispered. Ellen had also gone shopping – predictably, Aunt Louise had stripped the apartment of everything edible, presumably to force Lydia to the conclusion that she must accompany her aunt back to London or starve in the street – and had purchased, as well as coffee and rolls, a cup, a plate, and a set of cheap tin utensils to lay out on the cherrywood table in the breakfast-room (Aunt Louise had sent the Limoges back to Halfdene Hall as well). 'Oh, you dear!' said Lydia when she saw this repast laid out for her. 'You didn't need to fix up the breakfast-room for me! I can eat in the kitchen.'

'Never, as long as I'm in the house, ma'am! What your mother would say about that—'

'What my mother would say to Louise,' retorted Lydia, 'if she heard she'd abandoned me in Paris with the Germans gathering on the border, and changed the lock on the door—'

'What your mother would say—' the maid's brown eyes twinkled – 'is exactly nothing, because she was as terrified of Lady Mountjoy as everybody else is. If you'll give me a bit more money (and the cost of coffee is enough to make you faint!) I'll go out later to get some real groceries – the markets are still open, thank heavens! – and a newspaper.'

She bustled through the baize-covered door that led into the pantry and the apartment's kitchen quarters, leaving Lydia to contemplate the over-elaborate visiting card of La Belle Nicolette and wonder if Ellen had managed to salvage any of her – Lydia's – clothing from the trunks that Louise had ordered packed. If not, where might she purchase at least a camisole and drawers . . . and another skirt . . . and a middy – a middy would go with nearly anything . . . and some stockings. What would people be wearing, now that war had started? *Good heavens, I'll need face powder, rouge, mascaro, lip-rouge if I'm to be presentable at all . . . I hope Aunt Louise hasn't taken the laundry soap! Will two thousand francs be enough?*

The jerk of her head made her realize she'd drifted almost into sleep. She had dozed, uncomfortably, in the chair at Jamie's bedside for nearly three hours during the night, waking at intervals to see Ysidro motionless with his hand against Jamie's temple, his yellow eyes half-shut as if listening to voices far off. ''Twere best you continue as you have been,' he had said the first time she'd wakened, 'and come here at eventide. Thus I may keep watch over you both. I mislike this "William Johnson" of yours. He does indeed write like a German' (Lydia had brought to him the note that had come for her, repeating the previous invitation, before she had left the apartment) 'and we have no surety who is working for whom. Sleep here if you can.'

Rising now, she slipped across the main salon and down the hall to her bedroom, which faced east into the small courtyard in the center of the block of flats. Ellen had made up the bed – Aunt Louise's second housemaid had been stripping sheets and blankets when Lydia had sneaked away the previous evening – but there was no sign of a trunk, of Lydia's small valise that she'd brought from Oxford, or of anything else. This included, she noticed, the cardboard box in which she'd brought long swags of dried garlic flowers, aconite, and Christmas rose, plants universally acknowledged to be inimical to vampire flesh. *Did Aunt Louise pack them in my trunk with everything else? Or did she just have them thrown out?*

Sunlight streamed in through the tall window, so it probably didn't matter at the moment.

She pulled the pins out of her hair (twelve of them), sponged off her face powder and the artfully applied rouge without which she refused to be seen in public (using the hem of her petticoat for a towel – Aunt Louise had made off with those, too), and took off her shoes, skirt, and shirtwaist. With a certain amount of difficulty she loosened her corset, and finally – with profoundest relief – dropped on to the bed and slept.

And dreamed of a walking stick, bursting into flower.

'What did he say?' she had asked Ysidro last night, and for a long while the vampire had not replied. Had only sat with one hand on Jamie's forehead, the other on his wrist, as if looking into those dreams – *what was Jamie doing, having dreams that belonged to Ysidro?* – that had so disconcerted him.

'He heard my confession that night,' the vampire said at length, and in her dream now Lydia glimpsed him as he must have been in those days, with his white ruff and his dark velvet clothing, kneeling before the cross, hands folded in supplication. *So much for the legend that vampires can't look at the cross . . .*

'He said he could not grant me absolution, but must speak to his superior, the Cardinal Montevierde. Even that gave me relief, to know that I had put in train the opening gambits of my salvation. When I returned the following night Montevierde was there, a tall man, lean with fasting and smelling of old blood from the wounds beneath his clothing: the cilice, the hair-shirt, the weals of self-flagellation. I found it extremely difficult to concentrate on anything that he said to me, so absorbed was I in a storm of hunger and need. He believed in the Undead and knew that this was what I was, yet in him I sensed no fear of me.'

'Did he look on it as a test?' asked Lydia. 'Of his faith – or of yours?'

'Mayhap.' For a moment in her dream Lydia saw in his fleeting expression – as she sometimes did in waking – the young man he had been, emerging from behind the dignity of Spanish etiquette and the chill of Un-death. 'At the time I had the sensation that fear had long since been burned out of him by some incandescent inner fire.'

'Faith?' After half a lifetime studying medicine and suffering, Lydia had always been amazed by faith, as if she heard people speaking in tongues.

Ysidro's voice was quiet, and dry as paper. 'Ambition.'

'And did he absolve you?'

'He told me to seek out Esdras de Colle, who had been a nobleman in the region of Bordeaux and was the chief of the Protestant vampires of Paris,' said Ysidro. 'To seek him out, and kill him.'

At that point, on the previous night, footfalls had sounded in the corridor and Sister Thérèse's voice had echoed, indignant at the idea that any person had the right to express the opinion that the army was amiss in its strategy. 'That time is past, doctor! The might of the army – the spirit of our men! – is what stands between us and the Germans! Not by one word – for God's *sake*, Fantine, can't you even carry a tray properly? – not by one word can we diminish that spirit . . .'

And Lydia's dream folded itself away and she was in Oxford again, in the long garden of the house on Holywell Street, watching her daughter run races with butterflies. At two and a half Miranda would pick up, pursue, or examine anything, from bumblebees to chicken guts in the kitchen, and even after being told what these things were would make up alternative explanations for and uses of them ('Bumblebees make houses for butterflies!').

But even dreaming of her child, Lydia seemed to see shadows moving behind her, visible as a flicker in her peripheral vision – such peripheral vision as she had beyond the rim of her spectacles – and gone when she turned her head.

And she knew what she saw was a vampire.

Lydia had instructed Ellen to wake her at one, and she jerked from sleep with a gasp at five minutes before. *Where can I buy clean clothing before tea with La Belle Nicolette at four?* The lace-and-gauze shirtwaist she'd worn yesterday and last night was missing from the chair where she'd left it, and she guessed Ellen had stolen in and taken it to launder in the kitchen. But when she padded forth to the salon wrapped in the bedspread it was to find her handmaiden with a face like thunder, and an assortment of small parcels laid out on the salon's holland-draped central table.

'Invitations to visit gentlemen without telling anybody where you're going are one thing,' stated Ellen. 'And what your mother would say about *that* I won't go into, because you know as well as I do, with Professor Asher out of his senses and the German army tearing up the countryside . . . But any man who would have the brass-faced arrogance to send such things to a lady, and a married lady . . .'

She thrust an envelope at Lydia as if it bore the postmark of one of the upper circles of Hell.

'And like this "William Johnson" he's got foreign handwriting, too! Who are these people, miss? Ma'am,' she corrected herself – she'd have taken the trouble to correct herself, Lydia reflected, even if she'd had to shout *The building's being bombed, miss!* 'Do they have anything to do with poor Professor Asher?'

The handwriting wasn't the Teutonic style of the alleged William Johnson. It was the vertical, looped, rather spiky script of a sixteenth-century Spaniard:

> Mistress,
> Whilst you slept last night I took the liberty of communicating with various tradespeople with whom the Paris nest habitually deals, who are well used to such instructions. I trust the parcels which will arrive today will serve to replace some at least of what your execrable aunt bore away.
>
>   Ever thy servant,
>   Simon

Lydia tore up the note at once (Ellen was trying to read it over her shoulder). The packages – from Houbigant on the Rue de Rivoli, Madeleine Chéruit (*CHÉRUIT works for the vampires???*), Marcelle Demay, Hellstern and Sons, and an assortment of clothing merchants – were a shining tribute to the ready-made garment industry. Shirtwaists, camisoles, underclothing, stockings, gloves, a pair of jade-and-lilac pumps (*how does he know my size?*), and two extremely pretty afternoon dresses in the colors Lydia favored. Another parcel contained towels. A smaller one held cosmetics and a hairbrush; one smaller still, a pair of earrings, in emerald and pearl.

'Don't you *dare* put those on, ma'am! The very idea! Your Aunt Louise would have a stroke if she heard of it!'

'My Aunt Louise is the one who's responsible for me being obliged to accept these gifts,' Lydia retorted. 'They're . . . from a very old friend.' *About three hundred and eighty years old, in fact . . .*

Stanislas Greuze, waiting faithfully at the taxi-stand on the Étoile, kissed his hand and cried, '*Magnifique!*' as Lydia got into the cab and despite the total impropriety of accepting gifts of clothing and jewelry from a man not her husband – even if he had been dead for centuries – Lydia felt a good deal better about visiting an eight-spring luxury model courtesan knowing that she herself was just as expensively attired.

La Belle Nicolette's flat was smaller than Aunt Louise's – the same could have been said of Buckingham Palace – but was, as far as Lydia could tell without her glasses, far more stylishly appointed. Its drawing-room windows overlooked the Boulevard Haussmann, now surging with a steady traffic of military supply vehicles. Its furniture, upholstered in dusty yellow and amber, made one think of orchids and serpents. La Belle Nicolette, a dainty brunette, rose to hold out her hand to Lydia as the maid led her in. 'M'sieu Ysidro said that he might send a deputy, rather than come to tea himself. Please do be seated, madame.'

Since she was wearing L'Heure Bleue by Guerlain, Lydia could guess the approximate cost of the rest of her raiment and be glad she'd disregarded Ellen's admonitions about propriety. 'My name is Mrs Asher,' she introduced herself. 'I'm the wife of the gentleman – he may have called himself Asher, or he may not – who sought you out last week to ask you about old *hôtels particuliers*.'

Every trade, Lydia was well aware, has its ethic, and La Belle

Nicolette merely raised polite eyebrows. When the maid brought
in tea and madeleines, Lydia caught the subdued bustle and scrape
of activity elsewhere in the flat. *Packing for hasty departure?
Ysidro was right . . .*

Whatever the French government had decreed about the French
railroads, five hundred francs would go a long way with a woman
who planned to go a long way.

'Shortly after he spoke with you,' Lydia went on, 'my husband
met with violence, and I have reason to fear that those who hurt
him – he's in hospital now, unconscious—' the younger woman's
eyes flared with sympathy and shock – 'might still seek to do
him – or me – harm. We're trying to find them – trying at least
to learn who they might have been, and why they attacked him.
It doesn't appear to be . . . random. Not robbers or thugs, I mean.
And so far, the only clue we have in this whole business is his
investigation of these old *hôtels*.'

'*Tiens*!' Even at the width of the tea-table, La Belle's features
were little more than a delicate impression of rose and ivory, but
she sounded impressed. 'So this *histoire* of writing a book?'

'As far as I know, there is no book. My husband – did he call
himself Asher, by the way?'

The courtesan shook her head. 'He gave his name as Alexander
Prior, but you understand—' her silvery laugh implied that any
gentleman might do the same – 'so often men conduct business
under names not their own. So silly, when the business is
completely innocent – as indeed his was, madame, I assure you.'
She handed her a teacup. 'He gave me a little present to thank
me for my trouble, but truly, all he asked of me was to show
him my uncle's old *hôtel* in the fourth arrondissement, and to
introduce him to my Tante Camille, who lived there as a child.'

'Were you there when he spoke to your aunt?'

'Briefly.' La Belle considered the matter for a moment. 'I had
another matter which needed attention that day – it was the
twenty-sixth of July, and I was preparing to depart for Deauville,
you understand. All this—' she gestured toward the long windows,
the grating rumble of trucks passing on the Boulevard – 'seemed
. . . inconceivable! And of course now all the arrangements have
had to be changed!

'But your husband asked us both about how long the house

had been in the Batoux family, and who had first built it. Our family is a very old one, you understand, though we were never of the nobility. Our . . . I don't know how many greats, but my aunts on the *respectable* side of the family could doubtless tell you! Our ancestor Jacques Batoux was a moneylender, and his son it was, or maybe his grandson, who built the *hôtel* and was appointed to be an intendant by Cardinal Richelieu, and so founded the family fortunes. Of course the Marais was the most fashionable part of town then. Later the family acquired a much nicer place in Passy when we became *fermiers généraux*, but there were always some members of the family living in the old *hôtel*. It was usually some impoverished spinster or scholar or someone that the family was supporting. That's what Uncle Evrard is – my mama's uncle, and Tante Camille's.'

She held out the madeleines to Lydia, who dipped one into her tea and then set it down untasted.

'What your husband wanted to know was what the place was like inside. For his book, you understand – but now you tell me there was no book. But the idea that Uncle Evrard, of all people, might have . . . what? Hired thugs to assault your husband?'

'No, of course not,' Lydia hastened to reply, though La Belle had chuckled in genuine amusement at the idea. 'Who lives there now?'

'No one, as I told M'sieu Prior – M'sieu Asher, that is to say. Only guards. Uncle Evrard has a farm outside Perpignan – which Mama tells me he has not the faintest idea how to run!'

'Then he didn't own the house?'

'Officially he does – *on paper*, as the Americans say. In reality, no, I think not. His side of the family never has had a bean.'

In Peking Lydia had encountered a powerful underworld family who had kept a vampire as a permanent prisoner, under horrible circumstances . . . In the same city there had been a temple where the Master vampire of Peking had living priests to act, apparently willingly, as his protectors. She couldn't imagine Ysidro – or Grippen, the Master of London – putting themselves into such a situation, but keeping the living on hand to guard the Undead was clearly not an unheard-of strategy.

Unless Uncle Evrard himself . . . ?

'As I told your husband, Uncle Evrard and his family were

cast out of the house by solicitors after the German war in 1871. I presume these were the same people who put money into his bank account every month.' She made a graceful little shrug with hands and eyebrows as well as her silken shoulders. 'It was all supposed to come from "family investments" that nobody ever discussed, and Uncle Evrard and all his sisters and their husbands occupied this giant spooky old mansion on the Rue des Trois Anges, trying to live like gentlefolk on cabbage soup. They were killingly respectable, and they had all these rules that Uncle Evrard demanded that everyone follow.'

'What sort of rules?'

'Crazy ones.' The girl grimaced. 'Whole areas of the house were locked up, and God forbid anyone should go into them. One could be beaten even for being found near the doors, Tante said. One couldn't have company in the evenings, because everyone had to be in bed by dark. My other aunts – Tante Camille's sisters and cousins – and their husbands didn't dare disobey, because they didn't have the money to live anywhere else, really. Tante Camille finally had enough of it and got Gran'mère – Uncle Evrard's youngest sister, who had been seduced by one of Uncle Evrard's friends and thrown out of the house and went on to the stage – to introduce her to a protector at Maxim's.'

'That was your mama's mama?' Lydia recalled with a wince what her father's butler had said to her when – at her father's orders – he had refused to admit her to the house again on the day her father had discovered that she'd enrolled at Somerville College to study medicine.

'It was. By the sound of it, Gran'mère danced in the Opéra ballet for all of about forty-five minutes before a protector set her up in a flat, and after that she has only been in contact with the family through reading of them in the social columns of *Le Figaro*. Mama herself has never set foot inside the house nor spoken to Uncle Evrard or any of his side of the family. Certainly not the rich side of the family out in Passy.'

'Might it have been the Passy side of the family who gave him the house, and the money?' Odd rules about the operation of grace-and-favor dwellings were certainly nothing unusual among Lydia's Halfdene relatives, none of whom – to her knowledge – was numbered among the Undead. Though now she thought of it, nobody had seen Uncle Nugent for decades . . .

'I don't think so.' La Belle's delicate eyebrows puckered. 'Tante later got a friend of hers, a banker, to try to track down where the money came from, and it was so tied up in trusts and foreign accounts that he couldn't. But Uncle Evrard was always fighting with the Passy crowd, who wanted him to sell the house and divide the money with them. Tante Camille says also that Uncle Evrard seemed to get madder as he got older – he must be nearly ninety now – and that he never would tell anyone why he had all these little rules. Gran'mère said she thought he'd gotten them from *his* Uncle Raoul, who lived in the house before him, but he seemed terrified that if anybody disobeyed they'd all be thrown out on to the street.'

A vampire nest.

It has to have been what Jamie was looking for.

'As indeed they all were, in the end . . .'

Eighteen seventy-one, Lydia recalled, was the year Elysée de Montadour became Master of Paris and started creating her own fledglings. She also remembered the nebulous rings of men and women all through the poverty-stricken alleys of the East End upon whose services Lionel Grippen, the Master of the London nest, could call: publicans who lent money to men who needed it, men who thereafter could be called on for 'favors' without any need to explain why.

The same way, she supposed, that Ysidro could simply send out notes to tradespeople last night, secure in the knowledge that they'd arrange for two lovely frocks and assorted stockings, rice-powder, towels, and underwear to be delivered to Aunt Louise's . . .

Or ask a waiter at Maxim's to hand the woman before her a note containing five hundred francs in order to purchase an hour of her time and all the information she had to give about an old *hôtel particulier*.

And Jamie went there . . .

'And he wanted to know what the place was like inside?'

'It's what he said.' Again La Belle spread her hands with a dancer's gesture, an actress's wry little moue. 'The only person who would want to know that – aside from a man writing a

book – would have been a burglar, but as far as I know there's
nothing of value there to steal. Tante Camille said that she and
her brothers sneaked into the forbidden area looking for treasure,
about three years before the war with the Germans – this would
have been in 1867 or '68, then – and she told me the place was
nearly bare. Just old furniture, crumbling to pieces, and chests
and chests full of old clothes. I went with M'sieu Prior to Tante
Camille's flat that day and introduced them, and left him there
with her. I don't know if he returned the next day or not.'

*And the following night he was thrown off a church tower,
after being bled nearly to death . . .*

*How close is the church of Sainte-Clare to the Rue des Trois
Anges?*

'Is your aunt still in Paris?'

'Now you speak of it—' the young woman frowned, thinking
back – 'I don't think I have heard from her this week. Of course
things have been so upside down . . . she might very well have
left town – she has a place in Normandy. But that's very close to
the Channel, after all. It isn't like her not to send me a note.' She
glanced again toward the window, toward the trucks grumbling
their way in the direction of Belgium.

'Might I beg of you,' said Lydia, 'a note of introduction to
your aunt? I really think . . . there's something very odd going
on here,' she added, with a hesitation which she hoped sounded
genuine. 'And I'd feel much better if I could learn from her just
exactly what she told my husband about that house.'

SEVEN

'Already one finds it difficult to obtain petrol,' observed
Stanislas Greuze as he gunned the cab across the Champs-
Élysées. 'It is not only medicines that the army is buying
up all over the town. When I was very small I remember it was
like this, in the days of the last war. The streets silent, as the world
waited for news.' All along the edge of the Bois de Boulogne,
placards above the news-stands screamed with black letters.

The German army was shelling Liège. Britain had declared war. Clinging to the hand-strap in the back seat, Lydia felt a queer sensation of sinking, as if she'd somehow stumbled into somebody else's life.

This isn't supposed to be happening. Somebody was supposed to stop it at the last minute, like they've always done before. Something was supposed to get us out of it.

Her heart pounded hard at the recollection of things Jamie had told her about the new weapons of war: airships, poison gas, cannons that could launch shells four miles.

Or at the very least I was supposed to be reading about this while sitting with Jamie and Miranda in the parlor in Oxford, exclaiming, 'Oh, I do hope those poor people in Paris don't get shelled!'

She stared without seeing at the silvery gleam of the river, the black lace arrowhead of the Tour Eiffel against the slow-fading light of late afternoon.

Jamie, wake up!

What am I going to do?

Tante Camille's flat on the Boulevard de Versailles was within a half-mile of Aunt Louise's. The front entrance of the building was molded with the asymmetrical curves of a 'modern' door-frame, giving Lydia the impression of walking down the throat of an immense lily, like Alice in Wonderland. No one occupied the concierge's little booth in the lobby, but through its brass-grilled window she saw an inner door standing open, and heard voices within: '*Ça va bien, ça! Tu me déserts pour cette précieuse Patrie, et alors? Que se passe-t-il à tes enfants, si tu es sauté?*'

Three b, La Belle Nicolette had said. The elevator, around which the bronze-decked marble staircase ascended in graceful ovals, was likewise deserted.

Lydia climbed the marble stairs.

The silence above-stairs seemed absolute. She wondered if the inhabitants of these expensive flats had already packed and left, just as La Belle was packing (or rather having the servants pack), and if she'd find the apartment of Camille Batoux as empty as Aunt Louise's.

And then what? Go to the Rue des Trois Anges and try to get into the Hôtel Batoux myself? Return to the hospital and wait until some afternoon when there are so few on duty – or they are so exhausted – that they don't notice one of the vampires' human servants walking in, the way I just walked in, and killing Jamie in his sleep? Wait for the Germans to arrive? Should I take day guard, and leave Ysidro to watch through the nights?

Prior to meeting La Belle Nicolette, Lydia had made another attempt to see W.W. Streatham at the embassy. She had left after one look at the long line of stranded holidaymakers – penniless, and as weary as herself – that jammed the halls. Even had she succeeded, she reflected as she rounded the last landing and ascended through a little archway formed of two bronze caryatids to the stair-lobby at the top, *they'd only lie to ME.* She glanced around – though the place was as empty (*probably considerably emptier, come to think of it*) as an Egyptian tomb – and sneaked her spectacles on to identify the bronze emblem on the door as 'a'. A short hall stretched on the other side of the lobby, terminating in door 'b'.

Before her hand reached the bell, Lydia smelled it.

There was something dead in the room beyond.

She'd worked too long in the clinic at the East End charity hospital, in her days as a struggling resident, not to recognize the stink of rotting flesh. It would be stupid to knock – what human being would stay in a place with a corpse? – and she glimpsed beneath the door the corner of a piece of paper. Bending, she pulled it out.

> Madame,
>
> I beg a thousand pardons, but Giselle was not here to let me in today, and Madame Rotier would not oblige. Please send a note to let me know, should I come Tuesday?
>
> > With sincerity,
> > Anne Foucault

Charwoman. Lydia threw another glance back at the lobby behind her, silent as a stage-set in the slightly bleak north light, then pulled up her skirts and removed, from the slender packet buttoned to the bottom edge of her corset, the roll of picklocks that Jamie had given her. The proper thing to do, of course, would be to run downstairs, interrupt the domestic dispute between the concierge and her husband (the elevator operator?), and call the police . . .

How many police remain in Paris? wondered Lydia, maneuvering the smallest of the delicate hooks into the keyhole and probing around for the wards. *Have they all gone down with the hospital orderlies to volunteer?* And if Monsieur and Madame Rotier didn't detect the smell of decay – the concierge's booth had reeked of cheap tobacco, so there was a good chance they wouldn't – would they refuse to 'oblige' her as they had refused the charwoman?

She added another probe to the lock, listening all the while for the echo of a footfall in the stairwell, the rattle of the elevator mechanism. This close to the door the smell of death was distinct – not just rotting flesh but feces as well (*they must both have been killed in the flat*) – but not strong. If the flat was anything like the size of Aunt Louise's, the bodies – Tante Camille's and that of Giselle, who was presumably her maid (*did she keep a cook?*) – might be several rooms away from the door . . .

She felt the wards give, gently pushed the door open.

Tante Camille had been killed in the bedroom. The chamber was a sort of shrine to the wages of sin, which in her case had clearly been substantial. Naked bronze atlantes upheld the canopy over her bed; the ceiling was the sort of Moorish plasterwork that reminded Lydia of photographs she'd seen of the Alhambra palace in Spain. The chests, wardrobes, dressing-tables, and bureaux that jammed the room were themselves jammed with precious things: statuettes of bronze and marble and alabaster, Sèvres porcelain make-up pots, Tiffany lamps and boxes. Whether the room had been searched, or whether the old woman who lay on her back on the bed in twenty thousand francs' worth of Jeanne Paquin had been packing to leave Paris, Lydia couldn't tell. Certainly every drawer of the shoulder-high jewelry safe next to the bed was open and empty.

Given the heat of the week, and the oven-like stuffiness of the room, Lydia guessed the woman had been dead four or five days. It was hard to tell, for she had been tortured, in a fashion that brought the taste of bile into Lydia's throat. It was clear, however, that most of her blood had been drained.

Moving quickly, touching nothing – though the first thing she'd done on entering the flat had been to put her gloves back on again – Lydia checked the frame of the bedroom mirror, that universal filing place of visiting cards, invitations, and addresses. Nothing. She tried not to see in the glass the reflection of the twisted body on the bed.

The dressing-table and the mantelpiece – more bronze nudes, upholding rose-red marble from Spain – were tidy, a tribute to 'Giselle', but if the killing had taken place four days ago Lydia guessed that any information Jamie had left had not yet had time to migrate into a drawer. Though Camille's hairpins and false switches of hair had been put away in their alabaster bowls, the old woman had still been dressed, which meant that the vampires had come for her as she'd been preparing for bed. Sponge and wash-cloth lay ready beside the cold water in the basin and ewer. The electric lamps burned not only in the bedroom but in the salon, and tears of agony had left tracks in the rice-powder, mascaro, and rouge that still plastered the wrinkled, pain-twisted face.

Trying to learn something? Lydia wondered, catching the frame of the bedroom door to steady herself. *Or just for sport?* With vampires, it could be either.

She knew James was right, in his vow to destroy them all.

Beyond the door, in a sort of drawing-room, trunks stood half-filled with dresses. They'd clearly been gone through, garments of satin, lace, and silk tumbled on the floor, but the notes tucked into the mirror-frame above the mantel here were undisturbed. Lydia recognized her husband's handwriting at once.

Alexander Prior. 10 Rue Saint-Louis en l'Île.

I should search the rest of the flat . . .

Through the heavy golden curtains bars of sunlight lay at a strong angle, which didn't mean – Lydia was well aware – that she was anything resembling safe. She tucked the note into her glove, crammed all the rest of the cards and invitations into her handbag to be sorted through later (*and all of them thrown out, I should imagine, but one never knows . . .*), made sure that the front door was slightly ajar, and then hastened through to the kitchen quarters, to where she knew she'd find the back stairs.

As she suspected, she passed the maid Giselle, a woman a few years younger than Camille Batoux, dead on the kitchen table amid boxes of half-packed dishes. Wrists and ankles had been tied with silk scarves and she, too, had been tortured. A cup of cold tea stood nearby, with a sewing-basket containing a beige-and-black striped Poiret skirt. Very little blood was to be seen.

It must have happened immediately after Jamie came to visit.

Immediately after Tante Camille told him whatever it was she told him about the interior arrangements of the Hôtel Batoux.

Was that what the vampires wanted to know? Whom she'd told, and why he'd asked?

She quickened her steps down the tradesmen's stair, unlatched the door at the bottom, and stepped out into a narrow alleyway. The afternoon's advance had already left it in deep shadow, but at its end the Boulevard de Versailles glowed in late sunlight.

If I hurry, she thought, hastening her steps toward the red-and-yellow cab that still waited for her across the street, *I can make it to Jamie's rooms before the sun goes down.*

Shadows haunted the streets of Paris.

Against the starry sky – stars black and clear as Asher had seen them in the Dinarics – he could see the roofs of tall buildings, the occasional spires of churches; the stink of woodsmoke and the mud underfoot told him where he was. Asher was aware of the young man Simon flitting ahead of him like a shadow, invisible to the man he himself pursued. Of that man, Asher could see only the white of a small ruff at his throat, the occasional pale smudge of his face when they passed an ill-fastened shutter.

Of those who ringed them, like sharks trailing a lifeboat adrift in open water, he could see nothing at all. But he knew they were there.

Asher tried to catch up, tried to shout to that first man, *Watch out!*

Go indoors, go where there are people . . .

Run for the bridges and cross running water . . .

He fished through his mind for all the various things that folklore described as inimical to vampires: garlic, crucifixes, wolfsbane, Christmas rose. Knives with silver blades . . .

For a moment another memory tugged at him. *Shouldn't I be wearing a silver chain around my neck? That sounds like a good idea . . .*

The recollection of having done so, of feeling the weight and chill of it under his shirt-collar, scratched at his thoughts like a forgotten appointment. *Why would I have done such a thing?*

Or was that in some other dream?

Someone had taken it off him. He remembered that. Iron hands had held his arms. Rough fingers fumbling at the back of his neck.

Why am I dreaming about vampires in the days of Shakespeare – and in Paris, of all places?

I was in Paris . . .

The memory sank away. But just in case, he took the silver chains from his wrists (*Why am I wearing these?*) and wrapped them around his hands.

A blow from the silver will burn . . .

Burn whom?

The intended victim turned, in a tiny court blue with starlight that had no other outlet. Asher saw the sober dark clothing of a merchant or tradesman. He held up a book, thick and dark-bound, cried out, 'Keep your distance, spawn of Hell!' and the young man Simon's eyes flashed in the dim light. 'God will defend me!'

'Don't name God to me, heretic,' whispered Simon's soft voice from the darkness. 'You have led your last victim astray with your blasphemous sermons.'

With the shocking suddenness of a dream the pale-haired vampire was beside his quarry, clawed hand flicking toward the older man's throat. But in the same instant, it seemed, the other vampires materialized from the darkness: for the first half second only a ring of reflective eyes, then they were there, as if they'd dropped from the roofs or risen from the reeking mud.

They caught Simon's hands and arms, grabbed his hair in their unbreakable grip. The black-clothed man with the book stepped forward, grinning horribly: 'Well, well, demon, so your Pope dares call us heretics, does he? So you're going to try to silence the teaching of God's true word in the name of your Anti-Christ in Rome?'

Simon looked in shock at the vampires who held him. Like terrible ghosts in the starlight, two men and two women, grinning with their long fangs. Their leader, a stocky man with the thick mustache and localized chin-beard seen in portraits of James I, took Simon's jaw in his hand and looked for a moment into his eyes. His own eyes, gleaming in the starlight, were pale snow-water blue. 'He is a stranger.' His voice was like sandpaper on stones. 'A Spaniard. I've not seen him before. I doubt those hell-spawned devils at the Cemetery of the Innocents even know he's in Paris. He'll not be missed. And I'll not be trifled with.'

And the other vampires shifted on their feet like children eager for a treat.

The chief vampire unhooked a horn from his belt, long and slightly twisted, the end cut off so that instead of forming a drinking vessel it made a funnel. The others dragged Simon's head back, heedless of his frantic struggles, and forced the horn's small end down his throat, holding him still as the bearded vampire took a phial from a purse at his belt and poured its contents into the horn.

'Will it kill him, Brother Esdras?' The Protestant preacher stepped close to take the empty phial and sniff it. With a grimace he handed it back. The vampire called Esdras drew the horn out of his victim's mouth, returned it to his belt and the phial to its pouch. Simon tried to struggle again, but could not move in the grip of the other three. His yellow eyes were wide with fear.

'Nothing kills us, Brother Thomas,' returned the bearded vampire. 'That is our curse. Only the sun's cleansing fire. But this one—' with a weird tenderness he stroked the disheveled pale hair back from Simon's forehead – 'will very shortly lose all control of his limbs and go limp as a puppet whose strings have been cut. But his mind will still be awake and alive, as we carry him up the Hill of Martyrs and leave him at the top. There he'll lie watching the dawn lighten – little by little – in the sky, knowing that at any second his flesh will burst into unquenchable fire. A fit prelude,' he added with a chilly smile, 'to the eternal fire which will consume his soul in Hell. Would you care to come along and watch?'

'I should like that very much.' Brother Thomas the preacher nodded at the vampire's belt-pouch. 'What is it that you gave him?'

'An elixir Brother Emeric makes.' He smiled across at the

other male vampire, lanky and freckled with a nose like the root of a tree. 'Think you can run away, little Spaniard? Let's see.' He nodded, and the others released their victim's arms. Simon ran two staggering steps and fell. They followed him as he crawled toward the entrance to the narrow court, until he could move no more. But his eyes were open, living, frantic, as they lifted him shoulder-high and bore him through the starlit streets toward the city gates and the hills that lay beyond them. The Protestant preacher, Bible under his arm, followed gleefully behind.

'And let that be a lesson to you, my boy,' said Asher's father. '*Mali principii malus finis.*'

Asher found himself in his father's church at Wychford as it had looked in 1874 when he'd gone away to Bracewell's School in Yorkshire. The Reverend Arthur Asher looked as he had then, tall and thin – as Asher was himself – and, like his son, brown-haired and brown-eyed. Like his son also (Asher realized) capable of chameleon-like changes in voice and mien and manner, which only appeared when he preached: drama, passion, sound and fury, never seen at other times.

Now he was his non-preaching self, his shoulders stiff, his voice constricted, his eyes without expression.

'You'd think Brother Thomas would at least go along to pray for Simon's soul in those last minutes,' remarked Asher, who was – he was interested to note – his adult self, though he sat in the corner of the family pew which had always been his in his childhood.

'The boy was dead already, and damned.' The Reverend Asher shrugged. 'There was nothing that could be done for him. And he was taken at the moment of attempting a murder – completely apart from having sold his soul to evil to become a vampire in the first place. Don't talk nonsense, boy.'

'No, sir.' Asher knew that nobody had ever changed his father's mind on the subject of what one had to do in order to win God's approval or damnation. If this was 1874, calculated Asher, he was himself now older than the man who stood before him, the man who'd be dead in a railway accident in two years, without ever seeing his son again. The Reverend Arthur Asher had not been a believer in having children come home from school over the summer holidays, once they were dispatched to Yorkshire or (in his sister's case) Brighton.

Through the door of the church he could see the little cluster of vampires climbing the steep, wooded hill that Montmartre had been in the seventeenth century, the stumpy tower of Saint-Pierre church silhouetted against the paling darkness at the top.

'At least we could go along,' piped up Jürgen Schaumm, who had somehow transplanted himself from Rebbe Karlebach's parlor to this place and time. 'We could ask him what he knows, before he burns up. We have time for that, don't we?' He set down his green notebook, checked his silver watch.

Asher's own train for the school in Yorkshire would leave at seven in the morning, he knew. His father wouldn't accompany him to the station, nor would he permit his wife to do so. *Only make it harder on the boy*, he'd heard his father say.

I should go to the house and say goodbye to her, Asher thought, *since I won't be seeing her again.*

Yet he knew he had to follow the vampires up the hill, to speak to Simon before fire consumed him.

Simon knew something. He remembered that now. *I came to Paris to find . . .*

. . . to find . . .

Something that Simon would know, or might know . . .

But I'd better hurry. The sun will be up soon.

Schaumm got to his feet (like Asher, he was an adult in this dream, though they'd been of an age in the eighteen eighties so in 1874 he must have been a schoolboy too) and trotted to the door, notebook in hand. Asher rose and moved to follow, and his father snapped, 'Sit down. Where do you think you're going?'

'I need to find out,' he said.

'Find out what?' asked Lydia's voice, and Asher opened his eyes.

His mouth was dry and his head ached as if he'd been smashed over the skull with a coach-and-four. He said, 'Simon,' and his throat hurt as if he, and not the pale-haired Elizabethan vampire in his dream, had had the narrow end of an ox-horn shoved halfway down it.

Lydia pulled off her glasses, bent her head down, and pressed her forehead to his shoulder. 'Jamie,' she whispered. 'Oh, Jamie . . .'

He brought up his left hand – his forearm tightly bandaged (*what the hell did I do to myself?*) and stroked her shoulder, the bones delicate as a fawn's under thin silk, and flesh not much more substantial. He felt weak, drained of strength, *a puppet whose strings have been cut . . .* who had said that? 'Where am I?'

'St Antoine's Hospital.' She sat up at that, put her glasses back on, and, seeing the frown that drew at his brows, added, 'Paris.'

'Paris?'

I dreamed about Paris.

I dreamed . . .

He groped for the fragments as they were sucked away down into darkness.

'Jamie, the war's started,' she said softly. 'Germany invaded Belgium, just like you said they were going to; they're shelling Liège. We declared war on them yesterday. Everybody's declared war on everybody else. All the armies are marching. Aunt Louise left for England . . . I thought you were never going to wake up . . .'

'What am I doing in Paris?'

EIGHT

'I got your things from your room.'

Lydia replaced the empty water-glass on the stand between Asher's bed and that of the man next to him. The ward reeked like a workhouse in the hot night, and the only sound that broke the stillness was the rumble of trucks in the street, and someone coughing a few beds over. *If they've declared war – dear God, what happened? – they'll be pulling all the medical personnel they can into the Army . . .*

Francis Ferdinand. His mind groped at half-remembered fragments, as unreal as the conversation with his father in the church at Wychford or the weird farrago of dreams about Shakespearean vampires in Paris (all of them speaking very proper Rabelaisian French).

Somebody shot the emperor's nephew Francis Ferdinand . . .

And if Serbia was allied with Russia and Russia was allied with France and Austria was allied with Germany . . .

Like a horrible little song, the entangling alliances spun themselves into a chorus:

'And the green grass grew all around, all around, and the green grass grew all around . . .'

Did the Department call me over?

And I WENT?

'What happened to me?'

Her eyes widened, aghast. 'Don't you remember?'

He started to shake his head, but the slightest movement brought excruciating pain.

'I got a letter,' he said slowly. 'In Oxford.'

His study, the windows open into the garden. The July somnolence of the long vacation. The smell of cut grass and the tiny ice-crackle of flimsy German notepaper in his fingers. An address in Prague . . .

Yes, he thought. *Yes. Rebbe Karlebach wrote to me.*

Trying to remember was like trying to thread a needle with one eye shut and his fingers frozen. His head ached and he wanted nothing more than to return to sleep, but he forced his mind to pursue those strange, fogged fragments.

We'd – quarreled? Years ago. Why? He remembered most clearly his sense of relief and pleasure at seeing his old friend's jagged handwriting on the envelope, the motley assortment of Central European stamps . . .

'Was that why I came to Paris?'

'I think so.' She propped her spectacles more firmly on to her nose. She was thin, and looked harried, as if she'd not eaten or slept. *How long was I unconscious, leaving her alone?* 'The letter wasn't in your room – the room you rented here, I mean, on the Île Saint-Louis. At least I couldn't find it.'

Île Saint-Louis? That must have been the one near the Quai d'Anjou – the landlady had known him for years under the name of Prior. Why that one? With the river running on both sides it was easy to be trapped, easy to be followed. He made a noise in his throat like *hrmn*. 'That'll teach me to carry everything in my head.'

*   *   *

'Good lord, don't write anything down, boy!' Belleytre stared at him in shocked disapproval.

'It isn't as if members of the Auswärtiges Amt are going to be able to read Homeric Greek . . .'

'You'd be surprised.' Back at Oxford, Belleytre was always neat, with his graying ginger hair trimmed and his gray eyes sparkling with hidden humor. At the moment he was shaggy and bearded and clothed like an itinerant Greek monk, which was how Asher had encountered him in the summer of 1885 in the dusty streets of Belgrade – a town in which neither of them, as Englishmen, had any business.

Asher, journeying through the valley of the Drina, had thought it advisable – given the very real possibility at that time that Serbia was going to war with the Turks yet again – to let everyone think he was a Czech student from Prague, as he sought for tales of werewolves and witches, vampires and the goddesses who danced on Durdevdan night. So when he'd encountered the Modern Languages tutor who had, for the past year, been discreetly advising him to take courses in history and cartography as well as languages and folklore – and even at the age of twenty-one Asher had suspected him of not being the douce and retiring don that most people thought him – he had merely put a coin into his hand and had murmured in impeccable, idiomatic Austrian German, 'Bless me, Father, for I am far from home.'

For a moment their eyes had met, and Asher had known that he was right.

And in that moment – in the streets of the former Turkish garrison town that seethed now with rebellion, violence, smuggled weapons, and parlous information – Asher, dreaming, knew his fate had been sealed.

He'd followed the 'priest' back to his rooms at the local monastery, for what amounted to his first lessons in spycraft.

'Any man who knows his business can crack any code you can think up, before tea,' Belleytre had said, and had poured out for him coffee-black tea from the pot they'd begged from the brother in charge of the kitchens. 'You don't forget words, do you? You remember that on the Greek islands they call a visitor *episkeptis* and on the mainland *misafir*. God only knows how you tell your little witches and werewolves apart. No, my boy. You need to train your memory, like the old bards did in the Middle Ages – and still do, in these parts of the world. You write nothing down. No sense pretending to be a student from Prague if the Turkish authorities decide to strip you naked and find you've got some English importer's address tucked away in your sock. I promise you,' he added grimly, 'you won't like what happens next.'

So Asher had memorized a dozen names, to be delivered to a man at the embassy in Prague ('They'll know why those men are important'), and – he'd learned much later – in the few moments when he was out of the room Belleytre had concealed in his luggage two maps of the proposed Turkish railway route from Constantinople to the Danube. And though it had been another two years before Asher had made the decision to work for the Department, from then on he'd been careful what he wrote down and what he didn't.

And Lydia – the thought passed through his mind as he found himself again descending the tower stair in that shadowy *hôtel* to the pitch-dark twisting passageway below which he knew led down to the bone chapel – Lydia had not yet been born.

'Your husband paid a call on me,' said the green-eyed lady vampire of his dream.

Montadour? Lady Montadour, he had called her . . .

In another dream? The memory ran away like water.

His mind fumbled at legends, trying to separate French medieval tales of vengeful revenants from Byronic fables and literary poems. For some reason it seemed terribly important that he identify this particular legend. *It must have been important if I dreamed about her . . .*

He realized he must have fallen asleep mid-conversation, and opened his eyes.

She was standing beside the bed.

I'm still dreaming. They're not real.

It was clearly hours later. Lydia remained seated, keeping herself between him and Lady Montadour. 'Was it an oversight on your part that he survived, or was this supposed to be a warning of some kind?'

'*Et alors*, child, you don't think *I* had anything to do with his misfortune!' She reached out a hand gloved in lilac kid, and Lydia moved a little, to keep her from touching him.

The black eyebrows curved up. Her voice was childishly sweet and high, her French slightly old-fashioned. Asher remembered it from his dream. 'I promise you, had I wished to kill him he would not have left my *hôtel*, much less made it all the way to Saint . . .' She hesitated, for just a fraction of a moment too long. '*Where* did he fall from?'

'He was found in the old churchyard of St Clare's.'

He knew that new voice, too – male, whispering – and a shudder went through him. Simon, the vampire from his dreams . . . Simon, who had been given poison to drink by the other vampires, who had been carried to the top of the hill of Montmartre and left to watch the rising of the sun. Now he stood at Lydia's side – *had he been there a moment ago?* – calm and slender and as at home in a Jermyn Street suit as he had been in the dark velvet of seventeenth-century Paris. 'We thought – Mistress Asher and I – that you might have had something to do with it.'

'And what would I have been doing in that part of town, *en effet*?' She gestured her disbelief, hand-floreos like a flamenco dancer. 'Bourgeoisie who go to bed at nine every night—'

'What did he ask of you when he came calling, madame?'

'He said he came to warn me.' Madame de Montadour pouted with lips like a blood-gout in snow. 'He said one of my little ones, my nestlings, my little blood-spawn – or maybe more than one – was plotting with the Germans to betray me. I told him not to be a fool.'

The slight flicker of one of Simon's eyebrows embodied a world of disbelief, and she stamped her foot. 'They do not betray me! They are mine – I hold their souls in my hand! It is impossible for them to betray me! Impossible for them to drive me out!'

'Did he say which one?' inquired Ysidro politely.

'He didn't know.'

Asher studied her face, her throat, looking for . . . what? A burn?

He remembered his hand wrapped in silver chain, striking

flesh. Remembered a woman screaming curses as she jerked away from him. He didn't think it was this one.

'Or mention that whoever it was has made their own fledglings?'

Her green eyes widened with shocked fury. 'That's a lie!'

'Unless you've begotten new fledglings since last I walked in Paris, Elysée . . . homely ones, too. I know the beautiful Serge, the equally handsome Augustin, Évariste, Baptiste, Marin, Theo . . . Have you ever created a homely fledgling?'

'And why would I do that?' For a moment her eyes smouldered. 'There are as many handsome rich boys as there are ugly ones.'

'Let us not forget Hyacinthe and Marie-Jeanne. Though I haven't encountered Marie-Jeanne.'

'She came to misfortune.' Madame spoke the words like the chop of a cleaver beheading a chicken. 'Three years ago, it was. A stupid girl, though useful. Greedy and brainless. Who are these others you've seen?' Her eyes narrowed, and for a moment the silken pale youth of her face turned ugly, as if a mask had slipped to show what lay beneath. 'And where?'

'Montmartre.' He spoke the name of the hill without visible emotion. Was it only a dream, that he had been left there, paralysed, to die? *Is THIS a dream?* Exhaustion and lassitude dragged at Asher's thoughts so it was difficult to be sure of anything. *It has to be . . .*

Yet he was glad of it, because there was something that he needed to ask the vampire Simon. Something that Simon knew, that he himself had forgotten. Something important.

The war, he thought cloudily. *The war has started so it's doubly important. Vital tenfold . . .*

How could it affect the course of the war if it happened in Paris at the start of the seventeenth century?

'A man and a girl, hunting together,' said Simon. 'The man's a tough, and big. I suppose one could call him handsome, though not in your style, my dear Elysée. The girl's a child still, ten or eleven, by the look of her clothes a *nymphe du pavé*.'

Elysée de Montadour's red lip lifted like a dog's, to show a fox-sharp fang beneath.

'So if one of your get is creating fledglings,' went on Simon,

'I should say you might have done better to pay more attention to James's warning of an upcoming betrayal.'

Asher's thoughts slid away then, as if he were trying to crawl up the bank of a river with the water rising around him, sweeping him away. He was climbing the hill of Montmartre with Jürgen (*Father must be having a frozen fit of rage that I disobeyed him . . .*). He almost turned back, knowing the man would take his outrage out on his wife, but they were climbing the long flights of the Rue Foyatier, and looking down all he could see was the rooftops of the eighteenth arrondissement. *Surely these steps weren't here in 1602.*

'It's four thirty.' Schaumm checked his watch again. 'The other vampires must have fled by this time, so we can ask him what we need to know without interruption.' In their summers together under Rebbe Karlebach's tutelage Asher had found the gnome-like little German's obsessive collection of data amusing, but with the sky staining gray to the east above the Marne and the smell of dawn filling the air he felt a kind of angry distaste, even if, presumably, the vampire who lay on the hilltop waiting helplessly for the fire had murdered hundreds of people in the fifty years or so of his Undead existence.

But Schaumm scrambled up the steps ahead of him, and when Asher reached the top he found that it was, in fact, 1602. The white domes of the Sacré-Coeur were gone. There existed no trace of the Place du Tertre or the Lapin Agile cabaret or the myriad of bistros that formed the neighborhood. Only the church of St Peter crowned the stony hilltop, and a few thin trees concealed the dugout entrances to the gypsum mines that riddled the hills all around. A sort of outcrop of the native rock of the hill shouldered up from the soil a dozen yards before the church, like an altar, and on it the vampire Simon lay motionless. Beside him stood Brother Thomas, arms outstretched toward the east: 'Come, ye children, hearken unto me; I will teach you the fear of the Lord. What man is he that desireth life, and loveth many days, that he may see good? . . . For the arms of the wicked shall be broken . . . the wicked shall perish, and the enemies of the Lord shall be as the fat of lambs . . . into smoke shall they consume away.'

'The other vampires must be gone by this time,' said Schaumm briskly. 'We'd better hurry or we won't be in time . . .'

He scuttled toward the altar-like stone, calling out in his school-boyish French, 'You there, pastor! Hullo . . .'

Asher glanced around him – even though he knew in his heart there weren't real vampires, since this was a dream there was still a good chance that there were, despite Schaumm's insistence – and followed. But when Schaumm had only covered half the distance from the top of the steps and the stone, a figure appeared beside Brother Thomas, seemingly out of nowhere, a tall man in plain gray clothing, his long hair like a cloak of blackness on his shoulders. He caught Brother Thomas from behind, by one shoulder and his jaw, and with an effortless movement snapped his neck. As the victim jerked in dying spasms at the foot of the rock the newcomer scooped up the vampire Simon in his arms, and in what looked like a few effortless strides reached the church.

Schaumm cried protestingly 'Hey, now! Wait!' and ran after them. Asher followed more slowly, boots squeaking in the thin snow.

I know him. I've seen him . . .

Holding out ink-stained claws . . .

When he reached the church door, the sanctuary was empty.

A church . . . Panic flooded him at the memory of another lightless sanctuary. The memory of gleaming eyes, of hands gripping his arms . . .

'They'll be down in the crypt,' surmised Schaumm, polishing his thick-lensed spectacles where they'd steamed from the warmth indoors. 'Sunlight won't get them there.'

'Jürgen, vampires don't really exist,' pointed out Asher, and his fellow student dashed ahead of him across the open stone of the sanctuary floor.

'Yes, but if they *did* exist, that's where they'd be.'

Run, Asher thought, for a moment unable to move either forward or back. *They're waiting for you in the shadows. You can maybe get out through the tower . . .*

I DID climb the tower . . . They were between me and the door.

Was that this church, or my father's in Wychford? Or another, in another dream . . .?

He couldn't remember. *In any case they don't really exist.* He forced himself to cross the threshold, and by the time he reached the small crypt door beside the altar, Schaumm had vanished, as people appear and vanish in dreams. Asher descended the winding stair alone.

He half expected to find himself in the bone chapel again, but at the bottom lay only a tiny crypt. From its door he could see them – also in the fashion of dreams, for there was neither torch nor window in the dark little chamber. Not only the tall vampire in gray and the white-haired young Spaniard he had laid down on a carven sarcophagus that occupied the center of the cramped vault, but the others who had been in the streets of Paris, Brother Esdras with his bristling beard, freckled gangly Brother Emeric, and the two women who had held Simon's arms while the poison was poured down his throat. Black-clothed, hands folded, weird parodies of righteousness in their sober dark clothing, hair streaming loose over their shoulders.

Evil, he thought, his heart hammering. *Killers who drink the lives of the innocent.* He had seen them do so . . . *When? In other dreams?*

'You will listen to me,' said the gray-clothed vampire, 'and once and for all you will do as I say. I will have no conflict between Catholic and Protestant in my domain. None. I will have no war among the Undead.'

'Just because—' began the taller of the two women. The dark-haired vampire turned his gaze upon her, and the words were choked in her throat as if by a garrote.

'And what gives you the right—'

He turned his gaze on Brother Esdras at these words, cold, terrible, with the infinite power of an angel. 'Paris is mine,' said the gray-clothed one. 'It is mine by right; it is mine by virtue of my master who gave it to me. If you will not have it so, Esdras de Colle, you are free to leave it, if you think you can govern these my children who choose for the moment to follow you and your vision of God.'

His glance went for one moment to the taller woman, the other man, and they looked aside from him, abashed.

'But while you are in Paris – and should you travel to any of the other cities where I am Master, Bordeaux or Rheims or Brussels or Liège – you will remember that there will be no war among the Undead. Catholic, Protestant, Mohammedan or Buddhist, it matters not to me. We are all damned alike. We have all sought to circumvent the will of the God who decreed that men must die. Let us not be like the Christian fools who will continue to fight amongst themselves about the date of Easter when both are chained to the same rowers' bench in a Turkish galley. *I will not have it.* Do you understand?'

Esdras de Colle raised his chin under its stiff dark beard. 'I understand the God who delivered the unbeliever King Sihon unto the swords of the Israelites, the God who commanded Moses to avenge the children of Israel upon the Midianites, the God who delivered Jericho into the hands of Joshua whose belief was faithful and true,' he said. 'A man's heart is his own, Constantine Angelus, and God's. It isn't to bow to the belief of another man, much less to a devil such as yourself.'

'As long as we're quoting scripture,' returned the dark-haired vampire, 'I suppose I would be obvious if I spoke about sins and throwing stones.'

'I was made as I am against my will.'

'*I* made you,' returned Angelus. 'And I felt your will – your soul – your self clutch on to my mind with the grip of a starving child. When I offered you the refuge within my mind, while your heart ceased beating and your own brain died, there was nothing against your will—'

'I was a sinner then. I understood nothing of God. Now I have heard the good news of the Reformed Church, I will seek salvation.' De Colle staggered suddenly, head lolling. Asher could see his three minions had already sought the black corners of the crypt and lay sleeping on the bare stone of the floor. Thickly, the Protestant vampire continued, 'And the day will come when I shake the dust of this town from my feet . . . go into the wilderness . . . damned Spaniard . . .'

He lurched away, to lie down in the darkness.

The sun must have risen. Several of Rebbe Karlebach's books on the supernatural stated that vampires slept during the daytime. *If I'm going to dream about them, by all means let's follow the rules . . .*

So that's Constantine Angelus, is it? Where do I know that name from?

Angelus turned to the young man he had saved, laid a clawed hand on his chest. 'What is your name, friend?'

Through numbed lips, Simon mumbled, 'Simon Xavier Christian Morado de la Cadeña-Ysidro.'

'And did you hear what I said unto Esdras, Simon Ysidro? That I am Master of Paris. That Catholic or Protestant, I will have no quarrels among us, no madness of vampire slaying vampire. Not in Paris, not in any city whose night-hunters I have begotten, and my domain stretches from Flanders to the Garonne. I have given you your life, Simon Ysidro. Knowing nothing of you, only that you stood at the gate of fire, and cried in your heart to be saved. If God had put forth his hand to cover you in impenetrable shadow and let you live, would you give your life over to God?'

Simon Ysidro whispered, 'I would.'

Angelus looked down into Simon's yellow eyes. Into his heart, Asher thought. Into his life, his thoughts, his soul. Seeing all that he had seen, in life and in death. Knowing all that he knew.

'And would you give your life over to me?'

Again Simon whispered, 'I would. I do.'

'Then I say to you, so long as you remain in Paris, you are to me as if I had begotten you in blood, and taken your soul into my heart to carry you over the abyss of death. Do you consent to this?'

With agonizing effort, Simon moved his fingers, to touch the cold strong claws that rested nearby. 'I consent.'

'Sleep then.' Constantine Angelus laid a hand on his forehead. 'As you have no doubt learned by now, God has played a great joke on us all, we who were coward enough to barter our souls for the pottage of what we thought would be immortality. But though the day is full of arrows, and pestilences walk the night, rest as peacefully as you might, my brother. While I rule Paris, at least we who hunt the night will not have to fear one another.'

Asher opened his eyes in darkness. Only the glow of the light from the hall outlined Simon Ysidro's aquiline profile, and caught bronze glints in Lydia's red hair.

They are real.

The weight of that understanding fell on him like the beam of a stone temple, crushing his heart.

They exist. And I have indeed sworn to destroy them, for all that they have done.

Including Simon Ysidro.

Lydia was asleep. She lay across the foot of his bed, her hand curled under her cheek. With infinite gentleness, Ysidro removed her glasses from her face, folded them, and carefully held them in his long thin fingers as he sat back in his straight hospital chair. His face was expressionless as he looked down at her, but to the marrow of his bones Asher knew that she was safe in the vampire's presence.

What was it Solomon Karlebach had said to him? That for every day that he withheld from killing the vampire, the blood of the vampire's victims would be on his hands. Killing people was what vampires did.

Yet it didn't seem to matter to Ysidro, as he watched over Lydia's sleep, whether Asher had vowed to kill him or not.

They are real.

Beyond the black windows, the rumble of trucks in the Rue Saint-Antoine went on, bearing men north into the mouth of war.

NINE

'Who is the vile little man with the spectacles?' inquired Ysidro the following night.

Asher turned his head a little, but for a long time did not speak. Lydia watched him closely in the night hours when she was at the hospital. He was still very weak, and subject to crippling nausea and to falling asleep instantaneously and unexpectedly, and Lydia suspected that the other patients and their daytime visitors were giving him newspapers despite her insistence that he be kept absolutely quiet. (*No wonder he's having headaches!*)

But she saw, too, that there was something else, a deep and

weary watchfulness when Ysidro was present, as he looked not
only at the vampire but at the shadows within himself. He would
not, she knew, ask her to make a choice; he knew what side she
must choose, if choice were given, and how deeply that choice
would hurt her. But the matter at the moment was moot, and
this, too, she read in his silence, and the occasional flicker of
vexed irony in his brown eyes.

Nevertheless he seemed better tonight. The sweeper woman
Fantine had even brought him water to shave with, though Thérèse
Sabatier had taken from her the three francs Lydia had paid for
that kindness. ('The help aren't permitted to accept tips.')That
evening when Lydia had arrived, she had found him sitting up
in the straight-backed wooden chair beside his bed. He had risen,
very carefully, and kissed her, though the effort drained the color
from his face as if he'd had his throat cut, and he had recognized
Ysidro when the vampire materialized out of the shadows at his
bedside after Dr Théodule had finished his round in the ward
and gone on his way.

'Vile little man?' He seemed to come back from his thoughts
– to put aside the darkness – and frowned.

'You've dreamed of him four times now, and he does not seem
to fit the context of your dreams.'

Asher's frown darkened. He had asked Lydia earlier in the
evening if Ysidro had been entering into his dreams, as the older
and more skillful vampires were able to do. He did not remember,
he had said, much of his dreams, even as he had no recollection
of anything that had happened to him after he had left Oxford
in mid-July. But Ysidro had walked into his dreams before this.

Yet at the vampire's words he rubbed his forehead, as if trying
to reconstruct those vanished visions, or at least call to mind
someone who'd fit that description. 'Shorter than yourself?' he
said at last. 'Black hair pomaded straight back, square jaw, snub
nose, wide mouth, lobeless ears . . .?'

'Even he.'

'It sounds like Jürgen Schaumm.'

'Your fellow student at Rebbe Karlebach's?' asked Lydia,
surprised.

'I can't imagine why I'd be dreaming about him. I haven't
thought of him in years.' The troubled look retreated further,

before the challenge of a puzzle and the task at hand. 'A brilliant polymath with some jaw-dropping holes in his make-up. He could run rings around me in botany and the natural sciences, and read about twelve languages, most of them dead. But he was one of those men for whom, when in pursuit of one of his obsessions, it was as if neither food nor drink, neither sleep nor other people existed. He was in Prague originally to study early Hebrew texts, but by the time I came to Rebbe Karlebach's, he'd taken up the study of folklore as well.'

His brows pulled together again, as if the words had triggered some jagged line of connecting thoughts in his mind. For a time he was silent, trying to fit them together.

Evidently this didn't work. He shook his head, letting them go.

'Did he study vampires?' asked Ysidro.

'I – yes. Yes, I think he did. I know he read everything in Karlebach's library, and Karlebach had a number of volumes on the Undead. He'd come with me sometimes when I'd go on my walking trips into the mountains to collect legends,' he added. 'Wrapped up like a beekeeper to protect himself from the sun – he had skin like a mushroom. Last I heard he was teaching at the University of Göttingen. God knows where he is now.'

Lydia dug in her reticule and produced the last invitation of 'William Johnson'. 'Is this his handwriting?'

'Yes.' Then he read it over and glanced back up at her, thunderously angry now in the dim reflection of the single electric bulb burning in the hall. Lydia took the note from him, aware that the rush of anger would be followed by a splitting headache.

One more thing to worry about . . .

After the incursion of the lady Elysée de Montadour the previous night, Lydia had been more conscious than ever of how deserted the wards were at night. Of how people came and went in the daytime without ever encountering an orderly – most of whom were leaving for the army – and of Dr Théodule's growing exhaustion. *He HAS to be sleeping half this shift, if he's doing daytime duties as well!*

Only the squeak of Fantine's mop-head, far down the corridor, broke the stillness now.

With half the Paris police force reporting to their deployment stations as well, and nobody keeping track of random murders in the capital, does that mean vampires will be around the hospital in greater numbers, or lesser?

Her eyes returned to the note in Jürgen Schaumm's Germanic writing . . .

'That's why Karlebach must have written to you last month,' she said. 'He must have learned of some deal that Schaumm was making with the Paris nest.'

'With some of them, at any rate.' Ysidro perched on the edge of the bed like a well-dressed bird of prey. 'The man might be doing escort duty to German vampires, to take over Paris – it being preferable to rule in Paris than to serve in Augsburg, though personally I would have neither city, even presented to me on a golden plate. I observe in no correspondence does your *William Johnson* offer to meet you after sundown. Have you received further word of him?'

Lydia shook her head. 'He must think I left with Aunt Louise.'

'Be careful how you come and go.' Asher leaned back against his pillows, chalk-white, a line of agony between his brows. 'They will have killed Camille Batoux to silence her. God knows if Elysée will keep silent about you being here, or the fact that I'm conscious.'

''Tis to her advantage to do so,' remarked Ysidro. 'Yet no force on Heaven or Earth has ever served to stop that pretty mouth.'

Lydia glanced at the newspapers, folded (*that HAS to be Jamie*) on the small nightstand between his bed and the next. The Germans were still besieging Liège, whose hilltop fortifications the paper proudly claimed they wouldn't take in a hundred years. ('They're waiting to bring the heavy guns up by rail,' Jamie had said to her. For a man who wasn't supposed to be reading newspapers or anything else he was suspiciously well-informed. 'Once they get those emplaced, I doubt the fortresses around the town will last twenty-four hours.')

'I'll ask Streatham about Schaumm,' she said after a hesitant moment. 'He may know something, if I ever get to see him.'

Her latest attempt to do so had robbed her of most of her sleep that day without producing any useful result. The imposing eighteenth-century mansion on the Rue du Faubourg Saint-Honoré had been like a kicked beehive: tail-coated servants, morning-coated diplomats, and uniformed messenger boys strode through the patient hordes in the hall where Lydia had spent the hours between nine and six. Voices clattered and buzzed behind shut doors; telephones jangled without cease. Many of her fellow suppliants had been there for two days, living on what the servants would go out and buy for them at the cafés, and rationing their francs. Lydia had had to force herself not simply to hand them what she had in her pockets. Since her father's death, she realized, she'd grown used to having money to spend. She didn't know how long she'd be obliged to live on what she had left.

The confusion had still been going strong when Lydia had left at six, feeling as if she'd been slammed repeatedly against a wall.

On and off all day, when it had been possible to do so, she had read the pamphlets and treatises she'd taken from Jamie's rented room on the Île Saint-Louis the day before, purportedly written by Constantine Angelus. The seventeenth-century French was thick and difficult, and she had feared she'd find the subject matter – theology – thicker and more difficult still, but a bit to her surprise that had not been the case. The former Master of Paris had made his arguments for religious tolerance with light and logical concision, critiquing the degree to which Catholics and Protestants claimed to know the intent of God vis-à-vis their opponents, without deriding either group. He used simple, very direct French, cutting down the number of words she had to look up.

'Why Constantine Angelus?' she asked now, and Jamie's hand twitched involuntarily, as if the name meant something to him.

She almost thought he was going to answer her, as he had about Jürgen Schaumm's notes, unthinkingly.

But it slipped away – she could see it in the vexed folds of his eyes – and he whispered, 'Damn it.' And she wanted to slap herself for pushing him with yet another matter that required mental effort and strain. 'I don't know.'

'There were receipts from three different bookshops in your room.' She touched her satchel which contained the pamphlets and dictionary, though she hesitated to read them, even if he slept. The danger of falling asleep over them was too great.

'You paid almost two thousand francs for one of them . . . Don Simon says he was the Master of Paris. Who were the other vampires of Paris then?' She turned to Ysidro. 'And might one of *them* have survived, to be trying to . . . to reinstate himself, after making a deal with the Germans to leave him alone to hunt?'

'In a conquered city,' mused Ysidro after a moment, 'I suppose one could hunt the vanquished with impunity, particularly if one had a mandate from the victors to listen for murmurs of discontent. Yet had one of the Paris nest, as first I knew it, survived the Revolution, he – or she – would have no need of a German army to overpower Elysée de Montadour.' He drew from the satchel one of the broadside sheets, in its careful wrappings of cardboard and tissue, his fingers like colorless insects walking.

He was dear to me, Ysidro had said of the former Master of Paris. Lydia wondered if there were copies of these, also, in the dark, book-crammed library of his London house.

''Twas a smaller city then,' he went on in time. 'Yet the people of Paris believed in our existence. Thus greater care was needed, and there was wisdom indeed in Constantine's struggle to keep the Catholic and Protestant Undead from open war.'

Again Lydia saw Asher make the quick movement usual with him when he saw something out of the corner of his eye; one of the several things, she realized, that had made her wonder, even as a girl of fourteen, whether her uncle Ambrose's inconspicuous lecturer friend was indeed as unassuming as he appeared. But the next instant he winced with pain and frustration, and whatever it was disappeared as if the darkness of the dim-lit ward had swallowed it up.

'Constantine Angelus—' Ysidro folded the pamphlet again in its protective tissue – 'was a scholar at the University of Paris in the last days of the Capets. He was made vampire by Sybellia Torqueri, who was venerated as a saint in certain parts of the Île de France up until the Revolution. Constantine became Master of Paris when the English held the city during the long wars between England and France. Another of Sybellia's get, Raimund Cauchemar, claimed that Sybellia had a talisman of some sort – the *Facinum*, Cauchemar called it – that Constantine stole, which gave him power over the other vampires of the city. He,

Raimund, he said, had the true right to be Master of Paris. The Master of any city always has trouble dealing with his own master's leftover get.'

'As Grippen has trouble dealing with you?' Lydia smiled as she named the Master of London, and Ysidro looked down his nose at the idea.

'Constantine could have folded Lionel Grippen up like a napkin and put him in his pocket. The truth was that Constantine was one of the most powerful vampires that ever I met. He was a man of extraordinary strength of character, with the wisdom to choose carefully whom he made vampire. So many masters yield to the temptation to make fledglings of those who can give them property – which all vampires covet – or wealth. Or they take those whom they think they can control utterly. Contradistinct to this, Constantine would court a man or a woman sometimes for years, growing to know them, learning to trust or learning that this was a person whom he could not trust . . . and if he could not trust them living, still less would he trust them with the power of the Undead.

'He had made himself master of other cities, in France and in the Low Countries, and would periodically absent himself from Paris for years, before returning under another name. Thus he had a life in Paris, and living acquaintances who had no notion that the man they would meet in taverns, or in the churches after sundown, was vampire. Thus he took time and trouble, and carefully chose his friends. Many of these friendships were shattered when first Luther and then Calvin broke with the True Faith – as most things in the world were shattered. This was a great grief to him.'

'And who were these friends?'

'Ivo Chopinel.' The vampire's frown was barely a shadow. 'A gypsy woman named Zaffira Truandière. Anselm Arouache – a great disappointment, Constantine told me, for the man had been a scholar of Greek texts, but with the vampire state lost all interest in everything besides the hunt. Gabrielle Batoux. Françoise Rabutin. Emeric Jambicque was also a scholar, an alchemist who went over to the so-called Reformed Religion along with Esdras de Colle, who was one of the Bordeaux vampires, whom Constantine also made. 'Twas Esdras de Colle who led the Protestant vampires of Paris. He was the man I was instructed to kill.'

'Gabrielle Batoux,' said Asher quietly, and Lydia looked over at him in surprise.

'You remember?'

He coughed, and pressed a hand to his side – *DAMN it*, thought Lydia, *if he comes down with M'sieu Lecoq's pneumonia . . .*

'Not . . . not clearly. Not really. Her . . . her descendant, or her kinswoman . . .'

'La Belle Nicolette,' said Lydia. 'Simon arranged an introduction. He said you'd met her—'

'When a gentleman goes to Paris to make an assignation with the likes of La Belle Nicolette—' Asher cast a glance of mock reproach at the vampire – 'the least one can expect of another gentleman is that he will not inform his wife of it . . .'

And Ysidro returned a fleet, sudden, and completely human grin.

Lydia flicked Asher hard on the biceps with her fingertips. 'Did you manage to enter the Hôtel Batoux? I take it that's where you visited Madame de Montadour. I tried to see Tante Camille.'

She fell silent at the horror of what she had seen by the electric gleam of the bedroom lamps.

'She . . . it looked like she'd been tortured. I think it happened the day you were found in the churchyard. It was horrible. I–I sent for the police, or at least I left the front door half-open, so someone would be sure to go in and find them . . .'

She fell silent, seeing the look of anguish in his face.

'Do you remember her?'

He moved his head a little: *No*. 'Does that matter?' he added harshly. Stillness fell again.

'Gabrielle Batoux—' Ysidro's colorless gaze rested on Asher's face; it was Asher who looked aside – 'was the wife of a money-lender. An educated woman in the Renaissance fashion, though she, too, lost much of her interest in mathematics and Greek manuscripts from the first moment she drank of a human soul's dying paroxysm. She retained at least the good sense to limit her kills and draw no attention to herself, and 'twas she – a little to my surprise, I admit – who became Master of Paris when Raimund Cauchemar succumbed to a gang of witch-hunting beggars who developed a grudge against him during the upheavals of *La Fronde*. Her grand-nephew, I believe, built the *hôtel*, and I recall some rather curious rumors—'

'Raimund Cauchemar?' said Lydia. 'I thought the Master of Paris was Constantine Angelus.'

'Cauchemar became Master when Constantine perished.' Ysidro's voice turned cold and remote as starlight. 'Not a particularly good one. I am pleased to say he did not retain the position long – less than fifty years.'

'What happened to Constantine Angelus?'

'I have not the smallest idea.'

'Then could it be he—?'

'No,' said Ysidro, like the shutting of a door. 'No.'

TEN

'One of us should have a look at the Hôtel Batoux.' Lydia returned to the subject when a few hours later Ysidro, with Elizabethan courtliness, bowed over her hand in the deserted vestibule of the hospital to take his leave. 'I'll take an oath Madame de Montadour wasn't telling the truth last night.'

'I doubt she could identify Truth,' returned the vampire, 'if it came up to her and offered her a rose to put in her hair.'

Deathly stillness once again quenched the City of Light. All those tail-coated servants and uniformed messenger boys at the Ministry must be asleep by now; all those beaten, frustrated, frightened young couples and their children, all those exhausted grandmothers and uncles who'd innocently trotted off to take their usual two-weeks-on-the-Continent at the end of July . . .

Only the ambassador, the diplomats, and Streatham the spymaster must lie open-eyed on clammy pillows, Lydia reflected, calculating the days before Britain's Expeditionary Force could be ready to take ship for France. Ready to march away to war. They'd be wondering how many submarines Germany had in the North Sea, and counting the hours it would take for General von

Kluck to bring up the siege guns Jamie had described to her, so big they took two railway cars to carry and so powerful they could lob a shell nine miles. *And oh, yes, I suppose we've got to do something about all those people in the hallways . . .*

How can they AIM nine miles?

Jamie slept, like a corpse save for the wet, slow rasp of his breathing. Fever-spots stood out on his cheekbones.

Don't you dare, don't you DARE develop pneumonia!

When she'd come in at sunset – days ago, it felt like now – after spending the whole day in the Ministry vestibule, she'd found that M'sieu Lecoq was gone. Dead, Thérèse Sabatier had informed her briskly. In her absence that day all the other wards had been consolidated, and what had been space between the beds was now occupied by more beds and more men. Coughing spattered the room like gunfire, and the place stank of bodies unwashed, dressings unchanged, of piss and gangrene.

I MUST talk to Dr Théodule when I come back, about having Jamie moved to Aunt Louise's . . .

'And I think it should be me,' Lydia went on after a moment. 'Because I'd really rather you were here to keep an eye on Jamie at night. I can go in the daytime, and at least see what it's like now. I'll go in disguise – change my voice, I mean, and the way I walk. According to Mrs Flasket's guidebook, St Clare's church-yard is only a few streets away. It was a convent church, and I'll just bet you there's a sewer or a crypt or something left over from the convent, connecting the two. He has to have been on his way out, after seeing Elysée. Why not use the front door, I wonder?'

'Fear of her fledglings, I dare say. I like this not, Mistress,' the vampire went on quietly. 'Yet I agree that one of us must see this place, and the guards by day will be less of a threat than whatever we might encounter there by night. And with the crowds that come and go here unwatched and unchecked, my heart misgives me to leave James unguarded even by day. Could I walk about in the light, I doubt not that I could come in here in the middle of the day, kill half the patients in the ward and walk out again unremarked. Watch behind you – even in daylight, this Schaumm may not be the only living man employed by the Undead. You shall need this.' From his pocket he drew a wash-leather sack, which jingled when Lydia took it.

It was heavy.

Aunt Louise would lock me in my room for the rest of my life.

'Thank you.' She took the sack, put her hand on Ysidro's shoulder and kissed him, very gently, on the cheek. 'Bless you.'

The vampire smiled. ''Tis long,' he remarked softly, 'since any person has said those words to me, Mistress. They are good to hear.'

Through the hospital doorway she could see Stanislas Greuze's taxi, waiting for her across the empty street. It was after four in the morning and the city was utterly deserted, yet she removed her spectacles lest anyone see her with them on. When she looked back at her side, Ysidro had disappeared.

With Ysidro's money Lydia bought a day of the cab-driver's time, sent him off to stand guard in the hospital ward, and – after stopping to ransack the cupboards of Aunt Louise's maids – walked to the district once called the Marais.

Nicolette Batoux had warned her that the *hôtel* was difficult to find. It had been a fashionable suburb in the days of Cardinal Richelieu and still contained a number of elegant mansions whose stable blocks and extensive gardens had for the most part been sold away and the land built over with the cheaper lodgings of the poor. Fashion had moved across the city, to the newer districts around the Place de l'Étoile. Following the Revolution, the artisans' *quartier* of Saint-Antoine had spread to swallow this up.

Lydia had to walk along the Rue de Moussy three times before she saw the turning for the Rue des Trois Anges, which had been left off the three most recent maps of Paris. She'd had the same trouble the first time she'd tried to locate Don Simon Ysidro's London house.

Just before turning down the tiny street she took off one shoe and inserted a pebble in it to change her gait (and make sure she didn't forget which foot she was supposed to be limping on). The result was startlingly painful, and made her glad she'd also borrowed one of Aunt Louise's canes.

With Mrs Flasket's oldest dress flapping baggy around her thin frame and all her red hair skinned back carefully under a countrywoman's cap, she approached the shut gates, the sealed door.

No one responded to her knock on the gates. But when she put her eye to the crack (reflecting on what a relief it was to wear spectacles and not worry about who was seeing her because she was in disguise), her view of the cobbled courtyard beyond was almost immediately blocked by a man who emerged from the concierge's booth to the left. Lydia barely had time to step back before he opened the small wicket door. 'Whom do you seek, madame?'

'I'm seeking my niece.' Lydia made her voice as unlike her own as she could, with a whispered thanks to her governess and the mistresses at Madame Chappedelaine's Select Academy for Young Ladies for an almost flawless facility with French. She blinked nervously at the blue-uniformed guard through her second-best spare glasses, square-lensed and thick as bread sliced for sandwiches at tea; took in the unshaven jaw, the ill-buttoned uniform, the size and shape of the courtyard behind him, and the location of the house door, set beside the round, many-windowed tower. Guards in novels – and villains always seemed to employ scores of them – were generally tough, soldier-like, and formidable. This man looked like a retired butcher.

'Madame Lotier – Danielle Lotier – she's staying with the Peletiers. Rue de Moussy . . .' She squinted at a piece of paper she'd written on, and named the nearby street.

'Two streets up.' The big man jerked a thumb in the general direction of Montmartre.

'They don't mark the streets around here,' complained Lydia, turning at once to limp away. 'How they expect anyone to find anyone in this city . . .'

She changed her shoes at a café on the Rue des Francs-Bourgeois for another pair that was too tight, to remind her to keep her walk small and shuffling, and took a shawl and a wide-brimmed straw hat from her satchel. These alterations effected, she abandoned Aunt Louise's cane, returned to the neighborhood, and made a cautious circuit of the streets and alleyways around the old *hôtel*, to get some idea of its size and extent. It was hemmed in on all sides by later buildings, but past their corners and over their rooflines Lydia could occasionally glimpse the conical cap of the tower.

That done, she hobbled the short distance – and she calculated it was less than two hundred yards, though the layout of the intervening streets made it seem much longer – to the church of Sainte-Clare-Pieds-Nus.

Owing to the cutting of the Rue de Rivoli through the old Quartier de la Porte-Saint-Martin the church had been left standing a good distance back from the street, tucked behind a block of shops. Both church and churchyard were much neglected; Lydia looked up at its stumpy tower and a sensation like a cold hand around her heart overwhelmed her. *Jamie fell from there. He must have hit the roof of the porch and rolled before falling again.* The first row of windows was about thirty feet from the ground. More than enough to fracture a skull.

Oh, Jamie . . .

Though her feet hurt in her too-small shoes, she shuffled up to the door.

The church was as dilapidated inside as out. Windows which presumably had been stained glass before the Revolution had been replaced with murky, yellowish panes. Statue niches still stood empty. Above the main altar a bronze Christ gazed sadly at the passing centuries from his cross; in a side-chapel, money had clearly been spent on a painting of a young woman running out of a garden gate to follow a gray-clothed friar who stood in the road outside. Presumably St Clare, reflected Lydia, though she seemed to be wearing her shoes on this occasion. Lydia wondered if they fitted her properly. From a circular baptistry to one side of the main door a stairway wound up into the tower.

They MUST be connected underground. Jamie wouldn't have come here for refuge – he knows perfectly well that a church is no refuge from the Undead.

She stepped hesitantly into the dim gloom. *And the thought that he might have been meeting someone here is just silly . . .*

With his physical courage and half a lifetime of spying behind him, her husband could take very good care of his own skin.

He must have met Elysée at the Hôtel Batoux. He came in through here.

He could easily have picked the old-fashioned locks on the door.

There were nearly three hundred miles of sewers under Paris, according to Ysidro – and Mrs Flasket's guidebooks – and close to four hundred miles of tunnels that anyone knew about in the old gypsum and limestone mines that lay beneath its higher districts like Montmartre and Montparnasse. Even London had old Roman drainage tunnels, and the bricked-in culverts of small, forgotten rivers. Sunken crypts, the cellars of Roman temples and houses, the vaults of lost churches . . .

Jamie had told her he could cross nearly any city in Europe without coming above ground.

Beside the archway leading to the tower, someone had tacked a thick silver chain to the parish bulletin-board.

'FOUND . . .'

It was Jamie's.

She'd bought it for him herself, at the same time that she'd bought the one that circled her own throat under the high, old-fashioned collar of her shirtwaist. It wouldn't necessarily keep a vampire from killing you, but it was enough to burn one badly. Time enough to flee, if you were lucky. To scream, to grab a weapon if there were one available. She remembered the silver wrist-chains wound around his hands.

'. . . ON THE MORNING OF MONDAY 27 JULY . . .'

'My child?'

She pulled back from touching the chain. A tall, thin man in a priest's soutane stood behind her, a little basket of rags and silver polish in his hand. *Doesn't this church even have an Altar Guild or a Ladies' Auxiliary or whatever it is Catholic churches have?* She'd noticed that despite the cheaply replaced windows and the not-replaced-at-all statues, the inside of the church was spotless.

'Can I help you, madame?'

'I . . .' She struggled against the overwhelming urge to remove her glasses at once. *He's already SEEN you with them hanging on your face and besides, you're supposed to be in disguise . . .*

She took a deep breath. 'My name is Lavinnia Prior.' She held out her hand, and he shook it with genuine warmth. Despite his gray hair and deeply lined face, his grip was firm and powerful. 'My husband is the man who fell from your tower last week.'

She saw his quick glance ascertain that she was not in mourning. Mrs Flasket's oldest dress, like all the companion's clothing, was 'second mourning' for a husband long in his grave, dark (and much-faded) plum jollied up with cinder gray. This was close enough to actual mourning to cause the priest to say diffidently, 'He was badly injured when they took him from here. I trust . . .'

He left the phrase hanging.

'He has recovered consciousness,' said Lydia. 'But he recalls nothing of what happened. I came here to see . . .' She paused, gathering her thoughts and sorting out a story like a hand of cards.

'The thing is, Father,' she went on after a moment, hoping she remembered to cover everything, 'I have reason to fear that my husband was . . . was lured here. He stands to inherit a substantial sum of money, from an aunt who years ago disinherited her own son for . . . for conduct as shocking as it was violent. When they told me he appeared to have fallen from a church tower, I was baffled – why would anyone climb a church tower in the middle of the night? It isn't even a place robbers would choose.'

'I understand.' The priest glanced toward the baptistry, the door to the tower stair. 'I am Father Martin, by the way . . . And yes, that aspect of the accident puzzled me as well. I locked the doors myself when I left after Vespers.'

She widened her eyes and tried to look as if she'd never seen a picklock in her life. 'I'm afraid – from what Aunt Louise has told me of her son – that he might have . . . might have had something to do with all this. Because it's he who will inherit, if Jamie – Mr Prior . . .' (*is his workname James or John Prior? or something else Prior? –* she couldn't recall) '. . . should . . . should not recover. And of course with this frightful business happening in Belgium, the police don't have a moment to speak to me, and I can't even get in to see anyone at the embassy. It isn't as desperate as what's going on in Belgium, of course,' she added, and let her eyes fill with the tears that she'd been putting off as an unnecessary luxury for the past ten days. 'But it's desperately important to *me*. Knowing Jürgen – Jamie's cousin' (*I'll feel SUCH a ninny if this man turns out to be working for the vampires and I've just given the game away!*) '—is still out there somewhere . . . I thought I would at least come here and see where it happened . . .'

'Of course.' Father Martin set his basket on the nearest

bench-pew and offered her his arm. 'Do you wish to go up into the tower? After I looked around the chamber from which it is clear that he fell, the circumstances struck me as very queer. Watch your step here, madame, the stairs are very worn . . . But I could find no explanation that would suit the facts. The police said that your husband had lost a tremendous amount of blood, but there was none in the chamber – it lies between the ringing-chamber and the actual belfry, and is used for storage – and only a very little splashed just there.' He pointed to one of the worn, crooked steps just beneath a narrow door. 'I had meant to ask the police if there was further information.'

He opened the door, and with a shiver Lydia stepped into the room, illuminated from windows on all four walls (*we must be above the level of the church roof*). As Father Martin had warned her, the place was half-filled with boxes of what appeared to be parish records, neatly labeled, and an assortment of ecclesiastical bric-a-brac: old chairs, a rack of much-faded vestments, a narrow table piled with carefully sorted old clothes, and an enormous copper-bronze samovar enameled with flowers and birds.

'But with the onset of the current crisis, I must confess – and apologize – that the matter slipped my mind. The other priest attached to Sainte-Clare has gone into the army, just at a time when more of our parish have need of help and advice—'

'Please don't apologize!'

'This window was unlatched.' Father Martin walked to the narrow south-facing casement. 'The roof-slates just beneath it – that's the roof of the side-aisle – are much marked.'

Lydia found herself breathless, trembling, as she came to his side and looked out.

Not thrown. She gazed from the sill to the steep-slanted roof, eight feet beneath. *If he was caught by a vampire – or vampires – and managed to get loose . . . if he knew they followed him up the tower . . . he would have climbed out the window, hoping to drop to the roof and so scramble down to the ground. Hanging by his hands from the sill, his toes could just reach the roof . . .*

But it was too steep. And he was weak from the blood he'd lost. He couldn't hang on . . .

Stop it, she told herself as her stomach and knees both turned to water. *If it was somebody you didn't know you wouldn't feel like this.* She remembered Tante Camille's body, in the tangle of that gargantuan bed.

Father Martin, keeping close to her in case she should lose her balance, maintained a gentle flow of information about the church itself, to give her a chance to recover. Built as the chapel of a small convent in 1583 (*that's why the churchyard is so big; it must be the original cloister*), it had nearly been burned in the Revolution when the rest of the establishment had been torn down. Later it had been closed by the Commune revolt that followed the German war of 1871. 'They pulled up most of the headstones in the churchyard for the barricade they built on the Rue de Rivoli,' the priest explained, as he led Lydia down the stairs again. 'They also took the doors, and most of the church furnishings. And the Committee of Public Safety had the crypt searched for evidence either of taking commands from the Pope, or of a torture-chamber. It is – shocking—' he shook his head, troubled even after forty-some years – 'the sorts of ideas the ignorant have, who believe whatever their leaders tell them.'

Constantine Angelus, Lydia reflected, had written almost the same thing in 1597.

He nodded toward the small door at the side of the baptistry, when they emerged from the stair on to the ground floor again. 'We had most of the convent records still, there in the crypt. When the church was being used as an arsenal during the German siege a great many of those were simply burned. It was spring, and very cold. When I returned here after the army retook the city I gathered up what I could, but it was an irreparable loss.'

'Did you flee the city when the Commune took over?' Lydia thought of Uncle Evrard and his family, returning home to find themselves without one. Of Elysée de Montadour, Master of Paris, and the other vampires of the Paris nest, lingering in the beleaguered city to hunt in the chaos.

Lingering and dying, when the people of Paris had finally guessed who and what and most particularly *where* they were . . . *Why didn't they hide in the gypsum mines?*

'I was jailed,' said Father Martin simply. 'And came within two hours of being shot in retaliation for the execution of Communard hostages. And I saw what happened when the

Germans marched in. I read in the newspapers what is happening now, and am filled with the gravest foreboding.'

ELEVEN

*T*here has to be a way into the Hôtel Batoux from the church. Wrapped in her Japanese kimono, Lydia lay on her back, stared across at the muzzy suggestion of striped light on the wall of her bedroom.

They had been waiting for him in that dim shabby sanctuary, under the sad eyes of the bronze Christ. *It must have been the fledglings; Elysée de Montadour would have killed him in the Hôtel itself. The fledglings – with Jürgen Schaumm's help, if they got the silver chain off him.* It had been found, Father Martin had told her, in a dark corner near the confessionals. Lydia's fingers crept to her throat, where the chain – returned to her by Father Martin – now lay with four others of her own, warmed by the heat of her skin.

And afterwards they went and killed Tante Camille and her poor maid, for talking about crazy Uncle Evrard's house.

Or maybe to keep her from talking to anyone else about it.

Anyone else like me.

Most of the inhabitants of her aunt's building had departed. The constant soft vibration of footfalls, of activity, of water in pipes and windows opening and closing that had characterized the block of flats in the first days of her stay had all stilled. The Avenue Kléber, the Place de l'Étoile, the fashionable shops and usually bustling streets of this wealthy district, lay silent.

On the bed beside her that day's discarded newspaper, purchased on the way back from the Hôtel Batoux and the church of Sainte-Clare, blared the headlines 'GERMAN ZEPPELINS BOMB LIÈGE'.

I have to sleep. I'll have to remain awake all night, in case Ysidro decides to have a look at the Hôtel Batoux – or the church – for himself.

I have to talk to Dr Théodule about getting Jamie out of there.

She closed her eyes, and saw again the courtyard through the crack of the carriage gate, long and very deep between the wings of the house with its round Renaissance tower. Morning sunlight had glistened on the tower's many windows, modern additions even to Lydia's unpracticed eye – like modern handbills for soap pasted on eighteenth-century boiseries.

More than one guard, La Belle Nicolette had said. *They're probably under orders to get out of there come dark. Elysée can't afford gossip about the place and it certainly sounds like she can't control her fledglings.*

Lydia frowned, trying to remember all that Jamie and Don Simon had said about those fledglings.

Elysée took over as Master of Paris when her husband was killed . . . she had had to make all new fledglings, Ysidro said.

Murderers. Killing how many thousands over the years, how many tens of thousands?

Reflective eyes gleaming in the darkness. The silent whisper of movement, the chill laughter of the Undead.

The look she had seen in Jamie's eyes when he'd met Ysidro's gaze returned to her. His defeated silence in the face of the fact that they needed the vampire's help. *Jamie, I'm sorry . . .*

Ysidro's strong fingers around hers, and the brush of his lips on her hand. The quick flicker of the smile that echoed, like one mirror's reflection in another, the man he'd been in life . . .

He is a murderer, too. A vampire. Jamie is completely, absolutely right. That he saved your life – and Jamie's, and Miranda's – does not excuse what he is. What he does.

You mustn't feel what you feel.

SLEEP, she commanded herself. *You're going to need your wits about you.*

But all she saw was the pale scrape of boot-scratches through the crust of moss and slate on the church roof where Jamie had skidded, scrambled, bled white and too weak to catch himself as he slithered toward a twenty-foot drop.

Monsters. All of them.

Simon among the rest . . .

A floorboard creaked.

In the silence it was like a gunshot. She knew by the sound exactly what floorboard it was. When one walked across Aunt

Louise's large salon on the way to the hall there was one board that made that particular noise, like a sighing half-note on the clarinet.

Lydia grabbed for her glasses and her movement must have made enough noise for her visitor to hear, for the footfalls suddenly pounded in the hallway and she flung herself toward the window. *We're on the fourth floor . . .*

The embassy yesterday morning. Someone saw me there and realized I hadn't left Paris with Aunt Louise.

Ellen screamed, 'Ma'am!'

If Lydia had dashed to the window then (she estimated later) she probably could have gotten away.

But Ellen, by the sound of it, was grappling with the intruder in the hall – thumping, crashing, Ellen's scream, and a man shouting '*Schlampe!*' Lydia grabbed an elegant (and very heavy) bronze vase from the mantelpiece – cursing herself for having abandoned Aunt Louise's cane on the Rue des Francs-Bourgeois – and dashed into the hall in time to see a small black-haired man in spectacles slash open Ellen's arms with a knife and, when she fell back screaming and clutching the streaming wounds, grab her by the back of the neck to pull her into a stab.

The maid twisted, stumbled, her height – she was taller than her assailant – making his blow clumsy. Lydia stepped in and swung the bronze vase hard, but in the melee of struggling bodies only caught the man a glancing blow on the back. He threw Ellen violently against the corner of the open doorway into the kitchen and grabbed Lydia by the throat – it always surprised and terrified her how much stronger men were than they looked. She smote him on the side of the head, knocking his glasses spinning.

He yelled, '*Hure!*' and cut at her, and at that moment another man – taller, younger, and dazzlingly handsome – kicked through the hall doorway like the hero of a penny dreadful, gun in hand. Lydia didn't even see the gun until he fired it, and her dark-haired assailant buckled, staggered, dropped his knife, and fled through the kitchen doorway (tripping over Ellen, motionless in a pool of blood). Lydia realized she'd dropped her vase and dove to pick up the knife, and the newcomer grabbed her around the waist and put the gun behind the corner of her jaw.

Not the hero, anyway . . .

'Stand still,' he said 'Don't make a sound. There's nobody in the building to hear you.'

'Nonsense, there's the concierge – ow!'

He'd twisted her arm behind her back, shoved her against the wall, and taken the gun away for long enough to grab her other arm. Lydia writhed in his grip and he wrenched harder, her knees buckling as she sobbed in pain. 'Don't get cheeky with me, young lady. You be a good girl, and nothing will harm you.'

What felt like strips of surgical plaster were wound tight around her wrists, another one slapped over her mouth. Lydia twisted again in his grip, trying to see Ellen, but he jerked her to her feet and thrust her ahead of him into the kitchen, toward the open door of the back stairs.

'Your friend Herr Schaumm may be waiting downstairs,' added her captor, 'and I promise you, you don't want to meet him. All we want to do is talk to you. So if he tries to attack us at the bottom of the stairs, you'd better sit quiet and hope that I prevail. All right?'

She's hurt . . . She may be dying . . .

That was a *lot* of blood.

If I kick him he'll only stun me, and maybe do something to keep me from getting away later. Lydia twisted her head around one last time to see Ellen lying in the doorway behind her, bleeding, as Lydia was thrust down the dark of the back stairs.

At the bottom he pulled off her glasses and blindfolded her with his handkerchief (*Thank goodness it's clean!*), hustled her ahead of him into the alley and into a motor car. 'You're lucky I've been keeping an eye on Schaumm,' the young man went on as the car rocked and jolted over the uneven pavement, then cornered on to what Lydia guessed had to be the Avenue Kléber. He spoke French like an educated Parisian.

'Your friend Herr Schaumm . . .' We were right. No wonder Jürgen Schaumm came in and out of Jamie's dreams. The vile little man with the spectacles, Simon called him . . .

'He'll stop at nothing, you know,' her captor's voice went on. 'And the creature who's in league with him. If Madame hadn't thought to set a watch on the British Embassy for you, we might never have been able to save you. He's taking no chance that anyone but he – and that nigger cocotte – will lay hands on the Facinum.'

The FACINUM??? Lydia was so surprised she almost forgot to struggle. *Is THAT what this is all about? Constantine Angelus's magic talisman of mastery really EXISTS?*

'Madame' would be Elysée . . . *Have you ever created a homely fledgling?* Ysidro had asked mockingly. This young Prince Charming certainly looked like her 'type'.

And 'nigger cocotte'. Asher had spoken of one of Elysée's fledglings, a dusky, beautiful American girl – *what was her name? Hyacinthe* . . . Ysidro had mentioned her as well. Had spoken of Elysée's fledglings being rebellious, making fledglings of their own. Elysée had been livid at the suggestion.

They must have heard somehow about the talisman that what's-his-name – Cauchemar? One of the early members of the Paris nest? – believed Constantine Angelus possessed . . .

But why kidnap ME? And can I get to my picklocks before he stops the car?

As far as she could tell the vehicle was a saloon model, with a softly humming electric engine. She'd been shoved down on to the back seat while her captor drove, and going by his silence she was almost certain that he was alone. Cautiously, Lydia began to gather up the back of her kimono and petticoat where her fingers could reach them behind her. The sheer awkwardness of lacing and unlacing her corset had taught her long ago simply to sleep in it when it was only a matter of a few hours' nap. At Madame Chappedelaine's all the girls had been forced to do so all night, for the sake of their posture.

The car had turned right on to Avenue Kléber, but since that meant they were headed for the Place de l'Étoile she knew it would be useless to try to figure out the probable destination by counting turns. Even in the reduced traffic, she guessed her captor was going to be too occupied with driving to glance into the back seat.

The Facinum was nonsense, Ysidro had said. And while Lydia felt more inclined to trust Ysidro's knowledge than that of Elysée de Montadour, it didn't necessarily mean he was right. But a talisman of power sounded an awful lot like something out of one of those occult books that Jamie periodically had thrust upon him by members of theosophist covens in Oxford. Constantine's brother fledgling had believed in it . . . but he, too, could have been as credulous as the average table-tapper.

The picklocks were still in their discreet little packet, buttoned to the lower edge of her corset. After a great deal of squirming and twisting she got her fingers to the button that closed the roll, and selected – with the very tips of her fingers, which were all that she could maneuver into the packet – the two that she guessed would do her the most good: a hook pick and a diamond pick. The thin triangle of metal at the end of the latter would, she guessed, prove useful for sliding under the wretched surgical plaster around her wrists, if she were ever left alone.

She dropped the hook pick into one kimono sleeve, the diamond pick into the other (*clinking in the pocket at the end of the sleeve would give the game away . . .*). Gingerly she used her toes to tug her petticoat, then the kimono hem, back down.

Ellen, she thought desperately. *Ellen, I'm sorry.*

I should have sent you home. I should have insisted . . .

There's nothing you can do. Grief welled in her throat, and terror. *You may not even be able to save yourself.*

But I can make this awful man and Madame de Montadour very, VERY sorry they tangled with Jamie and me.

TWELVE

The car slowed and took a number of awkward little turns (*old neighborhood, narrow streets*) before coming to a stop at a slight angle, as if making a turn into a gate. *Yes* – the driver got out, and Lydia heard the muted clang of sheet metal. Drove in, stopped the car, got out (*closing the gate behind us*).

Hôtel particulier. Courtyard walls, muffled street noise beyond.

Not the Hôtel Batoux. No guards greeted them. Only stillness. *Somewhere else.*

She was sobbing and trembling by the time he stopped the car again and helped her out of the back seat. Arabella Howard at Madame Chappedelaine's school had used such techniques to deal with the instructors and Lydia had always despised them, but she'd observed that they did put assailants off their guard. The first thing her captor did was unhook and remove the silver chains around her throat.

Drat you, Elysée . . .

It's still daylight. I still have time . . .

'Don't scream.' He guided her indoors. 'There's no one in the house to hear you. I promise you, you won't be hurt.'

She shook her head and looked in the direction where she guessed his face was, with as pleading an expression as was possible behind a blindfold and a rectangle of surgical bandage. She knew the adhesive was going to hurt like the devil when he pulled it off – slowly, and what he probably thought was gently – and she was right.

'Don't hurt me,' she sobbed, and wilted against his grip on her arm as he led her over waxed parquet, up a flight of steps (long but unenclosed; *they must rise up from a central hall with a gallery around it, like Lady Wycliffe's town-house in London*), then into a room with good-quality carpet on the floor. He sat her down in a chair. Behind her back she could feel slick brocade under her fingers, hard upholstery . . . *Louis Quinze or Seize?*

No other footsteps, no doors closing, but no smell of mold or dampness. Her impressions – and the style of the chair – were confirmed when he took off the blindfold a moment later. He was, as she'd seen before, a few years younger than herself: like the Apollo Belvedere in an expensive suit.

'Please,' she whimpered (*am I laying it on too thick?*), 'please give me my glasses back.' She was prepared with more tears and a tale of how it terrified her not to see anything, but she didn't need them. He produced the glasses from his jacket pocket and put them carefully (and annoyingly askew) on her face.

'My husband told me nothing,' she added tremulously. 'Nothing.'

'You never heard him speak of the Facinum? The talisman of mastery?'

She shook her head and made her mouth quiver, an expression Arabella had particularly recommended. 'Nothing . . .'

It worked this time, because his intent eagerness softened a little, and he asked more gently, 'Or the chapel of bones?'

'No.' She blinked, to release two perfectly timed tears that trickled down her cheeks.

'Did he ever speak of Constantine Angelus?'

'Who?'

He sank into another chair beside hers and put his hands on her shoulders, looking into her eyes. 'Madame tells me your husband has recovered consciousness,' he said, which clinched it: 'Madame' was definitely Elysée. 'She says you've sat at his bedside all these nights. Did he say anything? Whisper anything in his sleep?'

'Nothing.' *How much has Elysée told him about me? How much of an idiot can I get him to think I am?*

'He didn't speak of the Hôtel Batoux?' The hungry glow reappeared in the young man's eyes and his grip tightened. 'Of what lies hidden there?'

She shook her head and tried to look terrified – not difficult, when she recalled what she'd seen in Tante Camille's flat. 'He tells me nothing,' she whispered. 'I saw your Lady only once, and did not understand a quarter of what she and my husband said to one another! You aren't – this Faci-whatever – she didn't enslave *you* . . .'

'It is my privilege and my honor to serve her.' The cerulean eyes shone with the ardent love which, Lydia was too well aware, vampires were able to create in their servants. 'I do my Lady's bidding in the daylight hours, when they sleep. In the nights she lets me follow their hunt, like running with leopards as they prey on the rabbits and rats of this world. They aren't what you think.' His voice sank to a reverent hush. 'They feed on the weak and the corrupt. They winnow out the fools who will only degrade the race, harvest those who don't understand love or creation. As Nietzsche says, the apes who think themselves happy, who look at the stars and blink stupidly. That scrawny degenerate Schaumm wants to use them – can see no more in them than something that he can trick or bribe or buy into service for one country in conquering another.'

'Schaumm . . .' Lydia stammered, as if she barely knew the name. 'He was the man who tried to kill me. Was he the man who tried to kill Jamie – my husband? Does he work for the – the vampires?' She hesitated over the word, as if still barely able to believe. 'Like you?'

'Not like me!' As she'd hoped, her captor drew himself up, insulted at the thought of being compared to Jürgen Schaumm. *'Nothing* like me! Listen, Madame Asher.' The afternoon light that filtered through the room's long windows past curtains of dull golden velvet gleamed on his golden hair as he leaned forward again.

'Jürgen Schaumm is seeking the Facinum, the talisman that gives one vampire mastery over the others. He's seeking the chapel of bones, the place where the Master vampire of Paris must bring those whom she would translate into the vampire state.' She could hear in his voice that this was a scene dreamed and daydreamed in his heart.

'He'll kill to get it – and he'll kill to keep others from finding it first. He has allied himself with this . . . this mongrel trollop who should never have been raised to immortality in the first place. She tricked my Lady into making her vampire, and by deceit she's learned of the Facinum. Now she seeks to use Schaumm to seize it for herself, this shallow, silly woman of a degenerate race—' *definitely Hyacinthe* – 'who's jealous of my Lady's beauty and power.'

'I . . .' Lydia whispered. 'M'sieu, I—'

'Modeste,' he said. 'Modeste Saint-Vrain. You can help us,' he continued. 'Your husband can help us – *must* help us. *You* must help us convince him that we're not evil, that we're not demons.'

In other words, I'm a hostage . . .

'What he's heard about my Lady is lies, concocted by those who are jealous of her power.'

'Monsieur Saint-Vrain,' pleaded Lydia, 'this is – I have heard nothing about this from my poor husband. Not before he went to Paris, not since I have sat at his bedside listening to his whispered ravings, for four nights now. The doctors say that he has brain fever—' an ailment beloved of novelists, which Lydia had never encountered in her medical experience – 'and that he may well remember nothing of the circumstances which brought him to Paris. I beg of you, let me go! You've killed Schaumm . . .'

Actually, since we didn't trip over him on the back stairs he probably has only a flesh wound. But he's out of action for a while anyway.

'. . . and whatever my husband may have learned is gone, wiped away. Please let me go back to my aunt's! My maid – a woman I've known all my life – was hurt, she may be dying! Let me go to her side, let me go to my husband's side . . .'

He looked uncertain at that, like an actor miscued. 'I'm sure – that is, Madame will have to . . .' Having claimed he wasn't a demon he looked disconcerted at having to live up to the assertion. 'I – well – Madame will . . . You'll have to speak with my Lady. But I'm sure you'll come to no harm.'

Lydia bit back the words, *Oh, really?* As a hostage, she was well aware of what her chances of survival would be, particularly if others of the Paris nest came upon her when Elysée wasn't around. *They want to learn what Jamie knows . . . But knows about WHAT? If they know about the Facinum already . . .*

'Then please—' Lydia blinked forth another pair of tears. 'Please, would you telephone the police and tell them to go to my aunt's flat? Tell them there's been a burglary, that a woman is badly hurt. The address is forty-eight, Avenue Kléber – please! Ellen has been my friend nearly all my life! She saved my life; if she hadn't stopped Schaumm he would certainly have killed me! They may yet get there in time to save her!'

He hesitated, laboriously calculating times and distances.

No telephone in the house.

'Or send a note to the nearest police station.'

His brow cleared. 'That's a good idea,' he agreed and, rising, hurried from the room.

Lydia heard the key turn in the lock. *Good, he won't be back in a hurry.*

And thank heavens Madame picks her servants for looks and not brains.

She probed down into her kimono sleeve and drew out the hook pick that she'd dropped there.

It took a good deal of twisting and fiddling with the pick to get it under a corner of the adhesive dressing that bound her wrists, but once that was done she was able to stick that corner on the wood of the chair in which she sat, and pull the bandage loose. While she worked her mind raced, calculating the time Modeste Saint-Vrain would need to write a note, carry it to the nearest police-station . . .

The lock on the door of the small salon where she'd sat was old, and she thought she could probably have picked it with a couple of hairpins, the way Jamie did, if she hadn't had her picklocks. The whole chamber – and the gallery beyond, above the stair-hall, on to which the door opened – had an old-fashioned air, the boiseries on the walls unpainted, the curtains clean and dusted but faded, as if they'd been hanging there by the long windows since long before 1871 when, presumably, Saint-Vrain's Lady had taken possession of this place.

And what the dickens could Elysée de Montadour want from Jamie that she doesn't already know? Something about this Facinum? To the best of her knowledge, Jamie had never come across anything of the kind in his research. *And anyway, Madame seemed to know all about it.*

She did a swift reconnaissance to make sure the room next door – a music-room, stuffy and disused – was unlocked, then returned to the salon. Its long windows looked out over the central courtyard – *DAMN it! I'll have to wait for him. Otherwise when he comes in he'll notice an open window.*

Only a minute later the wicket door of the gate opened and Saint-Vrain's elegant, broad-shouldered form stepped through. Lydia watched him until he disappeared into the building itself, then opened the window wide, dashed with soundless speed into the music-room and whipped off the stout silken cord that belted her kimono. The salon door opened inward, but the cord was long enough to reach across the gallery to the banisters. *If I can just get the door closed behind him and the cord knotted around the handle quickly enough . . .*

She heard his step on the marble semicircle of the stair as she was maneuvering the lockpicks to re-lock the door from the outside. She'd glanced around her, both in the salon and the music-room, for anything that could be used as a weapon, but her attempt to bash Schaumm over the head had led her to mistrust both her arm strength and her aim. Knocking someone out with a vase was evidently a great deal easier to do in music-hall melodramas. Intrepid heroines – depending on how intrepid they were – might conceal a paperknife from a convenient desk upon their persons and make sure of their captors with a single stab to the heart. But first, though Lydia knew where the heart was, she wasn't at all certain she could stab a man in it without hitting a rib or the scapula (depending on the angle), particularly not in an emergency. Second, she knew she'd be right up next to him if her blow went awry.

And though she was fairly certain that Elysée de Montadour would kill her – while Saint-Vrain looked on in awe at her superhuman stature and resolve, no doubt – Saint-Vrain had in fact saved her life, and had done her no harm so far.

She wasn't sure she *could* kill him. Not from behind, in cold blood.

So she retreated into the music-room and waited, and when he unlocked and opened the salon door and saw the window across the room open and Lydia gone, he dashed across immediately to look out (as Jamie said eight people out of ten would do), leaving the key in the lock.

Oh, good, I won't need to do that sash business . . .

She pulled the door shut behind him, locked it, and removed the key.

The stairway, as she'd observed on the way up it, was a long one, so the drop from the window would be a good twenty feet.

Tying her kimono as she ran, Lydia darted down the stair. The key to the front gate was in a drawer of the table in the front hall. She'd heard him open and close it on their way in. Though perfectly willing to dash through the streets of Paris (*I wonder what arrondissement I'm in?*) in kimono and petticoats, she was deeply appreciative of the presence of the motor car – a Babcock electric brougham, it turned out to be – in the courtyard.

She abandoned it in an alley two streets from her aunt's flat, and let herself in through the service stairs. That door was locked. *Someone must have been here . . .*

There was blood tracked everywhere – men's boots – but Ellen was gone.

Lydia stayed only long enough to put on a frock and shoes and fill up a carpet bag with clean linen, make-up, and all the money she could find.

She found a taxi in front of the Peninsula Paris hotel. '*L'Hôpital Saint-Antoine*,' she said.

THIRTEEN

Jamie was sitting up in bed when Lydia arrived. But though he smiled a greeting his cheeks were flushed with fever, and she could see by the crease between his brows that he was in the throes of another splitting headache. During her recital of the events of the afternoon he twice turned aside from her, racked with coughing, and when Lydia went out into the corridor in search of a surgeon she could only find Fantine, who told her that Dr Bloch – the only day surgeon who hadn't joined the army – had already seen the men in Ward B and was in the Contagious Ward at the moment.

'And is Ward B not contagious?' retorted Lydia. 'I need to speak to someone about whether my husband can be moved.'

The sweeper looked profoundly doubtful – as was Lydia herself. 'I'll let Dr Bloch know. Or Dr Théodule, should he arrive before Dr Bloch is done.'

'Today's paper,' said Asher when Lydia returned to his side, and winced as someone a few beds away yelled, 'And then will Sedan be avenged!' at the top of his lungs. It was late afternoon, and visitors crammed the crowded ward. 'If Ellen was no longer at the flat someone must have come and taken her away, and it doesn't sound like Schaumm would have had either the strength or any reason to do so. Somewhere in all this jingoistic hoo-rah—' his fingers flicked the three-inch headline 'LES DARDANELLES FERMÉES!' – 'you should find what hospital she was taken to.'

Denunciations of Austria for declaring war on France's ally Russia jangled the air around them, every visitor waving a newspaper at bedridden fathers, husbands, sons. Speculations about how long it would take General Bonneau's Seventh Army Corps to sweep the Germans out of Alsace and cut off Germany's supplies to its army before they reached Liège almost – but not quite – distracted Lydia's mind from her concerns for her husband and Ellen, and where she might take Jamie now that Aunt Louise's was clearly unsafe.

'Karlebach said something to me once that makes me think he's on at least speaking terms with the Master of Prague,' Asher went on, after Lydia had finished her tale. 'The Master may very well have told him about Schaumm soliciting the help of a rebel fledgling in the Paris nest – and yes, that certainly sounds like what I remember of Hyacinthe. Looking back, I'm guessing that at some point Schaumm established contact with some vampire in Prague . . . I wonder if Karlebach knew about it then?'

The line of pain between his brows deepened as he tried to delve into further memories. Lydia put her hand over his.

'And then will Sedan be avenged!' bellowed a man near the door, and the cry was taken up by seven or eight of Asher's fellow sufferers.

'I'll swear Schaumm never read anything about this Facinum or anything like it in any of Karlebach's books.'

'Saint-Vrain said that the Master of Paris had to create her fledglings in a certain specific place,' recalled Lydia. 'Because the Facinum was there, I presume. Don Simon's certainly never mentioned such a thing, though I'm not sure that he would, to me. The *Book of the Kindred of Darkness* . . .'

'Says nothing of them.' The decisive note in his voice indicated that whatever else had been obliterated by the blow to his head, at least he remembered reading that strange old text. *A good thing, too*, Lydia reflected. *What a bore, to have to go back and reread the whole book – in medieval Spanish, too! – because you'd forgotten every word of it.* In the course of the past year, since the volume had come into his hands, Asher had been working on a translation for her: slow going, because they were both annotating, with their own findings and recollections, the original account of what Johanot of Valladolid had learned during his years of service to the Prague vampires in the fourteenth century.

'This bone chapel he spoke of . . .'

He frowned at that, and pressed his fingers to his forehead. 'I've never heard of any vampire having to create its fledglings in a specific place,' he said in time. 'But there was something . . .'

'About a bone chapel?' Lydia recalled the bone chapels that she'd seen in Rome, beneath the Monastery of the Capuchins on the Via Veneto: the walls of one tiny chamber wrought of grinning skulls, those of another of banked tibias and radii. Pelvises decorated a third. Ceilings refulgent with twining foliations of ribs, with flowers fashioned out of coccyges and fingerbones. In the last of the suite – there were, she recalled from her visit as a fascinated fourteen-year-old, six separate chambers – the image of Death himself had hovered on the ceiling, a single skeleton in an aureole of vertebrae, wielding his scythe. She recalled her delight, in the face of her school-mates' horrified shrieks.

'I think – I don't know.'

When Ysidro arrived with the coming of full darkness he shook his head at once. 'This is absurd. 'Tis the master who creates the fledgling, not the spot upon which the transaction takes place.' His yellow eyes narrowed. 'Raimund Cauchemar used to claim that the Facinum was the only reason Constantine was able to hold power over him, Raimund . . . for naturally Raimund would never admit of another's mind being stronger than his. Yet 'twas not so. I know this. As to why Elysée would seek to trap Mistress Asher as hostage . . .'

'Does it sound to you,' said Lydia slowly, 'as if Elysée *doesn't know* where the Facinum is? Only that it's somewhere in the house. Then kidnapping me would make sense, if she thinks Jamie *does* know. And if Schaumm knows, and has made a bargain to set up Hyacinthe as the Master of Paris, using its power . . .'

Asher leaned back against the pillow, eyes sliding closed. Lydia looked around her again, at the shabby women, wives or mothers, some of them also coughing or spitting. *This place is a plague ward!* It was long past the hour when Dr Théodule should have appeared. From the hall came Thérèse Sabatier's voice, railing at poor Fantine, and almost in Lydia's lap a woman was explaining at great length to her son in the next bed how she'd walked ten miles through the wealthier neighborhoods and had found nothing – not one thing – which could be scavenged and taken home to remake into another garment or another blanket, and what were they going to do for food tomorrow? A few yards along the ward, another went on and on about how Germany must be punished for starting all this trouble, in a voice so shrill it could have cut glass.

Across the room someone roared, 'And then will Sedan be avenged!' to a cacophony of cheers.

The heat was insufferable, the smell of dirty clothes stifling. All Lydia wanted to do was put her head down on the pillow beside Asher's and fall asleep, but she knew this was impossible. The newspaper on her lap was folded open to the small article – barely two lines amid acres of war news – that spoke of a burgled flat in the Avenue Kléber, and an English maidservant found wounded. She'd been taken to the Hôpital Lariboisière, it said.

I have to go to her. And tomorrow I'll have to make arrangements to send her back to England, the moment she's well enough to travel. M'sieu Greuze may know some way to get her to Bordeaux.

Even as her whole exhausted soul sobbed with thanks that Ellen had survived, Lydia cringed at the thought of going anywhere or doing anything further tonight.

Can't I just PLEASE go to bed somewhere and get some sleep?

Not in Aunt Louise's flat, I can't.

Just rest a few minutes, she told herself firmly, as she had all those nights of doing clinic duty at that awful charity hospital in the East End. *A few minutes' rest and I'll be fine.*

Lydia raised her eyes to Ysidro's cool alabaster profile, saw him studying one bed after another – the women, the men – with enigmatic absorption.

Monster . . .

'You've said—'

At the sound of her voice he turned his glance to her. Human again, or nearly so.

'You've said Elysée de Montadour doesn't have the strength to be Master of a city like Paris.' She folded the newspaper, tucked it aside. 'So how did she come to it? And is that why this woman Hyacinthe hates her so much?'

'All fledglings hate their masters.' His voice was remote, as if none of this had anything to do with him. 'Some masters force their fledglings to love them – which of course only makes the hatred worse. Others solve the problem by choosing only those too dull-witted to cause them trouble. Elysée wanted a servant from whom she would not have to conceal her vampire state; the deception rapidly becomes fatiguing. Like most white women of her class she had not the slightest notion that a woman of color would have more brains than she did.'

'And this was . . .' Lydia fished in her memory. 'Right after the last war? When Germany defeated France? Didn't you say Elysée's husband was the only one of the Paris vampires to survive the Revolution?'

'One of the few. During the Revolution one could hunt in the city with absolute impunity, so long as one wore trousers rather than breeches, or cheesecloth rags in preference to corsets and petticoats. They would go into the prisons every night to kill, retail murder which barely raised an eyebrow beside the wholesale slaughter taking place in the Place de la Révolution.'

'Were you in Paris then?'

Ysidro managed to sneer without altering his expression. '*Please*. Those of the London nest – and of other places – who made the Channel crossing on purpose to join them got, I am gratified to say, precisely what they deserved for such stupidity. As I said, the poor of Paris believed in vampires. Once the revolutionary women of the *quartiers* became suspicious, the chaos in the city made it possible for them to hunt the predators unopposed – indeed unremarked – and to raise a mob of any size on short order and no provocation.'

'Why didn't they hide in the sewers?' asked Lydia. 'Or the gypsum mines, or the catacombs?'

'Some did, I believe. As I said, I was not here. But for many vampires, the kill is not only a necessity, it is an addiction: they will come forth to hunt even under conditions of danger. François de Montadour survived by passing himself off as a living man, which took a great deal of cunning, and even after the accession of Napoleon made people believe this of him for a surprising number of years. He took over the town mansion of the Master of Paris – Gabrielle Batoux, it had been – on the Rue de Passy, and her other hideouts as well, presumably the old Hôtel Batoux among them. He had a great deal of money, which was by then the only criterion upon which one was judged in Paris. In counterfeit of a living man he wed Elisabette Cloue, otherwise known as Elysée L'Alouette, a demi-mondaine of rather specialized clientele: the years just before Napoleon's seizure of the French government were a notoriously vicious time.'

'According to La Belle Nicolette, the Hôtel Batoux was the original home of the family. Members of it lived there up until the last war with Germany.'

'A risky arrangement.' Ysidro frowned. 'Gabrielle Batoux had hideouts all over Paris. Her Passy *hôtel* – the present Hôtel de Montadour, probably the place to which you were taken – is a honeycomb of secret rooms and concealed staircases. So far as I know, 'twas François's chief nest and remains so for his wife.

'François, though not a particularly intelligent man, was ruthless, and cunning as a rat. Like Gabrielle before him he chose his fledglings – and his wife – for what they could give him or do for him, men and women as greedy and self-centered as himself. He taught them few of the finer skills of the Undead, preferring to keep the arts and glamors of deception which he had learned from Gabrielle – the songs one weaves with dreams – as his own secrets, his means of controlling them. Why it never occurred to him that conditions of civil chaos would be as dangerous in 1871 as they were in 1793 – despite the excellent hunting to be had in a city virtually without law – I cannot say—'

'I think I can, though,' said Lydia. 'I think Gabrielle Batoux, and François de Montadour after her, didn't take refuge in the sewers or the mines – or didn't do so for very long – because they were unwilling to leave the Hôtel Batoux unguarded.'

Impatience flickered in his eyes. 'There is no Facinum.'

'But they didn't know that. And there must be something about the house that caused François, at least, to think it gave him power.'

'François de Montadour thought the house gave him power because he was a fool,' snapped Ysidro.

'No, listen. Schaumm heard about the Facinum somehow, and about Hyacinthe's hatred of Elysée – do vampires gossip amongst themselves? I'm sure they must. They have to talk about *something* besides hunting.'

'You demonstrate your ignorance, lady.'

'Whatever the case, Schaumm promises Hyacinthe he'll put her in power if she works for the Germans – not a bargain *I'd* feel safe making. Schaumm learns that Jamie is in Paris trying to trace the places where the Facinum might have been hidden – places where Constantine Angelus might have been – and learns that Jamie has been asking questions about the Hôtel Batoux. Jamie gets away by the skin of his teeth . . .'

'And Schaumm guesses that you will come, when you hear of his injury,' concluded the vampire softly. 'Hence the disposal of poor Tante Camille – and that silly "William Johnson" charade.'

'And when he saw me at the embassy,' said Lydia, 'he knew I hadn't left Paris with Aunt Louise, and came to finish the job. And so I need to get Ellen, at least, away from Paris.'

She got to her feet, shook out her creased and rumpled skirts. 'If you would be so good as to remain here and watch over Jamie tonight—'

'I can look after myself for one night.' Asher's eyes half-opened. Lydia wondered if he had been asleep at all. 'Don Simon, if you would go with her—'

'Don't be silly,' said Lydia, in chorus with Ysidro's rather stronger admonition.

'And you,' added the vampire, turning to Lydia, 'do not you be a fool either.'

Lydia opened her mouth to snap a reply, and Asher put in, 'Can you hire this man Greuze, this cab-driver you had watching over me yesterday, to go with you tonight?'

After a moment's silence, in which Lydia could see the struggle in his face, he turned his head a little to meet the vampire's gaze. 'Would Mrs Asher be safe in whatever dwelling you've hired for yourself, Don Simon? Does your reputation extend to putting the fear of the Lord into the Lady Hyacinthe?'

'It does.' There was something in his expressionless voice that made Lydia certain that the vampire Hyacinthe – and in fact any of the Paris nest – would think twice before going up against this slender gentleman in his trim gray suit. 'I assure you, James, your lady will be safe beneath my roof. Safer than you are—' his yellow glance touched the window – 'beneath this one.'

After Lydia's departure, Asher drifted again into feverish sleep. A year ago he had warned Ysidro that he would no longer abide or endure the odd partnership – close enough at times to border on friendship – that for the past seven years had existed between himself and the vampire. From what felt like an enormous distance he saw himself and Ysidro together by lantern-light in a dream he'd had of African twilight, and reflected that it didn't seem to matter to the vampire what he, James Asher, could abide or endure.

And the past few days had brought home to him that his own commitment to what was right – to the deserts justly due to this pale predator – wouldn't stand the test of expediency either.

And Ysidro knew it. Had known it from their first meeting.

Had he walked in my dreams and known that of me, before we met? Was that how he chose me as his tool?

He'd come back, a hundred times, from 'abroad', in the days of his service to the Queen, loathing himself and the things that he had done. Loathing his calm readiness to kill total strangers, his undoubted facility for theft, fraud, lies, and the betrayal of those 'enemy' civilians who'd trusted the man they'd thought he was. Like poisoned magic, the words 'for Queen and country' had always drawn him back. And the knowledge that he was good at what he did.

Thus he recognized that he was apparently perfectly willing to form a partnership with Don Simon Ysidro – knowing full well what Ysidro was and did – if those he, James Asher, personally loved were in danger.

He had done far worse, for goals less vital and true.

What does that make me?

He didn't know, and his head hurt too much to think.

In his dream he stood in his study in Oxford, holding the letter he'd received from Rebbe Karlebach. The paper was blank. He turned it over and found it blank on the other side, though curiously he could see the blots and marks of his old mentor's handwriting through the paper. The sheet was definitely written on – just never on the side facing him.

When he went to his desk, where the *Book of the Kindred of Darkness* lay open, it was the same. The age-stained brown pages were blank. When he turned them he could glimpse the 'lettre de somme' printing on other pages but, open it where he would, it was always to pages that were blank.

The Facinum has to be in here somewhere, he thought. *I have to have missed it.*

He went to the bookshelf, found there the much later 1637 Latin edition of that same work that had been in Karlebach's house (and indeed, in crossing the study to the bookshelf he found he had gone from his own house in Oxford to Karlebach's musty-smelling, heavily curtained cubbyhole in Prague), and opened it.

Ysidro is wrong. There is something in the bone chapel. François de Montadour knew it. Elysée knows it. Something that will change the course of the war. Something that will unleash the German armies on all of France, on Belgium, on England.

Something . . .

I knew what it was.

He remembered Elysée's drawing-room, on his first encounter with the Paris nest, in the Saint-Germain mansion that had been her husband's. Remembered the gold silk wallpaper, and theatrically beautiful vampires playing cards by thousandfold candlelight. Hyacinthe standing so close behind him that he could smell her perfume, her long nails brushing the skin of his neck.

Beautiful, as all the members of the Paris nest were beautiful.

Or was that only because vampires could appear beautiful to their victims?

Karlebach's copy of the book was blank, too.

In the center of one page he found a paragraph that was common to most – though not all – of the book's various printings:

> Seldom do the Undead entrust the living with the knowledge of who and what they truly are . . . and seldom do the dead employ a living servant for more than five years before killing him and all members of his family, to protect their secret.

But what, Asher wondered, *is their secret?*

'Jesu Mary, sir, I thought you'd come to grief sure!' The young man (*was he here a moment ago?*) sprang to his feet from a seat by the fire (*there wasn't a fire burning . . . and why is the hearth different from the one in Karlebach's house?*) as Simon entered the study (*what's Ysidro doing in Karlebach's study? But it wasn't*

Karlebach's at all, though just as crammed with books and just as tiny . . .).

The young man – tall, red-haired, and clothed in good brown wool, doublet and Venetian breeches – fell on one knee before the vampire and reached to kiss his hand.

'Get up, Tim. I have already pointed out to you that I'm not the Holy Father and this ring isn't a sacred relic.'

And Tim grinned, and scrambled gawkily to his feet. 'Did you find him, lord?'

'I did.' Cobwebs and dust smutched the black velvet of his doublet. Asher thought he looked drawn and ill. Tim evidently thought so, too. He took the vampire by one elbow and put his other hand, big and red and bony, on his shoulder to steer him to the chair by the fire, and Simon went, tamely as an exhausted child, Simon Ysidro who seldom – as far as Asher had seen – let anyone touch him . . .

'Are you all right, sir? Did you – did you do the deed?' Tim reached for the poker to turn the log, then looked back worriedly at his master's face. 'How would a vampire go about killing another vampire anyway, sir? I mean, to drive a stake through his heart you'd have to come on him by day when he's asleep, but then *you're* asleep as well . . .'

'One would lure him into an alleyway with a choice piece of prey whose sins are begging to be punished.' Simon's slender fingers touched the corner of his mouth, where a sharp-edged mounting on Brother Esdras de Colle's ox-horn had torn his lip. 'And come on him from behind with two or three like-minded heretic vampires, and force down his throat a philter that numbs him like a poisoned fish.'

He pressed his hands together hard, to still their trembling. 'Then one drags him to the top of the nearest high hill outside the city – with one's tame heretic priest reciting psalms all the way – and leaves him where the morning light will find him . . .'

'My lord!' Tim fell on his knees before him, seized his hands, stared up into his face, hazel eyes wide with shock. 'They never—'

''Tis well, my good Tim.' Simon disengaged one hand, stroked his servant's hair as a man would stroke a dog, like rusty silk in the firelight. 'Behold me unhurt. 'Tis well. The Master of this town has forbidden vampire to harm vampire, saying – indeed with truth – that we are all of us damned together.' He turned his face aside and stared for a time into the hearth, as if it were a tiny chink in the wall of Hell through which he could glimpse his punishment.

As though he could read his master's thoughts, Tim's hands tightened over the vampire's. 'And this Father Jeffrey of yours, he wouldn't . . . he wouldn't give you shriving? Like they do soldiers before battle, sir? If any deserves it, 'tis yourself.'

'He can't. This Cardinal of his, Cardinal Montevierde, perhaps could – he speaks for the Holy Father in Rome – but he will not. Not until I have proven myself wholly God's servant. Wholly willing to accomplish God's bidding, with unstinting heart.'

'But if you die in the attempt, sir—' Still kneeling before him, Tim pressed his forehead to Simon's hand again. 'If the Master of this town kills you for disobeying his command . . . is he a heretic? The Master? He has to be, doesn't he, sir, if he'd take a heretic's side?'

'I know not what he is.' Simon stroked Tim's hair again. 'I should send you home, my friend. I think the water is going to be very deep here. We may neither of us have the strength to reach its farther side. I'd not condemn your wife to widowhood, nor your child to grow up fatherless.'

'You can bloody well try, sir.' Tim stood up, and looked down at the vampire with a crooked grin. 'I'd have no wife, nor no child neither, if 'twere not for you. And you'd have to pour your witch-festering Protestant fish-poison philter down my throat to get me on a boat back to England, and then I'd still find a way to come and help you. So don't talk cock. You going out again tonight, sir?'

'I must.'

Tim angled his head, like a dog confronted by an incongruity.

'If I am to find a way to kill Esdras de Colle, against the Lord of Paris's command . . . I must.'

FOURTEEN

When Tim had left the study, Simon Ysidro turned his head and regarded Asher with ophidian eyes. 'What are you doing here, James?'

'I haven't the smallest idea.' Asher glanced at the book still open in his hand: *Seldom do the dead employ a living servant for more than five years* . . .

He wondered how long Tim had lived past 1602.

'If I'm going to encounter vampires and their servants in my dreams, I'd like to arrange to speak to Johanot of Valladolid. Or Constantine Angelus.'

'Why Constantine?' Ysidro sat up. Already he had lost the more human mannerisms he had displayed earlier in the dream. Save for the Elizabethan clothing he was precisely as Asher knew him in London, poised and expressionless, as if he had never shuddered with remembered terror, or bowed his head to one he hoped would save his soul from Hell. 'You spent a great deal of time and money seeking out his tracts.'

'I saw him,' said Asher hesitantly. 'A tall man? Black hair, longer than yours, over his shoulders and down his back; straight nose, narrow tip. Gray eyes, broad shoulders. Square chin . . .'

''Tis impossible that you could have seen him. He died in 1603. Died in fact, in truth. The Hôtel Batoux wasn't even built then.'

'I saw him in the bone chapel. I dreamed of it—'

'As you dream now. He is dead, James. He never set foot in the Hôtel Batoux in his life.' As if he heard the sharpness of his own speech, Ysidro folded his hands again and returned his gaze to the fire.

'I was seeking something in the Hôtel Batoux,' said Asher. 'And I was seeking information about Angelus. Are you sure about this Facinum that this Raimund claimed he had? Facinum – from *facere*, to make . . . To make *what*?'

''Tis only the Latin for "talisman". No such thing existed.'

Asher was silent, and let the vampire reflect upon the fact of his own anger. Ysidro's expression did not alter, but Asher could feel it – as if he saw the turn of that bird-like head, the lowering of the slender shoulders – when he relaxed.

'Can you take me there?' he asked at length. 'To Constantine's rooms?'

That brought Ysidro's gaze away from the miniature Hell of the hearth.

'This is the manipulation of dreams that you were taught to practice, isn't it?' Asher's gesture took in the book-lined study around them. 'You told me – when we first met – that you had but to look into a person's eyes, to speak to them later in their dreams. To bring them to you, though it be from the ends of the earth, you said. To enter your consciousness into theirs, the same way your master – Rhys the Minstrel of London – took your consciousness into his own brain when the physical tissues of your brain died and began to reconstitute as vampiric flesh. An alteration at a cellular level, Lydia postulates.'

'She and I have spoken of this.' Ysidro straightened the ruffles at his wrists with a movement of one nail, like a glassy claw, as he rose from his chair. 'She has said, when the cells of the brain have finished their alteration, only then does the master breathe back the soul, the consciousness, the memories of the fledgling into them.'

'And can another vampire – not your master – have this power over you?' He remembered Angelus looking down into Simon's eyes, in the crypt below the church of Saint-Pierre. Seeing all he had seen in life. Knowing all he had known.

Ysidro looked aside. 'Some can.'

'Could Angelus?'

The vampire did not reply.

'You've said to me also,' Asher went on, 'that this . . . this *interpenetration* of the master's mind with the fledgling's is why the master holds such power over those he creates. Because a part of them – a part of their minds, their souls – remains in his.'

Ysidro nodded, like the single shift of a grass-stalk stirred by a raven's wing-beat.

'Because I think this is why I'm . . . I'm seeing things that happened to you. This is what Angelus took from your thoughts.'

'*That is not possible.*'

'Can you take me to his rooms? As you knew them, as they exist now in *your* mind.' Asher set down the *Book of the Kindred of Darkness* on Karlebach's library table and tightened around his middle the sash of his dressing-gown, which was what he'd been wearing at the start of this dream, as he'd stood in his own study in Holywell Street. 'You knew them well?' he added, as Ysidro opened a small door to one side of the fireplace which had not been there moments before.

Asher had to duck his head to pass beneath its lintel.

'Few better,' replied the vampire. Like ghosts, Asher saw them sitting across the small hearth from one another: Constantine Angelus in the black cassock of a priest, Simon Ysidro physically identical to the vampire who stood at Asher's side. But in his movements and expression, and the intensity of his words, this other Simon, this younger Simon, seemed infinitely closer to his living self.

'But what *is* death?' that younger Simon was saying, and leaned closer to the Master of Paris, as if he would seize those dark sleeves and shake the answer from him. 'And what is life? And what, physically, happened to *us*, that our lungs no longer fill with air save when we speak, that our bodies excrete no waste, that neither our hair nor our nails grow, that our loins are cold.'

'This I know not, my friend.' As it had been on the top of Montmartre hill, Constantine's voice was deep and gentle, like the wind over open sea. 'When the living kill one of us, invariably they make sure of the death with fire, so that I have never had the opportunity to examine twice-dead flesh. I have read that when a vampire dies its flesh quickly transforms to dust, yet this I do not know of my own knowledge. And men may write anything . . . even write that the damned may be saved if they but endow the Church with sufficient money to gain the approval of the Holy Father. A cheap argument,' he added immediately, with a sudden, very human grin, as Simon bristled all over with indignation. 'Worthy of a cheap pamphleteer. Forgive me, dear friend.' He made a salaam of deep obeisance. 'Let us consider instead the life of animals, or the life of plants, to take it to a form more simple yet . . .'

'He was a great scholar.' The real Ysidro – the present-day

Ysidro, clothed though he was in the scuffed black velvet of Elizabeth's reign – led the way into the chamber, which was generously proportioned and lined with shelves of books in the manner that Lydia had told Asher was typical of every room in Ysidro's tall London house . . . only far more tidy.

'I have often felt regret that Mistress Asher had not the opportunity to discuss these matters with Constantine, nor with Rhys the White who made me vampire, and who had an even greater curiosity than I do concerning the vampire state.'

Neither the young Simon nor Constantine Angelus turned to look at them, as Asher and Ysidro passed within half a foot of the hearth where the two vampires sat in conversation. Like Scrooge and the Ghost of Christmas Past, Asher reflected. *These are but the shadows of the things that have been . . .*

He wondered if Ysidro had read *A Christmas Carol.*

'When all was said, he was a man rooted deeply in a different age. Constantine studied with every physician in Paris who would teach him, and made the journey regularly to Flanders – where he was Master of half a dozen cities – to watch the anatomists dissect cadavers, and to observe their experiments with lenses and mirrors and light.'

He led the way into a room beyond the study, a larger chamber which Asher guessed ran most of the length of a good-sized city house. Its ceiling slanted up sharply to a maze of cruck-work and raftering from which a couple of iron rings depended on chains, set about with candles, though probably too few to illuminate much. The windows, at the ends of gables and dormers of varying sizes, were for the most part tightly shuttered, but Asher knew that vampires were capable of reading and working in total darkness. The only light in the room came from a small forge about halfway along, its embers glowing red and, on the opposite wall of the workroom, a sort of cooking range where a bubbling pot gave off a smell of slowly dissolving meat.

'Few vampires retain the living curiosity about the world to pursue studies as he did.' Hands clasped lightly behind his back, Ysidro followed Asher around the long room, as Asher studied the contents of the shelves, opened the cabinets to examine the shells of conch and nautilus, the animal skulls and ostrich eggs, the sand-scoured bottles of ancient Egyptian glass and the bits of crystal and amber. The shutters of one dormer were open, and on a table before the window a telescope pointed to the black sky over the roofs of Paris, luminous with stars to the horizon.

'For this reason I think he took to me, as I to him. The nights are long, and in a city of four hundred thousand – even in those days of inexplicable illnesses – a dozen vampires must hunt with caution. The poor died every night, of cold or of starvation, and as ever the hospitals were easy pickings . . . yet in those days men believed in the vexations of the Undead. We hunted seldom. Sometimes the others – Ivo, Gabrielle, Raimund, Zaffira – would go far into the countryside to make their kills, barely coming back before morning light.

'For them, their talk was all of hunting, as men long celibate will dream of women. More so, indeed, for compared to the impact of absorbing the energy of another's death, mere coition is but a pallid reflection, a child's penny whistle after a Bach fugue.'

'If you think vampires are the only ones who talk about nothing but hunting,' observed Asher, gently unfolding a sheaf of notes written in Latin in a neat, fourteenth-century hand, 'you've obviously never spent three days at a hunt meeting in the shires with Lydia's family. I don't wonder that Angelus – if he retained the capacity to appreciate educated conversation – took you to his bosom. By Saturday night I'd have played chess with Satan, for the sake of a change in topic.'

'A perilous occupation.' Ysidro opened the door at the end of the room, which led to a sharp-angled little enclosed staircase, leading down into blackness. 'As my friend Father Jeffrey cautioned me many times.' He glanced back to the glowing doorway far behind them, at his younger self absorbed in talk with the Master of Paris. 'To Jeffrey's mind, 'twere one thing to ingratiate myself with the Devil's minion with an eye toward the salvation of my own soul through assistance to the Holy Church, and another matter entirely actually to love the man.'

'Did you?' They descended to what were clearly the living quarters of the house, simply furnished with the sturdy elegance of that era, carven furniture cushioned in yellow plush, bulb-legged tables and curtained beds, maintained to convince servants that the man whose possessions they guarded lived and breathed and went about his business like other men. 'Love him?'

Before a fireplace – this one cold and swept – a chess set of limewood and ebony, a lute, and a set of virginals.

'I did.' The vampire followed him from room to room on this floor, as Asher looked into cabinets, drawers, behind the curtains of niches. 'Many did. Gabrielle, with that portion of her mind which she could spare from planning where and how and whom she would next kill. She chose her victims months in advance, slipped into their houses to observe them in the evenings . . . sometimes sat beside their beds every night for weeks while they slept, drinking their dreams, before she even made herself known to them in those dreams. Gabrielle was deeply fond of him, as was Ivo Chopinel, a simple soul who had been his servant in life. Anselm Arouache . . .'

And as Ysidro opened a door into another chamber Asher saw them, startlingly, like ghosts in the firelight, as he had seen Simon and Angelus in conversation upstairs . . .

And yes, there were both Simon and Angelus, talking with the others of the Paris nest in a chamber set up to be an eating-room, with a long table and sideboards grinning with silver cups. Two women flanked the young Simon Ysidro, shockingly beautiful (*is that only because this is a dream?*), laughing and smiling with those long white fangs gleaming against pale lips. One had brown curls wired up and trembling with pearls, and something of the coldly seraphic look of Lydia's aunt Lavinnia – *Gabrielle Batoux*? The dark one, with her tight-laced bodice cut to show the henna-stained areolae of her nipples, must be Zaffira Truandière the gypsy, though her gown was every inch as expensive and stylish as that of her companion, with its circular farthingale and collar of stiffened lawn.

'Anselm Arouache was, as I have said, a Flemish scholar with whom Constantine long corresponded . . .'

The stout, fair gentleman in brown velvet who stood talking to Angelus near the fire gestured eagerly, and there was a greedy passion in his pale eyes that Asher could not associate with a discussion of spontaneous generation or phlogiston.

''Twas a deep disappointment to him – and a personal sadness as well, I think – when Anselm forsook the science that had been his life and became the most avid and greedy hunter of them all. Emeric Jambicque the alchemist – who had been a dear friend of Constantine's in life – continued his studies after he became vampire. 'Twas the fervor with which he embraced the so-called Reformed Faith that estranged him from Constantine. I know that Constantine never gave up the hope of healing the breach.'

Asher looked around the room, but the young Simon, Anselm, and Constantine were the only men present.

''Twas Emeric who brewed the stuff they poured down my throat, that first night in Paris.' Ysidro paused beside his younger self, like an odd image in a mirror, listening to the two women croon and sigh over a young laborer they were in the process of hunting, night by night, along the quays. 'So far as I could tell, it contained enough aconite and silver to penetrate vampire flesh—' his extended finger touched Zaffira Truandière's dusky cheekbone, traced the sable stormcloud of her jeweled hair – 'as well as a drug that numbed the central nervous system. 'Twould kill a man,' he added. ''Twould still the lungs, paralyse the heart . . . But our hearts have already ceased to beat, our lungs to take air. At one time Emeric enjoyed a great reputation as a natural philosopher . . .'

For a moment, it seemed to Asher that – dream-like – he could look from the room in which he stood surrounded by the vampires of Paris through a door or window into a small lecture-hall, its benches occupied by a scattering of young men in the dark, sober clothing of the middle class. Some were taking notes – in the old fashion, on boards smeared with dark wax – but others looked frankly bored. Lectures, Asher reflected, did not seem to have altered much through the years. At the pulpit-like podium at one end of the room a tall man in the dark old-fashioned robe of a scholar lectured in Latin on the properties of salt and blood. Though his hair, and his flowing beard, were silver instead of sandy, the freckles on his cheekbones, the enormous crude shape of his nose, were recognizable instantly from that night in the Paris alleyways when he had held young Simon's arms in an unbreakable grip while Esdras de Colle poured poison down his throat.

'He dyed the beard,' remarked Ysidro. 'Our remade bodies return to a state of physical prime, and Emeric found that more people listened to his words if he wore the guise of age. Because his teaching was proscribed as heresy no one questioned that he would lecture at night, in secret, and in shuttered rooms where the light was dim. Many heretics sent their sons to learn from him: anatomy, alchemy, the properties of the natural world.'

'And did he, like Raimund, believe in this Facinum?'

''Twould not surprise me to learn that he did. Raimund studied the arts of alchemy in his way, but he was lazy – and his mind was ever upon the hunt.' Emeric Jambicque's lecture-hall dissolved about them, as places do in dreams, leaving them once more in the house of Constantine Angelus. 'And upon his "rights" to be Master of Paris, of course.'

Asher searched cupboards, opened drawers, ran his hands along the mantelpieces of stone and wood in every room of Angelus's house, looking not so much for an obvious 'talisman' – he was aware that he saw only what Ysidro had seen before him – but for something familiar, something he had seen before . . . whatever that was.

And wherever it had been.

The Hôtel Batoux, almost certainly. The drawing-room with its sun-damaged boiseries, the candlelight in mirrors and in Elysée de Montadour's eyes.

'Where did this house stand?' he asked, as they descended a stone stair into the earth, the cold of the damp air down there like walking down into the water of a well. 'Angelus's. Where are we now?'

'Rue Poitevine. 'Tis gone now. 'Tis just as well. Even these days I would find the place difficult to pass.'

It was pitch dark, but Asher was aware of the stone walls around him, of low vaulting and cellars that had once contained wine. *Ysidro's perception again*, he thought. *I see what he knew. What he wills me to see.*

'Sybellia Torqueri had slept in the catacombs beneath a small convent on the Rue de l'Arbalêtre – 'twas a district of the city stiff with religious establishments. Even after she was killed the nuns kept that portion of the crypts locked for centuries. She had endowed them most handsomely. This house Constantine had built on one of the occasions on which he changed identities – it does not do, you understand, for those who know you to observe that you do not age. He had gone by other names before: Solomon d'Espiritu, Chrétien Montfort. When he died Raimund Cauchemar abandoned the house, and it was burned shortly thereafter.'

'Did he loot it?'

'I suppose so. I had left Paris by then.'

Eyes flashed in the darkness ahead of them, tiny spots of phosphor. Asher stopped, his heart cold in him, and though the vampire stood a few steps in front of him he heard Ysidro's voice say behind him, 'What do you here, Cauchemar?'

Ysidro – young Simon, clothed in different garments from those he had worn upstairs, gray-and-black striped silk rather than the dark velvet he'd sported earlier in the dream – passed both Asher and his older self, and around the gleaming eyes Asher saw Raimund Cauchemar's face, then the whole of his form, black doublet glittering with lines of braid, pale features framed in a black jawline beard and a close-clipped black mustache.

'Don't tell me you haven't been curious, little Spaniard.' Cauchemar turned and walked away down the corridor, which descended a flight of a half-dozen steps, forcing young Simon to follow. 'Don't tell me you actually believe that so douce and milky a priest as our Angelus actually has the strength to hold the likes of the lovely Gabrielle – the spitfire Zaffira – with the gaze of his pretty gray eyes?'

They passed into a small chamber, round and low-roofed, which contained half a dozen stone coffins. All had their lids pushed aside. In two, Asher could see skeletons, and the ragged scraps of rotted winding-sheets.

'Does it never occur to you to ask how it is that such a master holds sway over fledglings stronger than himself?'

'The only one of them who thinks him weaker,' pointed out Simon, 'is you.'

'Pah!' The older vampire made a gesture of closing his fist. '*Think* him weak? I *know* him to be so! *I* am the elder!' He swung around, hand upraised as if to take a vow. 'And I am the stronger! Stronger than Angelus. Aye, and stronger than that bitch Sybellia before him. Does it never cross your mind to wonder what the Devil gave that skinny trollop – what the Devil gave *her* master – to hold our minds in thrall? Are you truly that stupid? That blind?'

'As blind as those women who come to your shop?' Simon raised a pale brow. 'Who pay you for "inheritance powder", when in fact what they get for their money is the slow wasting of their father or their husband, without trace of poison because there is none involved? Who purchase talismans of Venus from you, only to have you send an erotic dream or two to the one they desire . . . so long as they keep on paying you?'

Cauchemar laughed, a hearty mirth that struck the damp walls like a hammer. 'Blind enough not to do the same, I dare say. But just because I trick you into paying me for an imaginary horse doesn't mean that horses don't exist, my purblind friend. And Sybellia made me vampire years before she drank the blood of that cold silver flounder who presumes to tell me when to hunt and who I can and cannot kill – decades! Without the help of the Devil he would have no power – no power over *me*, anyway!

'Has he spoken of it to you?' He stepped close to Simon, put a hand on the Spanish vampire's nape and leaned close, to look into the champagne-colored eyes. 'You who spend all those evenings being cozy with him by his fireside, playing chess and twiddling on the lute – faugh! He has walked a long way into your mind – has he ever permitted you to walk into his?'

And when Simon drew back Cauchemar's face darkened. 'Or are you the one who's doing the whispering? Trying to sweet-talk the Facinum out of him, the same way he sweet-talked it out of Sybellia? The way he got power enough to lord it over *me*, who by all right should have been able to crush his flabby face into the mud. Power enough to free *you*, maybe, from that deranged little elf that lords it over the London nest. Is that why you came to Paris? Is that what you seek? The Devil's Facinum? Else why are you still in Paris?'

Simon had moved to pull free of Cauchemar's hand, but now stilled. The older vampire's grip tightened on his striped sleeve and his dark eyes almost glowed with intensity in the blackness.

'You've been in Paris three months now, little Spaniard. Winter melts to spring, and the man they told you to kill is ashes. And still you linger. What are you seeking?'

He drew him close. 'And can you and I come to an understanding about finding it?'

FIFTEEN

The Hôpital Lariboisière stood in the tenth arrondissement, hard by the Gare du Nord. Even at this hour of the evening – and it was nearly midnight when Lydia, escorted by the stolid taxi-driver, passed beneath its arched gateway and crossed the long courtyard within – the streets surrounding the train station seemed jammed with all the trucks and motor cars that had vanished from the rest of Paris during the daylight hours. Men in the blue uniform coats and bright scarlet trousers of the infantry (*they're actually going to WAR in those trousers?*) filed into the station with knapsacks on their shoulders. Others, in the rough corduroys and wools of artisans, laborers, shopkeepers, stood under the electric glare of the station lights in quiet conversation with women, heads bowed to listen below the constant clamor, hands furtively entwined.

Bidding mothers, wives, sisters, sweethearts their long goodbye.

It's a wide highway that leads to war . . .

Lydia tried to remember where she'd heard that proverb.

. . . and only a narrow trail that comes back again.

Even in the wide courtyard of the hospital the noise of the station could be heard, though like the hospital of Saint-Antoine, once Lydia went inside (there was no one at the desk in the lobby) there was an eerie sense of deadness.

As at Saint-Antoine the wards were crowded, beds crammed in fewer rooms to accommodate the absence of staff. And as at Saint-Antoine, everywhere she smelled dirt and neglect, and heard the hacking cough of pneumonia.

Nobody could tell her how to find someone to direct her.

After asking in three or four wards (*and do the vampires of Paris lurk in the shadows here?*), Lydia simply returned to the main lobby, searched the desk there (in the continued absence of clerk, nurse, or anyone else), and finally found Ellen's name – spelled phonetically – jotted in the middle of a long list, with that day's date – 6 August (only by that time it was an hour and a half into 7 August) – scribbled at the top. In a different hand, someone had noted 'Aig-12'. Presumably *aiguë* – acute.

There was a map in the drawer of the desk.

As at Saint-Antoine, even at one thirty in the morning, both men and women clustered, muttering, around the beds of the women in the Acute Ward. A child was crying as he clung to his mother's hand, the thin, faded woman trying to comfort him; there didn't seem to be anyone else of the family there. By another bed, a harassed old man was trying to keep three obviously exhausted, squirming, fretful little girls calm and cheerful by periodically hitting them, in between blows exhorting the woman in the bed, 'But you must come home, Marie! With Jean going now to join his company and Louis gone, Annette has left – hush, Colette! – and these brats drive me distracted!'

'I'll try, Papa,' she whispered, and as she passed the bed Lydia could tell that this woman wasn't going to rise from her bed soon, if ever.

Ellen sobbed, 'Miss Lydia!' and stretched out her hand; Lydia dropped into the chair beside the bed, put her arms around the maid's big shoulders, and for a time they clung together like sisters. 'You're all right,' the maid whispered – as if Lydia had been stabbed, not herself. 'You're all right. Ma'am, we've got to get out of here . . .'

'We will. *You* will, as soon as I can arrange for your passage – M'sieu Greuze, if you'd be so kind as to bring up a screen . . .'

The dressings on Ellen's arms and side had been changed recently (*so at least SOMEBODY is doing their job around here!*), but Lydia removed them carefully, knowing from Saint-Antoine that the army was already making off with most bandages and basilicum powder. The worst cuts were on the maid's arms, but there didn't seem to be any tendon damage. Lydia guessed she had passed out from nervous shock and loss of blood, rather than any critical injury. Thanks to a good stout corset the wound in Ellen's side, though bloody, hadn't been deep. While conducting her examination, Lydia gave her hand-maiden a carefully edited version of events, attributing the entire attack to German spies ('I KNEW Professor Asher had to be mixed up with spies somehow, ma'am! The way he's come and gone – and it was German spies who kidnapped Miss Miranda last year, wasn't it?').

'Not a word,' cautioned Lydia, a little alarmed at Ellen's acuity. '*Not – one – word*, not to anyone. Not even to me.'

'Oh, no, ma'am!' Ellen's brows deepened into a frown. 'Somebody might overhear. You know how the newspapers say, those Germans have agents everywhere. And you know I'm not one to gossip, not even with Mrs Grimes.' She named the Asher cook, who, like herself, had formerly been employed by Lydia's father at Willoughby Close and had taken up service with the Ashers upon his death rather than stay and work for the second Mrs Willoughby.

She sank her voice conspiratorially. 'Was it German spies that threw Professor Asher off the church tower?'

'I think it has to have been.'

'And *him*?' She nodded toward the sturdy form of Stanislas Greuze, standing guard at the edge of the screen. 'Can you trust him? He's a Frenchman, when all's said.'

'He's all right.' Lydia whispered a mental prayer that the cab-driver didn't in fact turn out to be in the employ of either Jürgen Schaumm or the Paris nest, and wondered if there were any way of making sure. 'He's making arrangements for you to go south to Bordeaux, to get on a ship for home.'

'Oh, ma'am, I couldn't!' Ellen was aghast. 'I'm perfectly all right, and it wouldn't be fitting for you to stay here in Paris by yourself!'

'I'll be under the protection of the Department—' she could see that Ellen was impressed by the term – 'until Jamie's well enough to travel. I hope that's going to be soon, but I'll feel safer – and I'll *be* safer – once you're safely on your way back to England.'

'Ma'am, all the other ladies have already gone! You know how people talk!'

It took Lydia another hour to convince Ellen that nobody in England was going to think that she, Lydia, was lingering in Paris to carry on a clandestine *affaire* while her husband was in the hospital and the city was in a theater-less, cab-less, nearly restaurant-less uproar because the Germans were getting ready to invade ('But that isn't the point, ma'am!'). After a day which had included kidnapping, attempted murder, no sleep, and neither lunch nor dinner, Lydia had the surreal sensation of carrying on the argument in a dream, and wondered at what point she had fallen asleep . . . *Oh, and I forgot all about the church of Sainte-Clare this morning!*

Crossing the long central courtyard toward the arched gateway again, where Greuze's cab stood on the Rue Ambroise-Paré, Lydia marveled that the din of trains was still, at almost four in the morning, going strong. That people were still coming and going on the street, dark figures passing beneath the electric lights along the hospital colonnades . . . *To take care of their loved ones, as I'm taking care of Jamie? To steal medical supplies while no one's looking?* In the hours she'd been in the Acute Ward with Ellen she'd seen one nurse, once, and no physicians at all. There had still been no one at the lobby desk when she had passed it going out.

Something in the shadows caught her eye with a cold sensation of shock, a memory of horror or fear.

But turning, she saw only a woman walking in the direction of the hospital's door, long black curls hanging down her back.

She was wearing a black-and-beige striped satin jacket, like the skirt Lydia had seen crumpled over a chair in Camille Batoux's violated flat.

'Did you kill Esdras de Colle?' Asher asked, and Ysidro turned his face aside.

'No.'

But the vampire was lying, and the dream had changed. Asher remembered asking Ysidro about the chief of the Protestant vampires, back when he had been in Ysidro's portion of the dream – back in Ysidro's memories of Constantine Angelus's house – but things were less clear now, and the scene kept repeating itself. He'd finished searching the house for anything that he recognized – *only how would I recognize something in a dream that I only saw in another dream?* – and the shadows of the young Simon, and of Raimund Cauchemar, had faded, leaving himself and Ysidro standing in the crypt among the lidless coffins in the darkness.

And he had asked him, 'Did you kill Esdras de Colle?'

But with the changed dream he stood in the crypt again and saw that the coffins all bore their lids now, massive slabs of stone. Too heavy for a man to lift, unless he possessed a vampire's strength. Yet they were not heavy enough to muffle completely a man's screams of agony, repeated over and over. And then – when Asher found himself once again in his father's church at Wychford – he saw standing to the right side of the Wychford altar Constantine Angelus, his fingers torn where he'd scratched and clawed at the inside of his stone coffin, his face ghastly with nightmare, exhaustion, and pain. 'Help me,' he repeated. 'Help me.'

In quick succession, and as if from a great distance away, Asher saw a mob drag a woman off the street and into the courtyard of a Paris house – artisans and laborers, they looked like, men and women both. They stripped their victim naked and brought out kitchen implements they'd heated red-hot in a fire, pokers and spits and cooking-forks; for many minutes the woman prayed to Saint Agnes and Saint Lucy – women who had met torture with God-given strength – as they burned her, until at last she screamed out the location of a house on the Rue du Grand-Hurleur. Then one of the men said, 'You better be telling the truth, witch,' and they tied her and left her naked in the mud with five of the mob's women to guard her while they all raged out into the street and the tortured woman sobbed with pain, over and over, 'Forgive me, my lord. Forgive me.'

Later – his dream was fragments of darkness and daylight – he saw the vampires Zaffira and stout, fair Anselm Arouache chase through the dark countryside a man whom Asher vaguely recognized as one of those who'd been in the mob, letting him think he'd escaped before materializing again out of the shadows at his elbow, cutting him a little and letting him run before they caught him and cut him a little more. They drank his blood – absorbed his life – as he screamed, 'My God, my God, why hast thou forsaken me?'

'Did you kill Esdras de Colle?' Constantine Angelus asked, in the hacked and burned ruins of a desecrated parish church – two monks washing the face of a third who'd been beaten to death – and Simon turned his face aside.

'I did not.'

Then Asher saw himself – younger and bearded and incon-spicuously attired as a laborer – pacing the crowded platform in the Müşir Ahmet Paşa Station, watching for Enver, his contact in Constantinople. There were two tickets to Belgrade in his pocket and the Sultan's entire police force buzzed around the station looking for him. In Asher's pocket was also a set of papers proving that Enver was in fact a French citizen and not liable for arrest by Ottoman forces – that he hadn't had anything to do with an Englishman who asked questions about clandestine German loans to members of the Sultan's court.

He felt again the panic and terror of knowing that the police were closing in and that if he were caught his own papers wouldn't hold up to investigation. *If only nobody stops me before the train leaves* . . .

Like most trains in Turkey, it was late, and every minute that went by was one minute closer to capture and, he knew, the torture that Englishmen weren't supposed to undergo.

And one minute more for Enver to make it to join him. To get himself out of the jaws of the trap.

When the train started moving Asher got on to it, the car jammed to capacity with countrywomen, goats, Greek priests, drunken soldiers, crates of chickens, so that Asher had to cling in the doorway as he stood on the bottom step and the train picked up speed. And as it did so, he saw Enver come into the vast modern cavern of the crowded station and break into a run for the platform, for the train.

Police closed around him. Asher saw that sturdy Armenian businessman, who had served for years as the Department contact in Constantinople, try for a moment to fight free, his dark glance going to the departing train, to the man who clung in the doorway of the last car, and though they were separated by nearly a hundred feet Asher had the sensation that their eyes met. That Enver saw him leaving as he was clubbed to the floor. He remembered hearing later in London that Enver had been killed in the prison – which was too bad, his superiors said; now the Department would have to recruit someone else . . .

Could I have saved him somehow, if I'd stayed? He didn't know. It would have been against his orders.

Then the feverish images changed again and he saw Simon

kneeling before the chair of the white-haired priest Jeffrey Sampson, while the tall Cardinal Montevierde stood in the shadows behind them, like the red-draped image of a martyr, smelling faintly of crusted blood. 'You did well,' Sampson was saying, 'you did well. There is another of that evil tribe, spreading poison to the ears of the young . . .'

Simon shook his head. 'I cannot. De Colle is dead. I gave men the direction to do the deed, and it was done. But I swore. I gave my oath—'

'Gave your oath?' said the Cardinal. 'Upon what Testament? Gave your oath in whose name?'

'You said if I did as you asked—'

'Will God extend His mercy to any man,' said the Cardinal, 'who will refuse Him the small service He asks? A service that *God asks*?'

Simon looked up then, pale eyes filled with anguish. 'The innocent suffer with the guilty,' he said. 'Men in the pay of de Colle killed a woman who worked for Arouache the philosopher, killed her horribly, trying to find out where Arouache and Angelus slept. When they went to that place and found none sleeping there – 'twas the vaults of an old church on the property of the Filles de la Providence – they wrecked the church and the convent nearby, saying the monks and the nuns were witches. Now those who have used the nuns to guard them have killed some of them in the mob, and speak of seeking out others.'

'You refuse a favor to *God*?' repeated the Cardinal, stunned. 'You hesitate, even for a moment, to do as *God Himself* asks?'

'The monks, and the Daughters of Providence, are in God's hands,' added Father Jeffrey in his gentle voice. 'And if 'tis true they gave shelter to such demons in the vaults of their church, their sin lay heavy on them in any case. 'Tis best not to ask too closely after these things, Simon. We are but the servants of God.'

SIXTEEN

Lydia returned to the church of Sainte-Clare late in the afternoon, after nine hours of sleep and a substantial breakfast, served up by a woman who, Lydia surmised, had been hired by Ysidro along with the *hôtel particulier* to which Greuze had taken her from the hospital.

Lydia had traveled with Ysidro before, and had wondered at the time whether there existed some vampire version of Cook's Tours which specialized in hiring out inconspicuous residences in out-of-the-way corners of every city in Europe, furnished with lockable sub-crypts and servants who didn't know who they were waiting on and didn't care.

She guessed that this small house off the Rue Caulaincourt wasn't where Ysidro himself was sleeping, but Madame Istabene (at least that was what Lydia thought the woman said when she'd asked her her name) spoke no English and very little French, so it was difficult to tell. She had, however, upon Lydia's arrival at four in the morning, provided her with chocolate and croissants, for which she was weepingly grateful, and when she woke had drawn a hot bath for her, followed by the aforementioned breakfast.

Thus Lydia felt very much better when, some hours later, Father Martin led her down a little corkscrew stair to the vaults beneath the church of Sainte-Clare and helped her take down three of the banker's boxes that stacked one wall. 'As I said yesterday, the convent of Sainte-Clare covered nearly three acres back at the beginning of the sixteenth century,' he explained. 'Everything over to the Rue Bar du Bec was convent land. The records of the original sales were burned, but there's a map here of what the buildings were like in the fifteen fifties.'

He switched on the jury-rigged light bulb that hung from the center of the low vaulting at that end of the room. Lydia saw that at one time the crypt had served for convent burials, the floor a patchwork of carved names – unreadable now with the passage of feet – and the walls ranked with niches, like a catacomb, all clustered around an ancient altar carved with the worn sculpture of a lamb.

'As for what else might be here . . .'

'That's just the trouble,' said Lydia, who had given a certain amount of thought to her story over breakfast. 'I am virtually certain that Cousin Jürgen – if it *is* Cousin Jürgen who did this – lured my husband here in some fashion, and if I can find anything – any familiar name, or reference, or reason that he'd have come here – I may be able to trace him, to find out where he is and what name he's using.'

She looked imploringly into the old man's face as he guided her to a rickety chair and a card-table set beneath the light bulb. 'From things the nurse told me at the hospital last night, it sounds as if Cousin Jürgen is still . . . still seeks to do my husband some harm. I've tried to go to the police with all this, but even if I had proof, with half their men joining the army . . .'

'True indeed.' In the harsh shadows his blue eyes were bitter, and sad. 'They're saying the fighting will be over soon. That now that our forces have seized Alsace they'll be cutting the German supply lines into Belgium. Myself, I don't see it.'

Even the women's ward of the Lariboisière Hospital had been in an uproar when Lydia had gone there briefly that afternoon, with husbands and brothers all waving newspapers and shouting 'SEDAN EST VENGÉ'! All the way along the unnaturally empty Rue de Rivoli, from the hospital to St Clare's, in Stanislas Greuze's taxicab, Lydia had seen men in the cafés gesticulating, hugging one another, buying one another drinks over the fact that French forces had seized back the 'lost provinces' of Alsace and Lorraine that Germany had taken from her forty-some years before. Or at least they now had troops on the ground there – which, from what Jamie had been telling her for years, was really the only reason France had wanted to get into a war with Germany anyway. She wondered if all this would make it easier or more difficult to get Ellen out of France – and eventually Jamie and herself.

'Imbeciles,' Greuze had muttered the fifth time an intoxicated reveler had darted into the street to plaster the newspaper's headline against the window of the cab, as if the fact had somehow escaped Greuze's attention. 'Worse – dupes. Going out and dying because one group of wealthy men in politics wants to score points over another group of wealthy men in politics! Pfui! Jaurès – a great man, madame, a socialist and a man of peace – warned us of this! You know what the true definition of war is, madame? Eh?'

Lydia had shaken her head, disconcerted by the rage in the driver's voice.

'*A gun with a working-man at each end of it.* Only those who sell weapons – and those who are excused from slaughter because they are "too important" to go into combat – have cause to rejoice in these days.'

He'd glanced briefly over his shoulder at her, his ugly face dark with pity. 'And we kiss the rods that scour our backs, and name as heroes those who march away with the army and leave their families to starve. Those men who teach peace and hope, like Jaurès – *those* men they shoot in the streets for being without love of their country. And when all is over, nothing in this world will be as it was.'

The next moment he'd leaned out the window to yell insults at the driver of a military *camion* who'd pulled out of the Place de la Concorde into his path, and had driven on in silence.

Nothing in this world will be as it was . . .

Now she went on, 'We are obliged to stay in Paris until my husband is well enough to travel. I'm so sorry to trouble you about our family matters, Father Martin, but I believe the danger he's in is real.'

'Evil in this world is real,' returned the priest. 'As I have cause to know. And at the moment, the forces of civil order all have their faces turned away from the concerns of common folk. Let me know how I can help you.'

Lydia studied the yellowed paper that he'd withdrawn from one of the boxes and spread on the table, cracked and brittle and traced all over with notations in the hand of some long-dead city clerk. She'd dressed, as she had yesterday, in Mrs Flasket's borrowed clothing, and felt awkward and uglier than usual in her spectacles – *really I look no worse*, she tried to comfort herself, *than Jamie does when he's in one of his disguises.*

'My husband is an antiquarian,' she said slowly. 'Particularly of religious architecture. His cousin could have lured him here. Tell me . . . did the convent at one time include a bone chapel?'

*   *   *

For the fifth time in his laborious walk from one end of the ward to the other, Asher was stopped by the brother (or father, or in-law) of one of his fellow patients, had his hand shaken and his shoulder slapped. 'Splendid, splendid, monsieur! I never harbored a doubt that we would see the English come to strike their blows against the Hun! But you must be as glad as we, eh, that the contest is all but finished now. War is a terrible thing, but now that we have the Germans on the run . . .'

Asher politely disclaimed any personal involvement in bringing the British Army to France, and kept to himself the reflection that in fact the French, in invading Alsace instead of sending the larger part of their army actually to meet the largest part of the German forces, had probably guaranteed their own defeat, whether the British showed up or not. His head ached less than it had when he'd first risen from his bed two days ago, but by the time he'd dragged himself back there he was, as before, nauseated and so dizzy he was obliged to cling to the iron bed-frames along the way. When he sank down again he was trembling, and cold with sweat.

Not good.

How soon can I plausibly convince Lydia that I'm fit to make the journey to Le Havre, let alone across the Channel to England?

At the moment, even the thought of trying to get out of the building seemed to lie in the realm of those blood-and-thunder heroes who could brain villains with tins of condensed milk after they'd managed to recover from being beaten senseless and subjected to poison gas, just in time to wriggle out of handcuffs and swim clear of flooded cellars. (*What would it cost to have one's cellar piped to flood with that much water, anyway? I'm sure the London Water Board would have something to say about it.*)

Whatever Elysée thought he knew, and whether the Facinum existed or not, it was only a matter of time before someone was killed.

It was some minutes before he was even strong enough to lean down and reach the cardboard box beneath the bed. Lydia had left the four pamphlets he'd bought, faded italic type tenderly wrapped in bookstore tissue.

The French was old-fashioned, even for the last years of the sixteenth century – traces of the old oblique case in the nouns, the occasional use of *li* for *le*, and copious sprinklings of the letter 's' in unlikely words. But the writing itself was concise and well-reasoned:

> Without the support of the King's law, you may ask, how would the Holy Church command the respect of the people of Christendom? Would not men turn from the way of God and become as the beasts of the fields? Yet is not law a quality of God, and does not law proceed from reason, from those things which mankind has found to serve it, whether the men of Rome or the citizens of Cathay and India, who are not troubled by such things as anathemas, fish-days, and what God actually thinks about works of art?

And:

> Is it not enough to follow Christ's teachings and live humbly and with forgiveness in our hearts, without killing other men over His nature, His mother's nature, and the small facts about His life on earth?

Another pamphlet spoke of Kings, and whether a King would indeed be favored by God for embroiling the country in a war for no better reason than his own desire for power, 'or to show off to Europe how great his army was'. Asher leaned back against the pillows, struggling to get his breath back even ten minutes after he had lain down.

Dangerous stuff. In 1602, France had just been torn to pieces by two generations of religious warfare. Catholic Paris had welcomed Henry of Navarre as its king, not because they believed his conversion to Catholicism was genuine, but because he promised peace. The Catholic League, driven out of power, would have gone on fighting. Another of Angelus's pamphlets dealt – under a series of very thin pseudonyms – with the great House of Guise, the family whose fortunes and power underwrote the Catholic League, and whose founder's son had attempted to seize the crown of France. *Dangerous stuff for dangerous times.*

Years ago, when it had first become clear that governments might angle for the services of the Undead, Asher had asked

Ysidro, 'What can the Kaiser offer a master vampire?' What could any government – or, he had found out recently, American corporation; richer than many governments, some of these were just as irresponsible about what they considered important – offer the Undead that would be worth the danger of being recognized, of coming out of the shadows, of putting themselves in the position of being captured, imprisoned, threatened, used?

He closed his eyes, pressed his hand against the pain in his side (*broken rib? It didn't hurt this way the day before yesterday*), saw again the troubling fragment of last night's dream: Simon Ysidro on his knees before the priest he trusted, the Cardinal with his dark ring gleaming in the shadows. Father Jeffrey's hand on the vampire's colorless hair. ''Tis best not to ask too closely after these things, Simon. We are all but servants of God.'

Simon weeping.

Asher closed his eyes, and passed out like a snuffed candle.

'The original church of the convent was smaller than this one.' Father Martin's calloused finger traced the irregular polyhedron on the map. 'Its crypt held the relics that constituted the convent's greatest treasures, most of which did not survive the Revolution. That may be for the best,' he added with a sigh. 'In our day and age, Christians are better able to focus on the faith and virtues of the saints through teaching and catechism, and I'm afraid that the whole custom of venerating relics led to far more abuses than acts of faith. During the Revolution the nuns did manage to save a reliquary containing a lock of St Clare's hair, cut off, when she dedicated herself to God, by the hand of St Francis himself. In earlier days of course the convent had a whole collection of such things: a finger-bone of St Agnes, any amount of earth from the hill of Calvary, what was supposed to be starlight from the Christmas star preserved somehow in glass, as well as the obligatory fragment of the True Cross.'

He shook his head. 'When the current church – this building – was built in 1583, the old church was incorporated into a new house for the prioress. But the bone chapel remained – you can see it here on this map, which is dated 1590 – and novices were still required to meditate there on the night before taking their permanent vows. The land was sold sometime in the early seventeenth century, and by the time Turgot's 1739 map was made the old church and the prioress's house were long gone. I assume the bones – whether they were moved here or remained in a private chapel in the basement of whatever house was built on the site – were cleared out in the seventeen eighties, when all the parish cemeteries of Paris were deconsecrated. But I understand the chapel itself was of the usual type. The altar wall consisted entirely of skulls, and contained niches in which complete skeletons stood in for statues, that sort of thing. An odd taste.'

His white brows twitched together as if he could see the macabre altar, the floating shapes of skeletons overhead. 'I understand people from all over Paris came asking to be buried there, to share in the sanctity of the nuns.'

'Was there a way from this church into the older crypt?'

'I expect there was at one time. It would have been walled off when the property was sold, and heaven only knows how much of it survived the digging of the Métro. Would that be something that your husband was seeking?'

'I think so. He has a theory that a sort of secret cult existed in Paris in the seventeenth century. You have no idea how seriously academics take these things.' She widened her eyes and looked earnest. 'It sounds silly to me, but it would be child's play for someone to lure him here in the middle of the night just by sending him a note saying that such a tunnel or connecting crypt existed. *I have a key, I'll let you in . . .*' Exactly like 'William Johnson', in fact, she reflected. 'Poor silly man, he wouldn't have stopped to think twice!'

Lydia was rather proud of her story, and was much gratified when Father Martin nodded, and sighed at the machinations of the wicked. 'I've served in this church for forty-five years,' he said, 'and I've never seen anything like the doorway or tunnel you describe. But I'll show you all that's left of the original catacomb – it's used for storage these days – and the sub-crypt below this one. I expect,' he added, offering Lydia his hand as she rose from her chair, 'one could figure out where the bone chapel would lie by measuring the distance from this spot to the site of the old church, always supposing that map I showed you is to scale. It should be somewhere near the Rue de Moussy.'

Lydia had already mentally estimated the current location of the old bone chapel of the Filles de Sainte-Clare, and knew exactly where it lay.

It lay on the land now occupied by the Hôtel Batoux.

SEVENTEEN

D reams without light.

Fragments, like a broken window of stained glass, of the crowding houses of Paris, half-timbered and grime-dark with centuries of chimney soot, darker now with foggy nights through which only chinks and slivers of dim firelight struggled around bolted shutters. The smell of the river, of woodsmoke, of a hundred thousand overflowing privies and of black muck underfoot. Bells chimed, near and far, the churches of Paris praising God for another day survived, driving away the Devil for another abyssal night.

Asher made out, as at a very great distance, the white edge of a man's plain linen collar, and the dead-white blur of a vampire's face. A stiff brown beard, and the smell of blood on his clothing. He'd killed that night.

Ysidro drifted behind like a ghost.

Esdras de Colle. Asher saw his face when he stopped, turned, once, twice, as if he heard or felt or sensed the Spanish vampire's presence. Watching and wary. He stepped into a shadow and disappeared. Simon, invisible also in the dark between two houses, moved not. Asher heard the scurrying slither of rats.

He wasn't sure when Simon departed in another direction.

The dream repeated. Esdras de Colle crossed a triangular church-yard before a church with a stumpy tower, impossible to identify in the darkness. So many churches had been pulled down and rebuilt in the eighteenth century. He stopped as before, listening.

Simon in the darkness – Asher was aware of them both – motionless as the fog.

De Colle moved on. Simon passed like the shift of moonlight against the sooty beige-brown clay of the walls.

Under peaked blackness, thirty feet from the stumpy church, a door whispered on oiled hinges.

Another night, the wind sharp as frozen wire moaning through the black streets. Church bells ringing again, stars burning holes in the sky. De Colle looking about him as he blew through the twisting streets, suspicion in his ice-pale eyes, his harsh mouth. Simon above him on the steep roofs slippery with moss and soot. Through dirty window shutters Simon saw – Asher saw – a man and woman sleeping on a crude bedstead in a litter of grimy blankets, filthy old coats and skirts, with two or three children huddled for warmth. Though the chamber shouted poverty – a table and a bench, a small woodbox containing scant fuel – still a little altar had been fitted up with a cheap plaster image of the Virgin, swags of holy medals and pilgrim-shells, a crucifix and rosaries. The door opened and Esdras de Colle came in, a shadow in his dark clothing. With him was a young man in the plain dark garments favored by the Protestants, his face like a locked steel box.

'You know what you're asking of me, Gallard.' De Colle's voice would have been covered over completely by the whine of the wind across the roof, to any ears but those of another vampire and of that young man at his side. 'I've told you what we are, and what we do.'

'I have prayed over this, brother,' replied the young man Gallard. 'I do not think that I am being led astray. God needs warriors. Is it not proof, when the leader of our armies himself is willing to sell God's honor for the hollow title of King? The forces of the Anti-Christ in Rome are mighty, and are being drawn from the legions of the Devil. You have shown me what a Christian heart can do, armed with a demon's powers. We can do great good.'

'Watch, then.' De Colle walked to the bedside; it was barely a step from the door. The young man hung back, and the vampire's mustaches lifted a little in a half-smile. 'Have no fear, brother. They will not wake. I'll teach you to lay a glamor like this on their minds, so they'll slumber up till the moment you take them . . . so they'll fall asleep on their feet, if you want them to. Come close.'

Gallard did. Knelt beside the bed when the vampire knelt. 'It's

Mestallier,' he said, surprised. 'He works for Clopard, who owns the Magpie.'

'Clopard at the Magpie takes his orders from the Catholic League. 'Tis Mestallier who carries them out: to beat a Reformed minister, to wreck the shop of a man who speaks out too loud against popish tyranny. 'Twas Mestallier and his men who kidnapped Séverine Ratoire last week and took her away to a convent, saying she had expressed the desire to become Catholic. Now they are refusing to send her back to her parents. For that poor girl's sake alone, this man's life will be no loss. Hold him down.'

Gallard put his hands – gingerly, at first – on the sleeping man's shoulders; then when he made no stir, leaned down harder. De Colle pulled the blanket down to show the victim's heavy-muscled arms and, taking up the right one, used his claw-like nails to rip open the arteries from wrist to elbow and pressed his mouth to the gushing wound. Mestallier jerked in his sleep, and his eyes flew open; before he could cry out, Gallard hooked one arm around his throat, choking off his scream. De Colle didn't even raise his head, only drank and drank, his whole body shuddering like a woman in orgasm, while Mestallier thrashed and croaked, and the other sleepers in the bed stirred and muttered uneasily, as if in dreams.

Asher watched; young Simon watched. *This happened three hundred years ago*, Asher told himself in fury, as Mestallier's body began to buck and twitch in convulsions. *I can no more save this man than I could have saved Enver in Constantinople.* The left hand that had pounded and torn at De Colle's head and shoulder lost its strength and direction, flopping and flailing. It struck the woman who slept at his side, waking her finally. She stared in confusion, as if trying to decide whether this was a nightmare or not.

De Colle thrust Mestallier's body out of his way, down to the floor with a thump, and with bloodied beard, bloodied mouth, bloodied hands seized the woman by the hair and one wrist and sank his fangs into her throat.

Gallard stepped back, flushed with sexual arousal and trembling from head to foot. On the floor, Mestallier tried to crawl to his wife's aid and Gallard put his boot down on the man's

groping wrist. It was scarcely necessary. He was clearly too weak
to defend her, too weak to live. When De Colle was done with
the wife he turned back to the husband, dragged the bleeding arm
to his lips once more and finished him, with a moan of pleasure
that could have been heard all over the house, had the occupants
not lain asleep under the vampire's silent influence.

For a moment De Colle stared at his helper and his reflective
eyes blazed with sheer hunger and sheer lust. Wanting only one
more ecstasy, to take his life as well.

He turned away, his arm before his eyes. Still turned away, he
took a handkerchief from his breeches pocket, wiped the blood
from his beard. Sniffed the handkerchief, deeply, before he put
it away and turned back.

'This is the road that gives us our power,' he said.

Gallard's voice was thick with ecstasy and devotion. 'Then I
will follow it, that I may render over my power unto God.'

Lydia's voice made Asher open his eyes. The Spanish Inquisition
had invented a device – a sort of springy iron band to encircle
the victim's head, with spikes that pressed upon the temples. The
band was open at the back and could be ratcheted tighter and
tighter until the spikes were driven through the bone into the
brain. It felt to Asher as if one of these devices were being
tightened around his head. Though he was almost nauseated with
the pain it certainly wasn't the first time. He forced his eyes open
a slit against what felt like blinding light, and saw Lydia and
Ysidro sitting beside his bed.

'I passed by that door about three times before I finally saw
it,' Lydia was saying. 'And I was really looking hard, too. I mean,
I knew vampires – skillful vampires – could make people not
see things like doors or houses; whole streets, even. When the
convent sold the western half of its property that included
the old chapel, they bricked across the middle of the old catacomb,
but there is a door there. When I mentioned it to Father Martin
he stared at it and said, "Bless my soul! All these years, and I've
never seen it!" Of course it was locked . . .'

'There are three catacombs,' said Asher, his own voice
sounding like someone else's to his ears.

As they stared at him in surprise, his memory yielded up –

small and clear as dark glass, like those fragmentary visions of his dreams – a close-printed page – *where did I obtain it?* – in a yellowed old book: *Traité sur les maisons religieuses disparues de la ville de Paris . . .*

'The convent of the Filles de Sainte-Clare had three catacombs, connecting the new church with the old,' he said. 'They were dug in a line. The great Roman sewer that ran from the old Monastery of the Capucins on the Rue des Quatre-Fils to the river lay directly under them.'

'Did you go through them?' Lydia leaned close to take his hand. She drew back at once, then felt his face, her brown eyes widening with concern.

'I don't . . .' He struggled to recall. A smell of wet bricks, of sewage and the river . . . of hastening, stumbling, through clammy darkness. Shallow steps, an uneven floor, slipping as he ran . . .

Pain closed around his skull like a vise.

He shut his eyes. The light was unbearable. 'I think I must have.'

Ysidro's insectile fingers pressed against his face, like one of the glass spindles lacemakers used, left out on a freezing night. 'I'll find the doctor.' There was a little silence, in which one of the other patients could be heard arguing with someone: what the hell did we need *les Anglais* for, anyway? Asher realized he was shivering with cold.

Fleeing through the catacomb. Looking behind him once, twice . . . The feeble glint of his lantern showed almost nothing, and didn't catch in the glow of vampire eyes. *I must have eluded them in the cellars . . .*

They'd been waiting for him in the church. Statues that came to life among the pillars, eyes gleaming . . .

'He says he will come shortly,' said Ysidro's voice.

'The thing is,' said Lydia, and her hand – fingers almost as cold as Ysidro's – stroked Asher's forehead, 'Father Martin told me about the relics that used to be in the bone chapel, and it really sounds as if one of them *might* have been . . . been something else. He spoke of a glass that had been imbued somehow with the light of the Christmas star, which doesn't sound like any relic I've ever heard of. I mean, they're usually things like somebody's fingerbones, or the skull of John the Baptist—'

'Of which there are two,' remarked Ysidro. 'One in Amiens, the other in Munich.'

'By the sound of it,' added Asher, 'there are skulls enough in the bone chapel without that of John the Baptist.'

'Whatever's in there,' said Lydia, 'has to be what Hyacinthe wants. What she's willing to deal with the living – to put herself into the power of the living – to get at. Listen, Simon. The place is guarded during the day, but there's a chance that the vampires are out hunting at night. I think day may be safer – to go in there, I mean, and see the place. But if Schaumm has other living men working for him – and he probably does – we can't leave Jamie unguarded. I can get M'sieu Greuze to come with me.'

'Don't be absurd. Your good Jehu will be of no use—'

'I won't have Jamie unguarded while you come with me at night.'

Ysidro was silent for a time, in which Asher tried to guess from the sounds of the traffic on the Rue Saint-Antoine what time it was. It had a different note to it, a different rhythm: trucks rather than motor cars, streaming by on their way to the Front. He knew by experience that it would go on so all night. This early in August the last, deadly sunlight would not have gone from the sky much before ten . . .

The argument at the other end of the room had shifted to who in the neighborhood were German spies. 'They're all over the city, I tell you, hiding in the empty houses, the empty shops . . .'

'Elysée de Montadour is among the most brainless women I've met,' said the vampire at length. 'Yet she has a kind of cunning about things she considers hers. You know she is waiting for you. Even if her guards must be out of the place by sundown, beyond doubt they have orders to leave you tied up in some chamber, should they find you there. And we cannot guarantee,' he added grimly, 'that she will be the first of the nest to enter that room, come darkness.'

'I have to risk it,' said Lydia stubbornly. 'Someone has to see the place. At least to see what we're talking about . . .'

'There is a solution.' The vampire steepled his long fingers. 'Literally a solution, and one which I have used before, Mistress. There are elixirs, mostly containing silver nitrate and various plant alkaloids, which enable the Undead to prolong their wakefulness for a few hours into the morning. Emeric Jambicque used to make them – he was forever fixing up one thing or another; I am astonished he did not kill himself before he met his fate . . .'

His voice paused, hovering in a way that told Asher that the vampire was recalling something about Emeric Jambicque's fate.

'I can't let you—'

'Mistress,' said Ysidro patiently, ''tis *I* who will not let *you* visit a vampire nest alone. James, you say an old Roman sewer lies beneath those catacombs.'

He managed to nod, his mind skating along the edge of sleep.

'Thus 'twould be possible for me to come and go, and find refuge for the remainder of the day.'

'I've seen what that sort of elixir does to you!' protested Lydia.

An illness which, Asher knew, could only be alleviated by killing.

Lydia, he was aware, knew it too.

With the vampires, he reflected, *it always comes back to that. A few extra victims.* The price the German High Command was perfectly happy to pay . . .

Is that reason for me to wink at it? To thwart their plans, whatever they are?

'Yet I assure you, Mistress, there is no Facinum, no magical glass of starlight nor vial of saint's blood, involved in the making of a new vampire. Nor in the domination of the master's mind over that of the fledgling. You know this.'

Asher whispered, 'Hyacinthe knows it, too. It's in the bone chapel.'

'What is?'

Ysidro's voice was sharp. Asher's eyes drifted open for a moment as his mind groped for that last thought: the thing that he knew was there.

The thing Hyacinthe was looking for.

The thought slipped away and he slept.

EIGHTEEN

Ysidro *is right*, he thought.
   A master vampire makes a fledgling by a natural process.
   There is no talisman, no magic about it.

Unless one called it magic, to absorb the soul of a dying man into one's own brain. To breathe it back into the brain of that dead man, once the changes to the tissue began to spread.

In a dream-fragment tiny as a fingernail he saw the young Protestant Gallard talking with his wife, a young woman, dark and bespectacled and intense. Gallard paced back and forth across a stolid, bourgeois study as he talked, while the woman watched him with her dark eyes growing larger with shock as he talked. She shook her head, and shook her head, and reached out for him. He took her in his arms, said, 'It's for our daughter that I'm doing this, Dorcas! For all the daughters of the Congregation, for its sons and its descendants! The Catholic League will stop at nothing! They are strong, they have the wealth of a thousand years at their back, the Spanish gold of the Indies! They must be stopped!'

'You will lose your soul, Gideon! Your soul!'

'No,' he insisted, 'no. My feet are guided into this course. I know I am guided! *God can use anyone to His purposes.* I know this. I am called. I know I am called.'

And she wept in his arms.

Elsewhere, as if he were looking through several windows at once, Asher was aware of Simon patiently following Esdras de Colle through the night alleyways of Paris, observing where he went, risking his own immolation to follow him to the brink of dawn to learn where he slept. Stumbling, shuddering with terror, into his own lodgings, to fall into the coffin that his servant Tim guarded for him in the vaulted cellar.

'You can't keep doin' this, my lord!' the young man protested, as Ysidro sagged back on the rough cushions, closed his eyes. 'One day sleep's gonna take you before you can get back.'

Ysidro's hand closed briefly around his servant's. 'I must . . .'

And Tim folded the vampire's hands together on his breast and wound a rosary around them, its crucifix wrought of ivory and gold.

Stanislas Greuze took Ellen and Lydia to a house near the Gare Montparnasse that afternoon – Saturday – to introduce her to the family of his neighbor's cousin, who were leaving for Bordeaux the following day. 'They're nice people,' he assured her, 'good people. They'll look after your servant and, I promise you, the money you give them for doing so will make all the difference to them when their family down there takes them in. These are hard times, mesdames.' He left the taxi half-blocking the narrow lane, helped Ellen from the back seat, and collected her valise from the boot.

Lydia had her doubts about these informal arrangements – the journey was to be accomplished in the wagon of M'sieu Dupont's coal business and would take three days – but the Duponts were, as Greuze had said, clearly 'good people', a working-class family who seemed equally and amicably divided between Gran'père's devout Catholicism and the red-dyed bred-in-the-bone socialism of Gran'mère, M'sieu Dupont, and two of his sons who unlike every other young man in the neighborhood showed no signs of dashing off to the nearest recruiting office.

'Ma'am, I can't leave you!' protested Ellen, as one of the boys carried her valise into the house, where she was to stay that night. 'I know you're staying with Professor Asher, but—'

'I need you to look after Miranda for me.' Lydia tucked into Ellen's handbag a hundred francs – in addition to the three hundred she'd already given M'sieu Dupont – and the ticket she'd purchased that morning on the *Bolingbroke*, sailing from Bordeaux on the fifteenth, 'Until Professor Asher and I get there. We shouldn't be long.' She suspected this was a lie, and wondered despairingly if she would ever see her daughter again.

'And I won't really feel safe,' she admitted to Ysidro on Monday morning when she slipped through the door of the old crypt below St Clare's, 'until I get the telegram from her saying she's arrived in London. The paper this morning says German submarines are patrolling both the North Sea and the Channel. But barring a miracle the situation is only going to get worse.'

As she and the vampire had arranged, Ysidro had entered the church in the night. He had left the side door open for her, and when Lydia entered at eight in the morning – as soon as the last celebrants of early Mass departed – the ancient vaulting still seemed redolent of the incense burned the day before. Ysidro was shivering slightly, and looked – Lydia reflected – every day of three hundred and eighty-four years old. He was usually able to keep her – and anyone else – from noticing the scars on his face and neck. Now they stood out in savage ridges.

'I hate these elixirs,' he said, when she asked him how he felt. 'Vampire flesh resists change, so they must needs contain that which is poisonous to us, aconite or silver, in order to have effect. Even the mildest take a fearful toll. I can only hope and trust that for the next sennight neither your friend Schaumm nor that execrable hag Hyacinthe will make any assault on the hospital.' He led the way from the crypt through the small door which Father Martin had shown Lydia on her previous visit, and down three steps into moist darkness that smelled of clay.

'Like the meditations which open the way into others' dreams,' he continued, 'the making of such potions is a dying art among the Undead, if you will forgive me the vulgarity of a pun. Emeric Jambicque studied the art, but few have done so since. Even he was looked upon as antiquated. Why trouble oneself with thought and experiment in how to alter the limits of the vampire state, when 'tis easier in these days simply to go forth and make a meal of the poor?'

Behind the expressionless whisper of his voice Lydia thought she heard a wry weariness. But when she slipped further open the slide on her dark-lantern, she saw no reflection of that – or of anything else – in his face. She was, moreover, aware of his fangs, something she usually wasn't, and the reminder was a disquieting one.

And her unease – her horrified conviction that James was indeed justified in his enmity to the vampire kind – she saw reflected in Ysidro's bitter eyes. The elixir that permitted him a few hours of wakefulness to keep her safe from the guards, she understood, drastically reduced his ability to mask himself with illusion.

He will risk himself to protect me, she understood, *even to the extent of risking my revulsion and hate at seeing him as he is . . . Is that the act of a monster?*

She didn't know.

The catacomb of the convent of the Daughters of St Clare had originally – Father Martin had told her – been some eighty feet in length, by ten in breadth. The curve of its vaults barely cleared Lydia's head. As in the crypt above, three tiers of niches were let back into the stonework of the walls, swept clear at some point in the past and, Father Martin had said, formerly used for the storage of the old chairs and cartons of church records that now graced the little room in the tower. After the floods four years previously, they had not been returned.

A partition wall had been built when the convent land had been sold. 'Do you think the builder of the *hôtel* – Monsieur Batoux, I think La Belle Nicolette said his name was . . . Do you think he had the door put in?' Lydia was no expert in architecture, but the narrow demi-porte tucked into the darkest corner of the truncated vault looked at least three centuries old to her.

Three centuries of priests and sextons and volunteers lugging cartons of parish records had managed to miss it, not to mention the 1871 Commune's Committee of Public Safety in search of popish torture-chambers. Reason enough to believe it had been intended as an escape route for the Undead. 'I can't imagine the Master of Paris letting a good back door go to waste.'

'It does indeed sound as if Gabrielle sheltered with her brother's descendants from the first.' Ysidro ran a thoughtful finger over the decidedly modern lock, which clearly he had had no trouble in picking last night. 'Myself, I'd not have put the price of a glass of wine into the hands of *my* sister, much less my life – particularly not if my sister thought she might gain some advantage out of my vampire state.'

Lydia's heart beat faster as she raised the dark-lantern to illuminate the catacomb which continued beyond the old partition wall. Niter crusted the ceiling vaults and the edges of the burial niches. Along the walls lay dunes of clayey mud, and many niches still contained desiccated snaggles of bones, rags, hair. From others, these sorry shards of mortality had been pushed out on to the floor – long ago, to judge by the mud around them. In the middle of the room stood a coffin, the lid lying by its side.

Empty (*it's nine o'clock in the morning; vampires would be sound asleep anyway . . .*), and smeared inside with old mud. *The floods again . . .*

'There.' Ysidro touched her arm with a hand that shook. Her eyes followed his pointing finger to a corner near the farther door, where a round well was protected by an ancient grille of rusted iron. 'The way into the Roman sewer, I dare say, of which James spoke.' He went to it, knelt, and wrapped his strong white hands around it; Lydia saw the muscles of his jaw and neck cord up with the effort of wrenching the grille free. 'A back door indeed. If no such entry lies in the room beyond . . .'

He pushed open the door to reveal a second catacomb, as Asher had said, the level of its floor some twelve inches below the first and its ceiling-vaults a good deal lower still. Three coffins formed a line, end to end, down the center of the room: all empty, as Lydia gingerly ascertained while Ysidro sought out a second well that communicated with the sewers. 'All is well,' she punned, straight-faced, and Ysidro gave her a pained look.

'I have killed men for less, lady.' He wiped the rust and slime from his hands with a spotless handkerchief. His fingers fumbled as he put it away, and his stride was unsteady as he walked the length of the narrow chamber to the door at its farther end, as if he were numb with cold.

'With your permission, Mistress, I shall retreat like a rat into that hole ere you broach the door to the third catacomb, lest its farther door communicate with a stair open to daylight. By the sound of it—' he pressed himself to the desiccated wood of the door – 'the footfalls of men echo at some little distance, as if in a stairwell. The weight of the earth and stone around us make it difficult to be sure, but were I Master of Paris, or of any other city, and knew such a back door as this existed, I would lay some sort of trap against the Undead as well as the living.'

Vampire flesh toughened, he had told her, as it aged; she knew he could endure more light than the younger among the Undead. Still she shuddered at the thought of opening a door to an unexpected light-shaft, of seeing the man she knew, the friend she knew, auto-combust into unquenchable flame.

Even if he does deserve it . . .

He is risking that, for me. For Jamie.

For whatever it is that Jamie found out the Germans are looking for. Whatever Hyacinthe is looking for . . .

'Particularly would I lay some trap,' he added thoughtfully, 'if I believed my power over my fledglings derived from some imbecilic bauble. 'Twere best we hasten, Mistress. This elixir I have taken lasts but a few hours, and I would fain be back in a safe place ere I sleep. And sleep I will soon, like the dead. If we can enter this place at all, we shall have little enough time to locate the chapel, and less to search it, ere we are discovered by the guards.'

'You know what it is, don't you?' she asked suddenly. 'What's in the bone chapel?'

'No.' He looked aside.

They're bringing up the siege guns to Liège.

Asher heard them, though the marketplace around him – Liège's riverside Sunday market along the Meuse – was as it had been on an early visit to the Belgian city with Belleytre, whose sturdy gray-clothed form he could see moving ahead of him among the barrows of fruit, books, children's toys.

The sky was clear and the river sparkled. Around him the babbled mix of French, Flemish, and Walloon was an intricate joy, like a mosaic.

But it was cold, freezing cold, as if he stood in the dead of winter, and his chest tightened at the roar that was a thousand times louder than thunder. The big guns, the 42-centimeter monsters that they had to bring up in sections on railway cars, that could pulverize a building like a sledgehammer hitting an American soda-cracker. He'd seen the prototypes at the Krupp proving-ground at Meppen, seen what they could do. He shouted to Belleytre, 'It's started!' but his tutor – to the end of his days with the Department Asher had never thought of the little man as anything else – was thumbing through a yellowed seventeenth-century pamphlet at a bookstall. Asher tried to thrust his way to him through the crowd, but around him the city seemed to change and shift, those tidy buildings of red and buff brick fading to narrow gothic frontages of half-timbering and steep roofs. The

Meuse flung wide without embankments, bordered with mud and reeds, bobbing with hay-barges and cargoes of salt.

Ysidro's memories? The Spanish had held the city for years . . .

The guns turned to thunder. Rain pounded on shuttered windows, hissed in a wood fire; for a moment, in one of those dark glass dream-fragments, Asher saw Simon Ysidro and his servant Tim in the midst of a gathering at what had to be a tavern. Paris again, not Liège. They were speaking French – early seventeenth-century French, before Richelieu and Louis XIV got to it, full of chewed-up bits of Latin and Italian – and the men around them on the benches leaned close to listen. It was cold here, too. Asher moved closer to the fire, but it gave no heat.

''Twas he who killed Mestallier and his wife,' Simon was saying. 'He who killed poor Jeanette Roux last week.' He was dressed as a priest and looked absurdly young. Try as he would Asher couldn't see the long glassy claws into which the vampire state transformed human nails, or the cat-gleam of reflected firelight in his eyes.

I gave men the direction to do the deed, he had said.

And the men on the benches round the fire exclaimed – in almost incomprehensible Parisian argot – and traded glares of anger and enlightenment. Asher made out fragments: 'raped until she died of shame' and 'slew the babe in the cradle in the very chamber'. One man cried, 'Heretic monster!' and Simon leaned forward, fingers stretched as if he would take that rough artisan's horny hands in his own, yellow eyes somber with outrage.

'You speak more truly than you know, brother. The man is indeed a monster. Tomorrow he will lie, like a great leech swollen with his gorgings, in the crypt beneath his house on the Rue des Puits de la Ville, dreaming of the Devil who made him . . . of the Devil who delivered Jacques Mestallier and Jeanette Roux and all those others into his hand . . .'

And what more did he whisper, Asher wondered, seeing him look into each man's eyes in turn, *in each man's dreams at night?*

After the darkness of the first two chambers of the catacomb, the faint daylight that permeated the third made Lydia squint and blink. *Drat it*, she thought, *Ysidro was right. How is there daylight so far underground? There must be a shaft of some kind ahead. Is there a way to close it off? To get past it?*

The strong, pale gleam flooding through the doorway before her outlined the same dilapidation and mess that had characterized the chambers through which she'd already passed, though the coffins that formed a line along the center of this one were closed, and caked with old mud. As her eyes adjusted, Lydia saw through the open door at the far end of the crypt what looked like a vestibule walled and floored with stone and flooded with morning light.

Whatever happened now, Ysidro couldn't follow her. Couldn't help if the guards found her.

I should go back . . .

She closed the door behind her, gathered up Mrs Flasket's borrowed skirts, and, hurrying the length of the narrow chamber, put her head through the open door.

The foundation floor of a tower. She'd seen the same thing in a dozen old fortresses to which she'd been taken as a schoolgirl, at Carcassonne and Frankfurt and Foix. Heavy stone groinings, stone floor worn into runnels that marked the traffic patterns of centuries, low doors. A stairway wound upward to floors above. But the floors of the upper chambers had all been torn away and replaced by a metal grillework, gleaming in the sunlight that fell from above. *The tower*, she thought. That stumpy cone-roofed Renaissance tower in the courtyard, where someone had installed all those dozens of incongruous windows.

The grille was silver – *probably silver plate*; she gasped to think of the expense – and nearly black with tarnish. The trapdoor that blocked the stairway up was fastened with a silver lock.

No Undead intruder was going to come sneaking in by the back way without Elysée de Montadour knowing all about it.

But Jamie came this way . . .

Above the level of the grille a gallery circled the inside of the tower, which Lydia estimated to be some thirty feet in diameter. Presumably any guards who walked that gallery could look down and see her.

Yes, here comes one now . . .

She watched him from the shelter of the catacomb's door. A tough-looking man with a paunch, a military haircut and a shotgun – *why hasn't he run off and joined the army like every other man in Paris? Perhaps he's a socialist like M'sieu Greuze and the Duponts?*

Or is Elysée just paying him a LOT?

He made a circuit of the gallery, loafing and bored, and disappeared.

Lydia waited, counting the minutes on her watch, forcing herself to patience. *The longer he's gone, the better. But I have to know HOW long.*

She hoped poor Ysidro hadn't fallen asleep in the sewer. *How would I ever get him back to his hideout? Wherever THAT is.*

It was fifteen minutes before the guard appeared again.

At the foot of the stair, opposite the door of the catacomb where she stood, was another door, the shape of its opening almost certainly original to the building of the tower. Heart in her throat, Lydia darted across the sunny ring of worn stone, counted the minutes it took her to pick its silver-plated lock. *It's like surgery. You have all the time in the world . . . there's nobody's life at stake.*

A velvet curtain hung immediately inside. Lydia pushed it aside to reveal another, a foot beyond.

There's nobody awake in there . . .

Threads of light from her lantern showed her the stone walls of a gently descending passageway. Yet another curtain, a sharp turn, then a fourth. *Gabrielle Batoux has to have built this part.*

She put aside the last curtain. Her light slid across the knobbed shapes of skulls on the walls. Femur-heads and scapulae glimmered like slick brown pebbles beneath the sea.

She stepped inside, raised the light.

The bone chapel was smaller than any of those beneath the Monastery of the Capuchins in Rome, barely twelve feet wide by perhaps thirty in length. As Father Martin had said, the altar wall and most of the long walls to her right and left consisted entirely of skulls, relieved by shallow niches for whole skeletons where in an ordinary church the statues of saints would have stood. Like saints the skeletons upheld the instruments of martyrdom, frightful implements of iron and wire, or dismantled segments of the rack. The altar under its arch of skulls was faced with ribs, like wave-combed beach sand. Amid patterns of vertebrae and phalanges on the ceiling, skulls grinned from pelvises, a mockery of conventional Renaissance putti faces framed in wings.

A sarcophagus lay on a sort of dais at the opposite end of the chamber, flanked by thick stone pillars. Lydia's guess was that it was where Elysée slept, but the stone lid was closed and even had she been able to do so without it slipping and alerting the guards, she would not have touched it. But she saw that the stone of the lid was carved in vague shapes of men and women, worn smooth by the passage of years.

Was this room, too, immersed during the floods of 1910?

Where did Elysée sleep during that inundation? And did she have to replace all those velvet curtains afterwards?

And what happened to the workmen who did that job?

Candlesticks stood in the niches beside the altar, crusted thick with winding-sheets of spent wax. For the rest, the altar was clear, and blotted all over with dark stains.

She really MUST make her fledglings here.

She thought of the handsome Modeste Saint-Vrain, and winced.

Four square doors broke the skull wall behind the altar, reminding Lydia of the wall-safe her father had had in his study behind the very expensive (and very bad) painting of Achilles slaying Hector. Each was about two feet square, set in the wall at slightly above elbow height. Instead of the iron safe door at her father's these were closed off with grilles of silver, tarnished black, in an older style than the grille that closed off the stairway in the tower. Through them the lantern beam caught a fugitive gleam of gold.

Years of scientific education notwithstanding, Lydia edged past the altar-rail with the sensation that she'd be struck dead if she touched the altar. *Who was it in the Bible that happened to?* She clearly recalled her governess telling her the story, and because it had been broad daylight in the nursery at the time Lydia had retorted that such events must have made it very difficult to find anyone willing to dust the Holy of Holies . . . a comment which had earned her a good hour of standing in a corner of the nursery nursing her smarting hand. In a pitch-black underground chapel being stared at by approximately seven hundred and fifty skulls – allowing seven inches by nine per skull and adding in the putti skulls on the ceiling – the matter appeared a little differently.

On the other hand, does a chapel maintained by a vampire – who's murdered eleven thousand eight hundred and something people, give or take a few dozen, not to speak of throwing Jamie off the church tower – count any more as consecrated ground?

I'll have to ask Father Martin . . .

One of the reliquaries – Lydia pressed her face to the grille – was in the form of a foot, with ivory toenails and a sandal so crusted with gems that it was almost impossible to see that it was made of gold. Another was shaped like a huge heart, studded with cabochon rubies like immense droplets of oozing blood. In a third, box-shaped and faced with glass, Lydia could see a severed hand decorated with jeweled chains and gold nail-guards. The fourth, also roughly box-shaped and also glass-fronted, contained something veiled in white silk gauze.

A stone?

A glass orb containing the light of the Christmas star?

If I pick the lock, will bells ring in the guardroom and the chapel flood with poison gas?

Though Lydia suspected this was the sort of thing that happened only in stories recounted in the Strand Magazine, instinct kept her from the attempt. Besides, at well over half a pound per cubic inch she had serious doubts about being able to lift or carry the reliquary very far.

I should at least . . .

Something – like the faint whisper of clothing against stone, the tiniest trace of sound – made Lydia swing around, gasping, aware – aware to the marrow of her bones – that someone was watching her.

That someone stood at her side. Someone who knew her name.

There was no one.

He's here . . .

She had no idea who 'he' was and it didn't matter. *He –* someone – stood . . . in the darkness? In the shadows? In one of those statue niches pretending to be a skeleton?

To the right of the altar.

There was no one there.

She had meant to search the chapel to see if there were any way whatsoever that Ysidro could cross the dim daylight of the vestibule.

To find whatever it was that Jamie had been searching for, that Hyacinthe and her German spymaster had killed poor Tante Camille to keep her from talking about . . .

That Elysée was afraid that Asher knew about . . .

And find it, hopefully, in time to get Ysidro back to the safety of wherever he was hiding in Paris before he collapsed.

But the conviction that she was not alone in the chapel, that there was someone else there (other than Elysée asleep in her coffin), someone watching her, drove her back to the door. She'd lost track of when the guard was going to be by. *Do I have two minutes? Thirty seconds? If he raises an alarm will Ysidro come to try to rescue me and open that door and burn up in the sunlight?*

It took all her resolve to take the time to lock the chapel door before she darted back into the safety of the catacomb, trembling like a sapling in a gale and turning a dozen times to look behind her as she hastened along the narrow burial chamber (*as if I could see one of THEM if they didn't want me to . . .*).

Panic almost choked her as she tapped – very softly – on the door of the second catacomb chamber before opening it, but entering she saw no sign of ashes or fire.

Creeping to the iron grille that covered the sewer-well she whispered, 'Simon?'

No reply.

It took all her strength to wrest the grille up, and she flinched from the smell below and the furtive wet scurrying in the darkness. Nevertheless she lowered herself down and found him, about a hundred feet farther along the narrow tunnel, curled into a little ball of bones and hair, unwakeably asleep.

Like far-off chips of glass catching light, Asher saw, as he sank into blackness and bone-breaking cold, the Spartan chamber of the Protestant Gallard again. Again he seemed to be looking through a window, the images clear though he felt as if he were a great way off. This time the young woman Dorcas slept in the bed, dark braids limp on the sheets, and Gallard in his nightshirt knelt on the floor before the fire. Before him, against him, Esdras de Colle knelt, one arm encircling the young man's waist to hold him up. With the other hand he held Gallard's thick fair hair, forcing his head back while he drank from the vein in his throat, spilled drips of blood now and then falling from his beard to spot Gallard's shirtsleeve like blackish rubies. The sleeve was torn open, the arteries of the arm cut in three or four places, the wounds sucked white yet oozing still.

'Give it to me,' Gallard whispered. 'I beg – I beg . . . You said you would give me the vampire life . . .'

De Colle drew his head back a little and smiled, loving – Asher could see this in his eyes – to hear the words 'I beg'. 'Did I say that?' he taunted.

'You swore—'

'And you swore you would do anything. I wonder if you meant it?'

Gallard was fighting to breathe, fighting to keep his fluttering eyelids from dropping closed. 'Dear God, don't play with me!'

'You're telling me what to do now?' De Colle grinned, bloody-mouthed like a feeding wolf. 'That doesn't sound like the man who swore he'd obey me.'

'No, I – I'm sorry – I didn't mean it . . .' The young man was weeping now, weeping in terror as he felt his emptying heart labor to keep going. 'I will obey. In all things I will obey.'

The vampire shook his head in deep regret. 'You don't sound like a man who means it.'

He drank again, and Gallard wept and begged as his blood and his life seeped away. Only at the last de Colle laid him on the hearth, and with his long nails ripped open his own sleeve and the flesh of his arm beneath it, and laid the bleeding wound at Gallard's lips. The young man sobbed and sucked at the blood like a starving baby, begging forgiveness of his new master, stammering thanks, while de Colle chuckled with contempt.

Then he gathered Gallard up in his arms again, pressed his lips to the other man's, and with the slowest possible delibera-tion, a millimeter at a time, used his long nails to open the arteries of Gallard's throat.

And as he saw, in another dream-fragment, the spire of St Lambert's Cathedral once more against the smoke-roiled sunset sky, Asher thought, *Liège*.

Constantine Angelus was also the Master of Liège.

NINETEEN

'**M**adame!'

It was the sweeper Fantine.

Shivering with exhaustion, Lydia stopped on the sidewalk halfway between the doors of the hospital and where Greuze had left his cab on the Rue Chaligny.

It was full dark. Asher had been unguarded for nearly two hours. She forced herself to sound calm, gave the woman a friendly smile, and said, 'Hello, Fantine. I'm afraid I can't talk, I have to—'

'Madame, the police come looking for you.' She stepped in front of Lydia, blocking her attempt to resume her course toward the hospital.

Oh God, Jamie . . .

She headed Lydia off again as she would have run for the door.

'The police arrest M'sieu Asher.' The woman frowned, deeply troubled by this turn of events. 'They took him away. They say he's a spy – that you're a spy, too. You aren't, though, are you, madame?'

Lydia could only stare at her, too shocked to speak.

The last time Asher had been accused of being a spy – which of course he had been for much of his life – had resulted in his diving headlong through a window of the Grand Hotel des Wagons-Lits in Peking and spending a week hiding with Chinese gangsters, but that obviously wasn't an option now. *Schaumm,* she thought. *Or the Paris nest. Good heavens, in a prison infirmary it's only a matter of time before one of the vampires gets to him!*

'You're not a spy, are you, madame?' Fantine's face creased with concern. 'Spies are wicked and evil. But you're good to me. You speak to me as if I were a regular lady.'

Lydia fished in her mind for any remark she'd ever made to the woman besides a friendly *Good day, Fantine.*

How nasty did Thérèse Sabatier have to be for that to shine in comparison?

'Not a bit of it!' Greuze slapped a five-franc piece into the sweeper's hand, closed the hard fingers around it. 'It's a plot by the real spies. *Merci, madame*! Tell no one!'

Fantine shook her head vigorously.

'You haven't seen us.' As the sweeper went through a whole vocabulary of childhood signs of loyalty and silence, Greuze took Lydia's elbow and walked her quickly back around the corner to his cab.

Don Simon Ysidro, as was his wont, had rented for himself a small house in Montmartre, like a country *manoir* from the days when the hill had been a rural village. It stood on a stairway off the Rue Lepic, only a few streets above the house on the Rue Caulaincourt where he had installed Lydia two days previously, and their cellars connected through the old gypsum-mine tunnels that riddled the hill. Rather to her own surprise, Lydia had been able to drag and carry the vampire up through the well-like manhole that morning and into the central chamber of the old catacomb to lay him in one of the old coffins, confirming her earlier suspicions that whatever it was that was transmitted through vampire blood – presumably a virus such as those Chamberland, Pasteur and Mayer had investigated – it changed the cells of the body itself to some substance both stronger and less dense than living flesh.

She had been unable to lift the stone lid that she'd found among the detritus along the catacomb wall, and had to content herself with remaining at Ysidro's side through the remainder of the day. She'd sneaked out once to help herself to candles from the church storeroom, and a second time to steal paper and a pen in order to make notes about what she'd seen beyond the catacomb door and her speculations concerning tissue transformation with regard to cellular composition in the early stages of the vampire state.

She had earnestly hoped that Ysidro's consumption of whatever it was he'd drunk to remain awake wouldn't cause him to over-sleep come nightfall. He looked – as she held the candle over his face where he lay in the borrowed coffin – well and truly dead.

But he woke just after ten, and seemed so ill that Lydia had insisted on seeing him back to his own rented quarters off the Rue Lepic. On the drive there he had insisted that Greuze stop at a café for sandwiches and soup, which he bullied Lydia into eating once they'd reached Lydia's sanctuary on the Rue Caulaincourt. She had then half-supported him up through the mine tunnels from her cellar to his, and returned – her heart in her throat in the clammy dark of the mine – to her own house again, where they had left Greuze and his cab waiting outside. The result was that it was nearly midnight before she'd stepped out of the cab on the Rue Chaligny and encountered Fantine Boue twenty feet from the door of the Hôpital Saint-Antoine.

Do Schaumm – and the Paris vampires – know about the manoir on the Rue Lepic?

In Greuze's cab on the way from the church Ysidro had given her the key to his own hideout, an astonishing piece of trust considering Asher's stated intention of killing whatever vampires crossed his path. Returning after Fantine's warning, she'd had the driver leave her in the Rue Lepic and had climbed the stair straight to Ysidro's door: dangerous, but the thought of another walk through the mine tunnels, at this hour, was more than she could bear.

Ysidro was gone when she got there. *Hunting.* Lydia felt sick with horror and self-loathing. Sitting beside him in the catacomb through the endless hours of the day, she had known that it would come to this: that the wakefulness he'd purchased with Emeric Jambicque's philter, the wakefulness he'd needed to assist her, had brought with it crushing debilitation that could only be counteracted, later, by a kill.

Or several kills.

With half the Paris police scrambling into army uniforms and dashing to the Belgian frontier, it would be as easy for him as stealing apples from a vendor's stall.

Protecting Jamie – making sure he wouldn't be left alone in the night – cost someone in Paris their life. Lydia sank down on the worn brown velvet of the sofa – the old town-house was furnished like her grandparents' country place in Hampshire, part-way between a Regency salon and a Victorian rectory – and took off her glasses to press her palms to her eyes, as if to blot out what she couldn't bear to see.

Murderer. Monster.

He would risk his life for me . . .

She blocked from her mind the words she could not – *COULD NOT* – phrase, and thought instead, *I shouldn't feel about him what I do.*

Jamie.

New pain and new terror flooded in.

Where would they take him?

How well will he be guarded, particularly at night?

What kind of hearing are they going to give these spy charges, and what kind of evidence is there, and can I even get anyone at the embassy to listen to me?

The newspaper on the table bore the latest headlines: the German armies had begun bombarding the forts around Liège. *They must have brought their big guns up.*

She knew she should take the opportunity to investigate the rest of Ysidro's house – she'd only seen the cellar and the kitchen before going to the hospital. *At least I need to make sure that cellar door is locked. I will look around*, she promised, *in just a moment.*

She removed her spectacles and closed her eyes, to open them (it felt like) almost at once at the touch of a cold hand on hers.

'Mistress?'

'He's in the chapel,' she said, not knowing why: a fragment of a dream that disappeared like glass in clear water. She lay on the sofa, looking up into Ysidro's yellow eyes.

'Who is?' And he asked the question too quickly.

As if he already knew.

'Who is?' she repeated, even the memory of having spoken swallowed up.

'You said, "He's in the chapel."'

She shook her head, passed a hand across her face, not certain now who she'd been speaking of. The ebony clock on the mantel, elaborately carved as if it were part of a Poe story, showed it to be four thirty in the morning. It had read a quarter to one when she'd entered the room. She caught his sleeve. 'They've arrested Jamie.'

Ysidro looked wasted and emaciated, the scars on his face

standing out like sword-cuts and his eyes sunk into bruises of fatigue. Despite the heat of the night he was wrapped in his black greatcoat, lank wisps of colorless hair hanging down on to his collar and his hands like a skeletal bird's. She reached involuntarily to put her hand to his face and he drew back a little; she'd put on her silver chains again to go to Saint-Antoine's, and had been too tired to take them off afterwards.

Debilitated as he was, even at this distance they hurt him.

'I know,' he replied. 'I have just come from there. Large policemen snore all around Ward B, awaiting your appearance and thinking themselves cunningly concealed behind screens. When dark falls again I shall seek him in the three prisons of the town. But you, Mistress, shall remain here. The hag that watches o'er the wards there spoke of you, and of him, spying for Germany – being part in fact of a ring of spies tasked to destroy the depots of supplies destined for the army, and to assassinate such gentlemen as Messires Poincaré and Gallieni.'

'That's ridiculous.' Lydia sat up and rubbed her eyes. 'I couldn't pick President Poincaré out of a receiving-line and I haven't the slightest idea who Monsieur Gallieni is.'

'The general in charge of defending Paris. There is food in the kitchen, madame, but I am for bed. Yet I charge you, remain indoors and open neither door nor shutter. I doubt not that between them Mistress Hyacinthe and Schaumm can raise up a coterie of deluded Parisians to seek you as a German spy. There are some already, I dare say, dreaming this night of your wicked face and evil deeds. 'Twere an easy matter to convince them that you should be killed on sight rather than turned over to the police. Who is it you saw in the bone chapel?'

'No one,' said Lydia uncertainly. 'That is . . . there was someone there. I know it. I – I don't know who . . .'

'You saw no one?' Again he spoke too quickly.

He knows who's there.

She shook her head.

And fears him . . .

She opened her lips to ask him, but fell asleep – vampires could do that to people – as if the ceiling had fallen in on her, and slept like a dead woman until far into the morning.

*   *   *

'Where are you?' Asher called out into the darkness of the chapel.

He'd seen Lydia come in, seen the flash of her spectacles as she looked around her, the dark-lantern she carried held high. *She must have come in through the catacomb from St Clare's.*

Unlike the other dream-visions this one was clear and close, and as such filled him with terror. This was no second-hand recollection from Ysidro's memories, glimpsed through dark window glass. He recognized the frock Lydia wore, the simple dark-gray dress of a working woman; she'd had it on when she'd visited him in the hospital.

Get out of there, they're watching for you. Waiting for you . . .

'We will help you,' he said, frantic enough to promise anything, 'but tell me what you want!'

I'm seeing this through his eyes; he must have been standing right by the altar.

'Why didn't you speak?'

Lydia whirled, as if at a noise. Fled through the door . . .

Damn it, don't tell me you went there alone! If it was daytime Elysée's hired guards would have instructions simply to lock up intruders, leave them there when they left the premises at night. At least at night there was a sporting chance that the vampires themselves would be out.

Damn you, Don Simon, why didn't you talk her out of it?

If she comes to harm I really will kill you.

He shouted, 'Show yourself!'

But his dream had shifted, back to his own memories again. Memories of knowing he was being followed back across the footworn stones of the round vestibule, memories of fleeing through the catacomb: one door, two doors, three doors . . .

Of knowing they were following him.

Of guessing they'd be waiting for him by the doors of the church.

Of calculating other ways of getting out of the building, of reaching the relative safety of lights and people. There was, he knew, a window in the storeroom in the tower from which it would be possible to reach the roof of the side-aisle. It was steep, and probably slick with moss, but if he could make it across to the buttress he could scramble down . . .

The gleam of eyes in the darkness around him, closing in. He wrapped his silver wrist-chains around his hands . . .

TWENTY

L ydia woke at a quarter to ten, from uneasy dreams. Sometimes it was the old dream of searching through the big house on Russell Square in which she'd grown up, looking for her mother – the mother who'd suddenly grown so thin, just before she – Lydia, ten years old – had been abruptly informed that she was going to go stay with her Aunt Faith, and no, her mother was perfectly fine but wouldn't be able to come see her for a little while . . .

She had never seen her mother again, except once, when she'd sneaked down and looked at her in her coffin.

But now – as frequently happened when she had the looking-for-mother dream – the rooms in the house kept changing: to her own bedroom on Holywell Street in Oxford, to Miranda's nursery (*but I don't have a child, I'm only ten years old myself!*), to that tall strange moldering dark house in the East End of London that she could sometimes find and sometimes couldn't, where Ysidro slept when he was in England . . .

Waking – creased and cramped and grubby from sleeping in her clothes – she tiptoed to the kitchen at the back of the house, tightly shuttered as were all rooms in that big square *manoir* of pink-washed stucco, and found there a copper of water steaming gently at the side of the stove and an old-fashioned tin bath set ready behind a screen. A skirt, shirtwaist, underthings, and petti-coat lay folded on the pine table – giving her the impression of having stumbled into a fairy-tale, only she wasn't sure whether it was *Beauty and the Beast* or *Bluebeard* – and she found butter and milk in the icebox, cheese, bread, and sausage in tin boxes on a shelf. The bread was fresh.

She took a bath, washed her hair, and though her whole heart was screaming Jamie's name she made herself have breakfast ('If you faint from inanition I shall carry you to the curb and

leave you there,' Ysidro had told her last night), and she did feel
much better afterwards. Tea, not coffee, which Lydia couldn't
have made drinkable to save her life (*does he have Mrs Istabene
– or whatever her name is – come up here, too?*).

*Why would a Renaissance Spanish vampire ever need to learn
to make tea?*

*There is no chance – none – that you will learn where Jamie
is, or HOW he is, or even if he's still alive, until full dark, so
you might as well explore the house.*

The shuttered windows (in most rooms reinforced with curtains
of heavy velvet like those in the twisting passage that led to the
bone chapel), though depressing, gave her a sense of safety. Her
recollections of Jürgen Schaumm, and of Ellen lying in the kitchen
doorway at Aunt Louise's in a pool of blood, and of the handsome
and not terribly bright Modeste Saint-Vrain, were enough to keep
Lydia well away from even touching the shutters. She searched
the house from cellar to attics and found no trace of Ysidro's
coffin or of the vampire himself, though she had not the slightest
doubt that there was a sub-cellar or a wine-vault somewhere whose
door she was just temporarily not noticing no matter how hard
she looked for it. She couldn't even find the door in the cellar
that led into the tunnels. She did find the vampire's clothes in the
attic, three trunks packed with exquisite neatness and containing,
in addition to suits, shoes, gray silk ties, and endless quantities
of immaculate white linen shirts, an assortment of toiletries whose
variety would have shamed a London dandy and a dozen books
in Spanish, Latin, and Greek.

With them, she was interested to note, were three pamphlets
by Constantine Angelus. So far as she could tell, they were not
those that Jamie had bought.

One of the few books in English was *Gulliver's Travels*, and
after she'd thoroughly inspected the house and found two ways
besides the front door to get out of it in an emergency, this was
what she read, on and off through the afternoon between naps.
She slept a great deal. Though her dreams were troubled she
understood that she needed the rest, and in any case was certain
that she was safer sleeping here than she would be anywhere
else.

From the last of these slumbers she woke to find Ysidro at

the kitchen table, a wilderness of maps and notes spread out before him.

'James is in La Santé prison.' He rose and went to the gas-ring on the counter – the stove was the old wood-burning variety – to prepare coffee for her. 'A vile place: I have visited charnel-houses cleaner than their infirmary. If 'twas the intent of Schaumm and Hyacinthe to kill him in the prison they overreached themselves. He is well watched, and will be tried by court-martial within days, the guards say. Myself, I doubt it.' The long fingers operated the iron coffee-mill with deft speed, and measured the grounds into the pot. 'The man I spoke to said that he is not well.'

With a calm that surprised herself Lydia asked, 'What can we do?'

By the glare of the kitchen gas-jets Ysidro still looked far from well himself. Though the night was warm he was periodically racked by shivers. She could tell he'd fed – *at the prison?* – and hated herself for having the familiarity to know this. But the attempt to investigate the Hôtel Batoux by daylight had clearly been almost too much for him.

'Naught, tonight. Nor yet tomorrow. Save only that I spun the superintendent of the night watch there a tale of crafty Germans and the possibility that they will try to murder James in his bed to keep their foul secrets safe – laying it on, as your schoolboys have it, with a trowel. 'Twill make it harder for us to abstract him from the place, but will, I hope, keep him safer there until such time as I—*cagafuego!*' he added, as he fumbled in bringing the milk out of the icebox, and dropped it in an explosion of glass to the floor.

Lydia sprang forward, thrust him gently aside – he'd caught the edge of the table for balance – and squatted to gather up the larger fragments of the bottle neatly from the mess.

'Sit down,' she said. 'I'm terribly sorry, I didn't think – no, Simon, I said *sit down*. I'll get this. I didn't realize this potion you took has such a devastating effect.'

''Tis sometimes guesswork, how much of what to put into it. And, 'tis a year since I made it last, and a century ere that. Emeric used it often, and so knew how to control the quantities to within the weight of a poppy-seed. Cauchemar was ever trying to get from him the formula for it – the proper formula, for there were a dozen. And trying to get other things.' Ysidro sank down on to the bench at one side of the big table, and watched – with obvious discomfort – as Lydia swept up the remaining glass and mopped the floor with a towel.

'Did Emeric and Cauchemar ever use it to try to break into Angelus's house to search for the Facinum? There *is* something there in the bone chapel, by the way,' she added, coming back to the bench. 'At least, there are four reliquaries in sort of grilled cupboards behind the altar. And as I said . . .' She hesitated, groping for the words to frame what she had felt there in the darkness. 'I had a sense of something – some*one* – being there, watching me, even though I saw no one. It may just have been because Elysée was sleeping there, *if* she was sleeping there – the coffin was closed . . . I take it Emeric the alchemist was loyal to Angelus. You'd said they were friends.'

'They were – or had been,' replied Ysidro. 'What he was, was a member of the so-called Reformed Faith, and as such would not have given Cauchemar a map to find water if both were dying of thirst.'

'They really took that seriously?' Lydia recalled Filomène du Plessis, the only Catholic girl at Madame Chappedelaine's Select Academy in Switzerland, and the way the other girls would whisper about her when her aunt and uncle – who lived in Geneva near the school – would come every Sunday to take the little girl to Mass. Remembered the rumors that went around about Catholics worshipping the saints and having to obey whatever the Pope told them, so you couldn't trust them. Remembered all the whispering when word got out that Madame Oberholtzer's academy on the other side of town had actually accepted a Jewish girl.

The colorless eyebrows flexed.

'I mean,' said Lydia, 'you were all . . . vampires were all . . .'

'Damned?' Ysidro's expression did not change. 'God forbid *our* Hell should be sullied with heretics. 'Twas all Constantine could do, to keep open war from breaking out between the two faiths and destroying us all.'

Marrow freezing, waves of chills consuming him, Asher fought to surface from the darkness. But the darkness pulled him down, like water. Filled his lungs so that he fought for every breath, knowing that any breath might be his last, that the water might at any second prove stronger than his ability to fight his way upward . . .

In the darkness he heard a scream.

Then another, and somewhere the thick roar of flame and the stench of flesh charring. Echoes of pain. He had killed vampires and he knew that even sunk in the paralysis of their day-sleep, even with their hearts impaled with a hawthorn stake and their veins injected with silver nitrate, when dragged into the sunlight they screamed as they died.

And sometimes the masters who had made them – sunk also in their day-sleep – screamed too in the prison of their coffins, feeling the flames themselves and unable to wake.

'But the truth of the matter was, Cauchemar would not have allied himself with Emeric in such a search even had they been united in their faith. Any object which promised mastery over the Paris nest would give such power only to one. Not both.'

'I will not have it!' Trembling, Angelus turned from the light of the fire, faced Simon across the book-lined study. Through the windows Asher could see the dreary Paris rain catching the candle-light, could feel in his bones the deep chill of winter as he had felt it in Gallard's tiny room, in the Mestalliers' attic.

Simon replied, carefully expressionless, ''Tis little loss.'

'The man was my get.'

'He turned against you—'

'He did not!' The taller vampire strode to him, caught his pearled sleeves in the crushing grip of exasperation, almost shook him. 'Cannot I make you understand, Simon? We cannot be Catholic, we cannot be Protestant, no more than the poor living can who try to make sense of their lives which are, God knows, sufficiently complicated . . .'

And like an echo Asher saw them again, the woman burned by the mob and lying naked and sobbing in the mud, the two priests washing the face of the third in the sacked ruin of their church. *The monks, and the Daughters of Providence, are in God's hands*, Father Jeffrey's voice murmured . . .

'I watched them go to war with one another. I watched them tear this city apart. Were you in France thirty years ago, Simon, when the Queen and the Catholic League stirred up the faithful to massacre their Protestant neighbors? Common shopkeepers, men with sons and daughters of their own, would slit the throats of children whom they had known since babyhood, telling themselves that this was "all right" because the parents of those children – not even the children themselves! – had made the choice to believe that bread and wine are exactly what they look and smell like – bread and wine – and not the product of some Platonic miracles of essences and accidents that they do not even understand!'

The firelight turned Angelus's eyes to lakes of flame in the gloom. 'We kill. I kill, you kill . . . we kill because that is how we are made. We deceived ourselves into thinking that we had the right to live, for whatever reasons we gave ourselves . . . Or some because the smell of mortal blood drives them into frenzy and literally takes their minds away in that moment, in the moment of the kill, as the smell of brandy takes away the mind of a drunkard.

'We cannot start fighting amongst ourselves, Simon. You have a servant, de Colle has mortal men faithful to him, aye, and women too . . . I have those whose dreams I walk in, whose thoughts I nudge in one direction or another. Whose debts I pay and whose favors I sometimes ask, to do this deed or that for me in daylight. They as well as we will suffer if we start a war among ourselves.'

He stared into Simon's eyes, and the younger vampire returned the gaze with a deliberate blankness, as if shutting a door. 'How can you be sure the men who killed de Colle were guided by a vampire?'

Angelus waved the question aside. 'De Colle was crafty. He had been vampire for a century, he knew the old ways, the old skills to guard himself. He had living servants who watched his houses, he had a dozen ways in and out of any one of them. Even with things as they are in this city, he would have known if a living man sought him. He would have heard his footfall, even in his sleep. Recognized it if it passed a second time. He would have known a face glimpsed in a crowd . . . glimpsed again where it should not be, and a third time, maybe too soon after the second. Only a vampire could have known where he lay. Was it you?'

'One of the others may have betrayed him,' replied Simon. 'Or his fledgling may have led someone to him—'

'*Fledgling*?' The master vampire's brows shot together, deflected from his concern by wary anger.

'He made a fledgling. A week ago, maybe more . . .'

'You have seen him?'

'I have seen him,' Simon affirmed. 'Yesternight. 'Twas what I came here to you tonight to say. A man named Gallard, near the Port au Blé. I saw them speak and part, not eight hours ere de Colle was killed. He was undoubtedly vampire.'

And when Angelus did not reply, Simon laid a hand on the large well-shaped hand of the Master of Paris and added quietly, 'I think you did not know this . . . man—' and Asher knew he was originally going to say *this heretic* – 'so well as you thought.'

For a long time after that Asher wandered among dreams that made no sense. Sometimes he was a child, back in that ghastly school in Yorkshire, listening to rain or winds in the winter after his parents died. He'd taken up studying Arabic that winter, he recalled, to keep his mind busy during the holidays; saw himself on the station platform a year and a half later, when he'd finally gone south to visit his aunt. Mostly in his dreams he was 'abroad', as they said in the Department, amused and exhilarated at the people he met, the human foibles he encountered among the Germans and Czechs and Bosniaks and Arabs who thought he was one of themselves; occasionally scared out of his skin.

Once in his dreaming he encountered his Uncle Theobald, on the railway platform at Shantung of all places, a snuff-colored fussy man like a plump-faced version of his father. 'What'd you mean, no?' demanded Theobald, a fragment of a conversation which had taken place in another location at another time, because of course Uncle Theobald had never been in China in his life. 'What possible living can you ever make mucking about with those dirty old books, boy? We've paid your school fees for five years, and looked after your sister, and the first time we ask you for something we get, "No, that isn't what I want to do with my life.'"

He knew he was burning up with fever; knew he was drowning, an inch at a time.

Sometimes he was in Liège, with the distant siege guns still hammering the other forts around the Belgian city as lines of gray-clothed men scrambled over the rubble, coughing on the dust. Sometimes, through that dust, he saw Constantine Angelus, like a shadow among other shadows: the vampires of Liège.

He saw Simon when Simon returned to the priest Father Jeffrey, made his confession, and knelt before the old Jesuit and the tall Cardinal Montevierde. Heard him whisper to the candlelit darkness, 'De Colle is dead, lord. It is done.'

Montevierde laid a hand on Simon's pale head. The ruby in his ring glinted purple in the gloom. 'It is not done, Simon. Not quite. Not while the Protestant demons still walk the streets of Paris.'

'There is another of that evil tribe,' Jeffrey Sampson said, 'spreading poison to the ears of the young.'

Simon shook his head, aghast, as they put aside his description of the violence that had begun to spread between the followers of one faith and those of another – and their vampire captains.

'You refuse a favor to *God*?' The Cardinal's fingers closed on Simon's hair, when the vampire would have looked away from him. 'You hesitate, even for a moment, to do as *God himself* asks?'

''Tis best not to ask too closely after these things, Simon,' Father Jeffrey said. 'We are but the servants of God.'

And Simon bowed his head. Asher could see that he trembled.

'The alchemist, Emeric Jambicque,' said Montevierde. 'It is whispered in the confessional that he is one of them too. Is this true?'

'It is, Father.' His voice was an insect-scratch upon frozen stone.

Father Jeffrey knelt at Simon's side, pressed the vampire's clawed hands between his own. 'Will you stay in Paris, and do this for us?' he asked. 'Will you do this for God?' His gray eyes met the yellow, plumbing them deep.

'Will you do this for your soul?'

A shiver ran through the whole of Simon's flesh, and he put his hand over his eyes. He whispered, 'I will stay.'

TWENTY-ONE

The following day, through the louvers of the salon's shutters, Lydia thought she saw the sturdy figure of Stanislas Greuze pass the house on the Rue Lepic, climbing the steep street to the top of Montmartre hill. Saw him give the shuttered windows, the locked door, a quick sidelong look that missed nothing.

She wrote a note to him at the Café of the Ax and Bow in Montparnasse, and, a little awkwardly, dressed herself in some of Simon's clothes to carry it down the street to the yellow post-box, with her long red hair jammed up under a cap. If the house, the street, or the neighborhood were being watched (*surely Hyacinthe doesn't have THAT many people working for her?*) this was a danger, but it wouldn't help to have Greuze prowling around the district looking for her. Schaumm, or Saint-Vrain, might very well know – and be following – *him*.

She searched the house again after that, and this time she found the door into the tunnels – stoutly locked – and another small doorway that led (once she'd picked the lock) into the cellar of the house next door (*and have THEY ever noticed there's a door there?*). Still she could discover no sign of Ysidro or his coffin.

It only means that I'm missing something.

There's a door somewhere that he's able to keep me from noticing, the way he's kept city authorities from noticing the street that he lived on in London all those years.

No wonder the Germans want to get control of a vampire nest.

The summer day was long.

Lydia read the newspaper she'd bought on the way back from the post-box, and flinched at the news from Belgium and from the Rhine. She examined – half a dozen times – the notes

Ysidro had left on the kitchen table last night, as well as she could given that the few handwritten jottings on them were in Spanish (*probably sixteenth-century Spanish at that*). Maps of La Santé prison, close to where the Duponts lived (they had probably reached Bordeaux with Ellen by this time . . .), drawn with a neatness that reminded Lydia that Ysidro himself had worked as a spy. A few 'X's marked junctions of corridors and doorways – *guard posts?*

The fact that the vampire had managed to make any investigation at all last night in that debilitated state spoke volumes for his determination to get Jamie out of there as soon as possible. Lydia had to fight not to leap to her feet, to pace the kitchen – the whole of the house – like a caged animal. Not to send another message to Greuze and go out herself, to see the prison at least, to do *something* instead of simply sitting here, waiting for nightfall.

She'd done practicum in charity clinics. She could imagine what a prison infirmary would be by comparison. Even the hospital had been bad, with poor M'sieu Lecoq coughing his lungs out two beds over . . .

Stop it. Ysidro knows what he's doing. You can do nothing until he's well enough . . .

She closed her eyes, rested her forehead on her fist. *I should walk out of this house, have nothing to do with him ever again.*

She knew she'd be killed within a day. And Jamie within another, leaving their tiny daughter alone.

I was the one who called him to Paris, she reminded herself. *Knowing what he is.*

Darkness fell.

Lydia made a third tour of the house, but she assumed that Ysidro had left in secret so as not to remind her that he would hunt again. He was always very careful, she had observed, not to let either her or Jamie ever see him kill. *Was that something he'd learned?* That if one's human employees were ever brought face to face with that starkest fact of vampire existence – that they must kill in order to retain the mental powers they held over human perceptions – one could never speak to them again?

She whispered a prayer for Ellen's safe arrival in Bordeaux – and safe departure, in three days' time, on the *Bolingbroke* – and realized she hadn't eaten all day. Returning to the kitchen she wondered if she'd have any success with scrambling an egg, a skill which had eluded her in her student days at Oxford. She managed to make tea at the gas-ring, although the result was dire – how did Mrs Grimes manage to get it to taste so good? She settled at the table again, looking over the maps: one section of the wheel-spoke blocks of cells was marked in kitchen pencil. But even on the most cursory sketch there seemed to be a frightful number of walls and corridors to get through, and if Jamie were badly ill how on earth were they to get him out?

We need to . . .

She came to, suddenly aware that she'd been asleep.

'Mistress.'

Had she actually heard Ysidro's voice? Was that what had wakened her?

'Mistress!'

He called in a hoarse whisper and she stumbled to her feet, wondering how she had even heard him. Somewhere in the blackness outside . . .

He'd never have called to me unless he were in trouble . . .

She ran to the kitchen door, shot back the bolts—

Don't be an idiot!

Her hand froze on the handle as he called out to her again – a distance away, somewhere in the little alley that ran behind the house and around to rejoin the Avenue Junot further down the hill.

The hair prickled on her head.

He has other ways to get into the house. Why call out for me?

She glanced at the windows. The shutters in the kitchen were stout and solid, not louvered like those that looked down on to the street in the front. An oil-lamp burned on the table and she had happened to cross behind it, not between it and the window, when she'd risen.

She bolted the door, returned to her chair the same way.

Urgent, desperate, the harsh hushed voice called, 'Mistress, help me!'

If he's killed Jamie will die, and I will die.

Or is this just another version of 'William Johnson'?

She folded her hands hard together, sat like a statue in the wavering light.

He did not call again.

He came into the kitchen shortly before three in the morning, still looking, as the anatomy lecturer at the Radcliffe had been fond of saying, like death on a soda-cracker. ''Twas not I,' he said, when she told him of the voice. 'Hyacinthe, for a guess, or Elysée if she still seeks you as hostage. Either can call out to your thoughts from a great distance, and both are adept at such tricks. I had hoped to go to the Hôtel Batoux again, to see if I can get more from Elysée than lies. Yet at the moment I think my nights better spent treading the halls of La Santé and whispering to the dreams of the guards there. James is not well, the inflammation of his lungs devouring him with fever.'

'I knew it!'

'Hyacinthe has been there, though she took care not to cross my path. Doing the same as I, I think,' he added, as Lydia looked across the table at him in alarm. She recalled the form glimpsed in the darkness outside Lariboisière wearing Camille Batoux's striped jacket, which had clearly taken her fancy. 'Finding out where James is situated, and informing herself of where the guards are stationed, and of how many doors she must needs get through. Her task is easier than ours, I fear. For we will need to bring him away with us, whereas her goal is but to kill him where he lies. Fear not, Mistress,' he added, looking down into her eyes. 'We shall take the trick. But I think the hour has come to instruct your servant Greuze in the role he is to play.'

'He isn't my servant,' said Lydia quickly.

'Indeed? Nine days now you have paid him a wage that outstrips his earnings with his taxicab, with the understanding that he kick his heels at a café in Montparnasse awaiting your pleasure. Tell me how this differs from the occupation of your Aunt Isobel's footmen, save that M'sieu Greuze is required neither to wait tables nor yet wear a powdered wig. Wilt have tea, lady?' He reached for the pot.

She shook her head. 'It's cold – and it wasn't so very drinkable warm.'

For just a moment, when he smiled, his ravaged face turned human.

'I – I don't want M'sieu Greuze hurt.'

'And I don't want you hurt, lady. Nor our James. Had I a sennight to recover my full faculties ere attempting a jail deliverance I might accomplish such a feat with but the two of us. Had I a sennight, or half a month, to court and charm and secure the services of some worthless stranger over whose possible death neither you nor I would shed a tear, I would do so. But I do not.' He held up a finger against her hot protest that she would shed more than a tear, stranger or no.

'I think we must make our move the night after tomorrow and for that we will need this man Greuze's help. You must needs follow my instructions to the smallest detail, and so must he, and e'en so I cannot guarantee your safety, nor indeed my own.'

'You would do that for Jamie?'

'I would do it for you, Mistress.' He took up her hand and brushed the fingers with cold lips. 'And yes, I would undertake such an endeavor for James's sake. I have a constitutional dislike of having my servants killed.'

Lydia remembered Margaret Potton; Ysidro had – as he had described it – courted and charmed her and secured her services five years ago, when he had decided Lydia needed an escort on her journey to Constantinople.

'Do you really?'

His eyes grew remote, like crystals of sulfur. 'I do.'

There were six other men in the infirmary. Between bouts of fever that left him feeling as if flesh and bone had been put through a mangle, Asher was aware that word had gone around among them that he was a German spy. One of them had tried to kill him by holding a pillow over his face, and when he had been dragged away had yelled that it was any good Frenchman's duty to do the same. At some later point – day and night had long since ceased to have any meaning – Asher heard a man in the corridor say that Liège had fallen. That the Germans were on their way to Brussels and, after that, to Paris.

And some time after that – though it may have been a dream, it was difficult to tell – he thought he saw a woman's face appear

at the barred window of the door. The vampire Hyacinthe, beautiful as twilight and stars. His bed was nearest the door and he
could see her quite clearly. For an instant he thought that there
was a livid burn on one side of her face, and remembered striking
her – when? In one of those dreams of darkness inside a church?

Striking her with a silver chain wrapped around his hand?

Someone spoke in the corridor, and she was gone.

Why is the window barred?

He drifted back into dreams.

Dreams of Simon, sitting by the window in a corner of his
lodgings. Gray rain pittered on the thick tiny panes and leaked
around the frame. Candles burned on the mantelpiece and on the
table amid his books. His servant Tim paced the room, long-
legged and long-nosed like a stork, gesturing with his long arms.
'I can't let you do this, my lord!'

'I won't go against him.' Simon would not meet his eyes. 'He
saved my life—'

'God's teeth, my lord, we're not talkin' of your life! We're
talkin' of your soul!'

Simon said nothing.

Tim lunged to his side, dropped to his knees, took his hand,
long and thin and white, in his own big red ones. 'My lord,' he
said. 'My lord. I swore I'd serve you – more, I swore I'd care
for you. Without what you did for us when my brother was taken
for plotting against the bastard Elizabeth I'd have been killed
with him, and my Ann also. I'll never forget that you went and
found our Maggie where we'd hid her. If you hadn't got her out
of that cellar she would have starved, or been eaten by the rats.
How could I forget? How could I owe you anything less than
the whole of my heart? I can't let you do this.' And he shook
him, as if by doing so he could make him understand.

'You're not *letting* me do anything, my dear Timothy.' And
Asher heard, in Simon's voice, the echo of the frozen calm that
characterized the vampire he himself knew. 'I have made my
choice. I will not kill Emeric Jambicque. I encouraged men to
kill de Colle – I told them where he lay. But Constantine is right.
He—'

'He's bewitched you,' retorted Tim. 'Him and his cozening
words, and his pretty metaphysical arguments – faugh! Like them

pamphlets he writes, twisting up what a man believes and bringing up all them pagans and Greeks. It suited his purposes to get you away from the heretics and it suits his purposes to make you obey him! To keep you under his hand, though it puts your soul back into Hell!'

And when Simon looked away the servant tugged on his hand, like an importunate child.

'It's like that tale you told me, about what's-his-name the musician that went to Hell to fetch back his wife. And the Devil told him he could take her, so long as he didn't look back behind him . . . This Angelus, this master – who isn't even really your master! – he's calling to you to look back behind you, sir! To turn your eyes away from the light. And if you look back, it's you who'll fall back into the pit! And yet he'll do it . . . for his own ends. My lord, that's not the act of a friend!'

'Stop it.'

'I can't stop it!' Tears stood out in the taller man's eyes. 'And I can't not speak, sir. I love you, sir. I don't care what you've done nor what you are nor what they say. And I hope when I die I'll win through to Heaven . . . and 'twould break my heart, my lord – yes, and Ann's, and Maggie's too, after all the good you've done for us – if we should be in the bosom of God, and look down and see you trapped in flames, trapped for eternity, not for what you done but for what you wouldn't do because you let this Angelus command you. This man Emeric's a heretic, my lord! He deserves to die for that, and for whatever other reason Father Jeffrey and the Holy Father know of . . . You don't know what that might be! It's a trial of your faith, my lord . . .'

Simon turned his wrist, breaking effortlessly from his henchman's hold. 'Leave me.'

'Not to go and run back into Hell, like a spooked horse into a burnin' barn, sir! I won't—'

'Leave me.'

Tim shook his head, reached for his master's hand again. But Simon was gone.

Why do you show me this?

Asher turned, searching the shadows – of the room where it seemed to him that he stood? Of the ward where he lay –

where he thought now that he was standing beside the bed in which his own body twitched and whispered in fever, and vampire eyes gleamed reflectively through the barred window in the door? Of his house back in Oxford, the nursery where his tiny daughter had climbed, with infinite care, from her own cot to sit on the window-seat, looking out into the deeps of the night?

Why do you want me to know this?

Don Simon walked for a long time, through the streets of Paris.

Partaking of the vampire's memories, feeling behind them the shadow of another's thought, Asher saw what he saw: the close-crowding walls of half-timbered houses, held together only with caked soot and filth; the twisting alleyways of the market district, Rag-Dealer's Street, Coal-Heaver's Street, the Street of Mutterings. Saw the poor who slept in doorways, shivering in the spring cold; they appeared as shape and heat and scent in the darkness, as vampires saw them. Every window was shuttered tight, every house a fortress. Rats picked at the garbage in the streets. Cats stalked them with careful steps, taking care not to get themselves into a place where they could be swarmed. In one place Simon, cognizant of such things, glimpsed the woman Gabrielle Batoux standing in the stinking black mud of a street, eyes half-shut like a woman in a dream, hands stretched out to one of those tall closed-up houses.

As Asher watched – as Simon watched – a man opened the door of the ground-floor shop, emerged like a sleepwalker, leaving the door open behind him and treading across the black goo underfoot as if he did not feel it between his bare toes. Gazing only at the woman before him, shining like a goddess in the dark.

Simon walked to the top of Montmartre and stood long beside the flat gray stones where he had lain waiting for the dawn. Thin rain sleeked his ivory silk hair into the illusion of its former darkness. Paris slumbered below him like a bed of quenched coal, tight within its medieval ramparts, but from the towers of a thousand convents and monasteries rose the soft chiming of bells, a thousand voices calling the holy to night-offices in churches where the holy water was ice in the fonts.

After that he went to a house on the Rue de la Fontaine and stood outside a shuttered window, looking through a crack. The only light inside came from a range of charcoal burners near another window of the long chamber inside, the glow only enough to pick out the gleam of vampire eyes. A coal flared, caught the shape of the vampire alchemist Emeric Jambicque's hooked nose and tufted orange eyebrows as he brought up a wire cage containing half a dozen huge rats. This he set on the table, beside a vat with a faintly rotten stink and eye-burning vapors which drowned even the stench of the streets. The tall vampire grinned, took from his pocket a small sand-glass. He lifted the top from the rat cage, plunged one hand in, his grin widening as the animal he seized writhed, clawed, and bit his wrist until blood splattered down. He held it up for a moment as if enjoying its terrified efforts to escape, then turned the sand-glass and dropped the frantic animal into the vat.

Even outside the shuttered window Simon could hear – Asher could hear – the rat screaming: screaming and screaming as the sulfuric acid (though Don Simon identified it as vitriol) ate away its flesh. Emeric stood looking from the sand-glass to the vat, absent-mindedly wrapping a rag around his bitten arm, observing as the shrieks stopped. After a few minutes he took up a pair of tongs, poked, and stirred.

Simon turned away.

TWENTY-TWO

'Will you help me?'
        Stanislas Greuze studied for a moment the paper Lydia had given him. Morning sunlight buttered the Avenue du Maine, but there was little traffic; the Café de l'Arc et de la Hache was nearly empty. A few cab-drivers loitered, reading newspapers, and its proprietor had settled down himself with the most recent edition of *Le Monde*.

'MASS EXECUTIONS OF CIVILIANS IN BELGIUM'. (Lydia had seen the headlines before leaving Ysidro's house on

Montmartre. Without her glasses, they could have been announcing a Chinese invasion for all she knew.)

'FRENCH AND BRITISH FORCES RETREAT TO NAMUR'.

The Germans were coming.

The cab-driver's dark eyes flicked from the instructions to Lydia's face. 'Who is he?' he asked. 'This Spaniard you had me bring to Rue Caulaincourt Monday night? Who is the man in the hospital, the one you call your husband? The night I sat beside him he whispered of strange things.'

'He *is* my husband.'

'I dreamed about your Spaniard last night, madame. Dreamed I was at the rally last year in Montparnasse, when Jean Jaurès spoke against conscription and pleaded for peace. Telling us – and he spoke the truth! – that we must not be lured into a war. That war is how the rich trick our minds, distract us with words like patriotism and righteous hate, to keep us from demanding justice. He spoke of the world as it could be, with working men and women striving for their rights. Telling us that we must stand against those who would send us forth with the tactics of Napoleon against the weapons of Krupp. And your Spaniard was there in the front row, a few steps from me.'

Lydia looked aside, unable to answer, but she felt her face burn. Hating Ysidro. Hating herself.

'Only he wasn't, you know.' Greuze set the paper down. 'I have a good memory for faces, and your Spaniard has one that's hard to mistake. In my dream I saw Jaurès embrace him, Jaurès whom the so-called patriots murdered the day the war was declared, Jaurès who was I think this country's last hope for peace and justice for the working-men who're dying by the thousands now . . . That husband of yours was there, too. In my dream. So who is he? Who are they?'

He was silent for a few moments, hands folded, his ugly, hook-nosed face still. 'Who are you?'

'There is . . .' she began, and stopped. Vampires killed those who told their secrets. Those who knew them.

Ysidro would probably protect her, but whatever he said about not wanting to have his servants killed, she guessed it wouldn't save this man's life.

'There is a weapon,' she said, picking her words carefully.

'Not exactly a weapon, but it can be used by the Germans against us – against Britain, against France, against the Belgians . . . I know about it because my government wanted to get hold of it to use it against them. My husband and I – and Don Simon – are trying to keep it out of *everybody's* hands, because whoever gets hold of it will abuse it. We know this. I can't . . . I can't explain more fully than that, and I can't explain why I can't explain. And you have no reason whatsoever to trust me, or to believe what I say.'

'This thing – this weapon that isn't a weapon . . . it's whatever it is that lets your friend get into my dreams?' The edge of anger still glinted in his voice. 'Isn't it?'

Well, he should be angry, she thought.

'In part, yes.'

'You tell your friend: don't ever do that to me again.'

'I will. I'm sorry.' She looked up into his face. Across the avenue a man and two boys were nailing up boards over the windows of a tobacconist's shop. Though it was mid-morning the shops on either side were still shuttered as well.

The Germans were coming.

'He was wrong,' she said at length. 'He should not have done that. He should have trusted . . . I'd like to think that if he'd told me what he intended I'd have asked him not to, but we have very little time. My husband spied for Britain before we were married. That's how he knows about these . . . these people, who can do this. He quarreled with the Department and quit, years ago. The man who accused him is working for the Germans; they can kill him more easily inside the prison than they could in the hospital, where Don Simon or I could be with him at night when the danger was greatest. We have to get him out. Get him away.'

Greuze's fingers brushed the paper Lydia had handed him, along with a stack of silver five-franc coins. 'So I see.'

His gaze rested on her face again. Calculating the cost of that dream, she wondered: the dream and its implications against . . . what? A half-dozen encounters with her? Whatever it was Jamie had whispered in his delirium while Greuze sat at his side last – Monday? Tuesday? She couldn't recall. She prayed she hadn't done anything egregiously stupid or conceited while he'd been with her, but the days blurred together with exhaustion and dread, and there was much that she simply couldn't remember.

He put the money in his jacket pocket, glanced down at the instructions, and asked, 'Can you drive a car?'

Lydia took a deep breath, refrained from bursting into tears, and said, 'Yes. Not well . . .'

'There's no traffic these days, you should be all right. Your Spaniard says here he's rented a car for us, a Crossley saloon. That's a big car. You familiar with the streets in the fourteenth, madame? No?' He finished his coffee. 'You better come with me, then.'

For the next two hours Lydia piloted Greuze's cab through the half-empty streets of Montparnasse. Fortunately the area between the Place d'Italie and the cemetery was fairly straightforward (*I will never permit Mrs Flasket to speak ill of Baron Haussmann again!*), without the confusing tangle of older streets that one found closer to the river, and with a little practice Lydia could circle the prison in a matter of minutes. 'We don't know what's going to happen once we get past the guards,' remarked the cab-driver as Lydia swung around the bronze lion in the Place Denfert-Rochereau and turned up the Boulevard Saint-Jacques. 'It might be safer if you just wait in the Rue de la Santé from the beginning.'

Since Lydia knew that she'd be safer in a moving vehicle than sitting still where Hyacinthe – or one of the other members of the Paris nest, or Jürgen Schaumm – could come upon her in the fifteen to twenty minutes Ysidro had calculated it would take him to bring a bedridden and possibly unconscious prisoner to the gates, she only said, 'I think Don Simon is afraid that the car will be identified and traced if it stands too long.' The cab – a powerful little Renault – was harder to drive than her Aunt Isobel's Detroit Electric, but she suspected that even more strength would be required to maneuver the Crossley. The thought of tonight made her heart pound; when she returned to Montmartre, slipping into the house through the cellar as she had exited it, she lay down in the little bedroom she had taken, but could not sleep.

Nowhere, she understood, was safe now.

On Wednesday night Ysidro had taken her into the tunnels,

and shown her not only the one leading to her former safe house, but another that debouched on to waste ground behind the Café Arabie on the Rue Gabrielle. The light of Ysidro's lantern barely illuminated the gallery in which they stood, which was surprisingly high – as indeed was the ceiling of the cellar behind them, which Lydia realized had itself been part of the gallery at one time – and marked by a line of square stone pillars down its center, the living rock of the hill.

'These mine tunnels extend for miles,' the vampire said. 'One can go to the Cemetery of Montmartre and the Buttes-Chaumont. They reach beyond the Cemetery of Père-Lachaise, and have a hundred entrances into the Métro tunnels, and at various places about Montmartre itself. Be careful if you explore them.' From his pocket he took a hunk of white chalk, which he pressed into her hand. 'Though 'tis safe enough in the daytime. And take care you mark your way secretly, with signs not readily perceived by those who do not know where and how to look.'

'Do the others in the Paris nest know about this?' Her footfalls whispered away down the side drifts and passageways whose entrances were barely more than hints of deeper darkness. Of Ysidro's there was not even a shadow.

It was in these mines, she guessed, rather than in the house above, that Ysidro had concealed his coffin. *The cold down here, and the damp, can't be good for him in his condition . . .*

She wanted to slap herself for the concern she felt. The unwillingness of the various members of the Paris nest to hide down here suddenly became much more understandable, Facinum or no Facinum.

'Does Hyacinthe know?'

'She knows they exist. Hence the stoutness of the door that leads into the cellar. To the best of my knowledge she has never devoted her time to the arts of lock-picking.'

They had reached the entrance of a smaller gallery, which at one time had been fenced across with a desiccated wooden barrier. Lydia wondered at the optimism of whatever parents had thought such a thing would keep inquiring children from further exploration – such a fence wouldn't stop her daughter Miranda for so much as a moment. Old chalk-scribbles contributed by children of all ages enlivened the walls at varying heights. The light of

Ysidro's lantern fell on a childish scrawl of an arrow and the words 'Rue Gabrielle'.

'When you ascend at the end of this passageway, listen through the door to make sure the yard behind the café is deserted. The ground there used to be someone's garden. I think Communards used that entrance during the siege in seventy-one. If Elysée begot fledglings for their brains rather than their looks there would probably be someone in the Paris nest who knew Montmartre in those days, but in that respect we are safe. The vampires who remained in Paris to hunt during the days of the Commune are gone, and 'tis not a neighborhood she would have deigned to enter since.'

He'd taken her hand then and led her back to the cellar, and so up to the kitchen above. They had played cards for a time, and talked: she of her girlhood as an heiress, he of the Paris of his memories. ''Twas twice as large as London, and a thousand times more sophisticated. My servant was forever getting himself lost, and swore he learned of vices then that he'd never heard of . . .'

'Was your servant Spanish?'

'English.' A flicker of something – memory? – moved in the back of his yellow eyes. He looked away from her and drew more closely about his shoulders the Persian shawl he'd brought down from one of the attics. Though the night was warm he shivered, exhausted still from their attempt on the Hôtel Batoux two nights before. 'Timothy Quodling. A simple-hearted rascal.'

'I thought the English back then hated the Spanish.'

'Tim was of the True Faith.'

'Was that why you didn't return to Paris?' asked Lydia after a time. 'Because of the Protestant vampires?' She remembered what Jamie had told her, of his confused visions of the war among the vampires of Paris and their living followers.

'*Dios*, no. After I left in the spring of 1603 there was naught here that I wished to see badly enough to justify the risk of enlisting a traveling companion. By the time of my departure there were no Protestant vampires left in Paris.'

He had been worn out, and to Lydia's distress had very soon retired to curl up in a chair beside the fire in the salon like an exhausted old man, staring into the flames. Lydia herself, sitting in the other chair, had dozed, and when she'd wakened an hour before dawn it had been to find him gone.

To his damp coffin underground, she thought, with a pang.

STOP IT! He deserves no pity. He KILLED someone tonight.

One of the prisoners in La Santé? That's where he was earlier, finding Jamie, telling the guards to be extra watchful. Surely there are murderers there, rapists, two-legged beasts who deserve to die . . .

Or would he say that the guards there keep too close an eye on the prisoners for one to be found drained of blood?

She'd slept again, and had dreamed – or thought she'd dreamed – of those dark grids of passageways and galleries beneath the hill of Montmartre. And instead of finding them dank and fearsome, in her dream she'd felt a child's delight, such as she'd felt in the big old country houses of various branches of her mother's family, houses shut up and draped in holland covers, cobwebs, and dust. She'd run through them, exploring and finding wonders, and in her dreams of the old mines she could see in the darkness, and ran through that spooky world of endless night, marveling at its ancient complexity.

When she woke – early, with the first sunlight of Saturday streaming in white needles through the slits of the shutters – she bathed and washed her hair and put on her usual careful application of rice-powder and mascaro and the tiniest touch of rouge (even if she faced no more than a day of reading and prowling the house and wondering if Jamie were safe, if he'd made it through the night . . .), and the thought of the tunnels didn't leave her. Yesterday's inactivity had left her restless and aching, and the prospect of another endless summer day like the one before appalled her.

Besides, she thought, *I should find out where he's got his coffin down there, in case I need to know.*

So with the fascination of her dream still lively in her heart she located a compass in one of the salon's desk drawers, took Ysidro's chalk, the dark-lantern, and a map of Paris, and set off exploring. She took care, as Ysidro had cautioned her, to make her guiding marks well below eye level, and in places not obvious to the casual glance. (*Who down here is going to be glancing*

CASUALLY?) Those passageways that smelled of sewage she avoided, and shrank, shuddering, from those where she heard rats moving about in the blackness. Out of an obscure uneasiness she kept her dark-lantern closed down to the smallest possible slit, and stopped, often, to shut it entirely (rats notwithstanding) and listen.

In the silence she felt the far-off vibration of the Métro Line A, and calculated she must be somewhere near the Cemetery of Montmartre at the foot of the hill. If she made her way to her right . . .

Somewhere near her, echoes carried the whisper of voices.

And the thin edge of light bobbed into view on the black corners of the passageway ahead.

Lydia double-checked her own shut lantern-slide, wrapped her skirt tight around her legs, and edged forward. *It's broad daylight overhead, it can't actually be . . .*

'Where is she?' Spectacle lenses flashed in the reflected gleam of another dark-lantern.

DAMN it! Lydia hastily pulled hers off.

But now I can't see who it is.

But she knew.

The vile little man with the spectacles, Ysidro had called him.

A lightning peek around the corner confirmed it. In addition to two rounds of flashing glass she could easily make out the striped jacket, beige and black, whose matching skirt she'd seen splattered with blood in the apartment of Camille Batoux. The jacket she'd glimpsed – or thought she'd glimpsed – in the court-yard of the Lariboisière Hospital . . .

Hyacinthe.

And Jürgen Schaumm.

'She'll be here.' Hyacinthe's voice was dreamy, but its hard edge spoke of strain. 'Don Simon would never take a house that didn't open into the mines.'

If she's taken anything like what Ysidro took the other day, to remain awake into the morning . . .

'It's only a matter of time before the woman finds a way past Elysée's guards . . .'

'Shut up and let me concentrate.' The vampire's rough French had a sing-song note to it. 'I can hardly hear a thing, underground.'

In the dim halo of Schaumm's lantern-light Lydia could make out Hyacinthe's curly mane of dark hair, an impression of skin like bronze silk, and a dark area – a bruise? A burn? – on the side of her face. She was taller than the German, who besides being short was a little stooped. His black hair gleamed greasily, and a sling held one arm close to his body. *As I thought: M'sieu de Saint-Vrain's bullet only grazed him.*

'I know she's been twice to the church,' persisted Schaumm. 'Asher has to have told her. If she finds some way to put chloral hydrate into the guards' coffee before we can . . . You know they've got to be making coffee on their watch, or sending out for ginger pop.'

'We'll get her, little man.' The smile in Hyacinthe's voice masked – Lydia was certain – an overwhelming desire to make a meal of him and leave his body here for the rats. 'Nobody's going to get the Facinum away from us. I'll swear it's one of the relics in the chapel. And I'll take oath that dumb bitch Elysée doesn't even know for sure it exists. I bet she thinks the power's in the house itself. You should hear the stories she comes up with to explain why they must come to her there, to be changed. She took me in her dressing-room. The whole place reeked of Houbigant perfume, like a whorehouse. Serge, Augustin, Évariste she did in her bedroom there . . . I know she had hell's own time getting Baptiste into the place to do the deed . . . no surprise, in *that* neighborhood! Why go to that trouble, when she's got a damn palace out in Passy? Believe me, she thinks it's the house.'

She closed her eyes, her nostrils flaring a little, as if sniffing for the smell of Lydia's dusting-powder, Lydia's blood. 'Now you do your part, little man, and let me do mine.'

'How do you know they're even in this district? She didn't take your bait last night, when you called out.'

'They're here. Somewhere. She'll come . . .'

Under the ground or not, thought Lydia, *they'll hear me if I move.* This close, Hyacinthe – Lydia was virtually certain – would detect the rustle of her petticoats, the pat of her slippers.

It's only a matter of time before she smells the hot paraffin in the lamp.

A matter of time.

And the time one waits in the Métro station is about . . .

Far off, the shuddering rumble of the train came again along Line A, and the moment it started Lydia retreated soundlessly, hoping she hadn't turned and gotten herself disoriented and away from her last mark. Under cover of the train's passage she slipped away into the dark, put her glasses back on, flashed the lantern close to the floor, and found the little white squiggle that could so easily have been a boot-scratch, pointing back in the direction from which she'd come.

TWENTY-THREE

T hey took the Boulevard de Sébastopol to the Pont au Change when the final slits of daylight had faded in the wooden shutters. Stanislas Greuze was of the opinion that Lydia didn't need to deal with the tangled ways of the third and fourth arrondissements.

But turning on to the wide avenue from the Rue de Paradis the dark anonymous Crossley saloon was halted by a stream of trucks, motor cars, and even wagons like that of Greuze's neighbor's cousin Dupont, whose faithful horses had up until last week been hauling groceries or coal.

Now they hauled men.

'From Liège,' said Greuze quietly. He twisted in the driver's seat and cursed to see a number of cars pulled up behind them, boxing him in. 'They're coming in at the Gare du Nord. Let me drive. I'll see if I can get us out of here and around on the Rue Richer.'

Lydia got out of the car. There was a snarl-up where traffic from the Boulevard de Magenta came on to the larger thoroughfare. The line of makeshift ambulances was stopped in the blue-white glare of the electric street lighting of which Paris was so proud. By it she could see into the back of the nearest truck, where a dozen men lay on stretchers and benches, their bright red-and-blue uniforms indescribably filthy and soaked with gore.

Tourniquets stanched bleeding on limbs that Lydia could see at once were shattered beyond hope of anything but amputation.

Makeshift dressings oozed blood like a signal of the horrors they hid. The blood looked black in the cold glare. One man's face seemed to be held together only by a dirty strapwork of bandages, his eyes staring – conscious hell-pits of agony – from a gleaming mask of grime. Vomit, piss, feces mixed with the blood in the truck-bed and the stink nearly drowned out the stench of bodies and uniforms weeks unwashed. The sound of them was almost worse than the smell: individual sobs and curses and screams with each jolt of the truck, rising like stones above a constant flow of muffled animal wails.

Lydia had worked the night clinic in the East End. She knew the stinks of mortal flesh. But the sound was horrifying in the way it filled the night, the way it hung above the boulevard all the way back to the station. Blended notes of agony. Thousands of men trying not to scream, unmanned with terror and pain, and most not succeeding. Men who'd held their wives' hands at the train station only weeks ago, boys crying for the mothers they'd kissed goodbye. A woman got out of the cab of a stopped truck and grabbed a canteen hanging on its side, clambered up into the back, and bent over this man or that, giving them sips. Another woman leaned from the window of the other side of the cab and yelled in very un-genteel accents, what the hell was the hold-up, goddammit?

From another truck someone yelled back, 'École Militaire! Saint-Antoine's can't take more, they say.'

Another truck lurched to a halt and Lydia automatically assessed the men in the back. Even from a distance of fifteen feet she could see that several were dead, that two others wouldn't make it. *Save those you can save . . .*

'Machine guns.' Greuze came to her side on the pavement, a dark bulk in darkness. 'Damn imbeciles think what worked for Napoleon is going to work now.'

She took a step toward the woman with the canteen, climbing down from the back of the truck with a look on her face that Lydia knew – knew because it was her own. Fury, pain, helplessness. Hatred not against the enemy, but against the god of war himself.

'They need help,' Lydia had never liked practice in the night clinic and had never cared for the actual binding-up-wounds part of medicine. Heart and soul, she was a researcher, fascinated by the minute inner intricacies of kidneys, glands, nerves: the secret chemistry of brain and blood and tissue. But the impact of that ruin and horror, the sight of what shrapnel and machine guns could do, smote her with the understanding that every pair of kidneys, every tangle of nerve endings, every pair of lungs, every heart, every brain, belonged to a man who loved as Jamie loved, who dreamed as Jamie and Lydia and Stanislas Greuze the cab-driver and Ysidro the vampire dreamed . . .

'They're going to need every doctor,' she said, 'every surgeon. Everyone who can work an operating room without fainting.'

Greuze looked sidelong at her, dark eyes filled with pity, and Lydia, as if waking from a dream, glanced back to see Don Simon Ysidro in the back of the car.

Jamie.

They need every pair of hands . . . but Jamie needs ME. ME, because I know about those who hunt the night. Mosquito-bite drips, she thought, compared to this shocking Acheron of blood and pain.

And it has to be tonight. The effort Hyacinthe had made to call Lydia to her in the daylight hours, while Ysidro slept, meant that Hyacinthe herself would be as debilitated as Ysidro was, weakened and shaky from the effects of Emeric the alchemist's potions. But that didn't mean Hyacinthe couldn't find a way to dose the guards at La Santé and simply walk past them, and each night that James Asher lay in the prison infirmary doubled the chances that he wouldn't see morning.

Someone had evidently got the traffic moving again. With a hideous grinding of gears the trucks in front of her jolted forward, and men screamed or wept or shouted weakly over and over, 'Stop it! Stop it!' The river of pain began to flow again, toward whatever spaces in Paris would take them.

Every organ and blood vessel in Lydia's body seemed to wrench her toward the men in the trucks. *Dear GOD, how many of them are there?*

But she climbed back into the car, and looked over her shoulder as Greuze steered it away.

Asher guessed that he was dying. It took conscious effort now to breathe. If he slept, he sensed dimly that he would simply stop. The weight of exhaustion seemed to pull him into darkness, and he had trouble recalling why it was that he wanted to gather his strength to fight his way out of it again. The news that his parents were dead had come on him with a kind of cold shock; he had felt almost nothing when he'd gotten the letter from his Uncle Theobald about the accident. His father he barely knew. His mother he had loved dearly, but had never been in a moment's doubt that time spent reading to him, walking with him in the fields around Wychford, teaching him to play the piano, and playing those lively duets that had been the joys of his afternoons, was all time carefully husbanded, orchestrated around parish duties and the Reverend Arthur Asher's need for his wife's approval and company. In the weeks following their deaths Asher sometimes felt as if both his hands had been chopped off: painlessly, but with incalculable, irreparable changes to the whole of his life. When scarlet fever had gone through the school he had gone down with it almost casually, as if it were expected of him.

They're dead, so I should die too.

But I didn't die, he thought, *did I?*

Didn't I go to Africa?

To China?

To Prague?

Somewhere in the deeps of the darkness he heard screaming again, the screaming of a man trapped in sleep, locked in a coffin. Heard the sound of screaming, the thick roar of flame, and smelled the smell of burning flesh.

Incense.

When the chaplain came to give Danny Barrow the last rites, in the bed next to mine, they burned incense . . .

Simon opened the door of Father Jeffrey's house, climbed the stairs. He moved slowly and stopped halfway up, as if he would turn back. Asher knew, without knowing how, that the vampire had stood for a long time in the dark of the Rue de l'Épée de Bois before entering. That he had gone away twice, and twice returned, cold and shaky with the hunger that the Undead cannot describe to the living, almost sick with it. The narrow slot of the Rue de l'Épée de Bois was nearly pitch-black. Even the threads of candle flame that had earlier burned at the joints of shutters were quenched now, the fires in every kitchen in Paris banked for the night.

Rats scurried across roofs. A cat's eyes winked in the dark. The house where Father Jeffrey stayed had been locked, but Simon had already learned the skill of whispering to the dreams of the scullery boy who slept in the kitchen, and the youth unbarred the door to him without waking. The door to Father Jeffrey's room on the third floor was unbolted.

Though the mud in the street outside had been rimmed with spring ice and the priest's breath made a cloud in the light of the room's candles, still Father Jeffrey was stripped to a single garment, a coarse shirt of goat-hair whose edges and creases, driven into his flesh by his outer clothing during the day, had rubbed swaths of scarlet in his wrists and neck. He knelt before the crucifix, white hair damp with sweat, rocking a little on his knees, and did not raise his head when Simon entered the room. Only when the vampire spoke did he look up, and there was no surprise in his face.

'Jeffrey . . .'

'Simon.' Father Jeffrey got to his feet, staggered a little with cramp, and went to take the vampire's cold hands.

Simon backed from him, shaking his head. 'I need help,' he said, 'I need counsel.' He cast a look around the dark chamber. The bed, with its single threadbare cover cast back, showed, instead of a mattress, a couple of planks of wood with a thin strip raised in the middle like a cleat, that its occupant might not rest too easy nor seek to linger there when the world had need of his service. 'Cardinal Montevierde?'

'He's back at the palace. But he is most pleased with you.'

Simon, who had been about to speak again, fell back a step, nonplussed. 'Pleased with me?'

Father Jeffrey caught the vampire's hands, gripped them. 'It was well done.' And, when Simon only looked at him uncomprehendingly, 'Jambicque the alchemist. We heard of it this morning when his body was found. In the streets they're saying the Devil came to claim his own, but I knew it had to be you. For years we've been trying—'

'I did nothing.' Simon stared at him in shock. ''Twas what I came tonight to tell you. That I cannot . . .'

'It must have been you.' Jeffrey shifted his hands to his friend's narrow shoulders, studied his face with concern. 'Or men you instructed, as you set them on to kill de Colle. For years now we've been trying to find where he made his lair. Who but you could have learned of the house on Montparnasse, of the well which had been dug down into the old mines beneath it? Who but you could have traced the mine tunnels that went to the chamber where his coffin lay?'

'I found the place, yes,' whispered Simon. 'But enter it I did not. Nor did I stir others to the deed. I swore I would not break the peace among the Undead of this city. I couldn't—'

'I told you before, Simon,' said the priest gently. 'Cardinal Montevierde absolved you of any vow given to the damned. Such promises cannot hold back a Christian soul from salvation. And in truth,' he added with a slight smile, 'you can't be said to have broken that vow in the case of the heretic de Colle, now, can you? If you spoke of it . . .'

'I spoke of it to none. Nor do I think anyone followed me—'

He broke off, his eyes widening, even as Father Jeffrey went on, 'I think there is no need for either of us to speak to Cardinal Montevierde of what you tell me.' He gave Simon's shoulder a gentle shake. 'The simple truth is that Jambicque is dead. Does it matter whose hand struck the actual blow? You have brought about the death of an enemy of the Faith, Simon. Be assured, the Cardinal will be grateful. Sometimes God extends a helping hand to those willing to be guided.'

Simon shook his head, horrified by a truth that only he could see. '*No* . . .'

And was gone.

The man in the next bed cried out, 'Don't do it!'

Asher turned his head, shivering with cold but aware at least that he was awake. He still breathed, though it was like a knife grinding into his ribs. *The school infirmary* . . .

No. Not the hospital either – Saint-Antoine. Lydia had been there, and Don Simon Ysidro . . .

This room he didn't recognize. By the grimy glow of dimmed gaslights he could tell it was an infirmary of some kind, and that it probably wasn't in a regular hospital. The window in the door

was barred. The stink of vomit and rats, of bedpans unemptied
and dressings long unchanged. Somewhere close, the sick-sweet
stink of gangrene, unmistakable. Bars on the outside window as
well. The man in the bed next to his, a burly fair man whose
hair had all been cropped off, was chained in his bed with a
leg-iron fastened around the bed-frame.

The man, jerked from sleep, had sat up shaking, staring around
him wild-eyed. Asher moved a little, confused and weaker than
he'd felt since he'd had scarlet fever in school, and felt the harsh
rub of steel around his own ankle.

The Hôtel Batoux. Jürgen Schaumm. Elysée de Montadour's
green eyes gleaming at him in candlelight.

Descending the stair to the bone chapel . . .

'LISETTE!' At the end of the infirmary ward a man in another
bed screamed, thrashed with both hands at some invisible adver-
sary, and at the same moment another man shouted, incoherent
words of terror and shock.

Two more men began to shout, jerking at their shackles, and
the man who'd been dozing in the chair by the door leaped to
his feet and yelled, 'Shut up the lot of you!'

Bolts slammed back on the outside of the door, a man's head
framed against the barred judas. An instant later a guard strode
in from the corridor. 'What the hell's going on?' He and the
guard who'd been in the chair raged down the center of the
room banging on the iron bedsteads with truncheons and cursing.
'Eat shit, sons of whores! Quiet, or I'll give you good reason
to yell!'

The men in the beds began to yell back at the guards and
Asher, looking beside him, saw a woman enter the ward, slim
and dark and demurely smiling. No one else seemed to notice
her in the confusion, but he saw her, and knew her, with her
velvet smile and hazel-dark African eyes and the burn on her
face that vanished as he looked at her . . .

She reached down and brushed his unshaven cheek with her
nails. Smiled, letting him see her fangs.

Then she was gone.

'Turn up the gas!' Asher reached from his bed, caught at the
sleeve of the corridor guard as he stomped back to the door.
'There was a woman came in—'

He knew the minute the words were out of his mouth that they wouldn't believe him, and he was right. The man struck at his hand with the truncheon, 'What the hell you on about, you dirty German?' and the man in the next bed – who had recovered from the shock of his nightmare – guffawed. 'Like we'd have missed a woman! Yeah, Drouet, turn up the gas! Find that slut and bring her over here to me . . .'

Asher could smell her perfume, mixed with the whiff of blood. She was in the shadows, waiting for them to leave . . .

'Hey, Goubert, you hidin' a slut in your bed?'

'The Boche says a woman came in here—'

'Call the doctor, man, and make him give me what he gave the Boche to see women around here!'

Damn it! DAMN IT!

The corridor guard left. The door bolt slammed. 'You pigs keep your mouths shut!' snapped the door guard, subsiding again into his chair. 'First man make a noise, I'm gonna come over there—'

At once a chorus of mock farts exploded, except from one bed whose sleeper had been unable to waken fully and kept crying faintly, deliriously, 'Anna, don't leave . . . don't leave me . . .'

'Don't leave him, Anna!' squealed one of the men in falsetto, which got another general laugh, and curses from the guard.

Asher could see Hyacinthe now, standing in a far corner of the room, nearly invisible in dark velvet. Arms folded. Patient, as the Undead are patient.

She met his eyes and licked her lips with a pointed, pale-pink tongue.

A hallucination? His head still swam with fever and he couldn't seem to get any air into his lungs. Any minute, he felt, he'd slide back into seeing his parents, or a wall of grinning skulls, or the vampires who'd walked Paris's mucky streets three hundred years before. But he was awake now, lucid, or almost lucid . . .

The ward around him was falling silent. The guard's breathing deepened.

Shout to be taken to another room?

What would that get him but another whack with the guard's club? *Boche*, they'd called him, *sale Boche* . . .

Schaumm, he thought. *Schaumm accused me of spying, had me brought here where I'd be chained, waiting for her . . .*

Exhaustion, fever, delirium, drowning him like a wave. He fought to remain alert but couldn't.

Call for the chaplain? Demand last rites? As if any vampire in the world paid the slightest attention to a crucifix unless it was made of solid silver.

The light from the corridor, falling through the barred window, caught in the mahogany-dark curls of her hair as she walked – with that drifting movement that she alone, among the vampires, seemed to favor – to his bedside. He remembered her perfume: it had filled his nostrils as he'd fled up the church tower at St Clare's, seeking a way out across the roofs. *I see you . . . I see you, honey-man . . .*

She took his hand, slowly unwound the bandage from the barely healed claw wounds in his arm, stroked the thin skin above the vein.

'Can't run no more,' she whispered, 'can you?'

The corridor light brightened on her hair. Heads shadowed the light.

Hyacinthe melted once more into the darkness, close enough that he could still smell her perfume.

Outside, the corridor guard complained, 'This's a hell of an hour to transfer him—'

'Nobody wants trouble,' retorted another voice. 'And we heard there'd be some, if we wait till tomorrow. You got that stretcher? Come on, then, let's get this over with.'

The door opened. The corridor guard came in, with another man – *another guard? Why does he look familiar?* – in the blue uniform of Parisian law enforcement.

And behind them, bearing a sheaf of official paperwork and likewise uniformed (and it was this that made Asher wonder if he had slipped back into hallucination), came the slender form of Don Simon Ysidro.

TWENTY-FOUR

Asher was delirious again by the time they carried him through the mine tunnels – entered this time through the cellar of a house on the Rue Ravignan – and up to Ysidro's *manoir*. For three days Lydia sat beside him, barely aware of the newspapers that Greuze brought to her; the Germans had moved from the rubble of Liège to Brussels, dogged by Belgian *francs-tireurs* and systematically murdering civilians – either in retaliation or in fear – and burning villages all the way. From the street outside came only the occasional rumble of trucks and the voices of neighbors calling out now and then as one or another family loaded its goods into wagons or handcarts and moved creaking down the hill to begin the long road to the south. The Germans were coming. Greuze brought in what food he could, and stayed at Asher's bedside in the mornings while Lydia slept.

For Lydia those mid-August days had a sense of profound unreality to them, as if she had been locked in a prison herself, or stranded on a deserted island somewhere. In the mornings she would leave the house, disguised, through one of the secret ways, and walk the weirdly silent streets. On Wednesday morning she climbed to the Sacré-Coeur basilica and stood before it looking out over Paris, wondering what she should do, or could do.

I have to get Jamie away.

And then I have to come back.

Every hospital in Paris was choked with the wounded. Lydia thought of Dr Théodule at Saint-Antoine, of the crowded wards of Lariboisiere. Of Fantine faithfully mopping floors and changing bedding.

Of her daughter Miranda, sitting in the window-seat of her nursery back in Oxford, waiting for her mother to come home.

Of the men in the trucks.

They need my help.

Wondering if she'd manage to get away before the Germans came for Jamie.

'Fear not, Mistress,' Ysidro said to her that night when he returned – very late – from the silent streets and found her curled up in the carved bergère chair beside Asher's bed. 'One way or the other, I shall see you home safe.'

She took his hand – the long fingers warm with someone's stolen life – and found comfort in the clawed grip, though she couldn't imagine what it would be like to live without Jamie.

Ysidro had told her last night that Ellen had reached Oxford safely, and she believed him. She could imagine, easily, coming back to France and working in one of the hospitals, wherever they would be by the time she returned – *Bordeaux, probably*. And she cringed at the thought of all the dead and the wounded if the French and British fought the Germans all that distance . . .

Can they DO that? Can they endure that much slaughter and pain? Can anyone?

But she couldn't imagine what it would be like – might be like – to go back to England and not have Jamie there.

For Jamie to be dead.

As a doctor she knew that people died, especially people who had pneumonia in both lungs after falling off church steeples.

But not Jamie.

Not this soon . . .

'Will you leave Paris?' she asked softly, and Ysidro glanced aside.

'I will see to it . . .'

'No.' Her hand tightened on his. 'Will *you* leave Paris?'

His face was without expression. 'There is something here I must see to. Something I must see done.'

'What?'

'I can't—' He stopped the words – whatever they'd been – on his lips. Then: 'I don't precisely know.'

'What do you mean?'

'I mean I don't – know.' He shook his head, looked away from her again. The room where Asher lay was still shuttered tight in the heat, velvet curtains keeping the slightest flicker of her candle-light from being seen outside. On her walks it seemed to her that men who remained in the neighborhood clumped together in muttering suspicion and followed her with their eyes.

'What are you afraid is in the bone chapel?' she asked softly.

'This – this thing that you keep saying doesn't exist, the Facinum that will – supposedly – give Hyacinthe power over the Paris nest, including Elysée? Will it give her power over you? Is that what you fear is going to happen if Hyacinthe gets to it before you do?' She looked up into his face, worn and thin like a saint in alabaster but for the scars and the fangs. 'That she'll make you her slave?'

'Worse, I think.'

'*Worse*?'

He knelt beside the bed and brushed Asher's temple, very lightly, with the backs of his long claws, his eyes half-shut, listening.

Seeking whatever it was that he sought in Asher's dreams. 'I have walked the Marais for some hours tonight,' Ysidro said softly, 'endeavoring to get close to the Hôtel Batoux. Though I saw naught of Elysée or any of the Paris nest I sensed their presence everywhere, and had no wish to risk drawing any of them here. Indeed, Hyacinthe may e'en yet be recovering from the effects of the day-walking elixir she took. Many such things are considerably stronger than the one I made, and she is younger than I am, and frailer.'

The following afternoon, when she knew perfectly well she should have been sleeping, Lydia took a taxicab to the Quai des Célestins – expensive, but the thought of going underground frightened her even in the daytime and the Métro had taken to running erratically, if at all. There were still taxis, like red-and-yellow candy-boxes, zooming through the half-deserted streets. From there she walked past the Hôtel Batoux. The gates to its court were locked, but peering through the crack between them she saw one of Elysée's guards crossing the court, past Saint-Vrain's rather worse-for-wear electric brougham.

Even dressed in boys' things Lydia felt exposed and in danger out of doors, well aware that any of the men she saw in the cafés of the Boulevard de Sébastopol, any of the women hurrying silently along the sidewalks of the Rue du Renard with their shopping-bags of cabbages and peas, could be in Hyacinthe's pay or under her influence.

Having satisfied herself that the Hôtel Batoux was still under guard she hastened back to the Quai de Gesvres to find a cab back to Montmartre.

That night when Ysidro returned she asked him about Constantine Angelus and, a little to her surprise, he answered. *He must be more tired than I thought.*

'He asked me,' said Ysidro, 'early in my days in Paris, what I meant to do with my life, if indeed I succeeded in receiving absolution for all I had done. This was before Esdras de Colle's killing. Indeed, I was careful to keep my intent from him, first from fear he would stop me – for he could have killed me easily enough – and then because I could not bear to lose his regard.'

'What did you answer?' asked Lydia. 'What *did* you plan to do?'

Ysidro brought his hand away from the sleeping Asher's forehead, trimmed the candle that burned beside the bed, the sole illumination of the room.

'I told him I didn't know. 'Twas the truth. I knew I would have to give up hunting altogether, and suspected 'twould be my death. For as you know, 'tis the kill that feeds these glamors of the mind that we cast upon the perceptions of the living. Without the kill, we cannot cause men to think our faces resemble theirs. We cannot blind mortal eyes against those features that mark us out as Undead.'

He spread his hands, with their inch-long claws. (*Tissue alteration in the keratin of the nail*, reflected Lydia automatically. *The structure of the eye changes as well, not to speak of photo-reactivity of the flesh . . .*) Still weary from their attempt to enter the Hôtel Batoux, he could not keep her from seeing him as he was.

'I had excused myself theretofore by killing only heretics, damned in any event. Constantine pointed out to me that no man was worthier of damnation than Saul of Tarsus ere the Christ appeared to him and transfigured his heart. Did I consider myself worthy to judge the moment of another man's salvation? To forestall the eventual intent of God? But when I spoke of the matter to Jeffrey, he said that Cardinal Montevierde was of the opinion that I must do whatever would strengthen me to be of service to the Faith. That God would guide me to a victim who deserved such an end. In a word, that heretics were lawful prey.'

'That's—' began Lydia indignantly.

'—precisely what James's superiors in his Department told

him of his country's foes,' the vampire finished for her. 'And to speak truth, at this distance, I wonder if the Holy Father even knew of what Montevierde did. As I have said, the Cardinal was a man of ambition as well as piety, even ambition to the throne of St Peter itself. I doubt not that the notion pleased him, of having a baptized demon at his beck and call.'

Lydia said nothing for a time. Only regarded her friend with helpless anger mixed with a confused compassion, which – like so many other emotions she felt towards this bleached and mutated soul – she knew she should not feel.

'What did Angelus think you should do?'

'He knew no more than I did. But he begged me to keep accurate notes of whatever befell me, for I was treading, he said, where none of our own kind that he knew of had gone before.

'For my soul, I would not have disobeyed him. And so perhaps I deserved my damnation, for loving one whom the Church would have called murderer and unworthy of my love or any man's. Quite literally, I would have gone to Hell for him, which was indeed exactly what I proposed to do. And my servant Tim Quodling, who had loved me and watched over me e'er since I delivered his wife and his baby daughter from death.'

He shook his head at the memory of that man, that woman, that child.

'Tim could not bear it, that I should suffer damnation for the sake of such a friend. So he took it on himself to raise a group of men and to use the knowledge he'd gleaned from me of the mine tunnels that ran beneath the house of Emeric the alchemist, near the foot of Montparnasse. Without my knowledge they tore Emeric from his coffin and dragged him, stupefied in the dead sleep of daytime, up into the daylight to burn.'

Asher saw him running, soundless as shadow, through the night streets of Paris. If those who slept in their tight-shuttered rooms in those soot-black houses on the Rue des Tournelles and the Rue de la Bûcherie heard his passing in their dreams they dreamed he was a bat or a gigantic mantis whose wings clattered drily over their roofs or against their walls. Candles burned in the house he had rented in the Rue de la Harpe and he went from room to room, still silent as a ghost: the study where the books he'd brought from London had been added to fourfold, the table and the cupboard of pewter and plate, purchased lest those who entered the house wonder at a man who had no use for food.

Likewise he had purchased a bed, and on the bed Tim lay, the room in a blaze of waxlight. Tim's eyes were closed, his rosary of ivory and gold clenched tight in his hands as if he'd hoped at the end that it would protect him. His face was no darker than the wax of the candles all around him, dripping in pools from window-sill and chest edge to the floor. His shirt and doublet had been torn away. Claw marks showed where his wrists had been held, and his own bloodied and torn-out nails spoke of a desperate fight. His limbs had been carefully arranged on the bed and his face at least looked at peace. Wounds gaped in his throat, his elbows, and along his forearms to his wrists – wounds, but little blood.

Simon sank to his knees and wrapped his hands around those of his servant, enclosing fingerbones and holy beads alike, and laid his forehead on Tim's arm. He remained thus for a long time, not weeping – as he had wept before Jeffrey Sampson – but unmoving, while the candles burned down into the hollow pillars of their winding-sheets and dwindled out one by one. It must have been nearly dawn when the vampire finally got to his feet, bent over Tim's body and kissed his lips. Then he leaned to the last candle and blew it out, and in the darkness that meant nothing to vampire eyes descended all the stairs to the vaults below the house and lay down to sleep in his coffin alone.

At two o'clock Sunday morning Asher's fever broke. He opened his eyes many hours later to see broad slits of light lying across Lydia's red hair; she'd brought a divan over beside his bed, and lay there asleep. A man whom Asher vaguely recognized – *was he one of the guards who came into the prison infirmary?* – sat in a chair nearby reading a newspaper whose headlines shrieked, 'BRITISH, FRENCH FORCES IN RETREAT'. Newspapers lay all over the foot of the bed. *Lydia was obviously sitting up with me . . .*

Someone had said something about taking him to Fresnes prison. He recalled that much.

He was clearly not there.

He felt far weaker than he'd felt after the vampire attack, but his mind was clear.

He also felt extremely surprised to be alive.

'Where am I?'

The craggy-faced man lowered his newspaper and said, '*Eh bien, mon brave!*' Asher switched to French.

'How did I come here? I was in prison . . .'

With Hyacinthe's cold hand on his wrist. He glanced at it. Bandaged, but that could have been from the earlier attack.

'How is it the Americans say? We sprung you.'

'*We* being . . .?'

'Your beautiful wife, your tricky Spanish friend, and two guards who I swear were drunk or drugged or . . .' His single bar of brow gathered like a stormcloud. 'Or I don't know what. Is that what it does, this thing that you're trying to get at the Hôtel Batoux? Is that what it lets men do? Command the mind? Destroy it, my friend.' He shook his head. 'I know boys in Montparnasse, in Les Halles, anarchists. I can get gelignite—'

'It's underground.' Even the effort of speaking made him dizzy. 'Twenty, maybe thirty feet. You'd never get to it. They thought of that.'

'Son of a whore.'

'And there are guards.'

'So your lady tells me.' The man growled, then held out a thick brown working-man's hand. 'Stanislas Greuze, at your service.'

'Alex Prior.' Greuze raised his brows – Asher's Paris workname evidently hadn't been the one on his prison papers, but Asher was too tired to try to sort it out. La Santé, he thought it had to be, if they'd been talking about transferring him to Fresnes. 'What day is it?' He remembered, or thought he remembered, at least two nights in the prison, probably more . . .

'It is Sunday,' said Greuze, 'the twenty-third of August. There was fighting at Charleroi yesterday, and at Mons, on the frontier . . .' He gestured with the newspaper that still lay on his knee. 'Today again, and worse; your countrymen and mine. The Boche are coming across the Meuse as well. All morning the wounded have been pouring into Paris. The hospitals are full, they're putting them up at the hotels, at the Invalides, everywhere. It will be bad, my friend.' He glanced sidelong at Lydia, who looked worn down to her bones.

Elysée. Hyacinthe. Propped on his pillows, Asher reflected that even greater than his surprise at still being alive was his gratitude that Lydia, too, had survived. He could see, where the collar of her simple white blouse fell away from her throat, the glint of silver chains. At her wrist, too, where her hand pillowed her cheek. He stretched his own hand toward her, but drew it back, not wanting to waken her. If she'd been keeping company with Ysidro for – *good God, has it been three weeks?* – she'd be exhausted. Bruises of sleeplessness marked the thin flesh of her eyes. Greuze brought over a cup of broth from a table near the door, propped Asher while he drank.

'This is Don Simon's house?'

'He talks as if it's his, though I haven't seen him here. Rue Lepic. Montmartre. Back during the Commune a pal of my father's owned the place; they hid ammunition in the basement. Some of the boys hereabouts know it. I doubt our presence here will be a secret long. There's a way through from the cellar into the old mines.'

I'll bet there is. 'These boys of yours in Montparnasse – can they be trusted?'

'Not all of them.' Greuze shrugged. 'Trusted for what, eh? To kill the cabbage-eaters? Probably. To obey orders? Depends on who's giving them. To destroy this thing that you seek, this weapon that isn't really a weapon . . . this thing that tricks the mind, that whispers crazy things to you . . . I think yes. Not to ask questions . . .' He raised his heavy brow. 'Well, if we weren't bad boys asking questions we wouldn't be socialists, would we?'

'Think of those you can trust,' said Asher, as a wave of weakness, of exhaustion, passed over him. Like Ysidro's description of the vampire sleep in the daytime: *We sleep and we do not waken* . . . 'Trust to take orders. And thank you.' Asher glanced again at Lydia. 'Thank you for helping her. For serving her . . . and Don Simon.'

'Who is he?' Greuze's voice was hoarse. 'What is he?' And then, when Asher said nothing, 'Never mind. You'll just tell me a lie, won't you?'

'I'm afraid so.'

He slept again, like a candle going out.

TWENTY-FIVE

'**D**id you know a woman named Corsina Manotti?' Ysidro paused in the doorway at the sound of the name. Lydia looked up from her welter of old maps of Paris and carefully wrapped pamphlets printed in the Low Countries in the fifteen eighties and nineties, and set down her French dictionary. Somewhere in the deeps of the house the clock struck the half hour, between three and four.

'She sang at San Benedetto,' said the vampire at last; Asher recognized the name of the eighteenth-century Venice opera house. 'If 'tis she you mean. A coloratura. 'Twas her only beauty; she had a face like a bad turnip. Has still, for aught I know. A pleasure to see you again in your senses,' he added, coming into the chamber and settling himself on the foot of Asher's bed. 'Two days ago I feared that we were too late in delivering you – completely aside from the issue of Mistress Hyacinthe.'

'She was there, wasn't she?' Asher struggled to bring back the recollection of the prison infirmary. 'That wasn't just a dream?'

'No, she was there. I thought she would dissolve into steam with pure vexation when my minions and I entered with orders for your removal – for which a man named Kryzwiki, whose name I obtained from your rooms on the Île Saint-Louis, charged me two thousand francs. I wonder that your Department was in the habit of using him, at those rates . . .'

'He would give me a discount.'

'He gave none to me. Madame Hyacinthe retreated to the shadows and could of course say nothing. The door was locked behind us when we departed; 'twould have taken the guard at least two hours to fall asleep again, ere she could engineer an escape from the room, and by then 'twould be on the very heels of dawn. As I recall Orlando Dandolo, the Master of Venice, made Corsina Manotti vampire sometime in the seventeen fifties.

She took refuge in London during Napoleon's wars, and drove Lionel' – he named the Master of London – 'near insane with her gossip and talebearing, her tantrums and superstitions.'

'Superstitions?'

'The dead can be fools as easily as the living, Mistress.' Ysidro answered Lydia's tone of surprise with a slight inclination of his head. 'As I have lately described to you, I was myself prey to a shocking number of them, for the first fifty years of my present . . . condition. Corsina traveled a good deal, as I recall,' he added, turning back to Asher. 'She is one of those vampires – as I am, it shames me to say – who enjoys the company of the living, though for her the goal is always malice and the small dominations of making mischief. She always does end up killing them. Possibly because the others among the Undead find her so annoying, she is one of the few vampires who travel for pleasure. I should not be greatly surprised if one day it is the death of her, if it has not been so already.'

'Not as of this spring, it hasn't.' Propped on half a dozen pillows, Asher still felt as if he were rationing very tiny quantities of strength. The single candle beside the bed shed only a dim and wavering light. Beyond tight-closed shutters, the sound of ambulance vehicles coming and going along the Boulevard de Rochechouart, the clanging din of the train stations to the south, came faintly through the uncustomary stillness of the night.

'She was in Prague. The Master of Prague spoke of it to Rebbe Karlebach—'

'I thought Professor Karlebach would have nothing to do with the Undead!' Lydia exclaimed. 'Certainly that he'd never believe what they told him.'

'He wrote to me that he didn't know what to believe or whether to believe,' said Asher. 'Nevertheless, he felt he had to write. It seems that Corsina Manotti established a friendship with Jürgen Schaumm – whom Karlebach knew was in Prague this past spring – and she told him that Elysée de Montadour's power over her fledglings in Paris wasn't genuine. She, Elysée, of herself, did not have the strength to hold them. Rather, Corsina said, there is something in her lair that gives her power, not only over the Paris nest but over those of Liège, Brussels, and Bordeaux as well.'

'Constantine Angelus's Facinum,' said Lydia. 'Which Don Simon says doesn't exist.'

But she glanced at the vampire's face as she said it, and Asher saw the question in her eyes.

'Did he say what this was?' Ysidro's voice was barely a whisper.

Asher shook his head. 'This she learned – said the Master of Prague – when she was in Paris before the Revolution. From things Schaumm had said to Karlebach, Karlebach guessed that Schaumm had established a connection of some kind with the Paris nest, and because the Archduke of Austria had just been murdered and everyone started talking of going to war – and even complete ignoramuses like my cousins knew that the German armies were going to come through Belgium – Karlebach wrote to me. The story sounded absurd to me,' he went on after Ysidro had begun to speak, then fallen silent again. 'Yet when I reached Paris and started tracing the ownership of houses and guessing at the history of the Paris nest, I began to wonder. It was clear to me that the Hôtel Batoux was a vampire nest, and that it was probably the central nest of Paris – the place where Elysée's power, real or imaginary, was centered. I took a chance' – he grinned wryly at himself; not the first chance he'd ever taken, nor in fact the most dangerous – 'and paid a call on her.'

Even now, the memory was patchy. He'd entered the church in the daytime, and presumed he had concealed himself from Father Martin – he had no recollection of how or where, but the building abounded in hidey-holes – and made his way to the catacombs. Nor did he remember clearly how he'd traversed the sunlit vestibule at the bottom of the tower up into the house itself. He must, he thought, have hidden for a time in the bone chapel, timing the appearances and the pattern of Elysée's paid guards on the gallery above. He recalled nothing of this, nor of picking the lock on the grille.

He did remember lighting the candles in her salon upstairs. Recalled sitting on the carved and surprisingly uncomfortable Louis Quatorze armchair, watching the last of the evening twilight fade through the slits in the shutters. Watching the night come. He'd heard the guards lock up the rooms downstairs as they left. It was part of their contract – for which, he had ascertained a few days earlier, they were extremely well paid – that they were completely away from the premises before dark.

'We gathered that much,' said Lydia.

'I warned her that German agents would probably approach one of her nest to try to get hold of this Facinum. She brought up Hyacinthe's name pretty quickly in the discussion, so she can't have had much doubt about who it would be. Nor, it was clear to me, was this the first time the notion of the Facinum, or something like it, had crossed her mind.'

Don Simon said you were a man of courage . . .

The cold grip of her hand on his, crushing the bone. Candle flame reflecting the green of her emeralds in the green of her eyes. *Those stupid cabbage-eaters aren't going to get within a hundred miles of Paris . . .*

'There is no such object!' She'd tossed her head a little, an imperious coquette. 'My husband needed no *object* to rule this city like an emperor! There was no vampire, and precious few living men, who would deny him what he asked. He made his fledglings here in this house because it was the safest place in the city to do so. Certainly safer than those filthy mines! He knew how to claim the hearts as well as the souls of those whom he admitted into our world, into le Royaume des Morts.'

'And how did he do that?' Asher had asked. 'Always in the same place in the house?'

'Shall I show you?' Her hands slipped up over his shoulders as if to draw his mouth to hers. 'Species of pig!' She drew back sharply as the bare flesh touched the back of his shirt-collar, feeling through it the silver he wore. He was watching for her to slap at him and stepped back in time for only her long nails to graze his face.

'Why was that, Elysée?' he asked quickly, urgently, drawing her mind aside from her anger. 'Was it just his fancy? Did he always tell you the truth?'

That stopped her, and she stood looking at him with hatred in her narrowed eyes.

Hatred that was not for him.

But hate, he knew, was a tricky weapon, easy to turn from a distant target to whatever is present before the hater's eyes. 'Have you ever made a fledgling outside of these walls? Is this the same of other masters, in other cities? That they must beget their followers in a single place? I don't think so.'

Grudgingly, she admitted, 'I don't know. I never thought of it.' She shrugged, as if the matter had nothing to do with her. In a hundred and ten years of immortality, she'd never asked.

Asher understood then why Ysidro considered her stupid.

'And just because this thing doesn't exist,' he had persisted, 'doesn't mean agents of Germany won't come looking for it. This house was built by Gabrielle Batoux, with money from property left her by a man named Raimund Cauchemar. Since that time it's always been guarded by members of the Batoux family, always been rumored about as a place of ill omen . . .'

Elysée made a motion as if shooing flies.

'. . . and according to the Master of Prague, it was of old the headquarters of the Master of Paris, who also ruled the nests of the Low Countries. That's what the Germans want, Elysée. The Paris nest, yes – but what they really want is to control the vampires of Belgium and Flanders. To use them when they strike at France, so the Belgians won't slow down their armies. They want the vampires of Paris to do their bidding, so they won't have little armies of Parisians holing themselves up on Montmartre hill or in the old mines below the city. *Did* your husband command the vampires of Belgium?'

'I don't know,' she replied sullenly. 'None of them ever came here. What are Belgians, anyway? Chocolate soldiers, cake-eaters . . .'

'They're what's going to stand in the way of the German army,' said Asher, 'while the French are hauling back their troops from the Rhine to meet a juggernaut like the Day of Judgment. Just because you don't know what your husband did or planned or accomplished in the years before you knew him . . . how long was he vampire before he brought you into his world?'

'Seventy years.'

'That's a lifetime. Two, if they're short. All the time women wed men who have a decade or two they don't speak of, and get surprises . . .'

Like Lydia finding out I knew half the gangsters in Peking . . .

Or other surprises less benign . . .

'Just because you don't know doesn't mean the Germans won't

tear this house to pieces. It doesn't mean they won't kill you to get at whatever they think is hidden here. It doesn't mean they won't get one of your fledglings to work for them in the hopes of coming out of the war as Master of Paris.'

'I think she honestly wasn't sure if there was a power of some kind in the house until I spoke of the Facinum.' Recounting the interview had exhausted him. Though his mind was clear – Ysidro and Lydia didn't seem to change their size or distance from him, as those around him had appeared to during the worst of his fever – Asher had the sensation of sinking down into the pillows of the bed, that nothing he could do would keep him from falling asleep from sheer weariness. 'I told her to come to me if she remembered anything, if she changed her mind . . . *Is* there power there?' He met Ysidro's eyes.

When the vampire didn't reply, Lydia asked, 'Have you ever been in the house, Don Simon?'

Ysidro moved his eyes a little: *No* . . . 'I was never *persona grata* with the Paris nest.'

'You're the only one of us who's actually been in the house, Jamie.' Lydia turned to him. 'I saw relics in the bone chapel, locked up behind silver grilles. Elysée's minion said she makes her fledglings there. Do *you* think there's something there?'

Asher thought for a long time, the dreams of his delirium returning to him. Descending the stair to the catacomb with Elysée going before him, a branch of candles upheld in her hand. Being seized in the dark of the church, Schaumm pulling the silver chain from his throat . . . Hyacinthe and her fledglings closing in.

Only in some of his dreams it had not been like that. In some of his dreams he had descended the stair alone. The door of the twisting passageway that led to the bone chapel had been open . . .

A man had been standing in the doorway.

'Are you sure,' he asked at last, 'that Constantine Angelus is dead?'

'Constantine Angelus had been dead for nearly two centuries when I met him.'

Asher said nothing to this. Only held Ysidro's gaze, and it was the vampire who looked aside.

'I am sure.'

For some moments Ysidro stared into the darkness beyond the candle flame, the darkness of a world long gone, while the trains clanged in the distance beyond the foot of the hill, bringing the wounded in from the Front.

Then he said, 'I was the one who killed him.'

TWENTY-SIX

'Because of Tim?' asked Lydia softly.

'Not . . . entirely.' Ysidro shut his eyes for a time, as if he could not bear what he saw in the darkness. 'I understand why Constantine killed him. I understood it at the time. Tim was twenty-eight. I was seventy-two, and though at that time still a faithful son of the Church which called me demon, I had seen a great deal of the nightmare of the war between religions – not so much as Constantine had, I dare say. I thought that he was wrong, but I understood.'

He folded his hands, long and narrow and pale, with their glassy claws, sat with head bowed, as still as a stone upon a tomb.

'I understood. But I remained a believer. And I clung to my hope of salvation. Constantine had turned from hope in any world but this one, but his hope in this world was like a white flame. This was why he had become a pamphleteer. Like Leibniz and Erasmus he wrote of the folly of religious war, the insanity of men murdering one another over the nature of one who was purported to be a God of love. Of the delusional dream that any of us knew anything about the intentions or wishes of that God. And yet he killed for sustenance, as we all do. Killed so that he could maintain his strength, his hold over the nest. He was not innocent.

'When I went to Jeffrey the night after Tim's death Cardinal Montevierde was there. They were both filled with holy triumph at the news of Emeric Jambicque's death, and with promises that the Holy Father would look with favor on my service to the Faith.

Jeffrey comforted me for Tim's death, and assured me that in his way poor Tim was a martyr, slain for his act of selflessness and his loyalty to me as a weapon of the Church, a sword in the hand of Christ. I begged him instead to undertake arrangements to provide for Tim's wife and their baby daughter – arrangements which were not made, incidentally, as I found out when I finally returned to England. After Montevierde took his leave I tried to explain to Jeffrey why Constantine had killed Tim, though Constantine was of the True Faith and Emeric a heretic. Jeffrey was horrified, and showed me by logical argument where I – and Constantine – were wrong. He begged me not to allow myself to be corrupted.

'Corrupted.' Ysidro smiled, a terrible echo of a human expression, all the crystallized bitterness that Asher had always assumed to have been washed away by time now surfacing in the wake of memories. 'I. Corrupted. Because of course my next target, as Montevierde told me before he left – and, he implied, my last and greatest – was Constantine himself. I should have seen that coming, but I hadn't.'

'Because of the pamphlets?' asked Lydia, and Ysidro nodded, barely a movement of his eyelids.

'He was worse than a heretic, they said, because he corrupted others of the True Faith, and led them to damnation as well. Even, as Jeffrey said, as he was crippling me in my efforts to save my own soul through service to the Faith. Even as he had polluted the Low Countries, that hotbed of heresy where he was also Master, as he was Master of the heretic towns in the south, La Rochelle and Bordeaux. I had no argument against that. Only what I felt in my heart. Jeffrey told me my heart was wrong. I believed him.'

Dimly, Asher remembered it. Fragments of dreams, interleaved like the broken shards of vases at the archeological dig in Syria where he'd gone with Belleytre in 1887, one of his first field assignments. Four Cambridge lecturers bossing the inhabitants of two Arab villages as they transformed a canyon in the wastelands east of Palmyra into a maze of cross-cut trenches and sorting-sheds built of poles and brush while Asher and Belleytre pretended to take notes and actually made maps of all the countryside between Damascus and Baghdad and found out which local sheikhs would support a rising against the Turks if Britain happened to need such a thing.

In the evenings he'd sat in Professor Bergen's lamplit tent while that gentle, gray-haired elephant of a man had reassembled pottery from the broken bits sifted out of the trench-dirt. What had at first appeared to be only random snippets of blue and yellow slowly came together as pictures: kings slaying lions, battles between dragons and griffins fought beneath the cold eyes of goddesses who hovered on vulture wings.

So the fragments of his dreams returned to him while Ysidro spoke. Of Simon, still a believer and the sword in the hand of Christ, slipping into the ransacked house of Emeric Jambicque on the Rue de la Fontaine. Dogs and cats fled, at his footstep, from the corpse of a man lying in what had been the shop downstairs. By the smell, the blood was fresh. The floor of the small shed behind had been hacked up, and from the black pit below where Emeric had kept his coffin – hidden, he had thought – rose the stink of ashes.

Beyond that, in the thin starlight of the tiny yard, only a vampire's eyes could have picked out the heap of ash and half-burned pages where a bonfire had been made of books.

Simon turned his head, listening; then climbed the narrow stair to the workroom above. The vats in which Emeric had dissolved the flesh from the bones of rats – and larger animals as well, to judge by the strings of them hanging near the windows to air the stink of the acid away – were lined up on the table now, and the dark form of a man moved about, gathering bottles and pots from hidden cupboards, retrieving scalpels, cleavers, fine-ground Flemish lenses from beneath the boards of the floor.

Sooty moonlight flashed on his fangs as he turned. 'Simon!'

It was Raimund Cauchemar.

'Simon, thank God!'

Even in the fragment of the dream, Asher recalled, it had been impossible to see the vampire move.

'I feared he'd find you.'

Even in the fragment of the dream, Asher also recalled, he had found himself thinking, *Feared so much you took time off to loot Emeric's alchemical equipment?* But obviously Simon hadn't thought that way, at least not at the time.

'Who would find me?'

'Angelus.'

'I've spoken to him.' Simon sounded dazed, distracted, and Cauchemar gripped his shoulders in those powerful white hands.

'Did he bid you come to him later tonight?'

Simon nodded; the grip tightened on his arms.

'He will kill you,' said Cauchemar. 'What he said to you earlier, it was a lie. 'Twas he who murdered your servant—'

'I knew that. He told me.'

'I'll bet he didn't tell you,' returned the older vampire grimly, 'how the boy died.'

'He told me.' Ysidro's whisper was barely audible in the stillness of the candlelit room. 'Only later did I consider how clever was his tale. The tortures he described were all such as would not show marks on the outside of the body. And Tim's body had already been taken away by the daytime servants of our house.

'I loved Constantine. I would, as I have already said, have gone unshriven into Hell for the sake of his beliefs – for the sake of his friendship – even, I think, in the face of Tim's death, when I believed his killing had been quick, and of necessity. But the man that Cauchemar described to me – the man who would play so hideous a game of cat-and-mouse as he related – that man I felt I did not know. Cauchemar told me likewise that Constantine intended to kill me later that night, and had asked me to come to his house so that he could deny having done so, should others – like Cauchemar, Cauchemar said – ask after me. I was a fool, of course.'

Simon briefly put his hand to his lips, as if he feared some involuntary contraction of the muscles of his face might show something of what went on within.

'He gave me a bodkin, steeped in poison – the same poison Esdras de Colle had poured down my throat when they'd left me on this hill, only a few hundred feet from where we sit tonight, to burn up with the rising of the sun. Cauchemar had long wanted possession of Emeric's alchemical equipment, of his supplies – which Cauchemar had no idea how to procure – and of his books. He had managed to salvage a good part of them, though the men Tim got to break in and kill Emeric had burned many. I think 'twas even in my mind at that time that Cauchemar meant to take over the Paris nest, though I doubted he had the strength to command Constantine's fledglings.

'But in my shock and my horror – for I knew I had been the cause of Tim's death, and that he had died for love of me – I did not care, and thought only of revenge. In my horror, I believed him: that Constantine would kill me, that Constantine had tortured Tim before he died, and laughed at his terror and his pain. And I knew if I simply fled Paris I would lose not only my vengeance but my last chance of salvation. In killing Constantine, I would save my soul. Jeffrey had said so. Cardinal Montevierde had promised.

'And so I killed him.'

For a time, in silence, he studied his folded hands.

'I think perhaps I was the only one of the vampires to whom Constantine would have stood that close. He was ever watchful of his fledglings, even of those most dear to him, and Cauchemar of course he trusted not at all. But he explained to me, there in his study at the top of his house where we had talked all those nights of what we were and why men were given souls, where we had played chess, and observed the stars . . . He told me how sorry he had been to kill Tim, how he knew it would grieve me. But, he said, he had had no choice. And when I feigned to weep – or perhaps my tears were genuine, I no longer recall – and he bent over to comfort me, I pulled the bodkin from the bosom of my doublet and drove it into his body up to the knuckles of my hand. He seized me by the neck and would have snapped my spine – he was hideously strong, and fast as a striking snake – so that we would both have lain there immobile, and would both have died when the first blades of morning light pierced the shutters.

'But the poison was fast. His hands slipped from my throat and he fell to the floor, staring at me with his living eyes as I staggered back. He tried to speak and I saw his fingers twitch a little as he reached for me. I went around the study opening every shutter and window while he followed me with his eyes, knowing what I was doing. Maybe knowing that Cauchemar had put me up to it. I heard him try to speak. A small sound, but most terrible.

'I fled from the study and I knew he listened to my every

footfall as I raced down the stair, followed them through the stillness as I retreated along the street. Even in those days I would lie waking a little while in the blackness of my coffin, after the coming of first light. That morning in its safety I felt the sun come up, and knew that he was gone.'

TWENTY-SEVEN

The flood of wounded coming into Paris became an avalanche. When in the course of the next two weeks Lydia went out in the daytime – under Stanislas Greuze's watchful care – she saw lines of ambulances and wagons, carts, and private carriages rattling and jerking from the Gare du Nord, the Gare de l'Est, to a dozen makeshift hospitals. The stench of wounds, of gangrene, of filth, and of death hung in the hot summer air along with the steady, desperate clamor of men in thirst, exhaustion, and unspeakable pain.

Into the city also came refugees, Belgians fleeing with whatever they could carry, on their backs or loaded into barrows or carts. Most of those who'd had trucks or motor cars when they'd fled had left them, emptied of petrol, along the roads from Brussels or Liège. Some sheltered in abandoned buildings or set up squalid camps for a night or two in the Bois or the Luxembourg Gardens. Mostly they didn't stay. Parisians, similarly laden, swelled their ranks as they moved on toward the south.

On Tuesday the Germans burned Louvain in Belgium with its university and library, and killed hundreds of civilians – men, women, and children – for the crime of resisting the German invasion of their country. On the twenty-sixth, Wednesday, the retreating French army blew up the railroad bridges over the Mons canal behind them. Word was that the Kaiser himself had arrived in the Rhineland to oversee the German forces there.

During all this Lydia observed her husband with a doctor's eye, read the newspapers, and tried to calculate when the risk of a relapse from being moved would drop low enough to allow them to flee, and whether that would happen before the Germans reached Paris. Lying awake in the early hours of the morning she tried not to wonder about her aunts, frantically seeking news of whether she'd gotten out of the city after Aunt Louise had (she could just hear the words rolling off Aunt Lavinnia's tongue) 'abandoned her to her fate'. About her friends in Oxford and London, telegraphing her family for word and getting nothing. *When this is all over and it's 1920 or something, will Aunt Isobel gently tell Miranda, 'As far as anyone knows, your mummy and daddy were in Paris when the Germans shelled it . . .'?*

'I can't say it to Jamie,' she whispered, late one night, when Don Simon came in and found her weeping in the corridor outside Jamie's room so she wouldn't wake him. 'He has enough to do, to rest and get himself better.'

The vampire made no effort to tell her things would be all right but wrapped her in his thin arms and held her, like the cold, strong grip of a ghost. 'There is time and plenty to flee, Mistress,' he reminded her. 'In the worst case, we can retreat underground into the mines.'

'Won't the other vampires be down there too?'

'Once von Kluck's forces close in I misdoubt that Elysée and her fledglings will remain,' said Ysidro reasonably. 'And in any case, there are many miles of mines. I have put James's friend Kryzwiki the forger to work producing travel papers that bear not the name of Asher – these should be ready within days. As for James, we will contrive. At the worst, succumbing to pneumonia will not be worse than being dragged to a military prison and shot as a spy. Know you how to fire a pistol, Mistress? Then 'tis time you learned.'

He set up a target in the longest of the mine galleries and ordered Greuze to instruct her in the early hours of the morning, when both the vampires and the local *apaches* – who used the mines for their own purposes sometimes – would probably have gone to their rest. The shots echoed hideously in the confined space and both muffled their ears with scarves, but Lydia also guessed the branching galleries would diffuse the sound and make it almost impossible to guess its direction. It was hard to aim by lantern-light, but at least she learned how to handle Greuze's Webley revolver.

That was the day the German army came across the border into France, eighty miles from Paris.

'Stay out of the mines entirely once darkness falls, Mistress,'
Ysidro warned her that night. 'I have observed more and more
loiterers in this neighborhood, despite the number of people
leaving. Hyacinthe – and Schaumm – have men in their pay.'

'I know.' Lydia looked up from sorting through the grubby
envelope of forged travel documents. Greuze had told her that
day that some Parisians were managing to stow away on
outgoing trains that had brought food into the city. He had said,
too, that some rather surprising individuals were being given
'military' passes. Penniless Belgians were camped all around
the walls of the waiting-rooms and on the platforms of every
station, trying to beg enough money to continue their journey
south. 'I've dreamed more than once that there was something
down there that I had to find. The dreams feel very . . . very
clumsy, you know. Unconvincing. Is that because Hyacinthe is
still recovering from whatever she took that enabled her to try
to lure me in the daytime? Or is it that she's just not very good
at it?'

'She isn't.' Ysidro turned a British passport for 'William
Stephenson and wife' over in fastidious fingers. 'This is too
clean to be genuine, and the stamp isn't correct. What did you
pay for it? Hmph. I shall have a word with this Kryzwiki . . .
But the danger stems not solely from Mistress Hyacinthe, I fear.
Nor yet from Elysée, who is, I suspect, also seeking this place.
Vampires from Liège, from Brussels and Antwerp, have taken
refuge in the mines. Among the refugees camped in the Bois de
Boulogne this night I encountered two from Strasbourg, two
from Milan, three of the Venice nest, and a like number from
Munich—'

'*Munich*? *Venice*? But that's – those aren't anywhere *near* the
fighting!'

'And more coming in. They feed every night, two and three
kills a night sometimes: refugees, wounded, men coming into
the train stations who never make it to hospital. Once the
Germans take the city and settle in to rule it the Undead would
be fools to remain, for then people will be on the watch for
strangers and the anger of the people will vent itself on them.
But for now, with the city in chaos and no one taking note of
what is about them, they may feed as they please, like black-flies

in their season. And like black-flies, more will come, lady, and no one – *none* – shall even notice their depredations among the hosts of the anonymous dead.'

On Friday the Allied armies were driven back again and General Gallieni, commander of the city, declared Paris a military zone. Preparations were put in train for siege. Cattle grazed in the Bois de Boulougne. Huge depots of arms and ammunition were established in public buildings. The southern train stations – Saint-Lazare, Montparnasse, Austerlitz – crowded already with refugees, saw the sudden influx of flocks of sheep, to supply the armies should they be thrown back on to the city itself. Men of every suburb were conscripted to dig trenches and 'wolf-pits', in Clichy, Vincennes, Saint-Denis. Even the outlets to the sewers were barricaded and put under guard. Military observers – and any civilian possessed of binoculars – appeared daily on the Eiffel Tower and the dome of the Sacré-Coeur, watching the roads north.

'I want you to get Lydia out of here,' Asher whispered one night. He had wakened in the dead hours before dawn to see Lydia asleep, exhausted, on the daybed near the shuttered and curtained window; Ysidro had just moved a screen between her and the single candle, lest even that feeble glow disturb her. As he had in the hospital, the vampire stood looking down at her, his scarred face human and infinitely sad, like a man looking through a cell window at a country where he knows he will never set foot. With moth-wing gentleness he moved a strand of her hair from her eyes.

The floor around the daybed was littered, not only with travel documents, but with lists and steamship schedules and maps; Stanislas Greuze had promised to 'obtain' a small lorry and sufficient petrol to get them to Poitiers. This was far enough from the fighting, it was hoped, to ensure that more could be obtained there in order to continue to Bordeaux.

'She will not leave you,' the vampire pointed out.

'That's why I'm talking to you and not to her. There's no way – none in hell – that I'll be able to make the journey. I can arrange with Greuze to hide me. I have friends from my days with the Department who can—'

'James,' said Ysidro patiently. 'Even supposing that you actually think that your Department will help you (which I doubt and I think you disbelieve as well), under the most favorable of circumstances it would take a hardy man indeed to abduct your wife. On a number of occasions in the past three years you have sworn that you will kill me because I am a vampire, so you cannot be ignorant of the fact that, as a vampire, I must go to ground at first light or perish.'

Asher said, 'Hmn,' and subsided back into his pillows.

'As there is no passage through Flanders these days, an abduction must needs include several days' travel to Bordeaux, even without the complication of yourself and Mistress Lydia being sought as German spies. I have no desire to find my coffin parked in the first place that your wife considers "safe" while she hies back to Paris to be at your side, an activity I will be powerless to prevent. 'Twill be much simpler for the three of us to remain together and await events.'

Lydia stirred then in her sleep, and Asher fell silent. Later, when he himself slept, the others' voices slipped in and out of his dreams. Once he heard her say, 'I think I saw Modeste Saint-Vrain – Elysée's minion, you know – today in the Place du Tertre, walking about as if looking for something. And at all the cafés, and in the market, people are talking about German spies hiding in the old mines.'

'Are they so?' murmured Ysidro.

For centuries, Asher recalled, a mad vampire had haunted the mines, a vampire whom all the others had forgotten, whispering prayers as he sorted bones in the dark. But when he slid back into dreams it wasn't that strange little withered ghost that he saw but the long upstairs chamber in the house of Constantine Angelus and the gleam of the master vampire's eyes as he lay on the floor, paralysed by poison, listening as Simon fled down the stairs.

Leaving him alone to await the dawn.

And then, very soft – and it might only have been the creak of the sleeping house – the whisper of what could have been the footfalls of someone else ascending.

Then a great crashing broke into his dream, like terrible thunder, and he opened his eyes to daylight. Lydia knelt beside his bed, gripping his hand. Another explosion made the building shudder.

He guessed already what it was. 'Less than a mile off.'

Church bells rang, frantically sounding an alarm. Shouts of terror came from the street below. Lydia went to open the window, the diffuse daylight blinding after weeks of twilight. 'The hill's blocking the view,' she said. 'They say it's Zeppelins.'

'Get down to the cellar.'

'Don't be silly. If the house is hit being in the cellar won't save me, and if I go into the mine the chances are that horrible Schaumm person is lurking just on the other side of the door. They have to have figured out where we are by this time.' She closed the curtains again, came back to the bedside. 'The French have aeroplanes. I saw them a few days ago when I went up to Sacré-Coeur. All somebody would have to do is fly in close and shoot the gasbag with a pistol. Those things are full of hydrogen; it would go up like a barrel of gunpowder.'

She took his hand with fingers that felt cold.

Later that afternoon he forced himself out of bed, standing with the help of Greuze and Lydia, sweating and shaking with the effort, knowing that the time for rest was over. *I can rest when we're in England*, he told himself, clinging to his helpers with hands that felt like jelly. *I can rest when we're safe.*

But he knew that England would not be safe either.

He rose again in the night, with Lydia dozing by the bedside, and, dragging himself from one piece of furniture to another, made his way to the window. Only the faintest glimmer of the waxing moonlight came through the louvers. When he pushed open the shutter he saw above the black rooflines of Montmartre the arch of the sky soaked in starlight, all the lights of the city below quenched.

In the street below, the vaguest movement of a dark figure, the momentary flash of vampire eyes.

He closed the shutter and turned back, and saw in the door of the room the slim shape of a woman whose eyes also reflected the moonlight like the eyes of an animal. Even with the distance of the room between them he could smell blood, and Quelques Fleurs.

'You said to come to you if I had anything else to tell you about the Hôtel Batoux.'

Asher let himself slip into the chair he'd been gripping by the back. His legs already shook with fatigue.

'You certainly didn't make yourself easy to find.'

'What's there?'

Lydia, he thought. Lydia was asleep beside the bed. Elysée could lift her like a child and be gone before he could stagger that far. *Keep her talking . . .*

'I don't know.' Elysée's silk dress whispered as she came toward him into the moonlight, passing Lydia without a glance. 'I don't think François knew, either. But he knew there was something about the house that . . . that gave him strength in controlling his fledglings. That empowered him to make fledglings – a sort of place, or thing, where he placed the fledgling's – soul, I suppose you'd call it. He'd pass it through himself, through his own mind, and on into this other thing or place. He said those he'd make outside the house would never obey him properly.'

Her silvery voice was for once free of its affected tones, and her movements without artifice. When she came close he saw the genuine worry in her eyes.

'With Gabrielle it was the same, he said: Gabrielle was the master who begot him. She always made them in the chapel. I don't know why. And I don't know whether she passed the souls of her fledglings through her, into this . . . this *place* that François described, but I think she must have. She never would leave that house. In the end she was killed because the mob knew where to find her.

'Her family lived in the house for years. If there were children in the household Gabrielle would give them nightmares about going into the locked part of the house. But it didn't always work. And François was never very good at all that silliness with dreams. He told me Gabrielle brought him into the house through the old catacomb from St Clare's, when the night came for her to make him vampire. She took him on the altar, the way he later took me. For the first two or three nights – while my body was changing – he laid me in a coffin in the chapel, as Gabrielle had done with him. I felt the power then, the power that he held over me and over all the others. This . . . this thing, this place, the place where his power over the fledglings came from. I've never known whether that was because it was where

I was made, or . . . or for some other reason. I still sleep there, in the chapel, many nights.'

She stood close before him in the alabaster moonlight, her long straight hobble-skirt touching his knees. He'd seen her there, he recalled. Seen her lying in her coffin in the chapel, clothed in white, her hair spread around her on the pillow. *It must have been when I was waiting for the guards to pass.* He'd gone to the drawing-room to wait for her, fearing to be trapped in the chapel by others of the nest.

'What do *you* know?'

'Do you have any command over the Belgian vampires who've come to Paris now?'

She nodded, her green eyes troubled. 'They stay clear of me now, but when they first came into the city two weeks ago I commanded them to keep clear of the neighborhoods where I hunt – Montparnasse, and along the waterfront, and the railway stations. They didn't like it.' She grimaced. 'But I – I concentrated on that power – that *place*, or thing – that I feel when I make fledglings – called it to me with my heart. And I made them kneel to me. Even Cornelius, who was Master of Liège, and that stuck-up bitch of his, Marielle.' Her lips tightened for a moment with spiteful triumph, but the expression was fleeting. The haunted dread returned to her eyes.

'I don't know how I was able do that. But whatever it is, that *place*, that strength . . . is it this Facinum you talked about, when you came to me in July? Or is it the house itself? I know I'm stronger when I sleep in the chapel, as François used to do.' She shivered. 'It's a nasty place. The whole house is drafty and dirty. I've kept up a few rooms, but I hate the place. And the neighborhood is impossible. But he'd sleep there, once or twice a week. After he was killed I . . . I did what he did. Sometimes I'll dream . . .'

She passed her hand over her forehead, even in her upset state not mussing her hair, and seated herself with a kind of intimate, offhand casualness on Asher's knee. 'Is it one of the relics? I tried taking them over to our *hôtel*, the Hôtel Montadour in Saint-Germain, one at a time, and then all four of them – which took four trips and most of one night! – and sleeping with them in the vault where my coffin is. They're almost impossible to get

through that curtained hallway that guards the bone chapel, and
when one or another was out at the Passy house I was always
terrified it would be stolen. And then I had to be careful. My
lovely boys – and that bitch Hyacinthe – would whisper so, and
watch me . . . so I've never dared give up sleeping at Batoux.
Not for long enough to see if it was the relics or not. And as
long as I could get them to obey me, I didn't really care how.'

'But now you need to know.' *Ysidro should be back soon.*
While Elysée had been speaking Asher had heard the downstairs
clock chime midnight. Lydia had said that the vampire prowled
the streets in the early hours of the night, patrolling for other
vampires, and latterly making arrangements to cache the small
truck 'purchased' by Greuze's Montparnasse friends (which Asher
suspected had been 'purchased' from men who'd stolen it from
the French army), and – Asher was certain – hunting. And while
he didn't exactly fear that Elysée had come here to kill either
him or Lydia, he was very conscious of things that could too
easily happen to hostages.

There was nothing he could do to prevent it.

'Now I need to know.' She laid an arm over his shoulders, the
gesture that of a living woman. 'If the Germans get any closer
. . . and every single one of the High Command should be flayed
alive for the idiots they are! What in God's name were they
thinking, sending all those men to Lorraine and leaving the high
road to Paris wide open?'

Asher made no reference to her earlier remarks about the
armies of France cutting off those of Germany from behind and
leaving them lying in their blood, though he was tempted to
do so.

'I hear that the government's been advised to leave Paris.
Supposedly they're going to Bordeaux, the cowards. Old Henriette
– the only one of Gabrielle's get besides François to survive the
Terror – once told me that Gabrielle was also Master of Bordeaux,
that she had "inherited" that position, though I don't see how
she could have. She'd never been out of Paris in her life! And
Henriette implied that François also would be Master of that city,
though like Gabrielle he'd never set foot there. There!' she added,
straightening. 'I have told you what I know! Now tell me what
it is! This Facinum . . . I cannot carry off more than one relic,

you understand. We simply have not the room in our transport. And I cannot carry away the house itself.'

'Have you ever sometimes . . .'

Asher hesitated, knowing that even in terms of the world of the Undead his thought was mad. Yet the visions of a hundred dreams came back to him, whispers of delirium, memories not his own . . .

'Have you ever sometimes wondered if there were another vampire living in that house? A vampire you never saw?'

Just for an instant he saw it, before her exaggerated expression of startled affront. That small, telltale flinch.

'Why on earth would someone do *that*? It's insane – how do the Americans say? *Loony*!' She sprang to her feet, flung up her hands like a ballerina miming exasperation on stage.

But the flinch had been genuine.

'You've never heard anything there?' he persisted quietly. 'Seen anything there? Dreamed anything there that made you wonder . . .?'

'Don't be absurd! If *that's* what you thought was going on, what you came to warn me about—'

'It wasn't,' said Asher. 'I came, as I said at the time, because I had heard that there was something in the house that the Germans were seeking to get hold of. Only recently I've begun to wonder if it was not some*thing*, but some*one*. It's a huge house, large enough to hold an extended family and a vampire nest as well. What if someone did with Gabrielle what *she* did with her family? Used her – and your husband – and you – as blinds?'

'Why would anyone do such a thing?' She strode from him, turned back, gestured again like an actress. 'If he were a fledgling of Gabrielle's, why would Gabrielle have hidden him? And if not, why then the need to hide? Particularly if he held power over the Paris nest . . . And if he were afraid of Gabrielle's power, and then that of François, why not simply go and try his luck in Liège or Brussels or Bordeaux? You're delusional, my poor boy.'

Coming to his side again she ran her fingers through his hair and suddenly gripped tight, tilting his head back. Asher raised one wrist warningly so that she could see the silver around it, though he guessed that, without the ability to make it out of the room, he would be buying himself at most a second or two before she broke his neck.

'Or are you just trying to get me to let you into the house, so you can look around for it yourself? You and that white snake Simon? Lionel Grippen pushed him out of London and now he's looking for a way to take over Paris? You tell him for me that I won't have him play such monkey tricks. Now that I've found this place, don't think my minions here in town can't stir up this whole district and burn this house over his head. And yours, and that of your pretty girl over there.' She glanced across at the sleeping Lydia. 'With everyone in a panic and the newspapers closing down and rumors flying faster than the smallpox, even that idiot Saint-Vrain could get a gang to tear this place to pieces—'

'It can just as easily be done to the Hôtel Batoux, *corazón*,' murmured Ysidro's soft voice, and Elysée let go of Asher's hair and turned, with a startled speed that spoke volumes for the older vampire's stealth. 'Then if you choose to come to an arrangement with whatever government this city finds itself serving a month from now, you will have nothing to come back to.'

'Species of snake!'

'The serpent is in many ways an admirable creature, Elysée. It comes and goes without a sound and can kill its enemies before they are aware of its presence. Did you arrange for your fledglings to wait for James in the church of Sainte-Clare, by the way, after he visited you in the Hôtel Batoux?'

'No. I didn't even know that bitch Hyacinthe was aware of the back way in. I haven't seen the slut in weeks – another reason—' she turned back to Asher, who was cold and sweating with the effort of sitting upright in his chair – 'why I need to know: what is this thing in the house? Which of the relics is it?' She added sulkily, 'And you tell me now you don't know.'

'I never told you I did. If I could get a better look at the chapel—'

'You? You couldn't walk from here to the door.'

And she was gone – vexingly, vampire-fashion, like the vision in a dream.

TWENTY-EIGHT

'Were you indeed in the bone chapel, James?'

Ysidro had moved too. Vampires came and went, Asher had long ago learned, by creating blind spots in the human perception, periods of reverie which lasted up to several minutes in which one looked into space and thought nothing in particular, only to wake with a start and find the vampire either gone or standing at one's elbow.

Hence, he supposed, the tales of the Undead materializing and dematerializing in the form of mist, or flittering away as bats.

Ysidro put a hand under Asher's arm, drew him to his feet without appearance of effort and steered him toward the bed. Lydia stirred, brushed the back of her wrist across her eyes and said, 'Jamie?', then sat up and fumbled on her glasses. 'What—?'

'Elysée de Montadour has discovered this place,' Ysidro informed her. '*Cagafuego putada.* It means I shall have to make arrangements for another refuge, and as things stand in this city at the moment this will be difficult, particularly if certain members of my household precipitate themselves back into fever and unconsciousness by rising too early from their beds.'

'I'm not a member of your household,' grumbled Asher. 'And yes, I think I must have hidden there, waiting for the chance to pick the lock on the grille and get past the guards and into the main house. I remember . . .'

What do I remember?

What is it that I'm forgetting?

A man standing in the doorway of the bone chapel.

A clawed hand held out to him, ink stains on the fingers . . .

Did that really happen? Or was it like the jumbled dreams, of Jürgen Schaumm in his father's church at Wychford, or meeting his Uncle Theobald in the railway station in Shantung?

'What was the house like inside?' asked Lydia. 'Did you look around?'

'I did.' The memory returned to him, sudden and clear. Shut-up

rooms, bolted doors, chambers filled with the furnishings of a
family covered carefully in holland cloth: birdcages, baby cribs,
shelves of dusty books. And on the other side of the door, the
sparse furnishings of an earlier era, beds that had never been
slept in, rooms housing harps and harpsichords, chess sets and
card-tables, new fresh candles in silver holders set among mountains of dripped wax. Trunk after trunk of clothing: knee-smalls,
panniered dresses, yellow linen brittle as autumn leaves.

Who cleans the place? He'd wondered at the time, and
wondered still.

Corridors, salons, empty rooms upon empty rooms. Footfalls that
echoed as the twilight deepened around him, after the guards had
gone . . .

Attics above those, containing who knew what mazes of tiny
servant-holes?

*Would I know it if another vampire lay in a coffin in those
attics? Could anyone tell, if some little chamber had been carved
out between two bedrooms, windowless and curtained in layers
of velvet like the passageway to the chapel, large enough for a
coffin and nothing more?*

The house was built so that a family could live there. Several
families, indigent brothers and aunts and cousins who lived on
the money that mysteriously showed up in their bank accounts
under the condition that they never, ever try to open those doors
that were bolted from the other side. *Like living with Bluebeard,*
Camille Batoux had said . . .

His glance returned to Lydia, and to Ysidro as the vampire
eased him back into bed.

'It was like Bluebeard's castle,' he said, half-closing his eyes.
Feeling as if he were sinking into darkness, weariness devouring
his bones. 'Haunted.'

'By what?'

Another memory. Footsteps ascending a stair in the hour before
dawn.

Help me . . .

'I don't know.' But in the depths of his heart he knew that he did.

Grilling days. Stifling nights. The train stations still a chaos of
reservists pouring out, wounded pouring in, refugees clustering

on the benches, along the walls. Elsewhere in the city, closed shops, shuttered apartments, silence. The French and British forces fell back from Saint-Quentin, eighty miles from Paris, to Compiègne, barely forty. When Asher stubbornly dragged himself to the window, he saw through the louvers men loitering in the Rue Lepic, watching the house.

'They've come over the walls into the garden, too,' reported Lydia, when he spoke of it. 'Poking about, looking at the house. Toughs, they look like: *apaches*. They haven't tried the door yet.'

She sounded matter-of-fact and cheerful, but Asher could see that she wasn't eating – always a sign of stress – and when he'd wake in the night, or in the long hot still afternoons, it was sometimes to see her pacing from window to window or fretting over a growing pile of lists, books, newspapers around her.

The armies retreated to Chantilly, twenty miles away. Shortly after that they crossed the river Marne.

On September first Greuze reported quietly to Lydia – outside the door of the bedroom where Asher was supposed to be asleep – that he'd had to shift the hiding-place of the truck. 'A man was in the street there, a man I've seen around here lately, one of the porters from the ammunition store, I think. Better safe than sorry, eh? They're saying around the neighborhood that German spies are hiding in this house—'

'Oh, *please*!' Typically, Lydia sounded more annoyed than frightened.

'I figured I had a choice: I tell them they're crazy, and have people start saying *I'm* a spy and watching *me*, or I keep my mouth shut and my ears open. But I tell you, your Don Simon better find another place for you to stay until Professor Asher's well enough to travel, and quick.'

That night Asher put his eye to the louvers of the shutter to watch the shadows move along the rooftops in the glimmer of the waxing moon.

'There was one in the garden a little earlier.' Lydia's strong fingers wrapped around his. 'A young girl, she looked like – wasn't one of Hyacinthe's fledglings a young girl, didn't Simon say?'

'We've made it out of worse places.' His hand tightened on hers. 'I want you to promise me: if the house is attacked, either by spy-hunters in the daytime or by the Undead at night, I want you to flee. Don't try to stop and fetch me. Just run. Find a safe place.'

'In the mines?' A thin stripe of moonlight gleamed on her spectacles as she raised those huge brown eyes, mildly inquiring, to his. 'In the café down the street? Most of the police have joined the army, so I don't think anyone would stop the local *apaches* from beating me to death as a German spy. In a cupboard in the attic? I suspect the first thing they're going to do is burn the house. And if I do manage to get away and run all the way to Dieppe – always supposing I can get to Dieppe – there's still no way for me to cross the Channel. Besides,' she added, 'I'm not going to promise anything of the kind.'

'I don't want Miranda growing up an orphan.'

'*I* don't want Miranda growing up an orphan,' retorted Lydia. 'Nor do I want to have to deal with my aunts without a husband to protect me, so you just do as you're told and let me protect you.'

She turned her head sharply, as if at some sound. Listening, Asher heard it too.

'Is that thunder?' She moved to the window as he had done, eye to the crack, still unwilling to show more of herself to the watchers than she had to. Even at this hour Asher could just make out the shadows of two men standing on the pavement opposite.

Hyacinthe's servants? Elysée's?

Had the Germans not been so near, the military authorities would have been on the doorstep days ago.

Another rumble in the distance, a deep, sustained growling that did not fade.

'It's the German guns.'

Announcements appeared all over Paris the following day. Greuze brought one in that he'd torn off the shutters of the boarded-up Café Arabie, along with his usual ration of bread, fish, and pâté.

PEOPLE OF FRANCE!

For several weeks relentless battles have engaged our heroic
troops and the army of the enemy. The valor of our soldiers
has won for them, at several points, marked advantages; but
in the north the pressure of the German forces has
compelled us to fall back.
This situation has compelled the President of the Republic
and the Government to take a painful decision.
In order to watch over the national welfare, it is the duty
of the public powers to remove themselves, temporarily, from
the city of Paris.
Under the command of an eminent Chief, a French Army, full
of courage and zeal, will defend the capital and its patriotic
population against the invader . . .
Endure and fight!

'They left last night.' Greuze leaned one shoulder in the doorway
of the kitchen where Asher was slumped in a wooden chair, trying
to rally enough strength to drag himself back up the stairs to bed.
'I've been up the Eiffel Tower, as far up as I could get. The military's still up at the top, and the radio offices. You can see the
smoke from the fighting. The Boche are on this side of the Marne,
and the soldiers at the Tower say they're still falling back.

'How you feeling?' He looked across at Asher, grim meaning
in his eyes.

'Like running a long distance,' said Asher, though his stomach
sank at the thought. 'At speed.'

'We better do it tonight, then. Without even the chance of the
police stopping them, they have no reason to wait. Our friends
here last night?'

He jerked his head back toward the Rue Lepic.

'Till about one.' When he'd gone to the window again at three
he had seen no one, though he'd guessed that if either he or
Lydia ventured outside they'd meet one of Hyacinthe's fledglings,
if they weren't simply hanged by the local inhabitants from the
nearest lamp post.

His dreams after that had been troubled, recollections of his
flight – sixteen years previously – from the German enclave in
Shantung in a railway boxcar full of raw cow-hides. Only in the

dream the cow-hides had been crammed into monstrous trunks, like Ysidro's traveling coffin, and he'd known that Lydia was locked in one of the trunks and he'd forgotten which one. . . . But as he'd patiently picked the locks on trunk after trunk, hearing Lydia's muffled pleas and sobs from somewhere in the boxcar, he'd opened one trunk and found it full of rat bones, still wet with acid whose fumes made his eyes sting.

'Raimund Cauchemar, Rue de la Fontaine, Paris', the label had said, and he'd thought, *Oh, yes, Cauchemar was in Emeric's workroom looting things when Ysidro got there. He must have got the acid and the rat bones too.*

'I'll come at two,' said Greuze. 'They've shifted most of the patrols over into the northern suburbs. Those papers your friend Kryzwiki wrote up should get us out of town without the truck being confiscated.'

The thought of dragging himself down the stairs again made Asher's teeth ache. 'I'll be ready.'

When the taxi-driver left the room Asher murmured to Lydia in English, 'What about Ysidro?' He could almost hear Rebbe Karlebach shout, *Leave the monster to die!* But despite his conviction that Karlebach was right, his every instinct revolted at leaving behind one who'd helped them.

To say nothing of the fact that Ysidro could almost certainly get them past the patrols.

'He usually comes here before two,' she replied. 'We'll have to get his trunk somehow.'

The journey to Poitiers would be a nightmare, Asher already knew, and God only knew if they'd be able to get petrol to continue, always supposing the truck wasn't confiscated en route.

He'd meant to write a note to the vampire – who might merely check the house before setting forth on his nightly rounds without making himself known to its inhabitants – but by the time Greuze and Lydia got him back up to his room and to bed, his hands were too shaky to hold a pencil. 'What should I say?' Lydia asked, and Asher dictated, '"We must leave at one a.m. – speak to us at once." Leave it in the cellar, where he'll see it.'

And how we're going to explain the presence of a coffin in the truck to Greuze . . .

She sat at the small desk in the corner and spread out a sheet of notepaper, a shred of sunlight from the crack in the shutters turning the ends of her hair to molten copper. As if from a very great distance away Asher saw her pick up the pencil, but he was asleep before she finished the note.

TWENTY-NINE

I'*m forgetting something.*

Asher shoved five hundred krone into his jacket pocket and opened the drawer of the small desk in his room in the staff quarters of Frühlingszeit Sanitarium – the Department's safe house in the Vienna Woods – though he knew he'd burned everything in the chamber that had his handwriting on it. He'd also burned the three telegrams which, taken together, had let him know that his German cover was about to be blown and that the Austrian Auswärtiges Amt might be looking for him tomorrow.

There was a train to Milan this afternoon at six forty. He had just time to catch it.

He'd bought a ticket weeks ago.

But I'm forgetting something . . .

He opened another drawer. There were rat bones in it, glistening wet and smelling of acid.

Urgency drummed him. *You have to flee.*

You have to meet the Baroness Himmelschein – that smouldery-eyed tart from the cabarets – *at the Café Donatelle, so that the woman you love here in Vienna, who has begun to suspect that you are not as you seem, will think you fled the city as the result of a cheap intrigue, rather than that you really AREN'T what you seem.*

They may already be after you . . .

The feeling plagued him, tormented him, in the fiacre into town, and as he made his way on to the platform at the Westbahnhof, his every nerve telling him to run and his training and intelligence telling him to amble, arm in arm with the chattering Baroness. All the while he was wondering if he'd remembered to put on his false spectacles and to shave off the imperial he'd grown for his journey to Vienna. He had, though, and was moreover vaguely aware that this was in fact a dream. Because it was a dream he was uneasy that the whiskers had either grown back overnight or had turned into something else that would attract attention.

Lydia, he thought suddenly. *I've forgotten Lydia!*

Seized with panic, he let go of the Baroness's arm – *Wait, did I know Lydia then?*

I have to wake up.

'Lucien,' purred the Baroness, hastening to the train-car – that was the name on his papers that year. 'Lucien, darling, hurry, the train is leaving . . .'

I was supposed to get Lydia out of Vienna.

No, wait, this all happened before I met her . . .

Police were coming into the station (*That's wrong, that was Constantinople. I made a clean getaway from Vienna, albeit saddled with the Baroness*). As he hastened down the platform a man behind him said, 'James,' and he turned to see Constantine Angelus, his dark churchman's gown billowing in the engine's steam. The conductors were calling out, 'Alle an Bord!'

'I can't stay,' said Asher, but Angelus stepped in front of him, a wet cardboard box in his hands. 'I have to wake up.'

'You have to take this.' The vampire held it out to him. 'Take it and destroy it.'

Asher didn't touch it, for he saw that the sulfuric acid that soaked the box had eaten the vampire's flesh away, the bones of his hand emerging from the blackening flesh of his wrists. The box had no lid: he saw that it contained a human skull.

Steam rolled across the platform, but the smell of it was the smoke of burning, and from the direction of the waiting-rooms came the crash of breaking glass.

The train was leaving. *I'll be trapped. Killed, as they killed poor Enver . . .*

'You have to take this.' Angelus caught his arm with his skeletal hand. (*Why am I not wearing silver?*). 'Please.'

'I'm sorry,' said Asher, 'I have to wake up—'

'Jamie, you have to wake up!'

He opened his eyes. Smoke wreathed the afternoon light where it slitted in through the louvers, burned his eyes. Men were shouting in the street.

Bloody hell shit bugger goddam—

He hadn't the slightest doubt about what was happening.

Someone fired a gun downstairs.

Lydia dragged him to his feet. He caught his trousers from the chair nearby. 'You don't have time to . . .'

'They'll be looking for a man in pyjamas.'

'Oh. Is that something they teach you in spy school?' she asked moments later, as she helped him down the back stairs toward the cellar. 'How to get dressed in a hurry?' She carried his jacket over her other arm, his tie crammed in her skirt pocket. Men were ramming the locked kitchen door with something, probably the bench from the garden. The salon and the dining-room were already in flames.

'Most of my friends learned that at Oxford, yes.' He caught a stout walking stick from a corner of the kitchen, clung to it for balance as they descended the stair, the wood cool against his bare feet. 'So I suppose you could say so. Are there other exits marked?' he asked, as she unbolted the old door beside the coal bin. 'If any of the mob were Communards you know they're going to know about the tunnel behind the Café Arabie.'

'I know the way to the one in a cellar on Avenue Junot. Greuze' – more shots upstairs – 'says he'll get away and meet us there with the truck.'

'What about Ysidro?' He ripped the note Lydia had written from its tin-tack on the coal bin, crammed the paper into his pocket.

'He's told me two or three times if worst came to worst to flee without him. He said he could hide in the mines for a time. His coffin is down there somewhere . . .' She leaned Asher against the wall, scratched a match and lit the dark-lantern she'd taken from beside the door. Only then did she close the door, kneel to put his shoes on him, and then, rising, put her shoulder beneath his arm again. Even descending the stairs had left Asher dizzy. *I'll never make it all the way to the Rue Caulaincourt, let alone Poitiers.*

'Do you have our papers?'

'Pocket,' she said. 'Greuze said he'd repainted the truck, but if we meet an army patrol on the way out of town they may give us trouble. They're confiscating any vehicles they can get, and they'll certainly take the petrol if they see it. If that happens, I'll tell them you're dying and have to be got out of the city,' she added. 'So try to look fragile.'

'There won't be any trouble,' he panted, 'about that.'

They ducked under a low-cut entry to another tunnel, turned a corner, and walked straight into Jürgen Schaumm and three men with pistols.

Asher yelled 'RUN!' and Lydia – to his thousand silent blessings – obediently shoved him straight into Schaumm's pistol and bolted. The oldest of the henchmen – medium-sized, broad-shouldered, with 'Prussian officer' written all over him in letters a foot high – shouted in German, 'Don't shoot him, you fool!' and the other two – who looked like German army seconded to the Nachrichtendienst – bounded after Lydia into the darkness. The officer pulled Asher away from Schaumm in an instant, flung him to the ground against the wall and held his pistol on him while he kicked him, savagely, twice. Through a haze of grayness Asher heard Lydia cry out, and distant curses in German.

They got her.

Damn it. Damn it . . .

The grayness that covered his mind cleared. He tried to rise and sank down again in a paroxysm of coughing as the officer lifted the lantern, called 'Kraus! Mundt! *Herüber*!'

And to Schaumm, in a cold, crisp tenor, 'This is the man?'

'It is, Herr Colonel.' Schaumm knelt at his side and added, over his shoulder, 'I don't think we'll need to worry about him.' And giggled, a mannerism that Asher had always loathed.

The colonel – and despite a fawn-colored tweed lounge suit that wouldn't have been out of place on Piccadilly the man bore himself with the aggressive strut of a military aristocrat – stepped over, looked coldly down at Asher for an instant, and kicked him again as men emerged from the darkness with Lydia between them, her arm twisted behind her back. 'Kill the woman if either of them gives trouble. We haven't time to play little games.'

Schaumm dragged Asher into a sitting position, held him propped against the damp rock wall. 'I hope for your wife's sake you'll be sensible.' Behind thick polygonal slabs of glass his blue eyes burned with the restless urgency, the directionless anger that Asher well remembered from their summers together in Prague. 'Where's the Facinum?'

Asher was silent for a time, like a man struggling not to give up a final secret. 'In the bone chapel,' he said at length.

'One of the relics?'

He let another half minute go by, hoping Lydia would forgive him and hoping he didn't miscalculate either the colonel's patience or his character. Schaumm made an imperious gesture to the henchmen and Lydia sobbed in pain.

'Stop it! Let her go! It's the gold box – the gold-and-silver box with the veiling inside.'

Lydia had the good sense to gasp, 'Jamie, no! Don't tell him—'

'You've pounded Liège into gravel already,' he snapped, turning savagely back to Schaumm. 'You hardly need its vampires at your service any more. I take it Elysée de Montadour and her nest have fled Paris?'

'In the small hours of this morning. Listen to me, Asher.' Schaumm stepped back as the colonel (*I wonder what regiment?*) signaled for the beefier of the two henchmen to get Asher to his feet. 'Hyacinthe Delamare is waiting for us at the Hôtel Batoux. She told me to bring you there – both of you. She's the one responsible for the exacerbated tempers of the locals here, for the rumors of spies hiding in the house . . . I expect it's in flames by now.'

He flashed the nervous toothy grin that Asher recalled, and when he touched Asher's shoulder his fingers were trembling. He was wound up tight as a violin string with the nearness of his triumph. 'You thought they all had to go to ground with sunrise, didn't you? That they all fell asleep like the dead?'

Asher said nothing, but tried to look as if he was shaken by this information, and Schaumm emitted another pleased little giggle.

'I've learned a great deal about those who hunt the night since last we parted, James. You never did believe in them, did you? When did you learn differently?'

'Seven years ago,' said Asher. 'What does she want?'

'Exactly what I want,' said Schaumm. 'The Facinum.'

The colonel moved closer, gestured with his pistol toward Lydia. 'And you had best be telling us the truth.'

Asher tried to look slightly panicky – which he was – and as if there might be any way for the Germans to tell whether he was lying or not, which he was fairly certain there wasn't. To Schaumm he said, 'How did you find out about it?'

He was curious as to whether Schaumm's account of his acquaintance in Prague with the vampire Corsina Manotti would tally with what Rebbe Karlebach had written to him back in June, but the colonel snapped, 'This is no concern of yours, Professor.' Asher thought Schaumm looked a little disappointed at being cut off. *He always did like to show off his knowledge.*

'How did *you* come to know of it?' countered Schaumm.

'One of the vampires in the Paris nest spoke of it, last time I was here.'

Arrows had been chalked on the tunnel wall; Asher struggled to stay on his feet as he and Lydia were thrust along after the bobbing light of the colonel's lantern.

'The Negro woman?' Contempt flashed in Schaumm's voice. 'Treacherous and stupid, like all her race, and lazy as a slug. She told me they all whispered of it amongst themselves, the Paris vampires. But actually to go to the trouble of finding out what it was, or where it was . . .' He shrugged in distaste. 'I tried to reach the chapel this morning, when Mundt told me the guards there had abandoned their posts. We've kept an eye on the place, you know. But she was there before me. Hopped up like a dope-fiend on an elixir they take so as to remain awake into the hours of daylight . . .'

He shook his head like a street-corner preacher confronted with an actual dope-fiend. 'She insisted we bring you to her, you and your charming bride. She wanted to hear about the Facinum from your own lips.'

'Doesn't trust you, does she?'

The smaller man shot him a glance of simmering resentment. '*She* should hold herself up on the issue of trust! I'd be a fool – *we'd* be fools—' his eyes went to the colonel's straight broad back retreating before them in the darkness, and something deeper than resentment flickered in the momentary set of his thin lips – 'to actually put that power into her hands. But the rest of them are too afraid of that slut Elysée.'

Gray daylight shone ahead of them. Asher smelled the vague

melancholy stink of graveyard earth. A flight of crude steps – *nailed together by the Communards forty years ago?* – led up to the cramped confines of a tomb, through whose wrought-iron grille Asher could recognize the crowded tombs, the iron crosses and thick foliage of Montmartre Cemetery. *The place was a quarry up until Napoleon's time; of course there'd be ways into the mines.*

The colonel halted just within the tomb's door, turned back to Asher with his pistol leveled. 'Fräulein Hyacinthe is going to ask you,' he said in his calm, oddly boyish voice, 'which of the four relics in the chapel is the Facinum, the source of power for the Master vampire of Paris. You're not going to tell her the truth.' He must have seen Asher's glance go back to where Lydia still stood, her arms gripped by the soldiers Kraus and Mundt, for he went on, 'Your wife will remain in the motor car with us. We will inform the lady that she was shot, killed. It is up to you to convince her of this. I hope you are capable of shedding tears at will, Herr Professor?'

Asher felt his ears get hot and his hair prickle with anger. He said quietly, 'Like a crocodile, Herr Colonel.'

'You will tell Fräulein Hyacinthe that the Facinum is one of the other relics – I understand that there are four of them? A pity they cannot all be carried away this afternoon and melted down for gold, but they are bulky and the way out of the chapel, so Herr Professor Schaumm informs me, is difficult to negotiate. The Fräulein Hyacinthe demands to know which relic it is, for that reason: she can get only one of them out of the *hôtel* and to her own hiding-place. You will see to it that she takes the wrong one.'

Asher glanced sidelong at Schaumm, and saw again in his face the anger of one who feels himself cheated of deserved credit.

As if he saw the glance, the colonel went on, 'Herr Professor Schaumm informs me that the vampire is a subtle creature, capable of reading small signs in the human face and the human voice. If you believe you'll fare better by taking her side in this business rather than ours, I assure you that you will find this is not the case.'

Asher whispered, 'I do not so believe.'

Another man – like Kraus and Mundt, clearly a soldier in plain clothes – waited outside the cemetery gate in a Renault *camionette*.

With most of the city's banks closed, Asher guessed that anyone who had the Nachrichtendienst's money on hand could get pretty much anything he needed. Certainly Ysidro had had no trouble.

Asher tried to brace himself against the door as the colonel went around to get into the driver's seat. 'Let Mrs Asher go,' he said. The sensation of speaking through miles of dark tunnel to someone infinitely distant hovered around the edges of his mind, the pain in his chest less disconcerting than the feeling of literally being unable to bear the weight of his flesh on his bones. 'I'll tell Madame Hyacinthe whatever you want, but leave Mrs Asher out of this. She's had nothing to do with any of this.'

The colonel made a sign – almost bored, like a man telling his footman to drown a crying kitten – and one of the soldiers shoved Asher into the front seat beside the officer. Schaumm, Lydia, and the three soldiers got into the back.

'When I get – *we* get – the Facinum—' Schaumm leaned forward across the seat backs to speak – 'and Hyacinthe Delamare takes her own prize and leaves, then you and Mrs Asher will be free to go.'

The colonel glanced back at Schaumm in a kind of slight surprise. Surprised, maybe, reflected Asher grimly, that Schaumm would think for a moment that Asher believed this . . .

Schaumm added silkily, 'We have no quarrel with the innocent.'

From his fellow student's slight stammer as he delivered this line Asher could tell that Schaumm had no intention of letting him and Lydia go free. *He'll probably tell Kraus and Mundt to do it, somewhere he can't see.* He wanted to ask how *no quarrel with the innocent* applied to recent events in a number of Belgian villages, but knew he'd be better off pretending that he did, in fact, believe what he'd been told. Still he couldn't help saying, 'You know we're going to be extremely lucky if she doesn't kill us both.'

'Oh, I think I'll be able to get out of there well before the sun goes down. Certainly the colonel has taken the precaution of loading his pistol with silver bullets. Fräulein Delamare will be effectively trapped in the chapel until dark.' Schaumm giggled again. 'And I assure you, I'll be very careful not to let her get between me and the door.'

THIRTY

A sher really did lose track of the proceedings after that, aware only of the movement of the car through the silent streets and not even always of that. The car came to a halt and gates were opened. Around him lay the forecourt that he'd only gotten a glimpse of through the judas of the gate, back in another world, another city, another life where people rode in lacquered carriages and bought earrings for ladies of a certain reputation in shops on the Rue de Rivoli . . .

The Hôtel Batoux.

It was exactly as Camille Batoux had described it – he recalled the lavender scent of her perfume and the curious silvery gravelliness of her voice – when she'd told him of her very peculiar childhood: *We'd make up stories of who lived on the other side of those bolted doors – all shades of Poe and Mrs Radcliffe and Miss Havisham! – and sometimes we'd slip out of bed in the middle of the night and listen at the keyholes. Sometimes we heard voices, or thought we did. My uncle would beat us if he caught us . . .*

Asher had sipped the coffee she'd set before him and had thought, *If you were my child in such circumstances, I'd have beaten you too.*

But then I'd never, EVER have raised a child in such a house.

Even as he'd thought this, looking across the worn and exquisite coffee-set into those enormous hazel eyes, he had reflected, *Easy for me to say, whose father had a good living in the Church. Whose family saw to it that I got an education, though they tried their damnedest to make me go into helping Uncle Theobald run his shoe factory.*

Gabrielle Batoux had picked for the house's guardians the most indigent members of the family, those who would have been sunk in Dickensian poverty were it not for the money that mysteriously turned up in Uncle Evrard's bank account every month.

Now, looking back on the conversation, he thought, *And what*

*else am I doing to Miranda, every day that I don't hunt down
Ysidro and kill him while he sleeps?*

He had no answer to that.

'Get out of the car.'

Lydia cried, 'Jamie!' when he stumbled, unable to stand, and
tried to get out too. The guard beside her yanked her back.

Asher panted again, 'Let her go,' as he was dragged to his
feet. 'We don't know—'

'All in good time,' said Schaumm. 'I understand from Miss
Hyacinthe that the Montadour woman has taken her human
minions with her.'

'*They* are human,' said Asher wearily. 'The vampires. Human
beings, like you and me. Not demons. Not spirits. Until you
realize that, you cannot deal with them.'

As he was shoved into the house he glanced back over his shoulder,
saw the line of sunlight was more than three-quarters of the way up
the courtyard's eastern wall. Close by, the chimes of the church of
Sainte-Clare struck six.

The house was precisely as he recalled it, though the trunks
and cupboards gaped open, looted by the guards before they'd
left. The spiral stair descended the tower through a drench of
buttery sunlight that fell from a dozen incongruous windows.
'Mundt,' the colonel commanded, and the henchman who wasn't
half-carrying Asher knelt to pick the lock on the grille. The chapel
door, at the foot of the stair, was still locked, and bore no sign
of any attempt to force it.

*The chapel. What am I forgetting that I saw in the chapel? Or
felt there, that made me go upstairs to wait for her to waken?*

Or was that only a dream?

The colonel struck a match, rekindled his lantern. Turned the
many corners, put aside the heavy velvet curtains. Opened
the door.

Hyacinthe turned from staring at the altar and smiled in the
candlelight. 'You again, honey-man.' She was beside them in an
eyeblink and ran caressing claws from the side of Asher's face
down across his throat. 'Not so brave with no silver on your
person, are you?'

He shook his head, mindful that he was supposed to be a man
who had just brutally lost his wife. Numb, eviscerated . . . She

took his face between her hands, kissed his mouth, her body clinging to his like wet silk. He felt her stiffen with anger as he turned his face aside, but she was already looking past his shoulder at the door.

'Where's the woman?' All the syrup vanished from her tone.

'Dead.' There was enough spiteful satisfaction in Schaumm's voice to convince anyone. He enjoyed saying it. If he'd been working with Hyacinthe for over a month, Asher reflected, there was probably a great deal of pleasure in seeing her baffled rage. 'So much for your scheme of having the local hooligans drive them into the tunnels by burning the house over their heads. She had a gun, and tried to defend him.'

Hyacinthe yanked Asher from the grip of his guard, pushed him against the stone chancel arch. Her narrowed eyes blazed as they looked into his, and Asher looked away again. Framing in his mind what it would be like. What he would feel, would think. *You can't just cook up a story*, Belleytre used to say to him, in Paris or Prague or Damascus, when they were sorting out fake passports and dressing up as whoever they were supposed to be on that trip. *You have to BE that person. To remember what that person remembers: losing a wife, losing a child, hating the British . . . WHY do you hate the British?*

She is dead. I loved her and she is dead. His heart was a desolation, as it had been when he'd first realized he loved her, and that it was impossible for that love ever to come to anything.

It probably wouldn't have fooled Ysidro, but he saw the flex of satisfaction on Hyacinthe's bronze lips. She was glad he was in pain.

'Then tell me this, honey-man.' She let him sink to the floor at the base of the pilaster, sank down with him to her knees, her hands circling the gray stem of the stone behind his neck. Her voice lowered to a croon, but where her wrist touched his cheekbone he could feel her trembling, slight and constant, and he could see clearly the burn on her face and throat where he'd slapped her with his silver wrist-chain wound around his hand in the dark church of Sainte-Clare. Barely checked madness glittered in her eyes. 'Tell me this and I swear to you, whatever happens to you, I'll kill him – and I'll make him beg me to do it. There is a magic hoodoo someplace, isn't there?

That Facinum they talk about? That Elysée used, to make her Master?'

He nodded, like a man to whom nothing has meaning any more. She had been awake, he calculated, since nine or ten o'clock the previous evening, when she'd learned that Elysée had fled. Had taken heaven only knew how much of what substance to ensure she stayed awake. She hadn't the strength to turn his mind aside from the disfiguring wound, nor the acuity to detect his lie. The pain in her flesh must be driving her insane and for a vampire there was, he knew, only one cure for that pain.

'Gabrielle Batoux had it,' he whispered. 'The Master of Paris who built this house. It belonged to Constantine Angelus. I don't know where he got it.'

Her eyes shifted toward the altar with its four massive silver doorways, the candle flame glittering on the gold within. 'Which one?'

He raised his voice just slightly and looked aside from her eyes. 'The second from the left.'

Her nostrils flared, as if snuffling his blood. She caught his hair and forced him to look into her eyes, but he only held her gaze for a moment, then looked away again.

'Well.' She stood, and with her slow, drifting step crossed to the altar. The soldier Mundt tried to shrink away from her as he picked the silver-plated lock on the door left of center – Asher guessed the locks were simple Chubbs – and with a teasing smile on her dark lips she stood close beside him as he worked, fingering lightly his sweat-damp hair and touching his shoulders to see him squirm.

But once, suddenly, she turned, as if at a sound, and for a moment Asher could see fear in her eyes.

Rank on rank, the skulls of the wall looked back at her. From the elbow-high dado of pelvis-winged death's-heads up to the curving vault of the ceiling, the skulls formed a silent chorus of mortality.

Watching with empty eyes.

I looked into those eyes.

Why did I do that?

She backed quickly away as Schaumm hurried forward and wrestled the relic from its niche. He could barely move the enormous heart, glittering with rubies and a-shimmer with enamel, purple and red and black; the colonel waved Mundt forward again with his pistol and, unwillingly, the soldier helped lift the thing and move it to the altar.

But Hyacinthe, picking it up, showed no such difficulty. Its size made it awkward in her arms but she cradled it like a baby, pressed her face to the blood-colored jewels. Her mouth quivered with the uncertain expression of one about to laugh or cry crazily, and her eyes burned in the lantern-light as she turned them upon Schaumm. 'Thank you, little man.' She nodded toward Asher. 'Save that one for me. I'll see you tonight.'

She stepped back, the shadows of the chapel seeming to engulf her.

If she thought I'd told her the truth she'd have killed me.

She must realize that there's a chance they haven't got the real location from me yet . . .

The colonel seemed to startle a little, as if waking from a dream to find her gone, and Schaumm passed his hand over his eyes in momentary confusion.

He hasn't learned to shut his mind to that illusion, thought Asher. *To watch them when they move . . .*

Schaumm turned (*yes, he's going to do it!*) to the far right niche and poked the picks into the silver lock. The colonel was right beside him, almost visibly itching to grab at the relic, and Asher, still sitting on the floor beside the pilaster, calculated his distance from Kraus, the nearer of the two guards, and how much strength he'd be able to muster for a dash to the door . . .

'Lying bastard ditch-pig!'

Asher had been watching the shadows where Hyacinthe had stepped back and disappeared – only he had still been able to see the gleam of her eyes – and even he didn't see her until she was at the colonel's side. The colonel and Schaumm were both engaged in lifting the heavy golden box-relic – the veiled Star of Bethlehem – from its niche and neither of them, clearly, had been aware that she was still in the chapel, hidden by the darkness and by her own powers of illusion. She took the colonel first and Schaumm dropped the golden box with a crash and a splintering of glass, and ran for the door like a rabbit. The German colonel screamed when Hyacinthe ripped his throat open with her claws and made a horrible, gurgling gasp as she fastened her lips to the spouting wound and drank.

The soldier Kraus yelled '*Scheiße!*' and fired, shattering bone fragments from the wall. Asher flung himself at the man's legs with all his strength, rolling – it was all he could do – and knocking him sprawling. He caught Kraus's gun as it clattered to the floor, fired at Schaumm as Schaumm whipped a knife from his pocket and dove, not at Asher – who was farther away – but at Kraus, the nearest target and still down on the floor.

Schaumm stabbed him in the neck – clumsily, inexpertly, but enough to release a gush of blood – and then fled through the chapel door and into the dark of the passageway, leaving the guard behind him as bleeding bait.

Hyacinthe will go after him first.

Mundt fired twice at Hyacinthe and then lunged to drag her off the colonel. Kraus staggered to his feet, ripped the gun from Asher's hand, and kicked him back against the wall before stumbling toward the struggling forms beside the altar. Asher had managed to crawl four feet toward the door when Lydia and Greuze whipped through the black curtains and fired at Kraus as – still bleeding like a stuck pig – he spun and loosed off a shot at them.

Asher had enough strength to roll toward the nearest pillar and cover his head. He heard Greuze gasp '*Dieu alors!*' and then a man's harsh scream. Greuze and Lydia reached his side in a single swooping dash (*Greuze must have followed Schaumm's car – good work!*), caught him as if to flee, and then ducked behind the pillar again, Greuze firing . . .

Hyacinthe looked up from Mundt's spasming corpse, blood streaming down her chin and breast and eyes burning with ecstatic delight.

Kraus had fallen, one hand pressed to the wound in his neck. He rolled over and emptied his revolver at the vampire woman as she rose from Mundt's corpse, and she smiled, orgasmic with the two lives she had drunk. Asher doubted if, between panic, shock, and the erratic beam of the colonel's kicked-over lantern, any of the terrified man's bullets even hit her, but knew that they'd cause very little damage if they did. She laughed, soft and throaty, and purred in the Creole French of her childhood, 'Oh, you little bunny, Mama's gonna eat you right up.'

Kraus flung the pistol at her and began to crawl toward the door.

'When she fastens on him,' breathed Asher, 'run.'

'I'm not—'

'Damn it, RUN! Get to the light in the vestibule . . .'

Hyacinthe looked up, a few feet from the frantically crawling guard, and met Asher's eyes. She almost chuckled as she whispered, 'No, you don't.' She glanced down at Kraus. 'This one isn't going anywhere in a hurry.'

She walked toward them. Slowly. Smiling.

Greuze fired twice at her and this time Asher saw the shots hit her, slow dribbles of blood from a heart that had ceased beating decades ago. She looked tickled to death at the prospect of a quarry who'd entertain her and Asher knew he and Kraus were going to be the last ones to die.

Hyacinthe turned. Quickly, as she had at the altar, as if at a noise. Dark brows plunging . . .

She started to turn back toward her prey and halted again. 'Who's that?'

Silence, and a thousand empty eye-pits staring out of the darkness. The flicker of the lantern put movement in the hollows.

'Who is it?' She swung around with such violence that she staggered, cat-gleaming eyes sweeping the shadowy room. She moved her hand as if trying to find support or brush away something she could not see.

Greuze whispered, '*Qu'est-ce que c'est que ça?*' and Asher tightened his hand on the cab-driver's wrist.

Knowing what it was.

Knowing sudden and whole.

Hyacinthe stumbled toward the door of the chapel, thrashed again with her hands. 'No!' She turned and twisted, as if trying to break some invisible grip. 'Don't! DON'T!' She flung herself to the floor, crawled toward one of the pillars, then reared up to her knees, struggling against some invisible force like a roped mare. 'Don't! Stop it! I'll be good! I'll serve you!' She jerked to her feet, staggered toward the curtained door, sobbing now, screaming 'Don't!' again and again. 'No! I swear it, I'll do whatever you say! Don't! Stop it!'

She almost fell through the curtains and Asher could hear her in the twists of the lightless passageway, screaming in terror, begging as she fell against the walls, but, he guessed – he knew – making her way, slowly and inexorably, up toward the last of the evening sunlight in the vestibule.

With an almost stealthy movement Lydia pulled up her skirt and ripped a strip from the hem of her petticoat, crawled swiftly over to the guard Kraus, and made a pressure bandage on the wound in his neck. The whole darkness of the chapel stank of blood. Even in his pain the German knew enough not to make a noise, and even the layers of velvet curtain couldn't muffle Hyacinthe's sobs and pleas. 'Don't – oh, God help me, DON'T—!'

Asher could tell when she reached the last curtains, the last doorway; heard the dim clatter as she tried to cling to the curtains and instead ripped the rods off the wall.

He didn't hear her open the door, but her shriek as the sunlight hit her flesh was like the damned falling, a thousand miles, into the burning lake of Hell.

Which he supposed – as Greuze's grip crushed his arm in shock and horror at the sound – that that was exactly what it was.

Hyacinthe screamed for a long time. Even through half a dozen layers of velvet curtains, the smoke of charred flesh permeated the air.

The silence afterwards – as summer darkness fell outside – seemed to last even longer.

At length Lydia whispered, 'We should go. We ought to get Sergeant Kraus to hospital – I do hope he's got French credentials . . .'

Asher said, 'No.'

'I at least must go.' Greuze sat back against the pillar – he had been crouched, as if ready to spring up and fight – and wiped the sweat from his face. 'The word has gone out, my friends. Air-scouts confirm it: the German army has turned east at the Marne, trying to surround our troops. They have left a gap in their lines. Gallieni has put out a call for troops, reserves: it is our chance. We can take them in the flank! Stop them! The whole of the Twenty-First Corps is coming in, and more are marching in from the Third Army. Every truck and transport is already at the Front, so Gallieni has put out a call for every taxi in Paris to take men to the Front—'

'Taxis?'

'We will not charge them, of course,' responded Greuze.

Lydia smiled. 'I thought you despised the war.'

'I do, madame. As I trust—' he glanced from the bodies of the colonel and Mundt, bled out and motionless, at the foot of the altar – 'that you despise these creatures with whom you have such dealings. One does what one must.'

'One does what one must,' Asher agreed quietly.

For King and country . . .

Hating the vampires – every single vampire – but glad to the core of his soul that Lydia was alive.

'I will leave the truck here in the courtyard. If you go soon you can probably still make it out of Paris. I'll even take this one here—' he nodded at Kraus – 'to hospital, so that you need not delay. It will be dark soon.'

Lydia glanced inquiringly at Asher.

'We'll wait,' he said. 'Ysidro will be here before long. There's something here that he needs to do.'

THIRTY-ONE

It seemed like hours, after Greuze left, before Ysidro appeared, though Asher calculated later that it was only about ninety minutes. Lydia found the heart-shaped reliquary in the far corner of the chapel where Hyacinthe had left it when she went to drag the bodies of Mundt and the colonel to a less visible spot. Even her experience with cadavers hadn't inured her completely to the presence of corpses, if they could be tidied away somewhere.

'You knew she'd pretend to leave, to see if Schaumm was lying about me being dead, didn't you?' she asked, shaking bits of broken glass out of her skirt hem as she returned to sit beside the pillar. 'I mean, that story he came up with sounded fishy even to *me*.'

'I was pretty sure she'd guess what was going on, yes.' Asher's chest and back felt as if he'd been through *peine forte et dure* and he doubted that he'd make it to Bordeaux without the pneumonia coming on again. At the moment it was good just to lie on the uneven stone of the floor with his head on Lydia's thigh and the momentary, peaceful certainty that the only vampire left in Paris was not going to murder them.

He wondered if the Twenty-First Corps would make it to the Marne in time to take on the Germans – von Kluck's forces must be stumbling with exhaustion by this time, after thirty solid days of marching, along with fighting and murdering Belgian civilians. He wondered if this would be enough to turn the tide.

Or at least hold it off until he and Lydia could reach England.

If they could get past the submarines in the Channel.

After a little time Lydia said, 'Jamie . . . after we get to England . . . you know I'm coming back.'

'I know.' His hand tightened over hers.

'It isn't that I don't love you,' she went on hesitantly. 'Or that I don't love Miranda. It isn't that I even want to. But there are so many of them. Thousands and thousands. A quarter of a million, the newspapers said. And it's only been a few weeks. With Schaumm gone the spy charges can be dealt with, and I know Dr Théodule will help me get a place.'

'You don't have to explain it, best beloved.' He looked up into her eyes, huge insectile rounds of spectacle glass in the dimness. He heard the tired bitterness in his own voice as he added, 'I think we're both going to be back.'

'Oh,' she said softly. 'Oh, Jamie . . .'

He shook his head, knowing there was nothing to be done. Knowing that, like the hospitals, the Department was going to need every pair of hands – every brain and pair of eyes – and wasn't about to waste a trained man.

And he would go, for King and country, putting aside all that he knew and felt about them as he put aside all that he knew about Ysidro, when Lydia was in danger.

'I'm sorry,' he said. 'And I'm sorry for Miranda, who's going to have a very strange childhood because of it. Like our friend Greuze, one does what one must.'

Lydia sighed, and for a long time held his hands tightly as the world outside grew dark.

At length she said, 'So the relic that shattered – the thing that was supposed to contain starlight from the Christmas star . . . that was the true one?' She glanced toward the altar, the shards of broken glass around it twinkling dimly in the lantern's failing light. 'And now that it's broken – it looks as if it was a glass ball painted with quicksilver on the inside – does that mean Elysée has lost her hold over her fledglings?'

Behind the grilles still closed, fragments of lantern-light slipped over the gleam of gold, the dark flare of jewels. The two open niches seemed to echo the empty black gaze of the skulls that surrounded them. Wall, altar, glass, and the stone of the floor were flecked with blood.

'What *was* it, anyway?' Lydia's voice was hesitant. 'I mean, really? Did you ever even find out?'

'I haven't the faintest idea.' He reached up – it took all his remaining strength – and touched her cheek. 'But it has nothing to do with the Masters of Paris.' He moved his head a little and saw Ysidro standing just within the black curtain of the doorway. He didn't know how long he'd been there. 'Does it?'

Ysidro whispered, 'No.'

He started to come into the chapel, then turned his steps aside and walked to the altar. And stood almost where Hyacinthe had stood, just to the right of the altar, looking at the wall of skulls.

Asher said softly, 'Do you know which one it is?'

Ysidro reached for one of the skulls – a little larger than the others – set about half a head above his own eye level. But before he could touch it he folded his long fingers together and stepped back, his fist against his lips.

Only stood looking up into the sockets of the empty eyes.

'Did you know?'

The vampire shook his head, a slight motion. 'I – began to guess,' he said. 'When my memories began appearing in your dreams. Constantine was the only one who would have been able to walk into my thoughts. And it made sense.'

'Because Cauchemar took over as Master of Paris?'

'He shouldn't have been able to,' said Ysidro. 'He was just not that strong a vampire. In truth . . .' He fell silent.

'In truth,' said Asher, 'it wasn't Cauchemar or Gabrielle Batoux or François de Montadour who were the Masters of Paris in their turn. The Master of Paris was always – and is still, I suppose – Constantine Angelus.'

Ysidro closed his eyes. Lydia, who had risen as if to go to his side, sat down again hastily, shock visible on her face.

After a time Ysidro said, 'Father Jeffrey said that he was the last enemy of the Faith that the Church would have me kill for them. The last foe of my portion of the battle against unbelief. I knew that without hunting I probably would not live long, but I would have the comfort of salvation when I died. That was important to me, then.

'I think Cauchemar followed me that night,' he went on. ''Twas he who – who told me that Constantine had tortured my servant Timothy before he killed him. Looking back I cannot imagine that he would have done so, even if he did indeed kill him . . . as I believe he did. But I was angry, shocked, shaken, a condition in which it is easy to believe plausible lies. Cauchemar followed me, the only person who could have gotten close enough to Constantine to stab him with a poisoned blade. And when I left the house, Cauchemar took him – paralysed, conscious, betrayed – back to Emeric's workroom, which he had taken over. There he created his own Facinum. He took for himself the power Constantine had over the vampires of Paris by enslaving him physically. By cutting him in pieces, and dissolving the flesh off his bones.'

'*Alive*?' whispered Lydia. 'I mean . . .'

''Tis well-nigh impossible for us to die,' returned Ysidro in a voice like the passage of wind across ruins. 'Save in the light of the sun. Nor do we lose consciousness, during the hours of the night. Even in the daytime our sleep is not sleep as the living understand it.'

'Elysée said that she used a power here in the chapel to focus her own thoughts,' said Asher. 'To . . . to guide the souls of the fledglings she made to that place of power, rather than holding them herself. When Cauchemar was killed, Gabrielle took possession of the – skull? Are there more bones here?'

'I sense only the skull.' Ysidro put his hand out again to touch the brown curve of the brow, but again drew it back. 'There may have been more at one time. She must have known 'twas the source of her power and destroyed the rest lest one of her fledglings steal one and use it for the same purposes. Obviously Elysée did not know, so I think her husband didn't, either. Only that the Hôtel Batoux was in some fashion the heart and center from whence their power flowed.'

'When I spoke of the Facinum she scoffed,' said Asher. 'But she got her minion Saint-Vrain to start looking for it . . .'

'He knew you.' He turned to regard Asher, and some of the stricken stillness seemed to pass from his expression. 'Constantine.'

'I saw that skull – that particular skull – when I was here in the chapel, hiding from the guards. The others were the skulls of the nuns – many of them young girls – but physiologically I could tell this was a man's. I was drawn to it . . .'

'I have often thought,' remarked Ysidro, 'that you and he would have dealt well together – despite your vow to destroy us all.'

'He must have known, then, that you knew me.'

'He saw deep into the thoughts of both the living and the Undead – even the Undead not of his own begetting. Like me, he was not a man to let his servants come to harm.' With great care, then, Ysidro worked loose the skull from its place in the wall by the altar. The dark gap seemed to Asher like one more hollow eye socket among all those other skulls, each of them a girl whose life had been dedicated to what her parents and preceptors had considered holy, or at least convenient for themselves. Like their sisters in the catacombs that joined the church of Sainte-Clare with this place, they had lived and died within those walls, and what they had thought of that life – or how they had looked upon the world – flickered with the movement of the lantern flame within the watching sockets of their empty eyes.

Like his own parents, reflected Asher, and what they had wanted for him.

Ysidro crossed the little room and put his friend's skull into Lydia's hands. 'Will you do me a great kindness, Mistress?' he said. 'And him also, I think. When dawn comes, would you smash this into pieces and leave them where first light will strike? They should burn quickly. And then he should be free to go where he is destined to go. If such a thing as Purgatory exists, and sin may be expiated by suffering, I suspect out of all of the Undead, Constantine alone stands a chance of finding his foot upon an ascending stair. He would make notes of the experience, if he could.'

A fragment of a half-remembered dream, a man in the chapel doorway, holding out his hand. *Help me* . . .

You must destroy this . . .

'We'll see it done,' Asher promised.

'Thank you.' The vampire hesitated, then extended thin, cold fingers to touch Asher's hand. 'With your permission I shall accompany you to the outskirts of Paris and do what I can to get you passed through the ranks of the Twenty-First Corps as they converge. Then I shall leave you. In the absence of our good Jehu I believe Mistress Lydia will have occupation enough getting a stricken husband to Bordeaux, without the further complication of explaining a coffin in the back of the truck. If the German army has indeed been turned aside at the Marne, I expect Elysée and her minions will return to Paris by Christmas. The sight of the ensuing struggle for mastery of this city, though perhaps entertaining, will probably be more than I can stomach. I will make my own arrangements, and depart.'

'Will you be—' Lydia stopped herself, confused. Not wanting, Asher knew, to say, *Will you be all right?* Knowing – as they both knew – what was necessary for a vampire to be *all right*. Knowing that he could not be other than he was.

But she looked into his eyes, caught, as she always was, between what she knew and what she felt.

'Come.' Ysidro took her hand as she stood clasping the skull to her middle. 'The nights lengthen, but still the dawn will be here too soon, and we have far yet to travel by starlight.' He bent and kissed her hand. 'What I shall be, Mistress, is at your service until the final sunrise of my life.'

Stooping, he drew Asher up and supported him to the darkness of the shrouded corridor, rank with the stink of burned flesh. Lydia picked up the lantern and came behind, her feet crunching Hyacinthe's calcined ashes, the skull of the Master of Paris cradled in her arm.

Years later, on an afternoon in Oxford, Asher recalled suddenly a dream he'd had – in Paris, he thought, at the beginning of the war, though his recollections of August 1914 were never completely clear. At times he felt as if he'd journeyed to Paris in the calm noon of one century and wakened there, startled and disoriented, deep in the heart of another.

He had dreamed, he thought, of the dark streets of Paris, and of Don Simon knocking at the door of Father Jeffrey's lodging in the Rue de l'Épée de Bois. It must have been early in the night, for a servant admitted him and showed him upstairs. Cardinal Montevierde, somber and smelling of dirty blood, was practically gloating with glee. He had clasped the vampire's hands. 'It is excellent!' he said. 'The word has come from a dozen quarters that he's gone.'

'Then I have paid my debt?' Simon asked in a constrained voice.

The Italian's dark brows shot up. '*Debt*? One doesn't speak of the salvation of one's soul as some kind of . . . of market transaction. You have proven yourself a good and faithful servant of the Holy Father, and he is extremely pleased with you. He – and I – have great faith that your next foe, your next target, will be worthy of your skills. Henri, the Duc de Rohan, is rising in leadership of the schismatics, particularly in the south. His forces will soon become a threat to the Faith in this kingdom.'

'Henri of Rohan?' Simon looked from the cardinal to the priest. 'He has nothing to do with the Undead. Nothing to do with—'

'He is an enemy of the Faith!' retorted Montevierde. 'That is all that you need to know, my friend.' He draped a familiar arm around Simon's shoulders. 'The falcon asks not at which game his master sets him to fly.'

Simon looked as if he might have said something else, but didn't. In the candles' wavering light Montevierde was smiling as if the matter were a fait accompli; Father Jeffrey hastily rose from his chair, took Simon's arm, and led him to the darkness of the hall outside the room.

'What is it, Simon?' the old man asked gently. 'You've served the Faith in a small matter, and done extraordinarily well. Do you doubt that we will give you every assistance? You shall command what you need: servants, gold, authorizations—'

'I want none of those things,' returned Simon. 'I want . . . my soul. I want the blessing of the Holy Father.'

'And you shall have it!' He clasped Simon's hands. 'Every step you take, every deed of service you do, is one step closer . . .'

The vampire drew back. 'Is that then what this is about? My "deeds"? My "service"? You asked me to kill an enemy. I did it;

it was the price, you said, of my soul. But then it wasn't: I had to kill a man who was almost a stranger to me.'

'A heretic,' Father Jeffrey reminded him. 'You've been killing heretics for years. And a murderer.'

'As I am a murderer. And that was to be the price of my salvation. Only it wasn't. You asked me to kill my friend.'

'He also was a heretic, Simon. His writings were pernicious.'

'He was not a heretic. He never embraced the so-called Reformed Faith. He only asked questions. And still that wasn't enough. So I must ask you, Jeffrey . . . and I must ask you to tell the truth. When will it be enough? How are the murders that you ask me to commit different from the murders for which my soul stands condemned? How is the Duc de Rohan, whom I don't even know, different from those I've killed simply to survive? To feed my appetite that is a part of this condition—'

'The condition which you accepted. Freely, of your own will, and for your own benefit.'

Simon only stood looking at him, grief and anger and bafflement slowly crystallizing to cold nothingness in his yellow eyes.

'Simon,' urged the priest. 'To achieve salvation, we must accept what we are told by those who understand these things better than we do. It is sufficient only that we trust, and obey.'

He reached out his hand to him again, but Simon drew back, like a ghost in the blackness of the hall.

Gently – sadly – Father Jeffrey said, 'You cannot ask these questions, Simon. You must have faith.'

Ysidro closed his eyes for a moment; *seeing what?* Asher wondered. Constantine Angelus lying on the floor of his study? The pre-dawn flush in the gray sky above Montmartre hill? Tim Quodling's face, not bloodless and twisted with pain but grinning brightly in the firelight as he set out a game of draughts?

'Wilt bless me, Jeffrey,' he asked, very quietly, 'as you used to do?'

Father Jeffrey looked away. Knowing, Asher supposed, that he should say, *You know I cannot*, and yet unable to bring out the words. Knowing, like the Pope in the Tannehauser legend, that a soul sent into the darkness does not come back, and with no amount of seeking can he ever be found.

When he looked up, with words on his lips, Ysidro was gone.